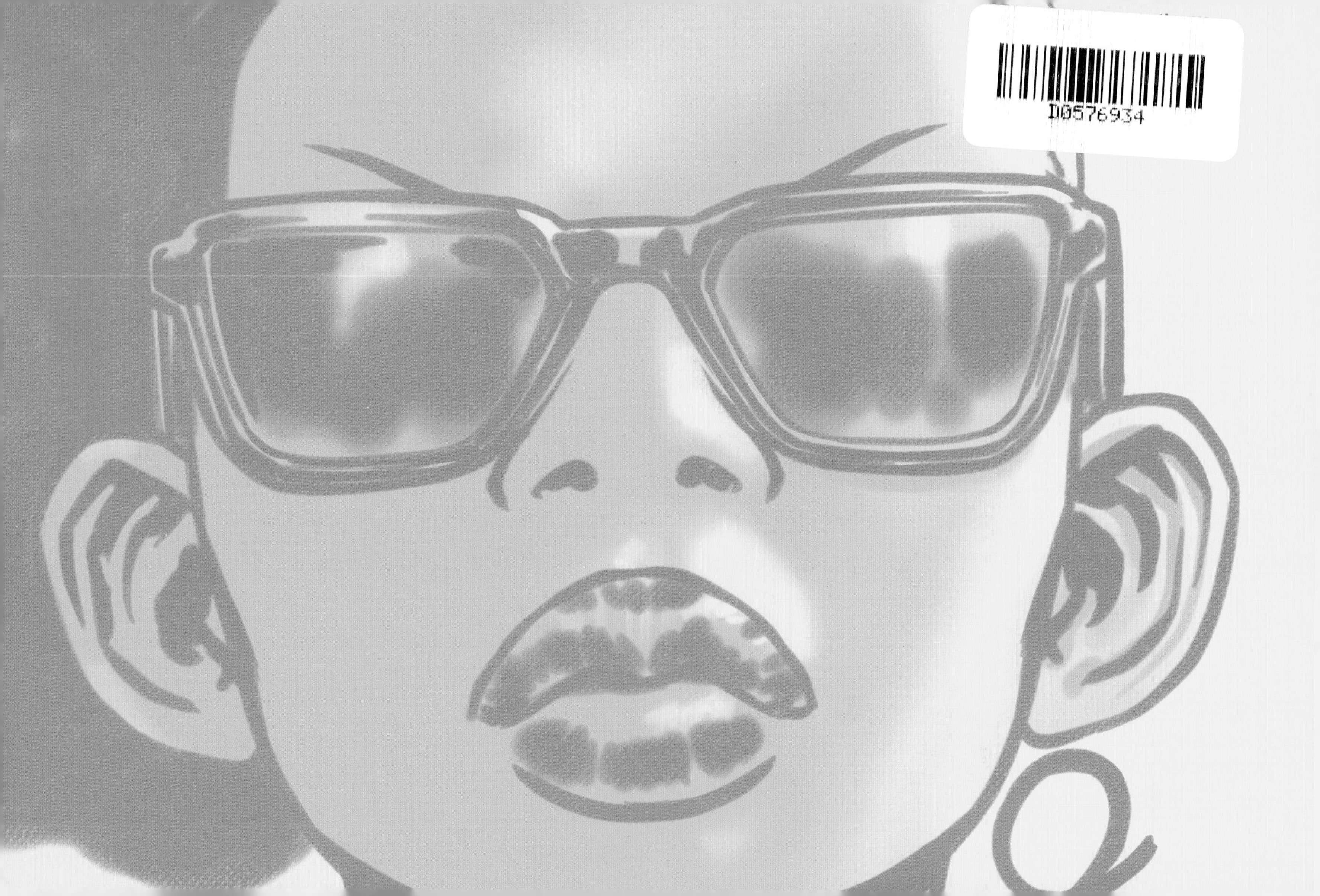

BLACKHAND & IRONHEAD

WRITER AND ARTIST **David López**

COLORS **Nayoung Kim**

SCRIPT TUTOR **David Muñoz**

LOGO **Cris Castañ**

TRANSLATION **Stephen Blanford**

ADAPTATION FOR THE AMERICAN AUDIENCE
Melissa Gifford • Shanna Matuszak
Briah Skelly • Hilary DiLoreto
Tricia Ramos

PRODUCTION & DESIGN
Erika Schnatz

IMAGE COMICS, INC. • **Robert Kirkman**: Chief Operating Officer • **Erik Larsen**: Chief Financial Officer • **Todd McFarlane**: President • **Marc Silvestri**: Chief Executive Officer • **Jim Valentino**: Vice President • **Eric Stephenson**: Publisher / Chief Creative Officer • **Jeff Boison**: Director of Sales & Publishing Planning • **Jeff Stang**: Director of Direct Market Sales • **Kat Salazar**: Director of PR & Marketing • **Drew Gill**: Cover Editor • **Heather Doornink**: Production Director • **Nicole Lapalme**: Controller • **IMAGECOMICS.COM**

Introduction

There's a classic trope about people looking like their pets. You know the one? You see it in old magazine cartoons a lot—a lady with a pointy nose and a fancy hat, for instance, walking a giant poodle with the same profile. There are modern memes versions too. You know what I'm talking about, don't you?

Well, my dear friend David López is like that, only... how do I want to put this? Instead of looking like his pet, he draws like he acts. Or... no, that's not quite it. Maybe "he *feels* like his books *look*"...? Uh... he's the flesh and blood embodiment of the espresso-fueled energy of his work! He's human chewing gum! Wait, no, I got it—

David is exactly who you see on the page.

I'm being silly because it's fun to tease my friend, but as big and expressive as his line is, there's a vulnerability to it, a genuine quality. And that's a Crazy Big Deal. What I'm talking about is *honesty*. And honesty is at the heart of artistry.

Working in fiction is a weird way to make a living. Lawrence Block calls it "telling truths by telling lies," and I've never found a way to phrase it that made more sense than that. Crazy thing is, sometimes the further a work of art gets from naturalism, the closer it gets to an essential truth. Think about Opera. Or Commedia dell'Arte. Think about Shakespeare.

(Breathe, David. I'm not saying you're Shakespeare.)

David lives life at the far end of the dial, and he puts that aspect of himself on the page in ways that are expressive, ridiculous, but somehow—magically!—incredibly human.

This book is a prime example of what I'm talking about. It's ostensibly about super-powered kids finding their way through a dangerous future full of liars and bullies. But really, it's about two complicated, scared young women searching for their truths.

The job of the artist is one rife with contradictions. We tell truths by telling lies, we come closest to universal understanding when we are the most specific, and when we are the most vulnerable? That's when our work is the strongest.

I'm proud of my friend for what he's made here. And I know you're going to enjoy it.

Best,
Kelly Sue DeConnick
Portland, OR
November 2018

Chapter One

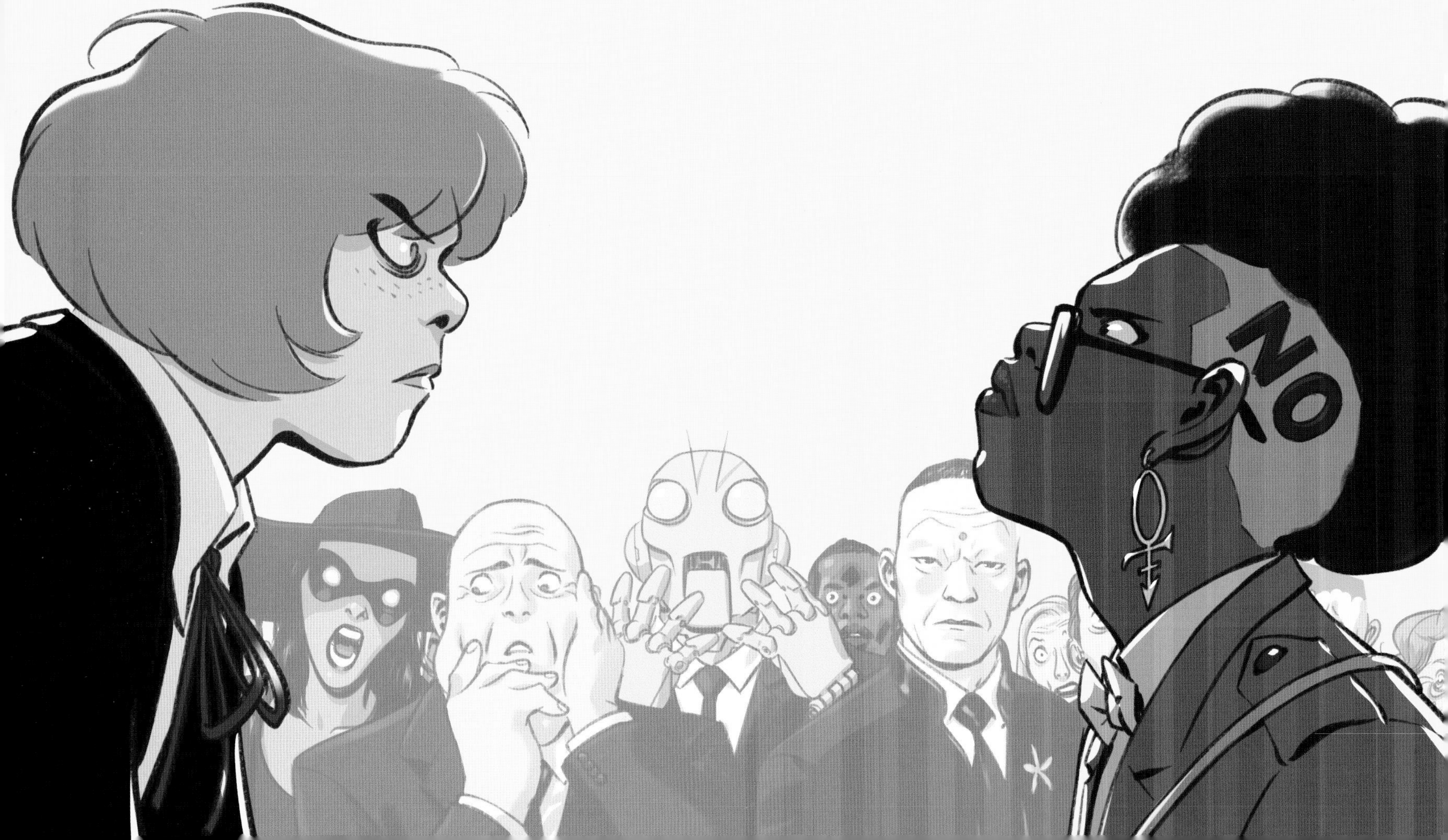
NO

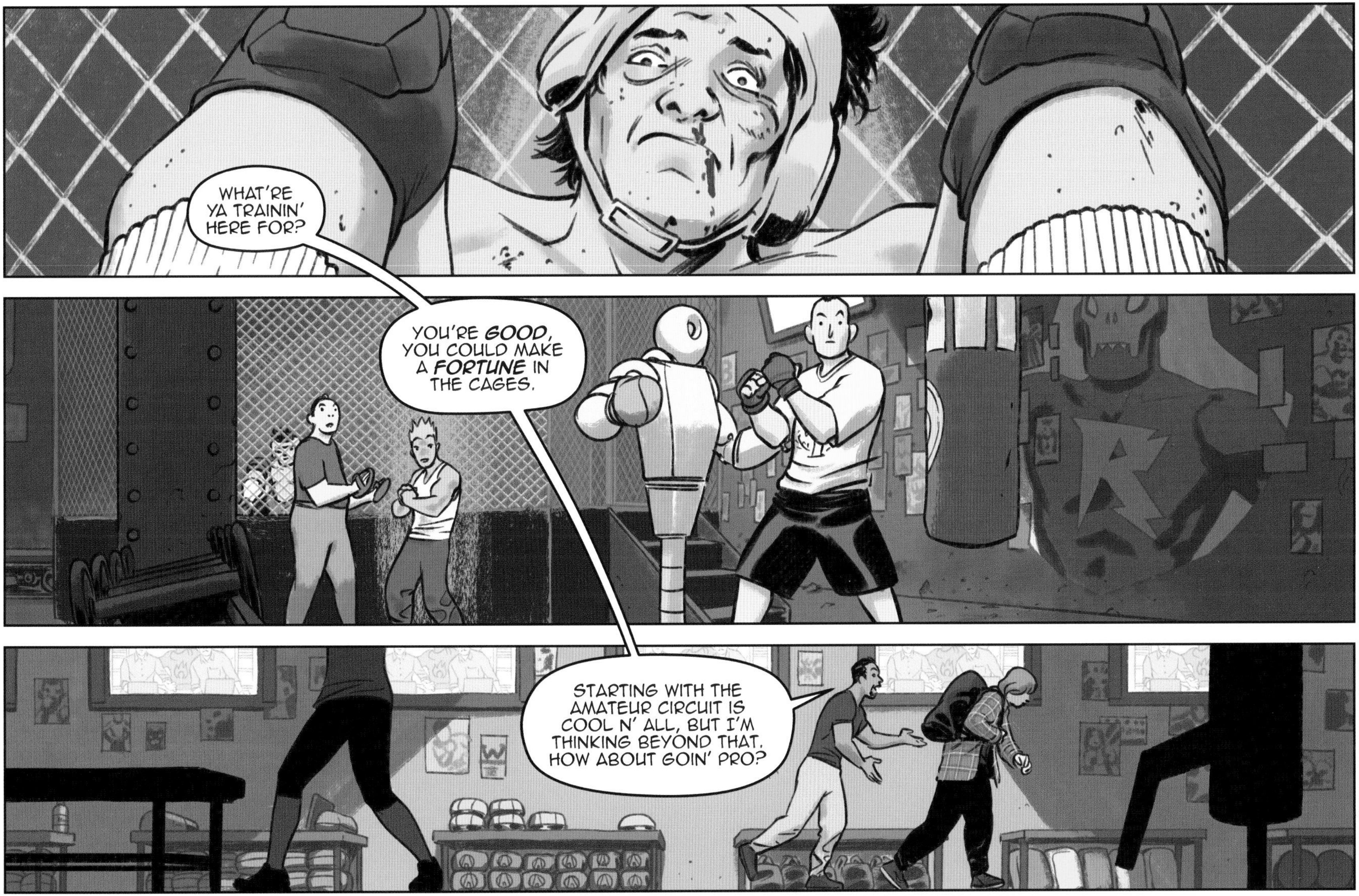
WHAT'RE YA TRAININ' HERE FOR?
YOU'RE **GOOD**, YOU COULD MAKE A **FORTUNE** IN THE CAGES.
STARTING WITH THE AMATEUR CIRCUIT IS COOL N' ALL, BUT I'M THINKING BEYOND THAT. HOW ABOUT GOIN' PRO?

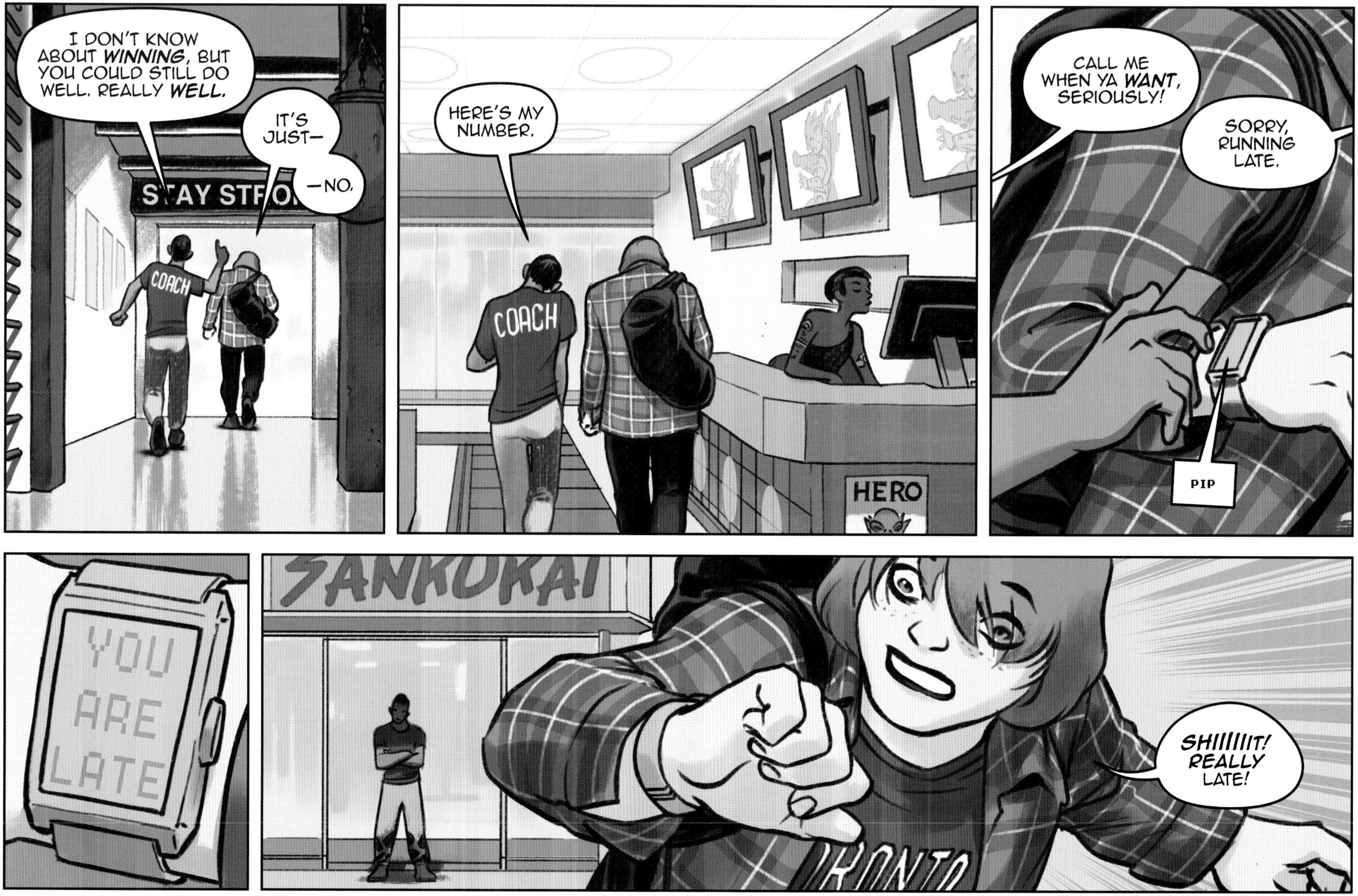
I DON'T KNOW ABOUT *WINNING*, BUT YOU COULD STILL DO WELL. REALLY *WELL.*
IT'S JUST—
—NO.
COACH
HERE'S MY NUMBER.
COACH
HERO
CALL ME WHEN YA *WANT*, SERIOUSLY!
SORRY, RUNNING LATE.
PIP
YOU ARE LATE
SANKOKAI
SHIIIIIIT! REALLY LATE!

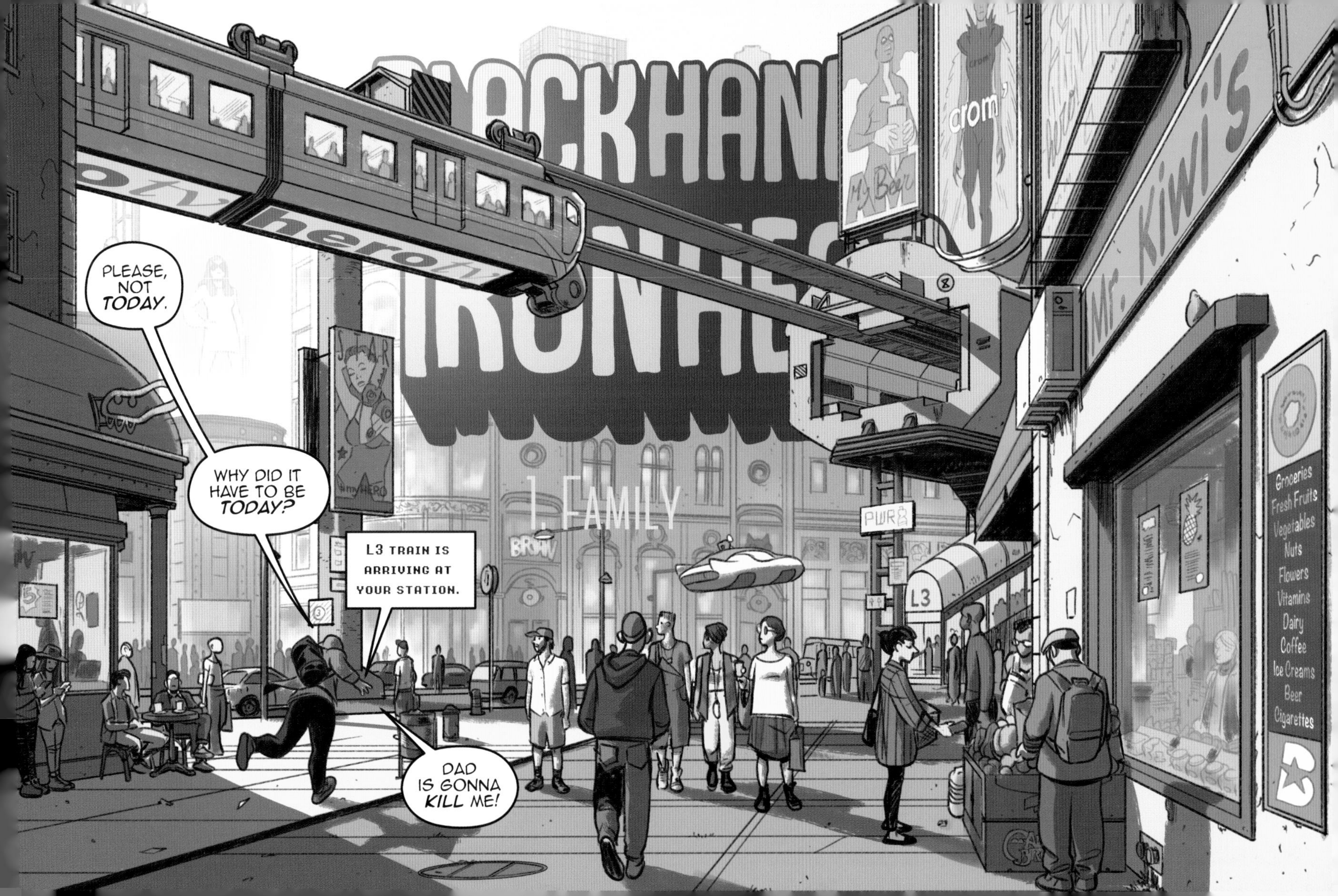
1. FAMILY
PLEASE, NOT *TODAY*.
WHY DID IT HAVE TO BE *TODAY?*
L3 TRAIN IS ARRIVING AT YOUR STATION.
DAD IS GONNA *KILL* ME!
Mr. Kiwi's
Groceries
Fresh Fruits
Vegetables
Nuts
Flowers
Vitamins
Dairy
Coffee
Ice Creams
Beer
Cigarettes
crom'
My Beer
STAR
#myHERO
PWR
L3

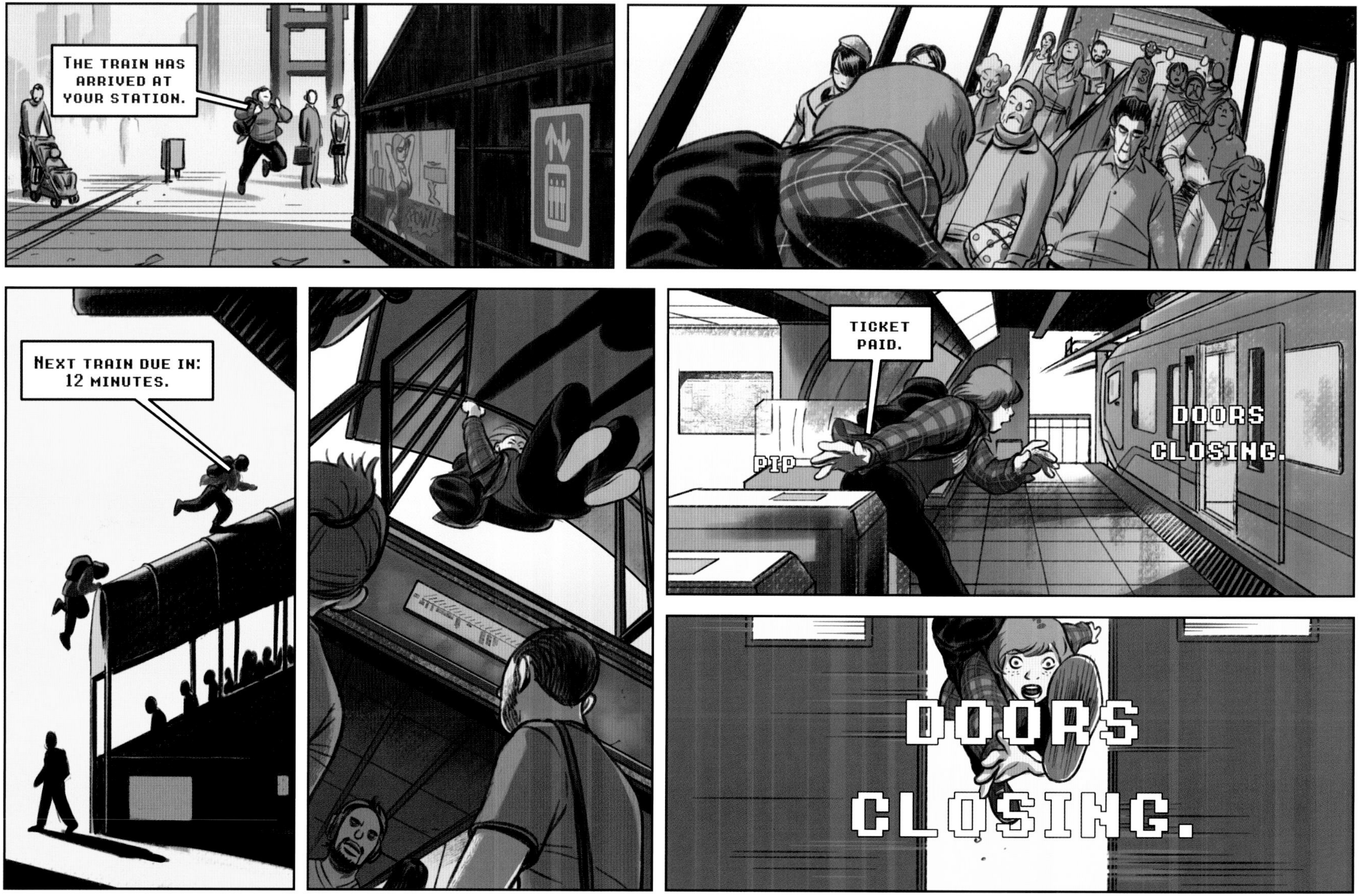
THE TRAIN HAS ARRIVED AT YOUR STATION.
NEXT TRAIN DUE IN: 12 MINUTES.
TICKET PAID.
PIP
DOORS CLOSING.
DOORS CLOSING.

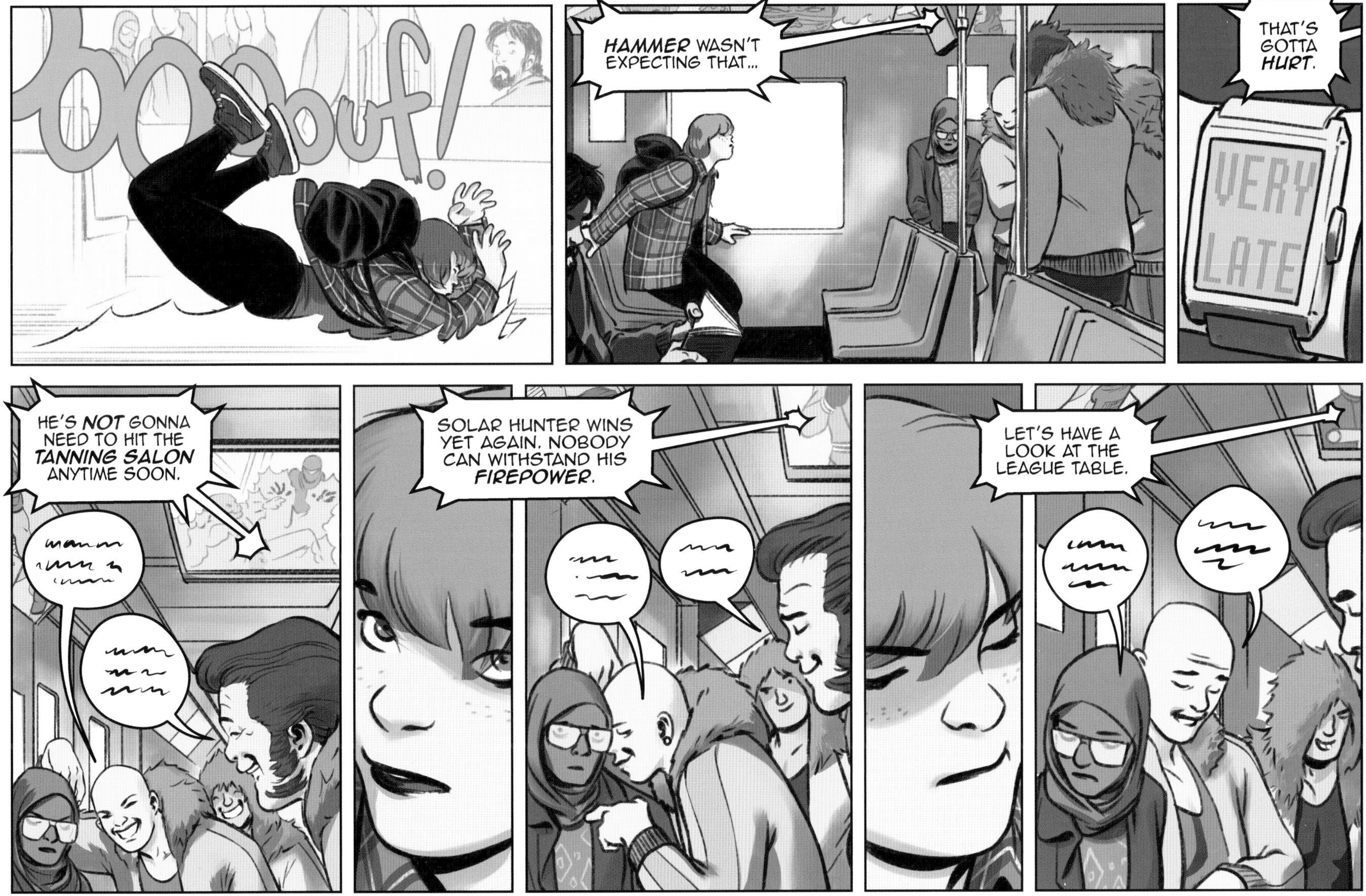
OOOOuf!
HAMMER WASN'T EXPECTING THAT...
THAT'S GOTTA HURT.
VERY LATE
HE'S NOT GONNA NEED TO HIT THE TANNING SALON ANYTIME SOON.
SOLAR HUNTER WINS YET AGAIN. NOBODY CAN WITHSTAND HIS FIREPOWER.
LET'S HAVE A LOOK AT THE LEAGUE TABLE.

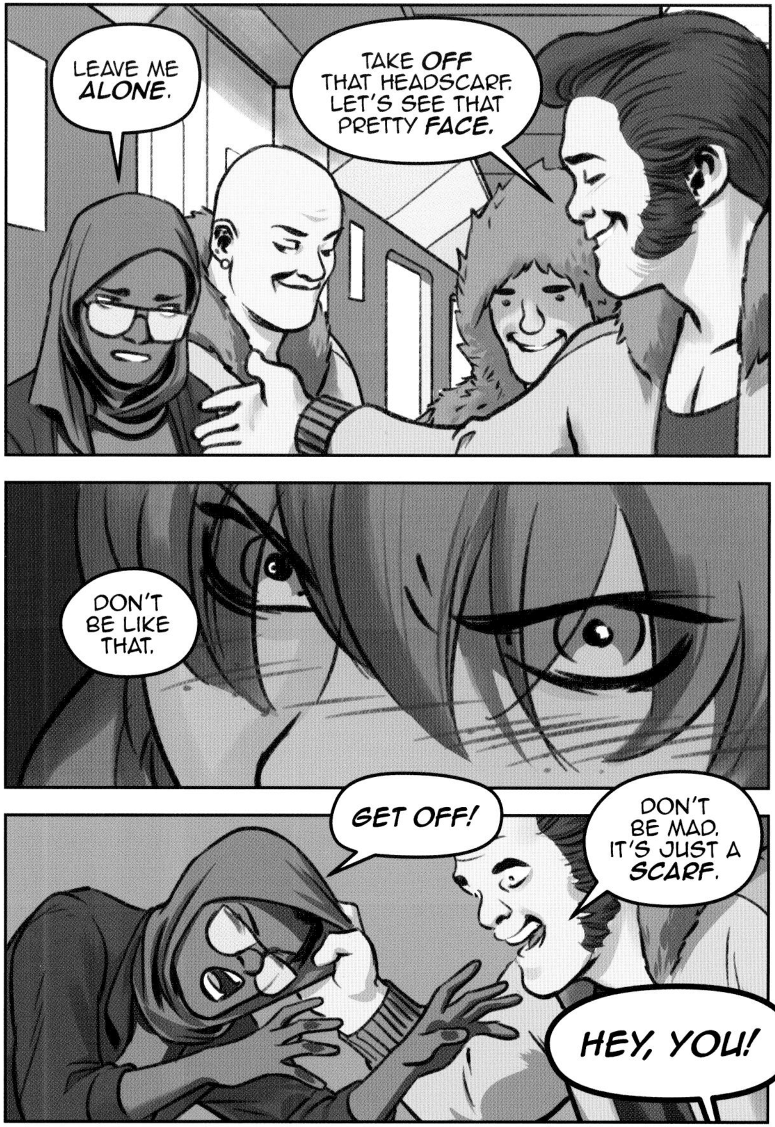
LEAVE ME ALONE.
TAKE OFF THAT HEADSCARF. LET'S SEE THAT PRETTY FACE.
DON'T BE LIKE THAT.
GET OFF!
DON'T BE MAD. IT'S JUST A SCARF.
HEY, YOU!

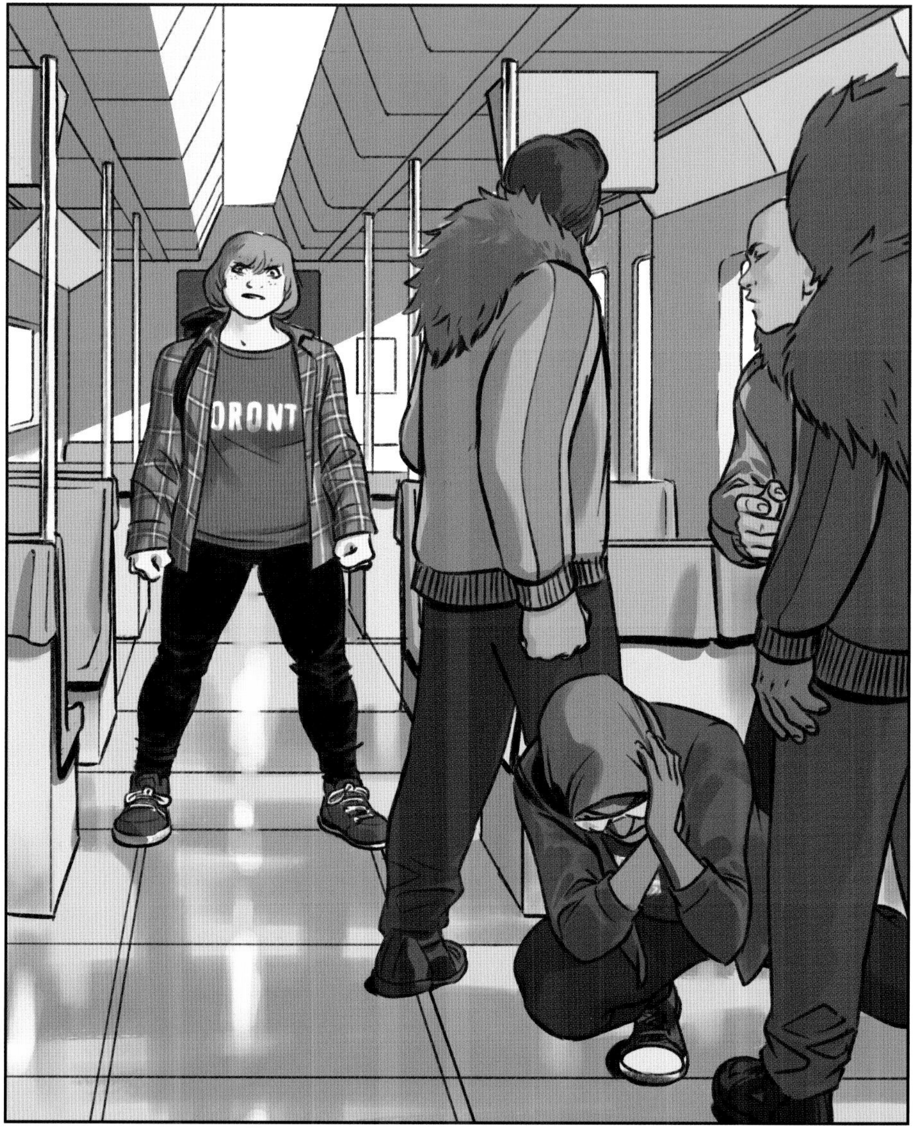
ORONT

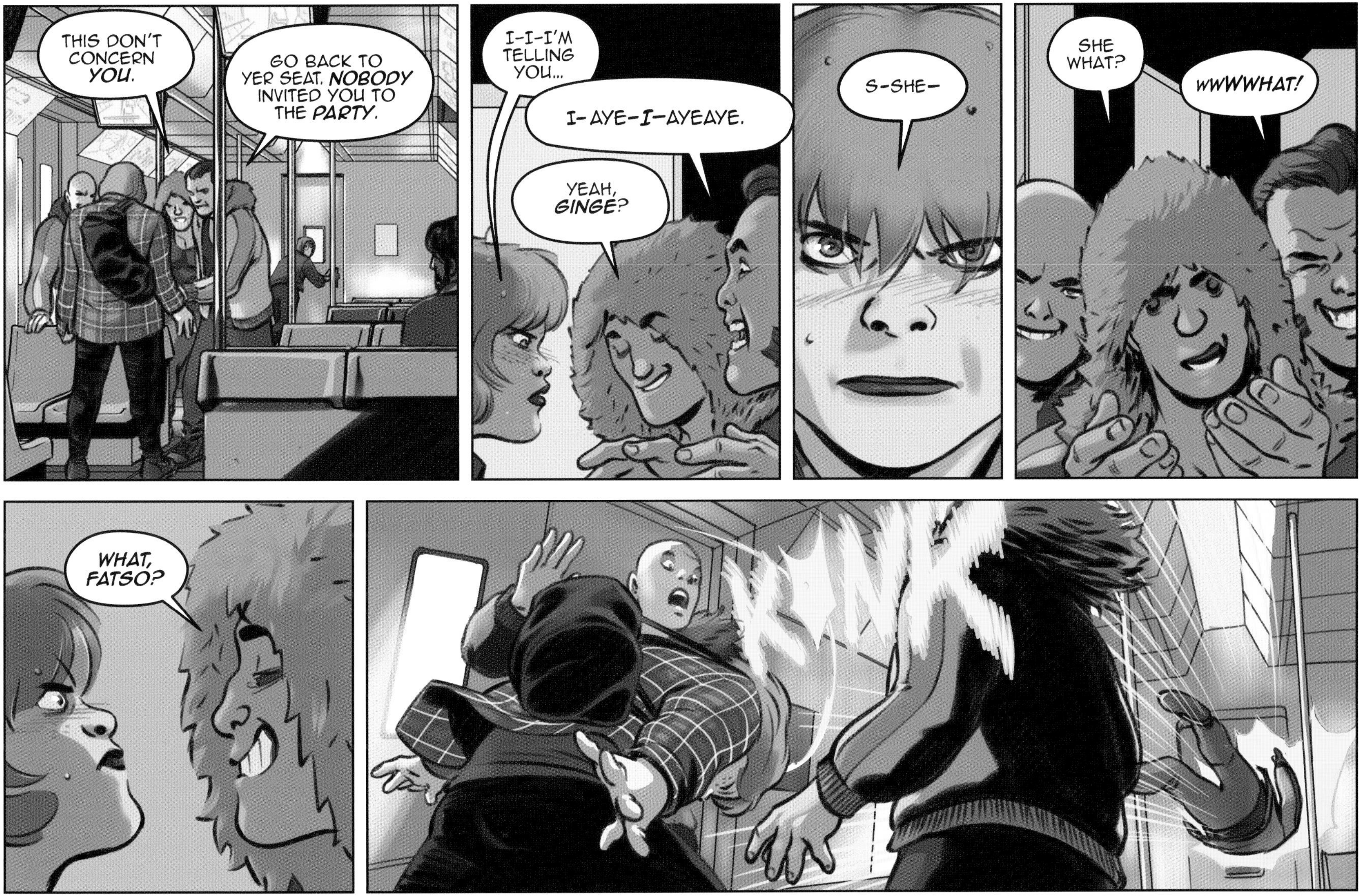
THIS DON'T CONCERN YOU.
GO BACK TO YER SEAT. NOBODY INVITED YOU TO THE PARTY.
I-I-I'M TELLING YOU...
I-AYE-I-AYEAYE.
YEAH, GINGE?
S-SHE-
SHE WHAT?
WWWWHAT!
WHAT, FATSO?

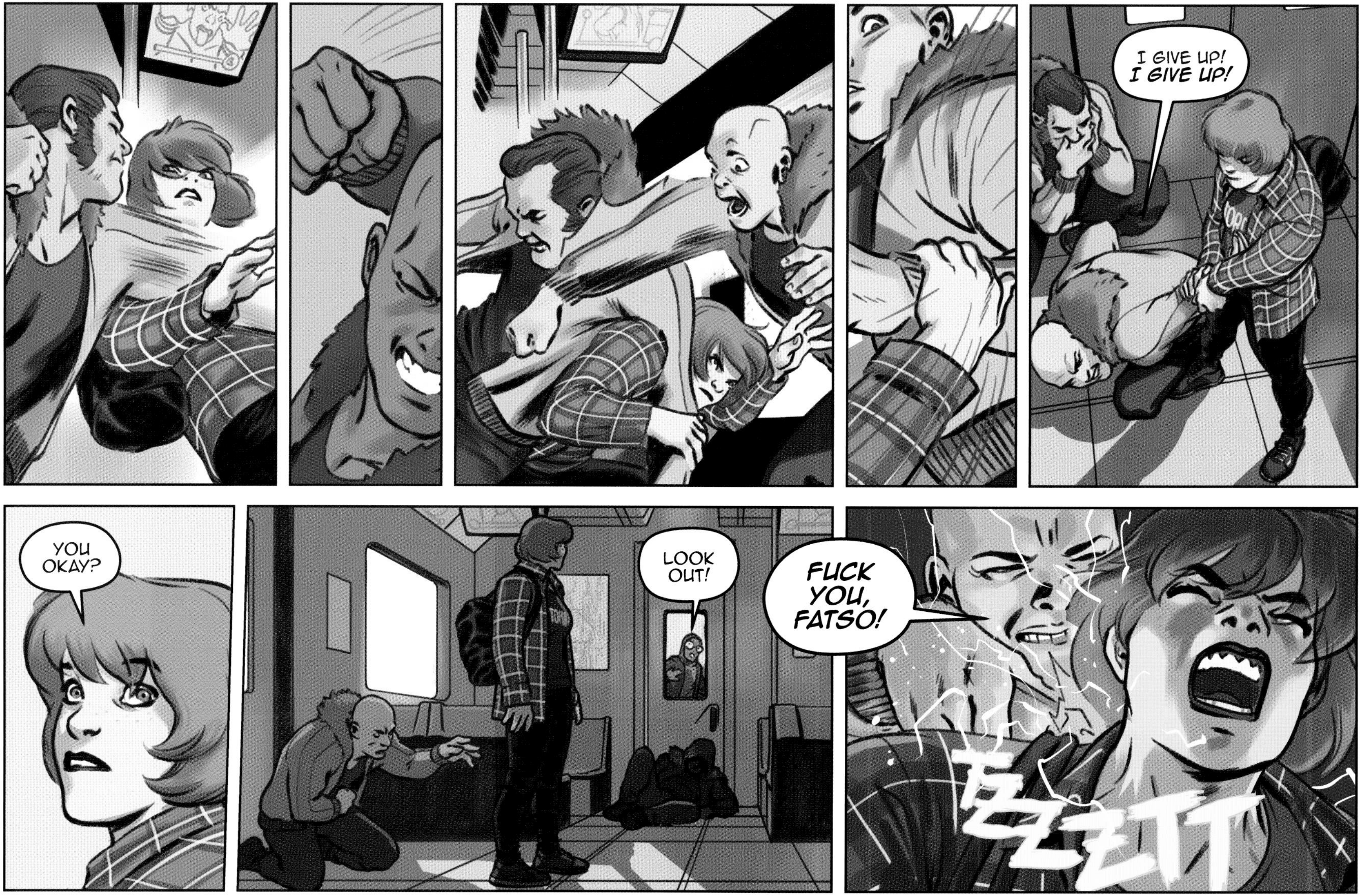
I GIVE UP!
I GIVE UP!
YOU OKAY?
LOOK OUT!
FUCK YOU, FATSO!
TZZZTT

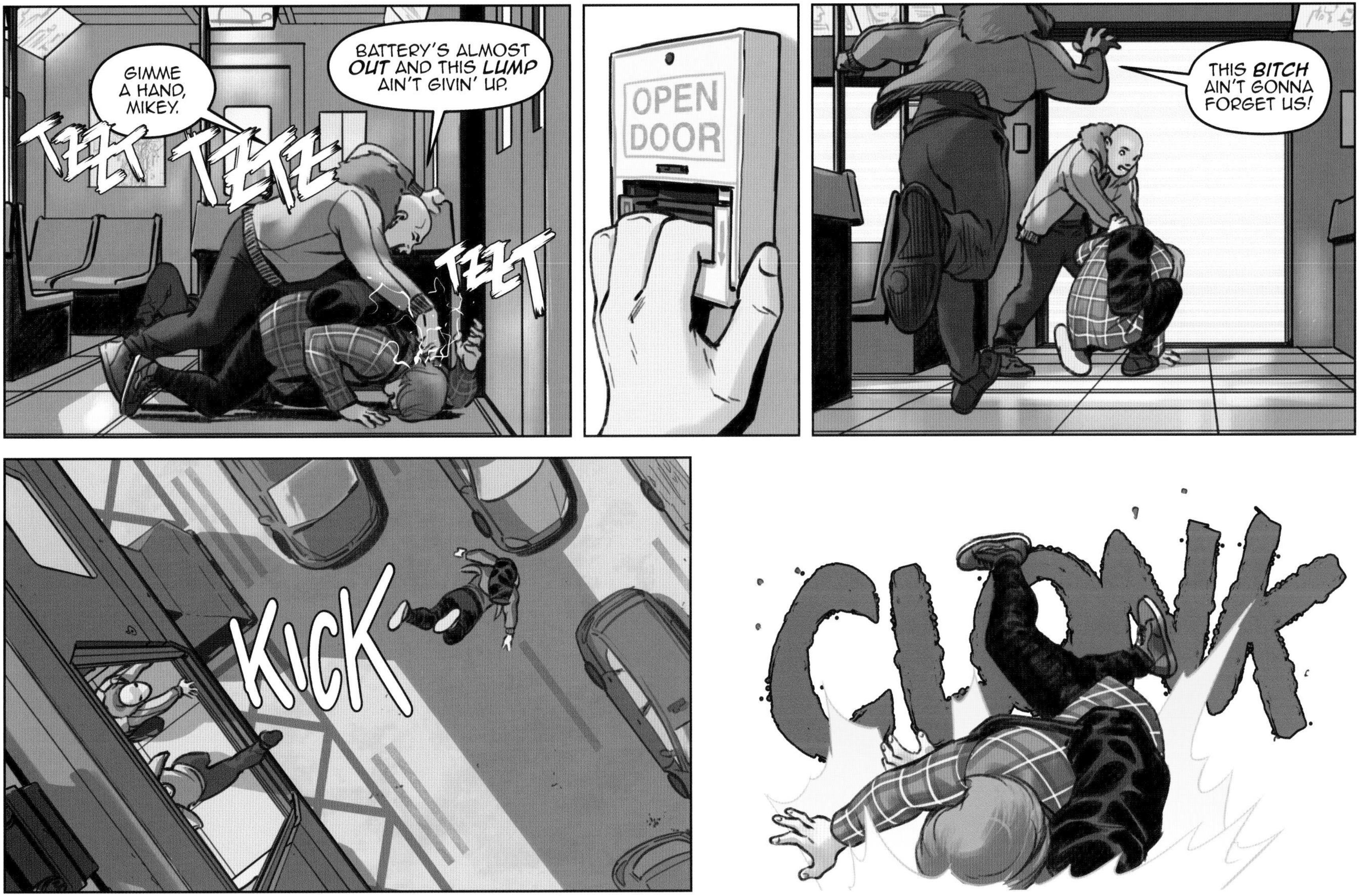
GIMME A HAND, MIKEY.
BATTERY'S ALMOST OUT AND THIS LUMP AIN'T GIVIN' UP.
TZZT TZZTZ
TZZT
OPEN DOOR
THIS BITCH AIN'T GONNA FORGET US!
KICK
CLONK

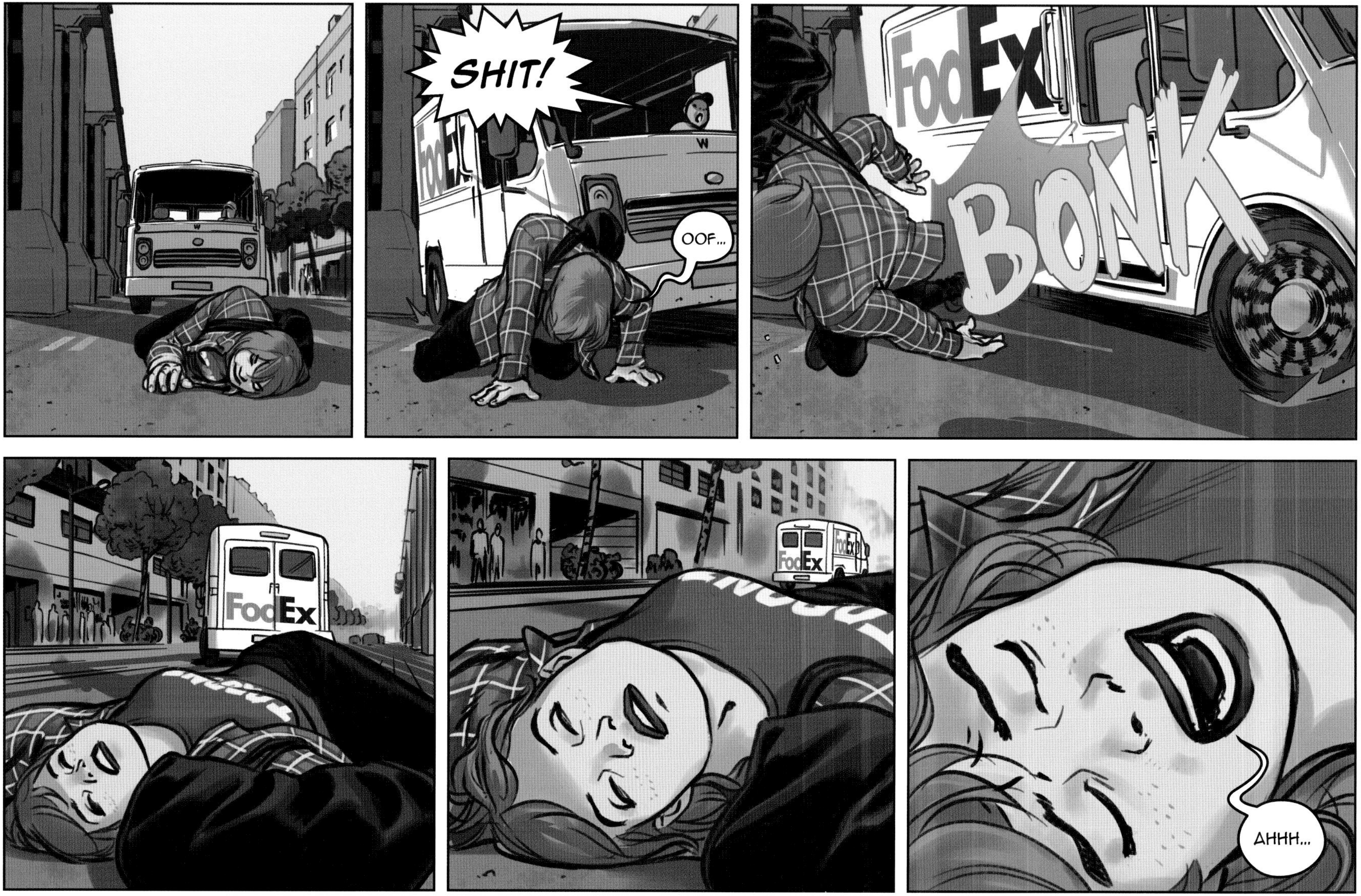
SHIT!
FodEx
OOF...
FodEx
BONK
FodEx
FodEx
AHHH...

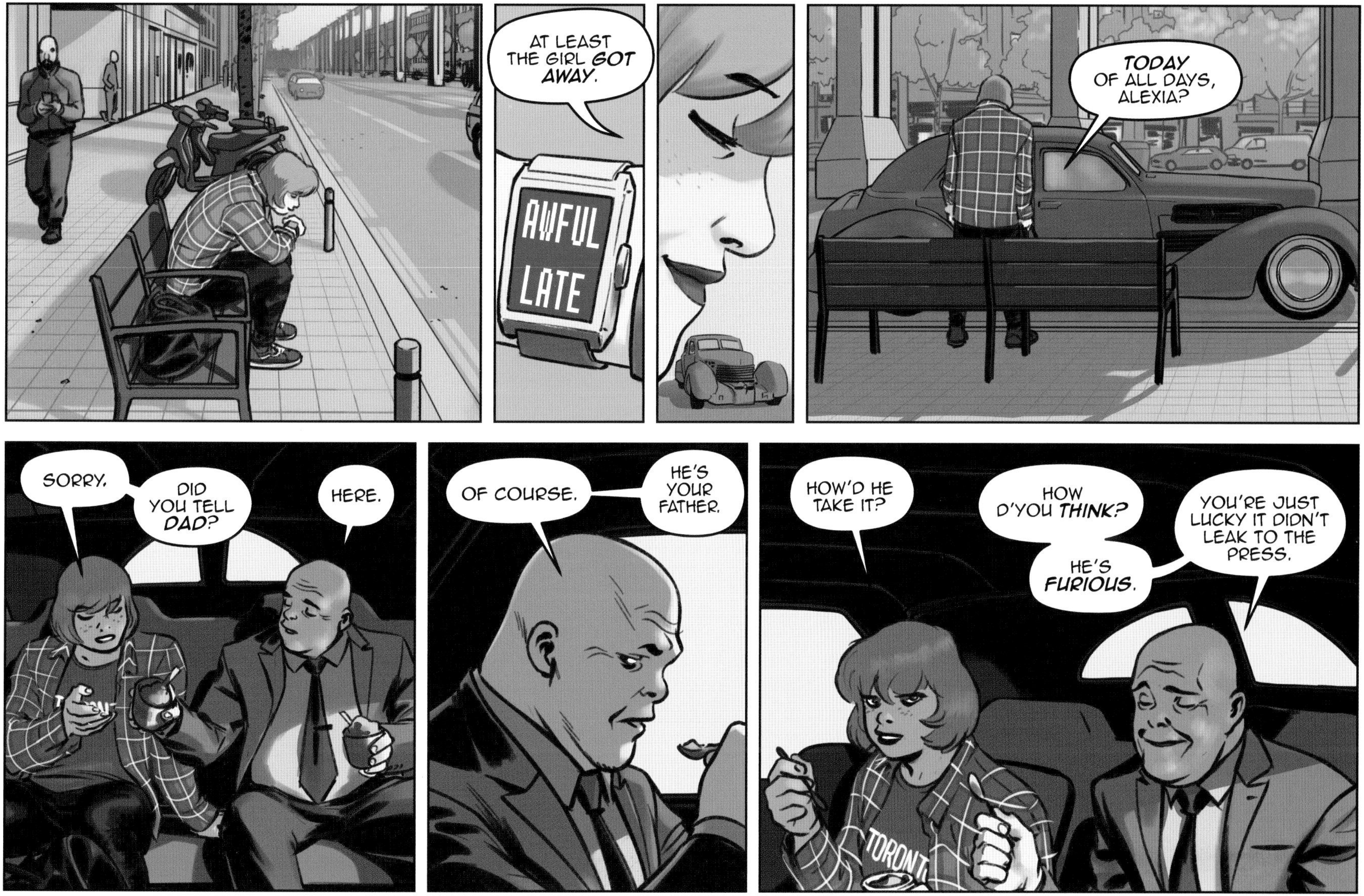
AT LEAST THE GIRL GOT AWAY.
AWFUL LATE
TODAY OF ALL DAYS, ALEXIA?
SORRY.
DID YOU TELL DAD?
HERE.
OF COURSE.
HE'S YOUR FATHER.
HOW'D HE TAKE IT?
HOW D'YOU THINK?
HE'S FURIOUS.
YOU'RE JUST LUCKY IT DIDN'T LEAK TO THE PRESS.
TORONT

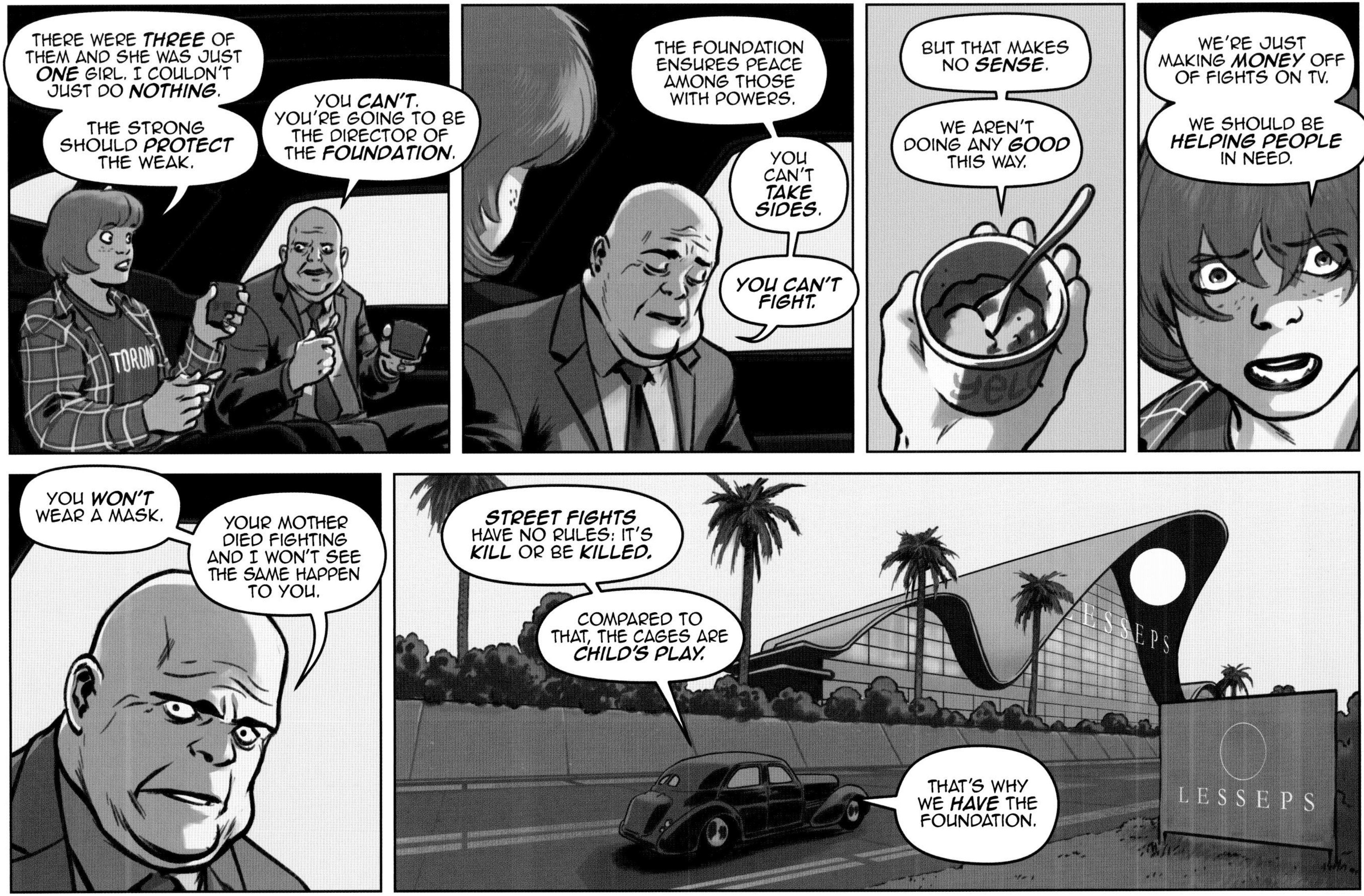

THERE WERE THREE OF THEM AND SHE WAS JUST ONE GIRL. I COULDN'T JUST DO NOTHING.
THE STRONG SHOULD PROTECT THE WEAK.
YOU CAN'T. YOU'RE GOING TO BE THE DIRECTOR OF THE FOUNDATION.
TORON
THE FOUNDATION ENSURES PEACE AMONG THOSE WITH POWERS.
YOU CAN'T TAKE SIDES.
YOU CAN'T FIGHT.
BUT THAT MAKES NO SENSE.
WE AREN'T DOING ANY GOOD THIS WAY.
WE'RE JUST MAKING MONEY OFF OF FIGHTS ON TV.
WE SHOULD BE HELPING PEOPLE IN NEED.
YOU WON'T WEAR A MASK.
YOUR MOTHER DIED FIGHTING AND I WON'T SEE THE SAME HAPPEN TO YOU.
STREET FIGHTS HAVE NO RULES: IT'S KILL OR BE KILLED.
COMPARED TO THAT, THE CAGES ARE CHILD'S PLAY.
LESSEPS
LESSEPS
THAT'S WHY WE HAVE THE FOUNDATION.

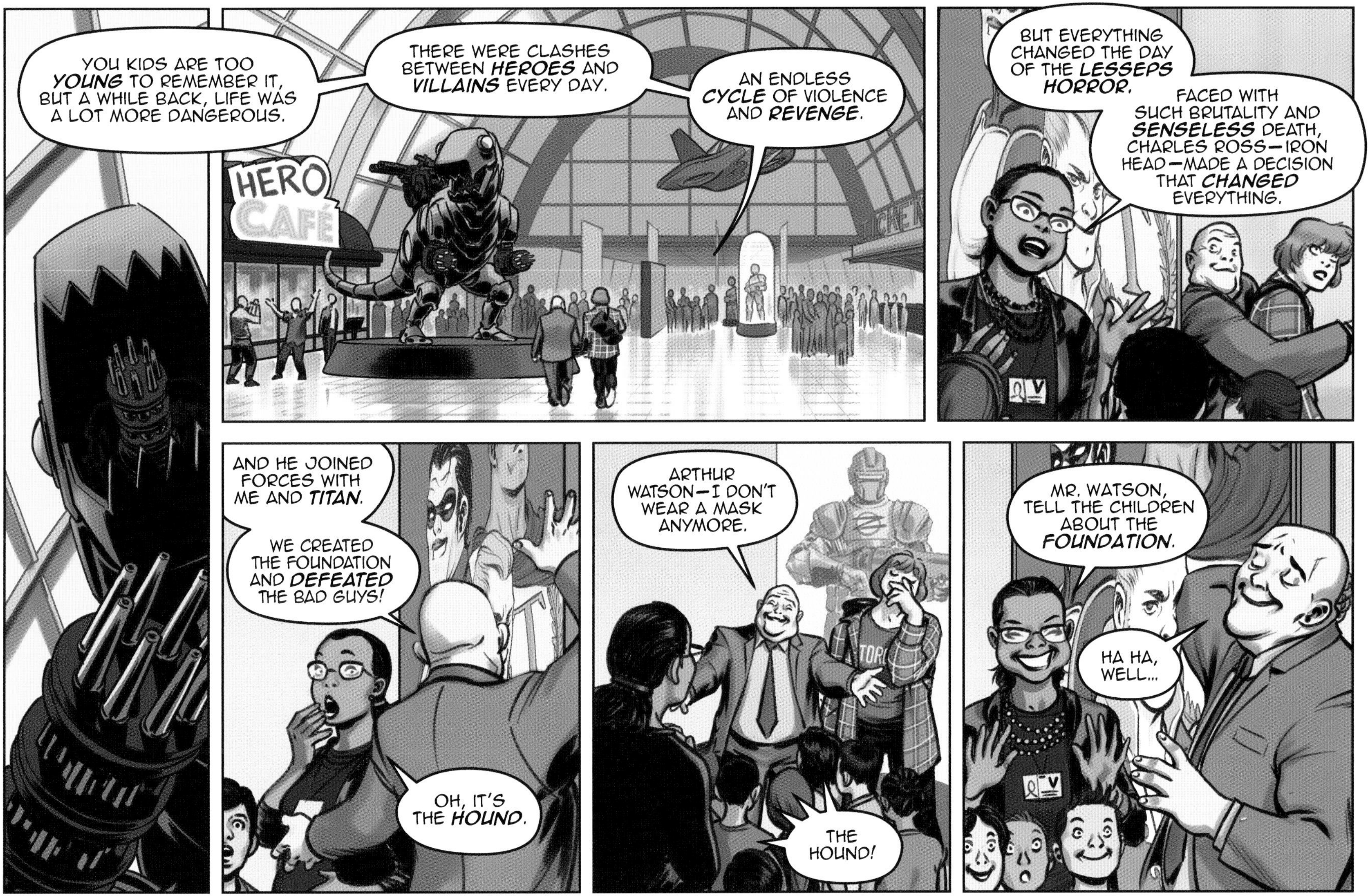

YOU KIDS ARE TOO *YOUNG* TO REMEMBER IT, BUT A WHILE BACK, LIFE WAS A LOT MORE DANGEROUS.
THERE WERE CLASHES BETWEEN *HEROES* AND *VILLAINS* EVERY DAY.
AN ENDLESS *CYCLE* OF VIOLENCE AND *REVENGE*.
HERO CAFÉ
BUT EVERYTHING CHANGED THE DAY OF THE *LESSEPS HORROR*.
FACED WITH SUCH BRUTALITY AND *SENSELESS* DEATH, CHARLES ROSS—IRON HEAD—MADE A DECISION THAT *CHANGED* EVERYTHING.
AND HE JOINED FORCES WITH ME AND *TITAN*.
WE CREATED THE FOUNDATION AND *DEFEATED* THE BAD GUYS!
OH, IT'S THE *HOUND*.
ARTHUR WATSON—I DON'T WEAR A MASK ANYMORE.
THE HOUND!
MR. WATSON, TELL THE CHILDREN ABOUT THE *FOUNDATION*.
HA HA, WELL...

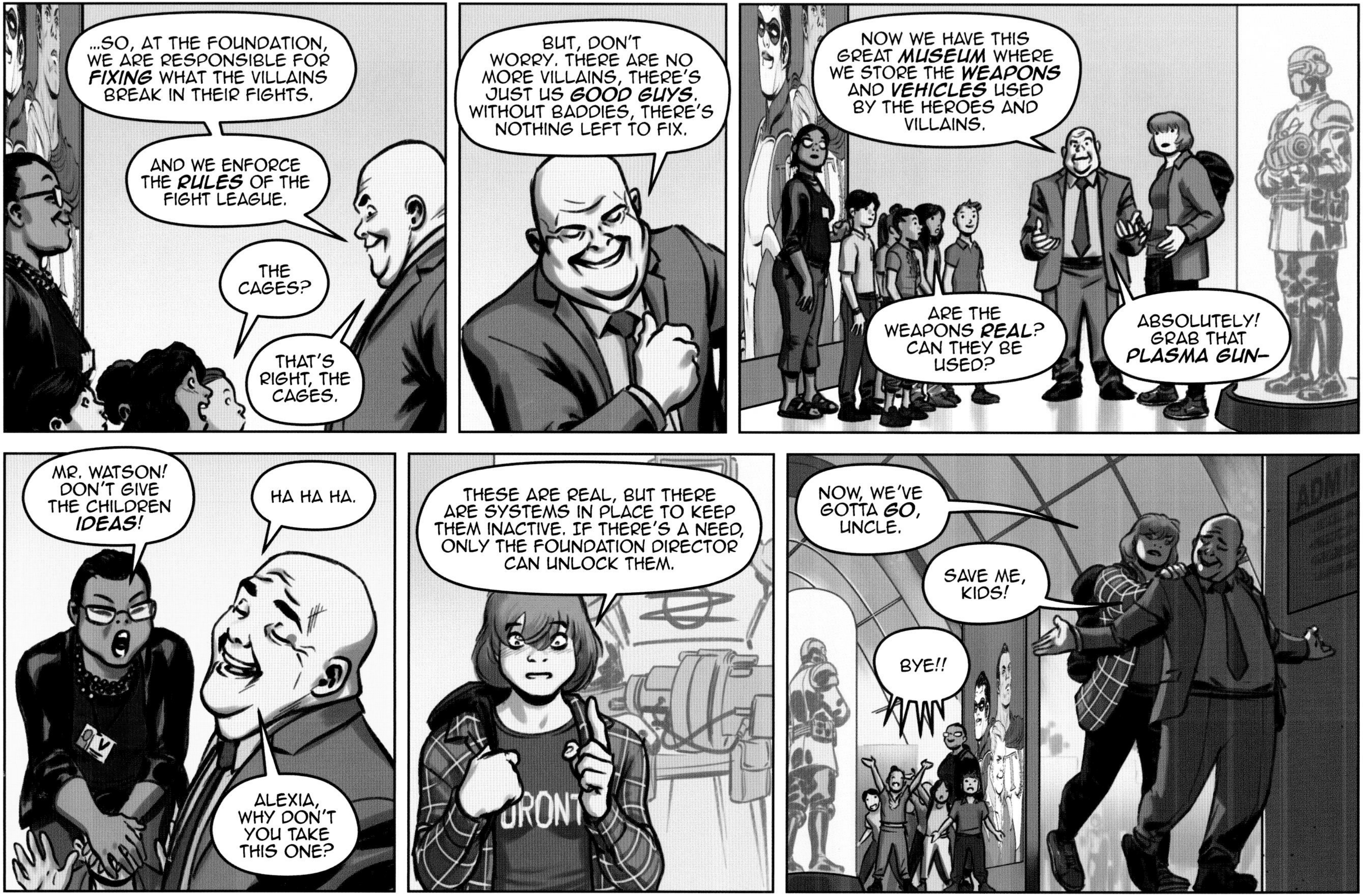
...SO, AT THE FOUNDATION, WE ARE RESPONSIBLE FOR *FIXING* WHAT THE VILLAINS BREAK IN THEIR FIGHTS.
AND WE ENFORCE THE *RULES* OF THE FIGHT LEAGUE.
THE CAGES?
THAT'S RIGHT, THE CAGES.
BUT, DON'T WORRY. THERE ARE NO MORE VILLAINS, THERE'S JUST US *GOOD GUYS*. WITHOUT BADDIES, THERE'S NOTHING LEFT TO FIX.
NOW WE HAVE THIS GREAT *MUSEUM* WHERE WE STORE THE *WEAPONS* AND *VEHICLES* USED BY THE HEROES AND VILLAINS.
ARE THE WEAPONS *REAL*? CAN THEY BE USED?
ABSOLUTELY! GRAB THAT *PLASMA GUN*–
MR. WATSON! DON'T GIVE THE CHILDREN *IDEAS*!
HA HA HA.
ALEXIA, WHY DON'T YOU TAKE THIS ONE?
THESE ARE REAL, BUT THERE ARE SYSTEMS IN PLACE TO KEEP THEM INACTIVE. IF THERE'S A NEED, ONLY THE FOUNDATION DIRECTOR CAN UNLOCK THEM.
NOW, WE'VE GOTTA *GO*, UNCLE.
SAVE ME, KIDS!
BYE!!

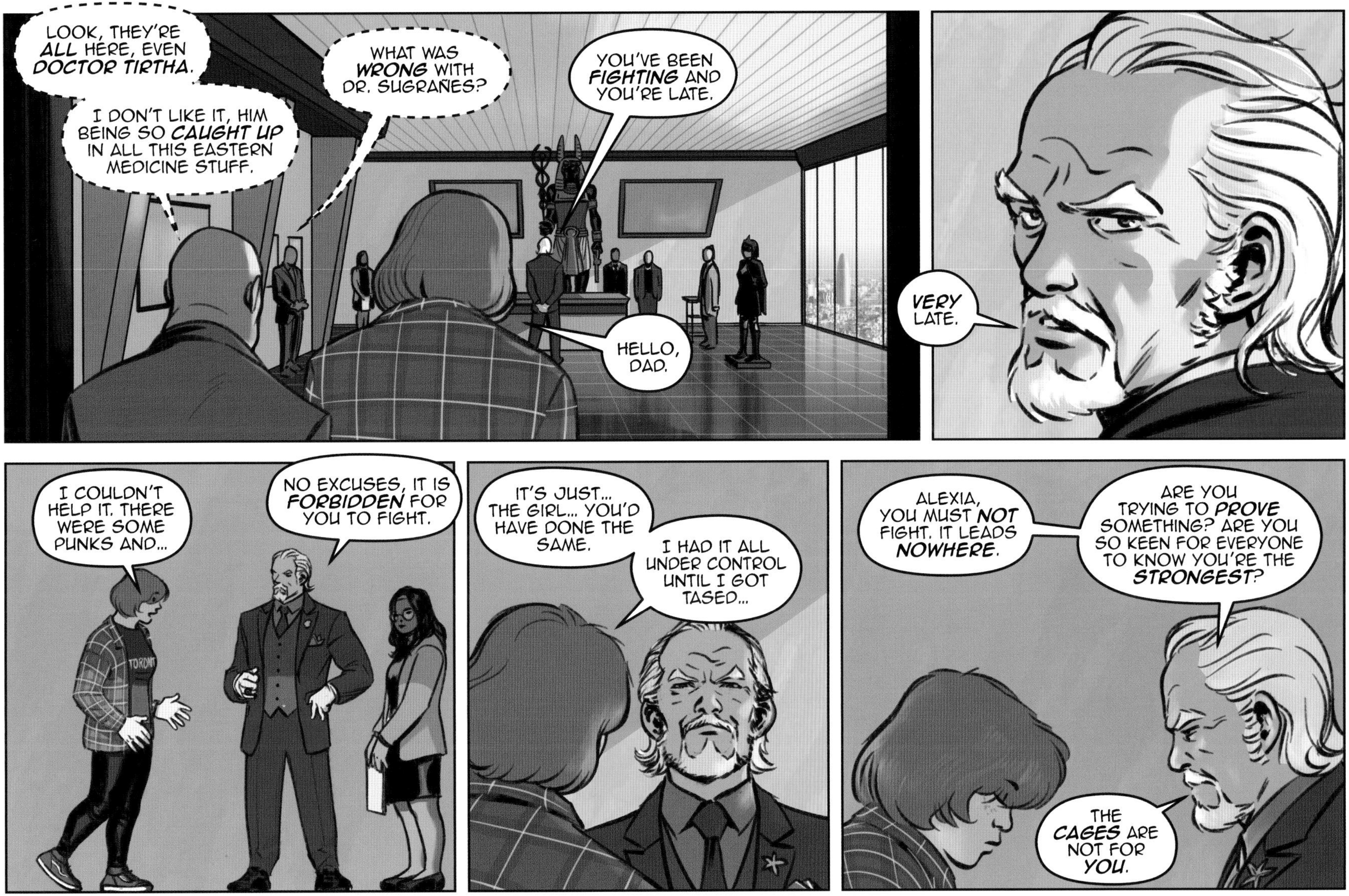
LOOK, THEY'RE ALL HERE, EVEN DOCTOR TIRTHA.
I DON'T LIKE IT, HIM BEING SO CAUGHT UP IN ALL THIS EASTERN MEDICINE STUFF.
WHAT WAS WRONG WITH DR. SUGRAÑES?
YOU'VE BEEN FIGHTING AND YOU'RE LATE.
HELLO, DAD.
VERY LATE.
I COULDN'T HELP IT. THERE WERE SOME PUNKS AND...
NO EXCUSES, IT IS FORBIDDEN FOR YOU TO FIGHT.
IT'S JUST... THE GIRL... YOU'D HAVE DONE THE SAME.
I HAD IT ALL UNDER CONTROL UNTIL I GOT TASED...
ALEXIA, YOU MUST NOT FIGHT. IT LEADS NOWHERE.
ARE YOU TRYING TO PROVE SOMETHING? ARE YOU SO KEEN FOR EVERYONE TO KNOW YOU'RE THE STRONGEST?
THE CAGES ARE NOT FOR YOU.

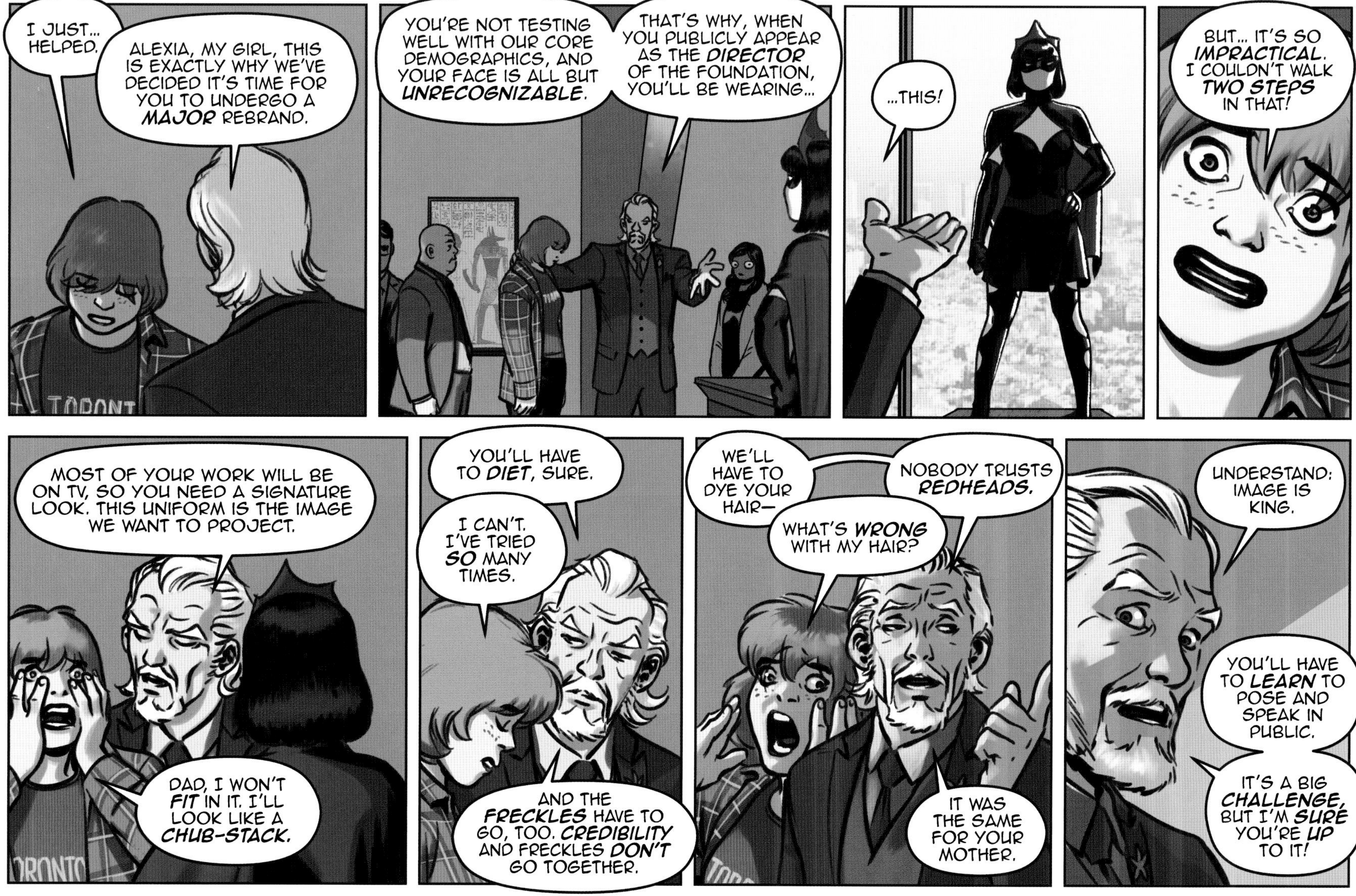

I JUST... HELPED.
ALEXIA, MY GIRL, THIS IS EXACTLY WHY WE'VE DECIDED IT'S TIME FOR YOU TO UNDERGO A *MAJOR* REBRAND.
TORONT
YOU'RE NOT TESTING WELL WITH OUR CORE DEMOGRAPHICS, AND YOUR FACE IS ALL BUT *UNRECOGNIZABLE*.
THAT'S WHY, WHEN YOU PUBLICLY APPEAR AS THE *DIRECTOR* OF THE FOUNDATION, YOU'LL BE WEARING...
...THIS!
BUT... IT'S SO *IMPRACTICAL*. I COULDN'T WALK *TWO STEPS* IN THAT!
MOST OF YOUR WORK WILL BE ON TV, SO YOU NEED A SIGNATURE LOOK. THIS UNIFORM IS THE IMAGE WE WANT TO PROJECT.
DAD, I WON'T *FIT* IN IT. I'LL LOOK LIKE A *CHUB-STACK.*
TORONTO
YOU'LL HAVE TO *DIET*, SURE.
I CAN'T. I'VE TRIED *SO* MANY TIMES.
AND THE *FRECKLES* HAVE TO GO, TOO. *CREDIBILITY* AND FRECKLES *DON'T* GO TOGETHER.
WE'LL HAVE TO DYE YOUR HAIR—
NOBODY TRUSTS *REDHEADS.*
WHAT'S *WRONG* WITH MY HAIR?
IT WAS THE SAME FOR YOUR MOTHER.
UNDERSTAND: IMAGE IS KING.
YOU'LL HAVE TO *LEARN* TO POSE AND SPEAK IN PUBLIC.
IT'S A BIG *CHALLENGE,* BUT I'M *SURE* YOU'RE *UP* TO IT!

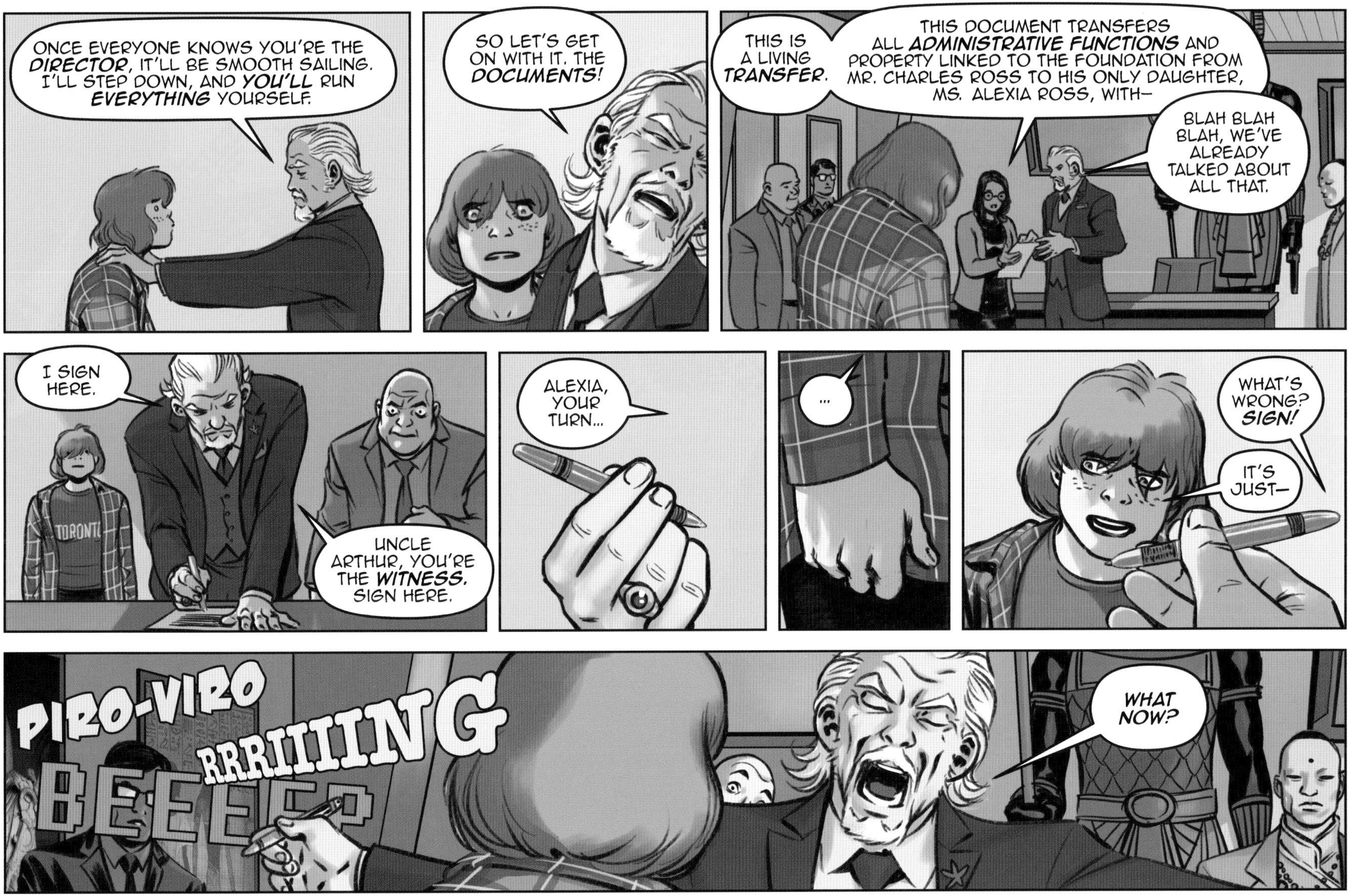
ONCE EVERYONE KNOWS YOU'RE THE *DIRECTOR*, IT'LL BE SMOOTH SAILING. I'LL STEP DOWN, AND *YOU'LL* RUN *EVERYTHING* YOURSELF.
SO LET'S GET ON WITH IT. THE *DOCUMENTS!*
THIS IS A LIVING *TRANSFER*.
THIS DOCUMENT TRANSFERS ALL *ADMINISTRATIVE FUNCTIONS* AND PROPERTY LINKED TO THE FOUNDATION FROM MR. CHARLES ROSS TO HIS ONLY DAUGHTER, MS. ALEXIA ROSS, WITH—
BLAH BLAH BLAH, WE'VE ALREADY TALKED ABOUT ALL THAT.
I SIGN HERE.
TORONTO
UNCLE ARTHUR, YOU'RE THE *WITNESS.* SIGN HERE.
ALEXIA, YOUR TURN...
...
WHAT'S WRONG? *SIGN!*
IT'S JUST—
PIRO-VIRO
RRRIIIING
BEEEEP
WHAT NOW?

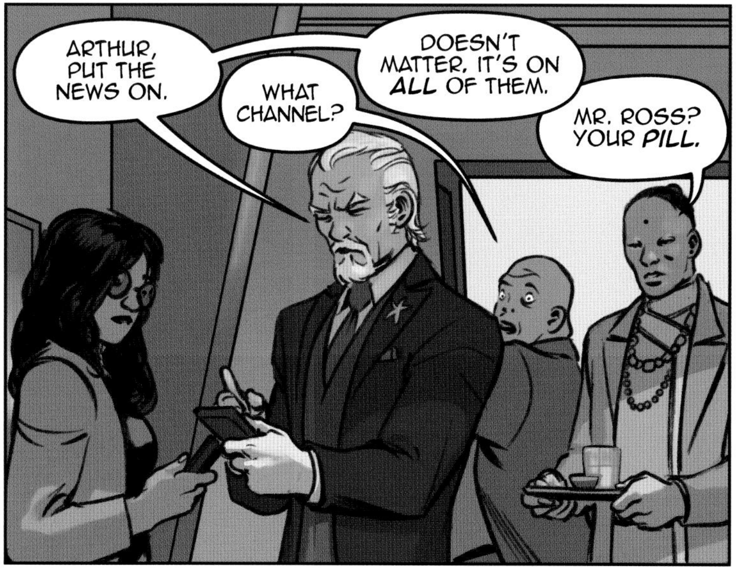
ARTHUR, PUT THE NEWS ON.
WHAT CHANNEL?
DOESN'T MATTER. IT'S ON ALL OF THEM.
MR. ROSS? YOUR PILL.

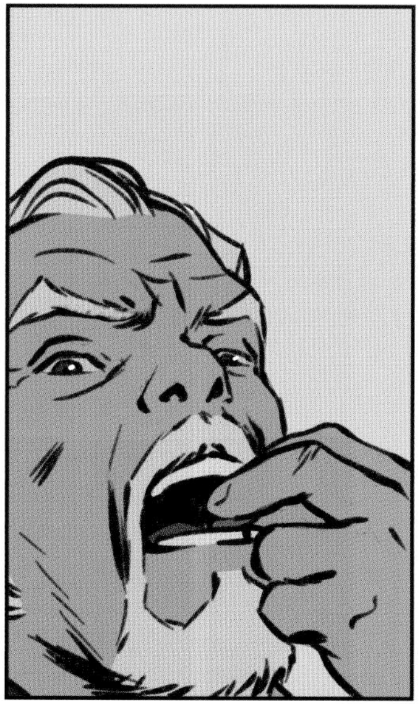

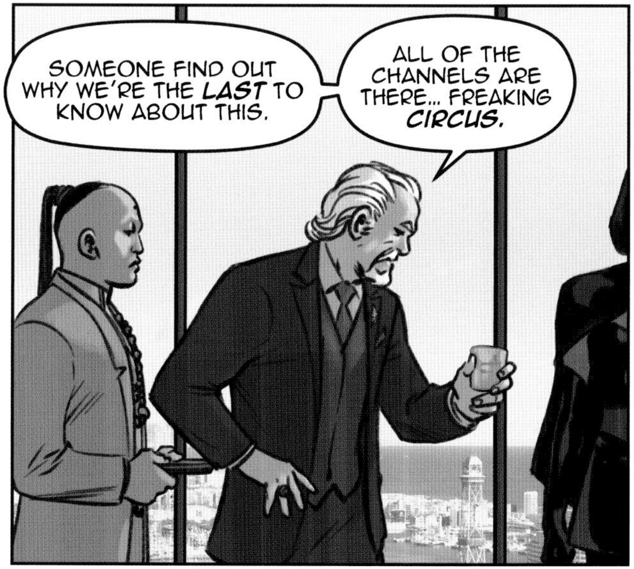
SOMEONE FIND OUT WHY WE'RE THE LAST TO KNOW ABOUT THIS.
ALL OF THE CHANNELS ARE THERE... FREAKING CIRCUS.

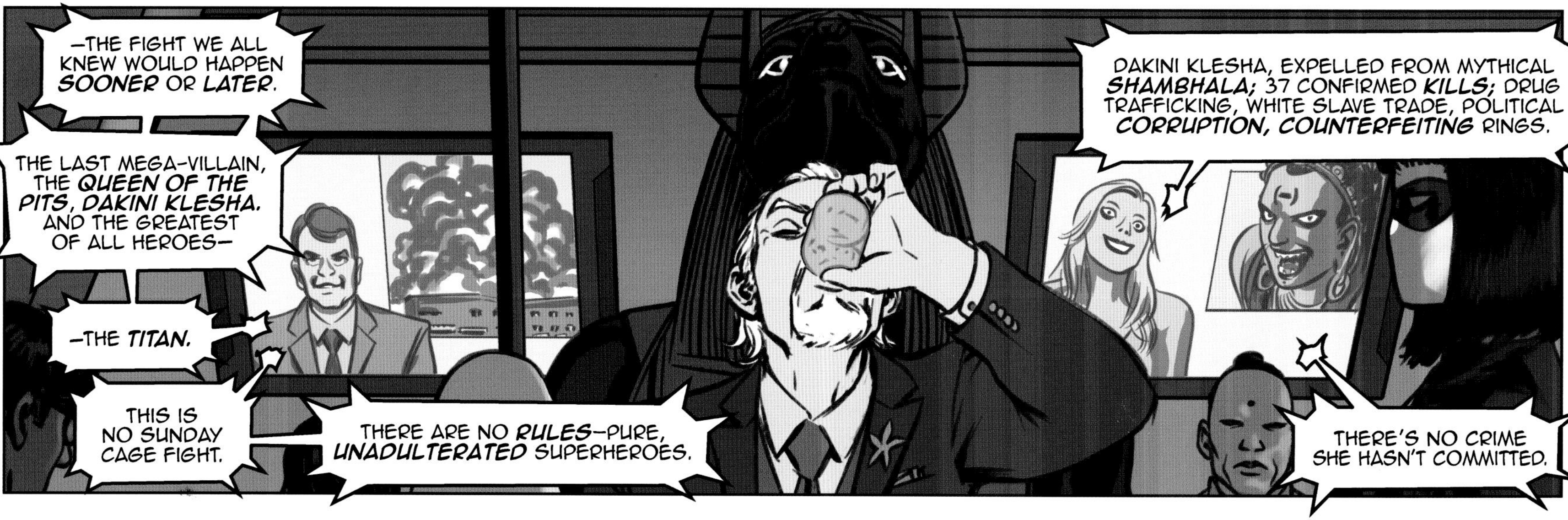
—THE FIGHT WE ALL KNEW WOULD HAPPEN SOONER OR LATER.
THE LAST MEGA-VILLAIN, THE QUEEN OF THE PITS, DAKINI KLESHA. AND THE GREATEST OF ALL HEROES—
—THE TITAN.
THIS IS NO SUNDAY CAGE FIGHT.
THERE ARE NO RULES—PURE, UNADULTERATED SUPERHEROES.
DAKINI KLESHA, EXPELLED FROM MYTHICAL SHAMBHALA; 37 CONFIRMED KILLS; DRUG TRAFFICKING, WHITE SLAVE TRADE, POLITICAL CORRUPTION, COUNTERFEITING RINGS.
THERE'S NO CRIME SHE HASN'T COMMITTED.

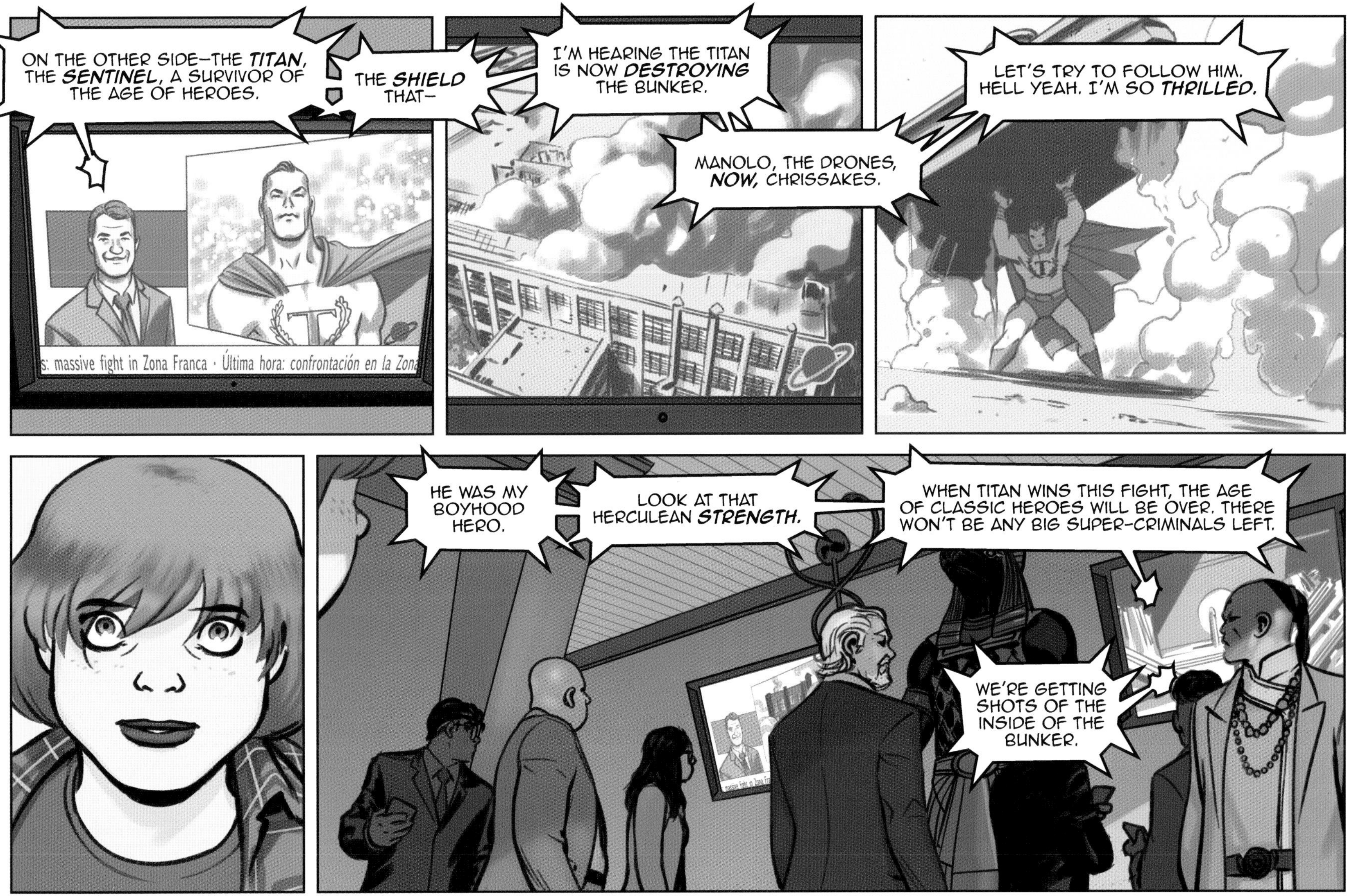
ON THE OTHER SIDE—THE TITAN, THE SENTINEL, A SURVIVOR OF THE AGE OF HEROES.
THE SHIELD THAT—
s: massive fight in Zona Franca · Última hora: confrontación en la Zona
I'M HEARING THE TITAN IS NOW DESTROYING THE BUNKER.
MANOLO, THE DRONES, NOW, CHRISSAKES.
LET'S TRY TO FOLLOW HIM. HELL YEAH. I'M SO THRILLED.
HE WAS MY BOYHOOD HERO.
LOOK AT THAT HERCULEAN STRENGTH.
WHEN TITAN WINS THIS FIGHT, THE AGE OF CLASSIC HEROES WILL BE OVER. THERE WON'T BE ANY BIG SUPER-CRIMINALS LEFT.
WE'RE GETTING SHOTS OF THE INSIDE OF THE BUNKER.

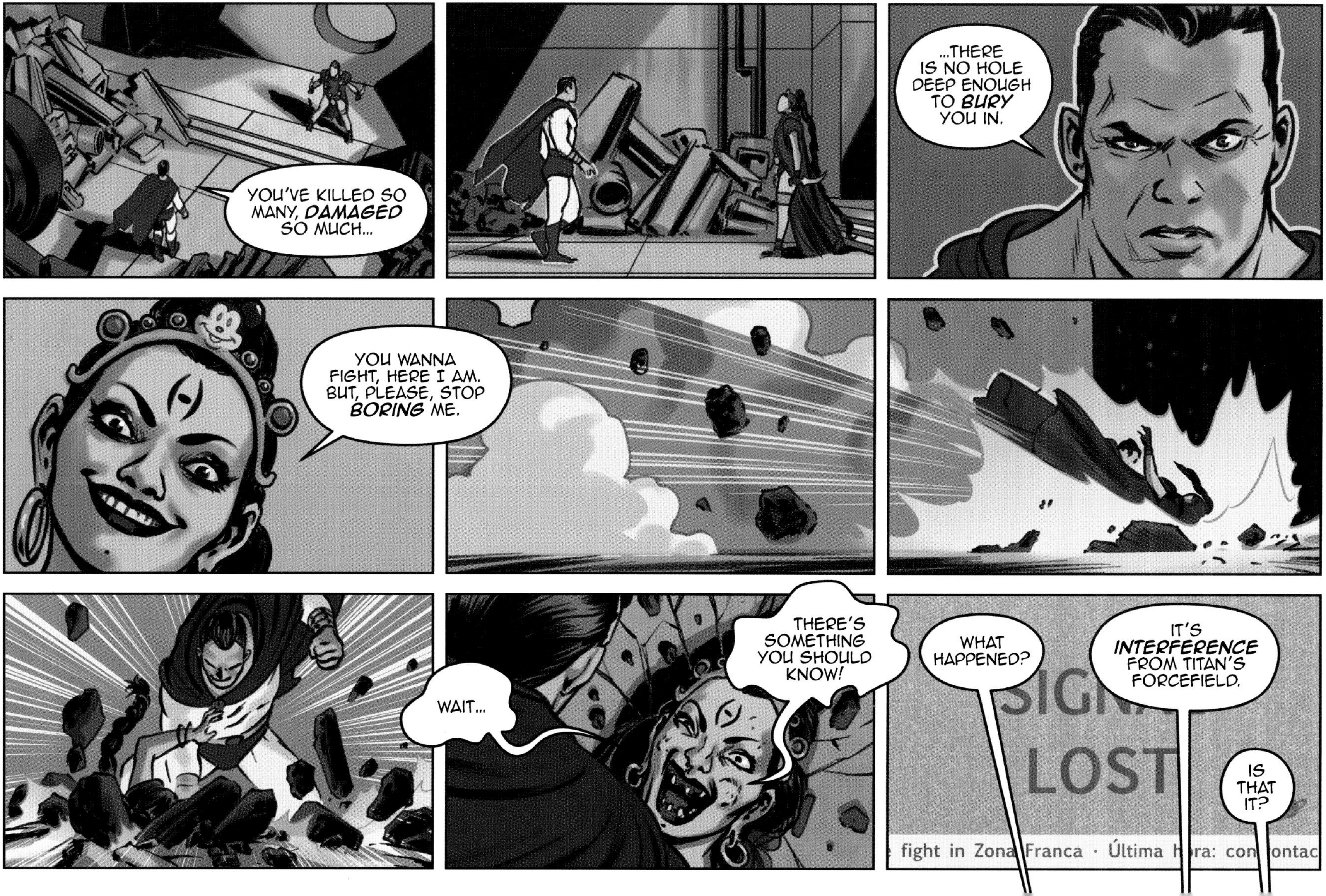

YOU'VE KILLED SO MANY, *DAMAGED* SO MUCH...
...THERE IS NO HOLE DEEP ENOUGH TO *BURY* YOU IN.
YOU WANNA FIGHT, HERE I AM. BUT, PLEASE, STOP *BORING* ME.
WAIT...
THERE'S SOMETHING YOU SHOULD KNOW!
LOST
fight in Zona Franca · Última hora:
WHAT HAPPENED?
IT'S *INTERFERENCE* FROM TITAN'S FORCEFIELD.
IS THAT IT?

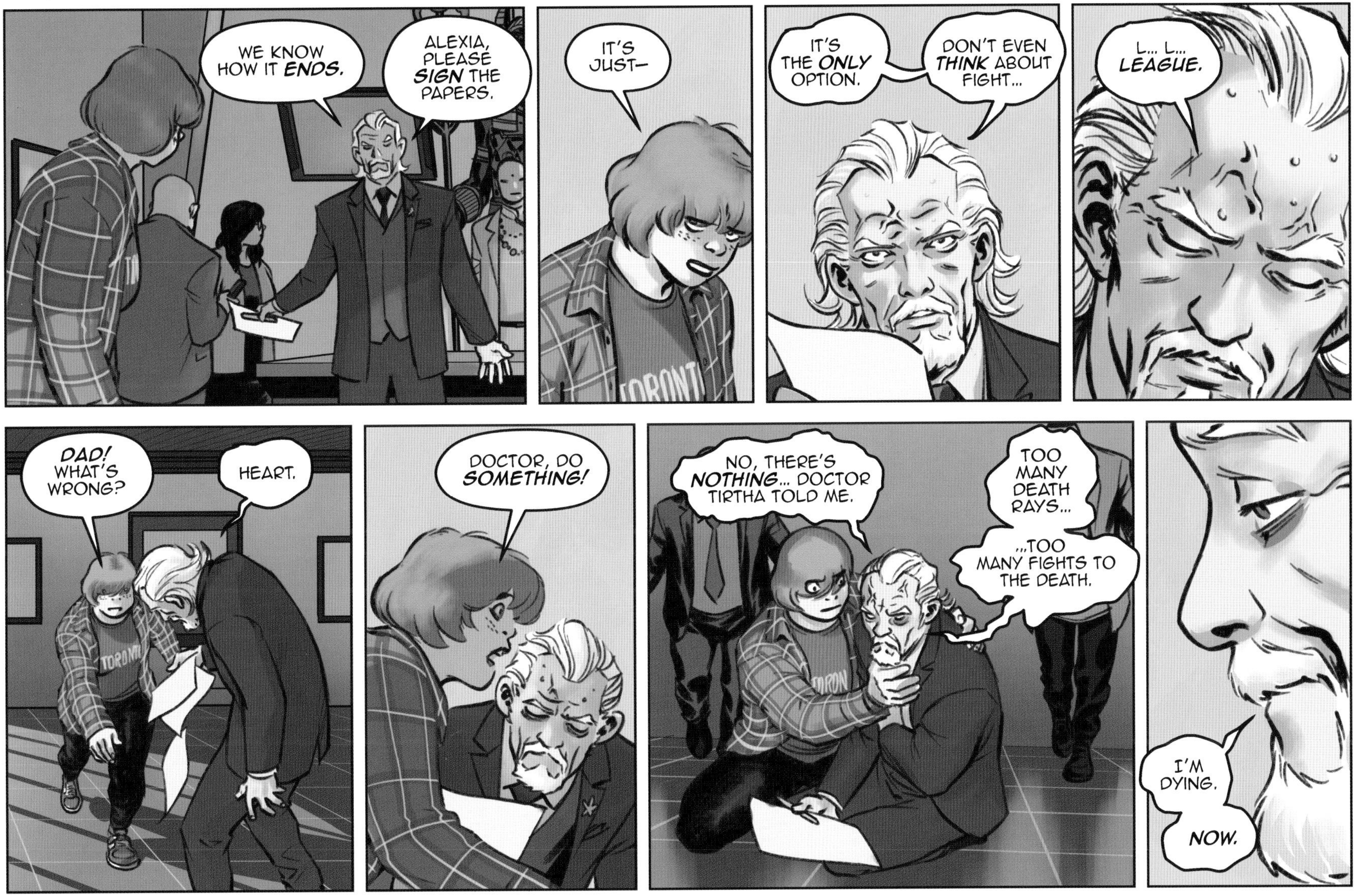
WE KNOW HOW IT ENDS.
ALEXIA, PLEASE SIGN THE PAPERS.
IT'S JUST–
IT'S THE ONLY OPTION.
DON'T EVEN THINK ABOUT FIGHT...
L... L... LEAGUE.
DAD! WHAT'S WRONG?
HEART.
DOCTOR, DO SOMETHING!
NO, THERE'S NOTHING... DOCTOR TIRTHA TOLD ME.
TOO MANY DEATH RAYS...
...TOO MANY FIGHTS TO THE DEATH.
I'M DYING.
NOW.

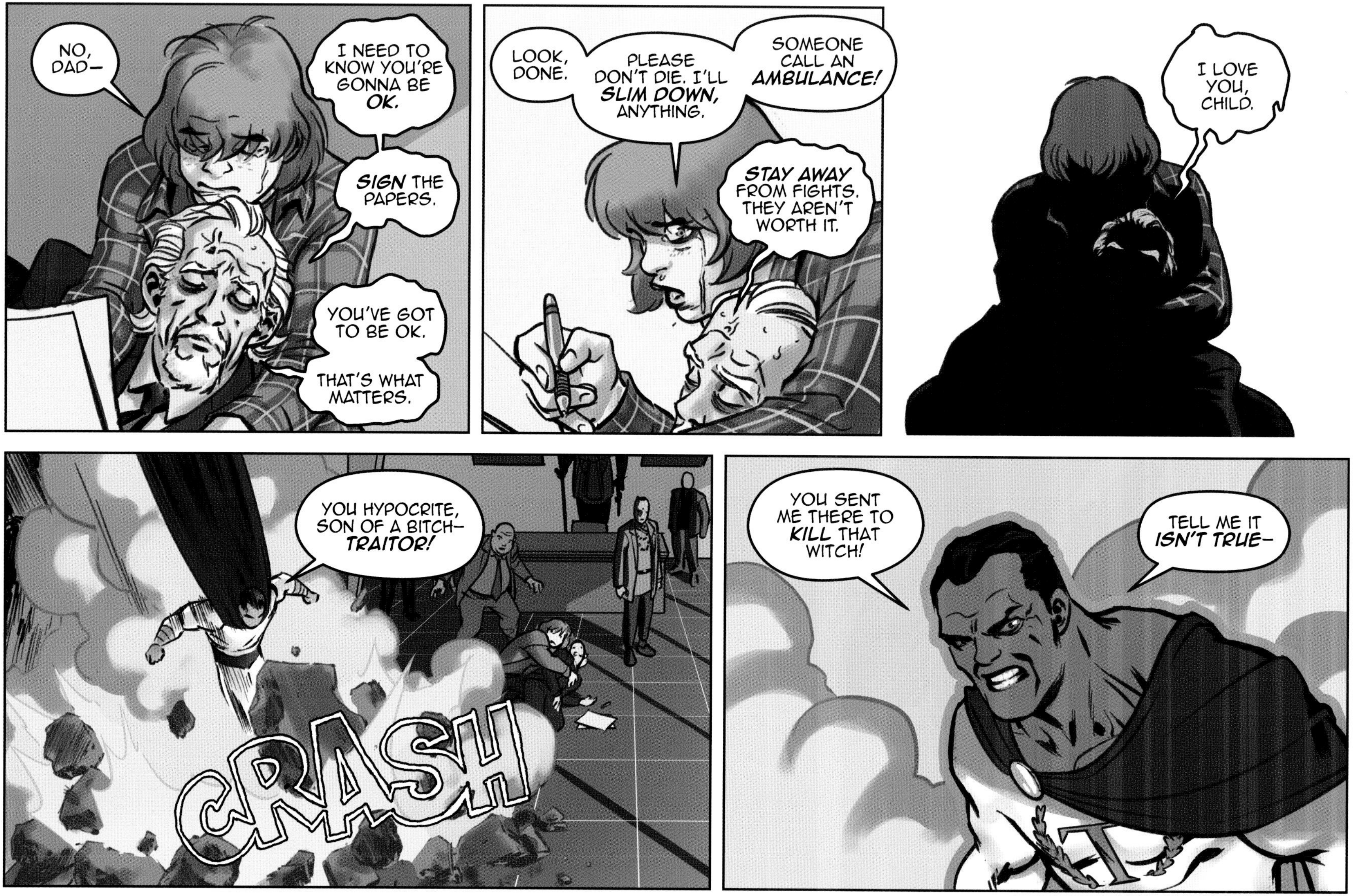
NO, DAD–
I NEED TO KNOW YOU'RE GONNA BE OK.
SIGN THE PAPERS.
YOU'VE GOT TO BE OK.
THAT'S WHAT MATTERS.
LOOK, DONE.
PLEASE DON'T DIE. I'LL SLIM DOWN, ANYTHING.
SOMEONE CALL AN AMBULANCE!
STAY AWAY FROM FIGHTS. THEY AREN'T WORTH IT.
I LOVE YOU, CHILD.
YOU HYPOCRITE, SON OF A BITCH– TRAITOR!
CRASH
YOU SENT ME THERE TO KILL THAT WITCH!
TELL ME IT ISN'T TRUE–

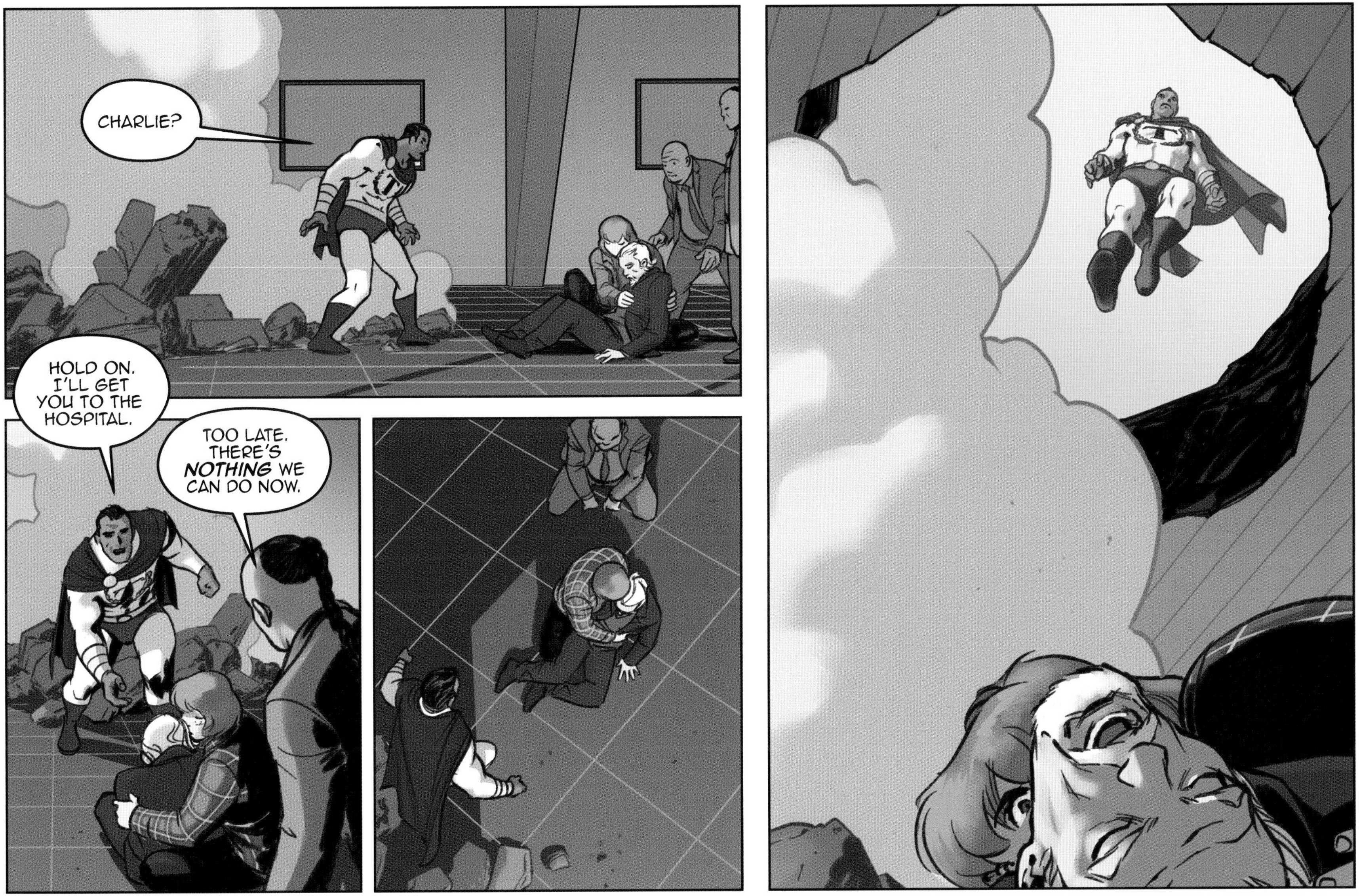
CHARLIE?
HOLD ON. I'LL GET YOU TO THE HOSPITAL.
TOO LATE. THERE'S *NOTHING* WE CAN DO NOW.

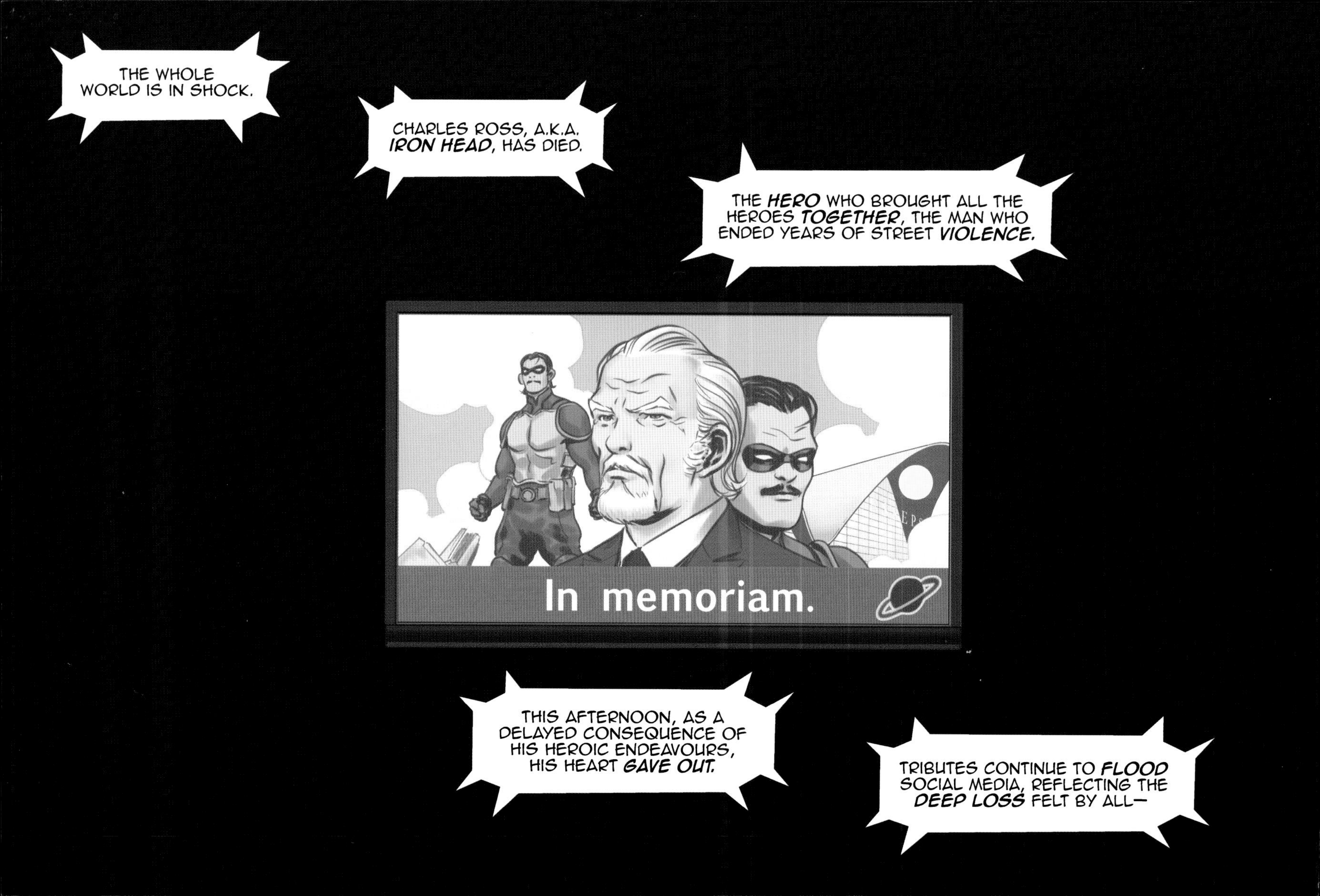
THE WHOLE WORLD IS IN SHOCK.
CHARLES ROSS, A.K.A. *IRON HEAD*, HAS DIED.
THE *HERO* WHO BROUGHT ALL THE HEROES *TOGETHER*, THE MAN WHO ENDED YEARS OF STREET *VIOLENCE.*
In memoriam.
THIS AFTERNOON, AS A DELAYED CONSEQUENCE OF HIS HEROIC ENDEAVOURS, HIS HEART *GAVE OUT.*
TRIBUTES CONTINUE TO *FLOOD* SOCIAL MEDIA, REFLECTING THE *DEEP LOSS* FELT BY ALL—

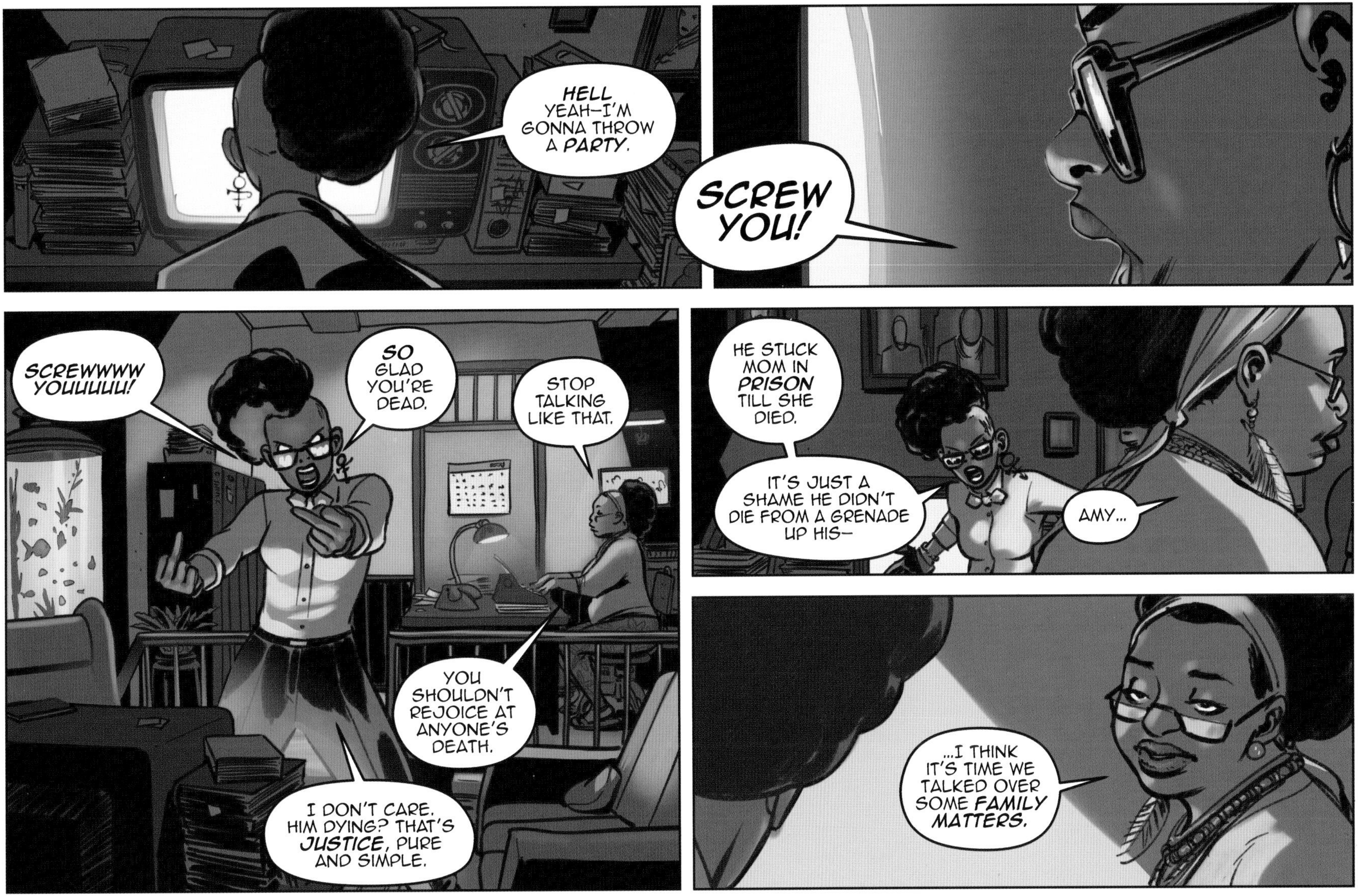
HELL YEAH—I'M GONNA THROW A PARTY.
SCREW YOU!
SCREWWWW YOUUUUU!
SO GLAD YOU'RE DEAD.
STOP TALKING LIKE THAT.
YOU SHOULDN'T REJOICE AT ANYONE'S DEATH.
I DON'T CARE. HIM DYING? THAT'S JUSTICE, PURE AND SIMPLE.
HE STUCK MOM IN PRISON TILL SHE DIED.
IT'S JUST A SHAME HE DIDN'T DIE FROM A GRENADE UP HIS—
AMY...
...I THINK IT'S TIME WE TALKED OVER SOME FAMILY MATTERS.

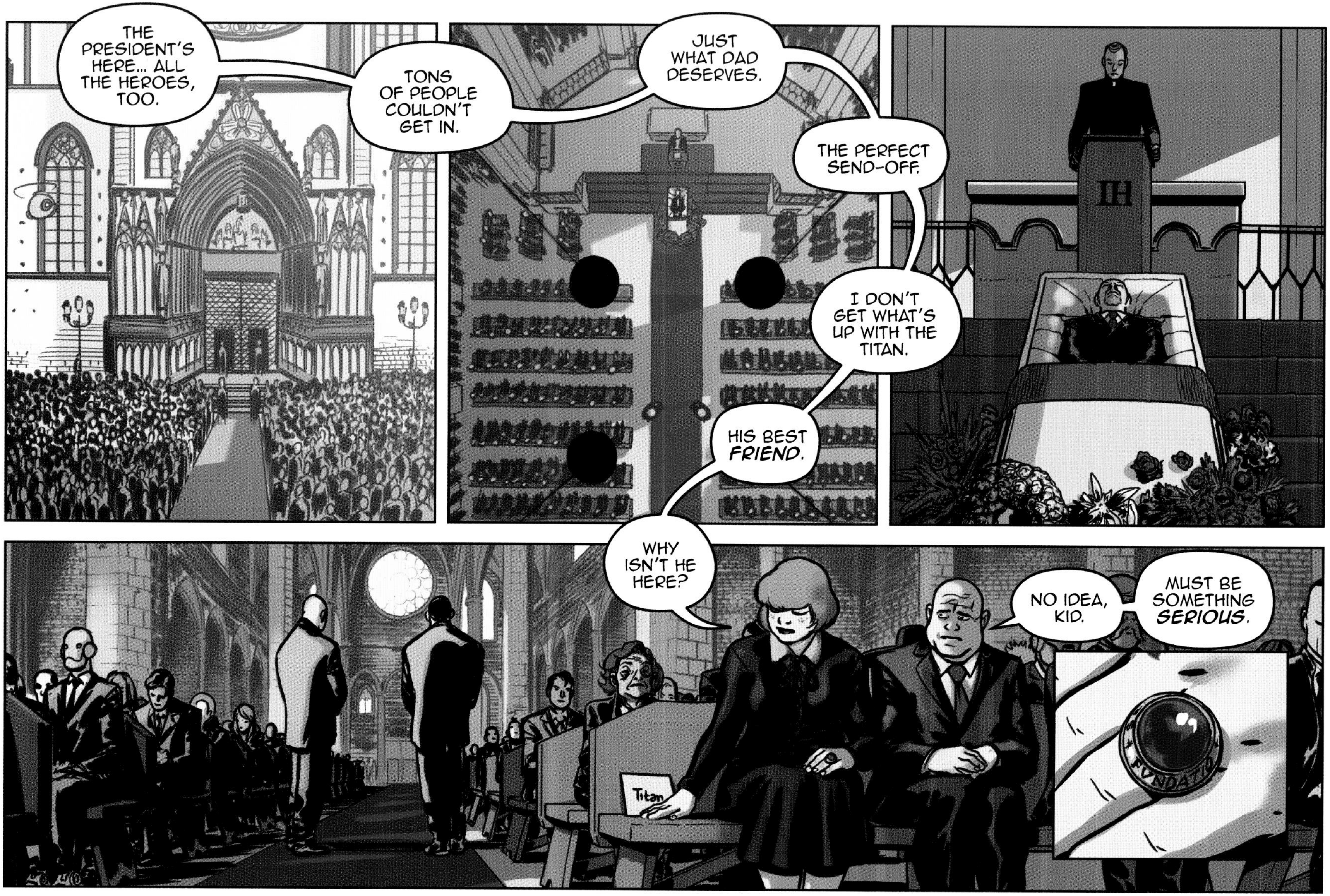
THE PRESIDENT'S HERE... ALL THE HEROES, TOO.
TONS OF PEOPLE COULDN'T GET IN.
JUST WHAT DAD DESERVES.
THE PERFECT SEND-OFF.
I DON'T GET WHAT'S UP WITH THE TITAN.
HIS BEST *FRIEND*.
WHY ISN'T HE HERE?
Titan
NO IDEA, KID.
MUST BE SOMETHING *SERIOUS*.

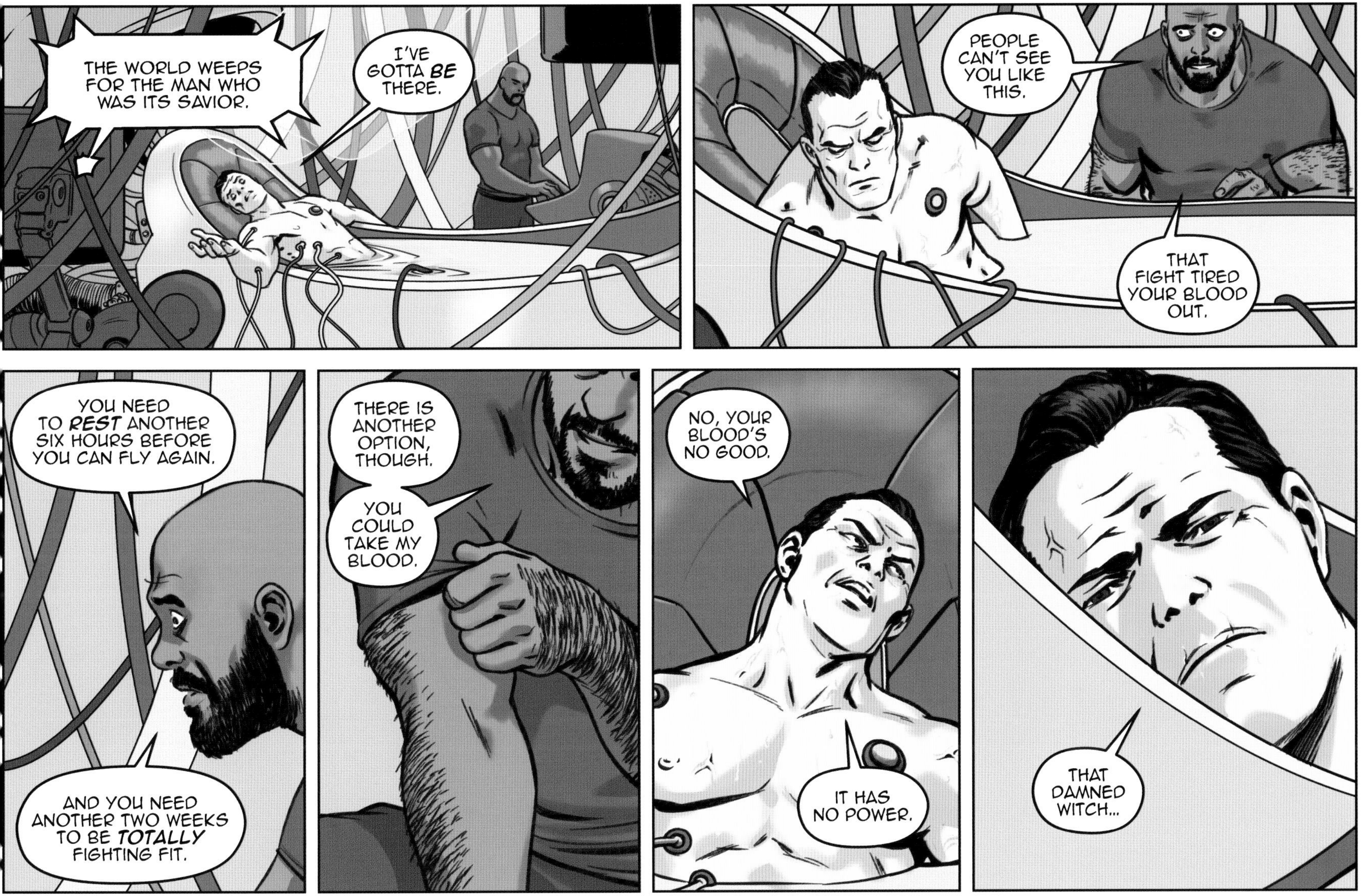
THE WORLD WEEPS FOR THE MAN WHO WAS ITS SAVIOR.
I'VE GOTTA *BE* THERE.
PEOPLE CAN'T SEE YOU LIKE THIS.
THAT FIGHT TIRED YOUR BLOOD OUT.
YOU NEED TO *REST* ANOTHER SIX HOURS BEFORE YOU CAN FLY AGAIN.
AND YOU NEED ANOTHER TWO WEEKS TO BE *TOTALLY* FIGHTING FIT.
THERE IS ANOTHER OPTION, THOUGH.
YOU COULD TAKE MY BLOOD.
NO, YOUR BLOOD'S NO GOOD.
IT HAS NO POWER.
THAT DAMNED WITCH...

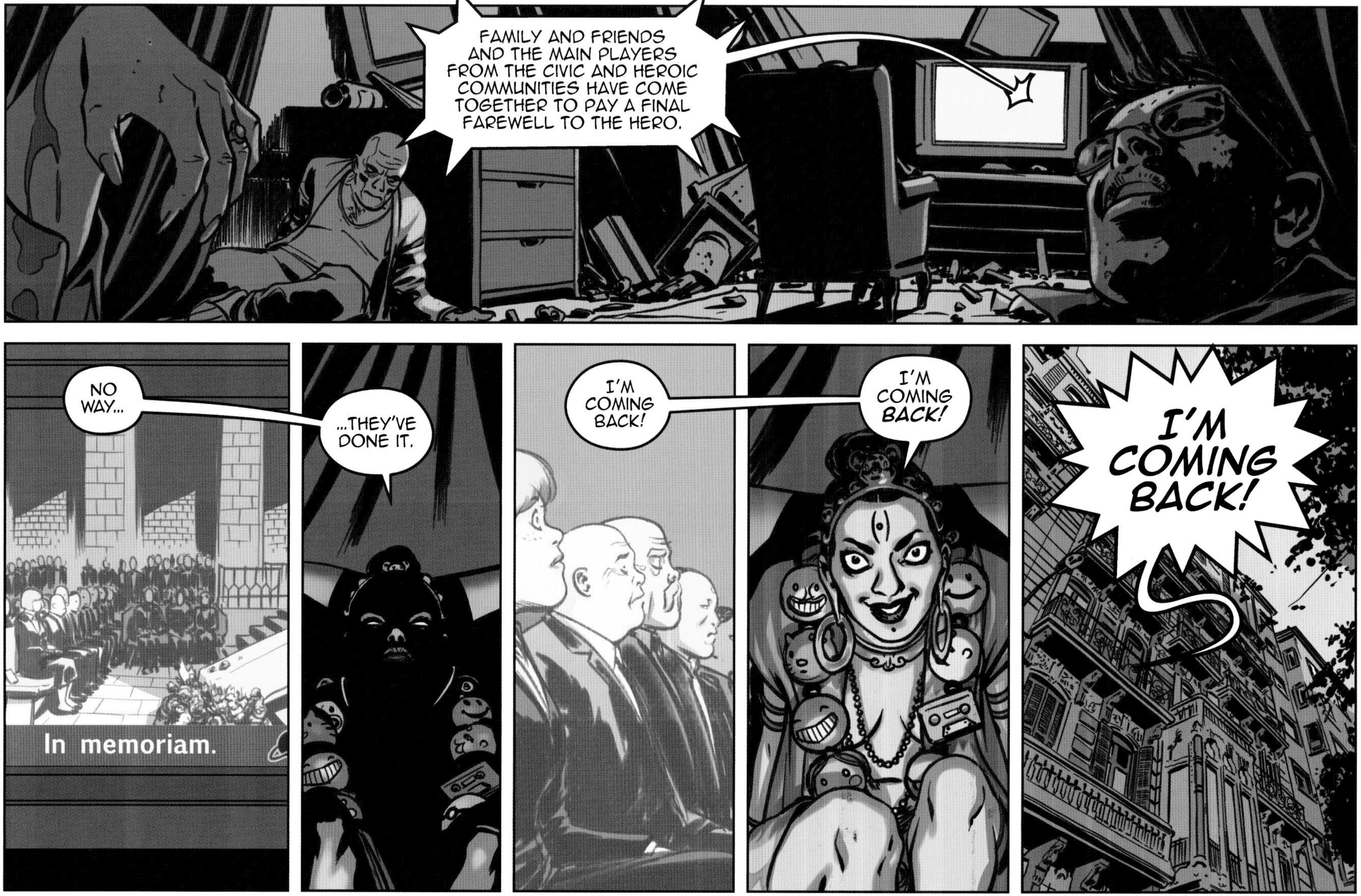
FAMILY AND FRIENDS AND THE MAIN PLAYERS FROM THE CIVIC AND HEROIC COMMUNITIES HAVE COME TOGETHER TO PAY A FINAL FAREWELL TO THE HERO.
NO WAY...
...THEY'VE DONE IT.
In memoriam.
I'M COMING BACK!
I'M COMING BACK!
I'M COMING BACK!

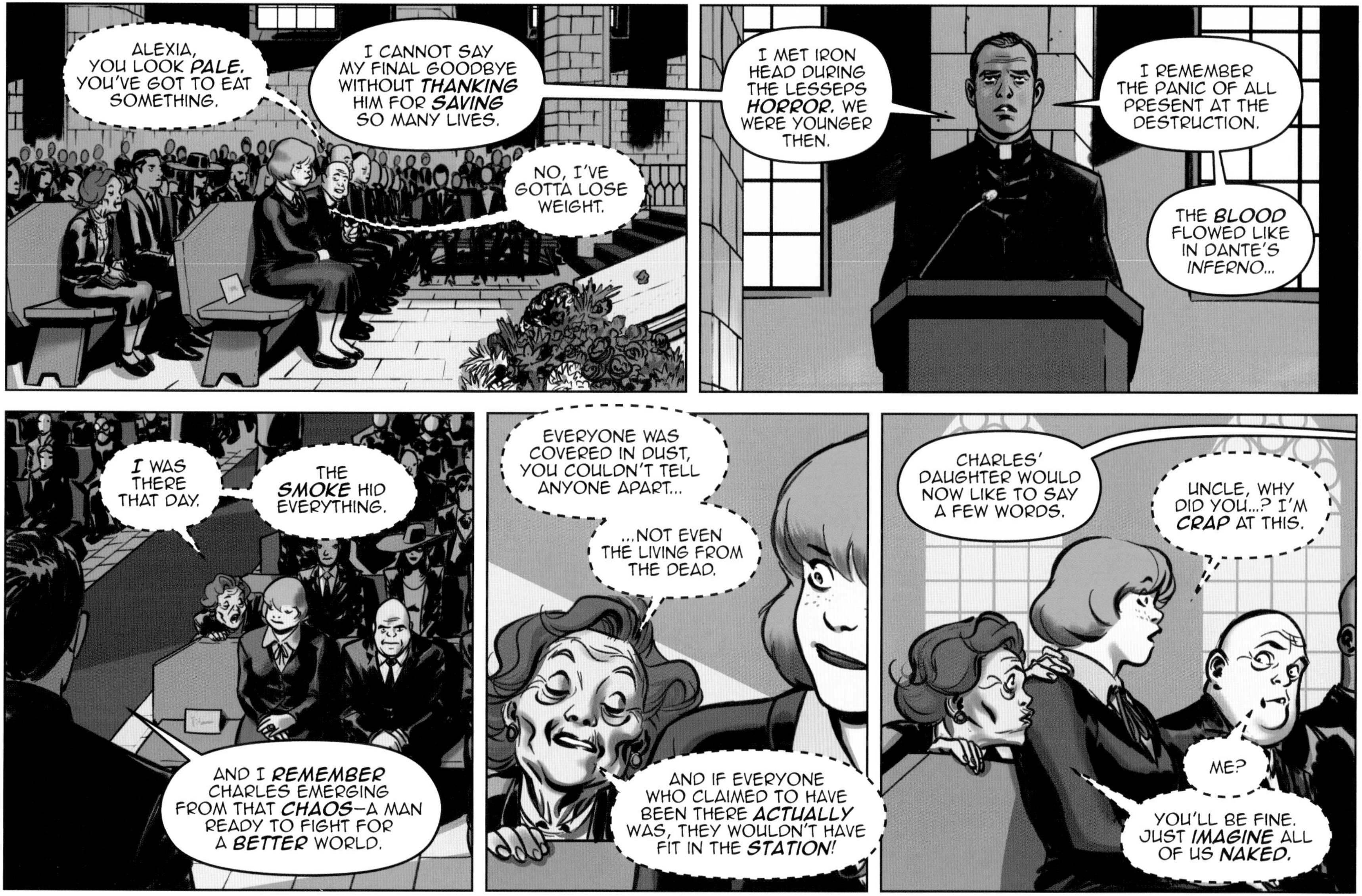
ALEXIA, YOU LOOK PALE. YOU'VE GOT TO EAT SOMETHING.
I CANNOT SAY MY FINAL GOODBYE WITHOUT THANKING HIM FOR SAVING SO MANY LIVES.
NO, I'VE GOTTA LOSE WEIGHT.
I MET IRON HEAD DURING THE LESSEPS HORROR. WE WERE YOUNGER THEN.
I REMEMBER THE PANIC OF ALL PRESENT AT THE DESTRUCTION.
THE BLOOD FLOWED LIKE IN DANTE'S INFERNO...
I WAS THERE THAT DAY.
THE SMOKE HID EVERYTHING.
AND I REMEMBER CHARLES EMERGING FROM THAT CHAOS—A MAN READY TO FIGHT FOR A BETTER WORLD.
EVERYONE WAS COVERED IN DUST, YOU COULDN'T TELL ANYONE APART...
...NOT EVEN THE LIVING FROM THE DEAD.
AND IF EVERYONE WHO CLAIMED TO HAVE BEEN THERE ACTUALLY WAS, THEY WOULDN'T HAVE FIT IN THE STATION!
CHARLES' DAUGHTER WOULD NOW LIKE TO SAY A FEW WORDS.
UNCLE, WHY DID YOU...? I'M CRAP AT THIS.
ME?
YOU'LL BE FINE. JUST IMAGINE ALL OF US NAKED.

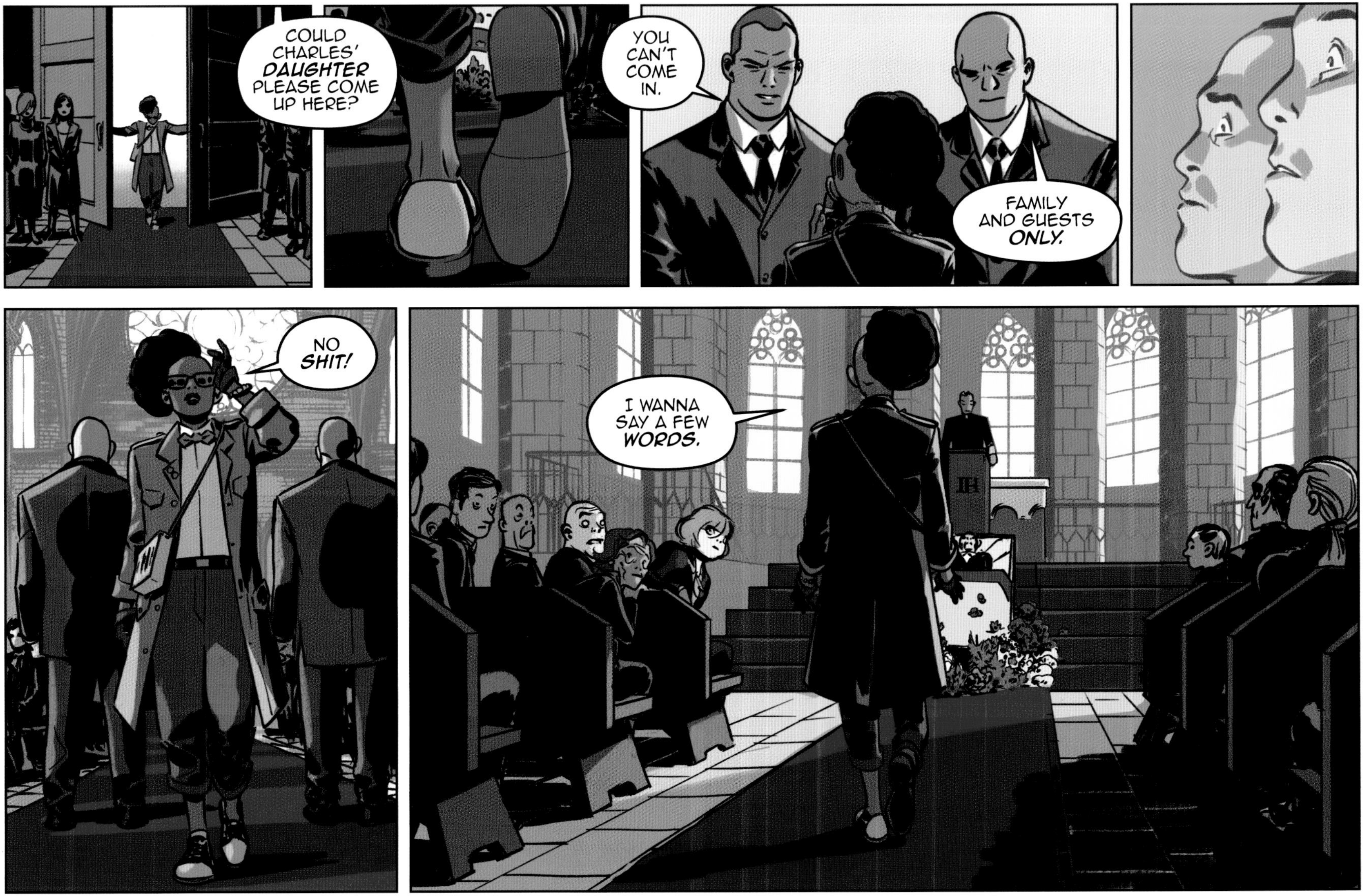
COULD CHARLES' DAUGHTER PLEASE COME UP HERE?
YOU CAN'T COME IN.
FAMILY AND GUESTS ONLY.
NO SHIT!
I WANNA SAY A FEW WORDS.

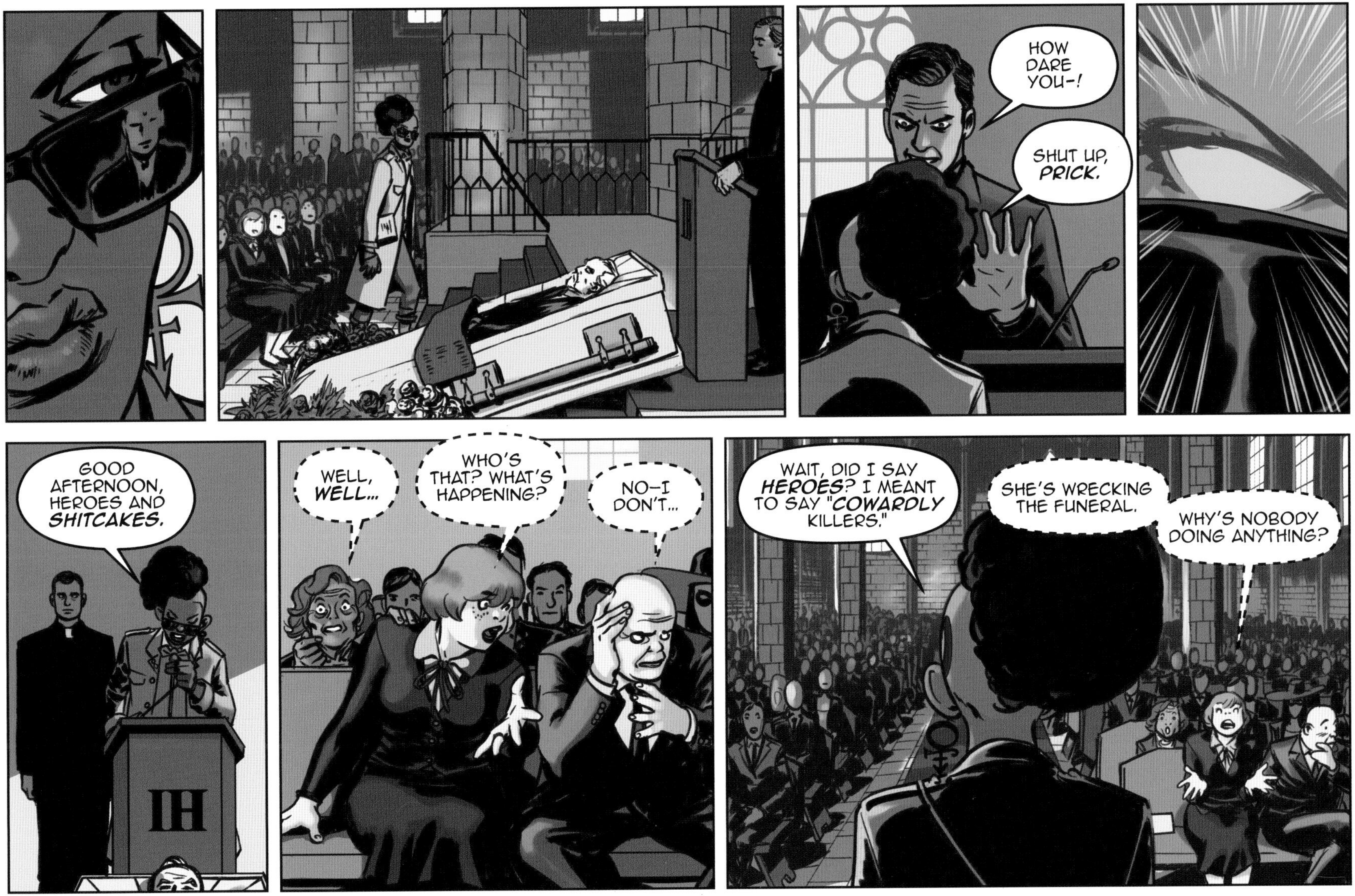
HOW DARE YOU-!
SHUT UP, PRICK.
GOOD AFTERNOON, HEROES AND SHITCAKES.
WELL, WELL...
WHO'S THAT? WHAT'S HAPPENING?
NO-I DON'T...
WAIT, DID I SAY HEROES? I MEANT TO SAY "COWARDLY KILLERS."
SHE'S WRECKING THE FUNERAL.
WHY'S NOBODY DOING ANYTHING?

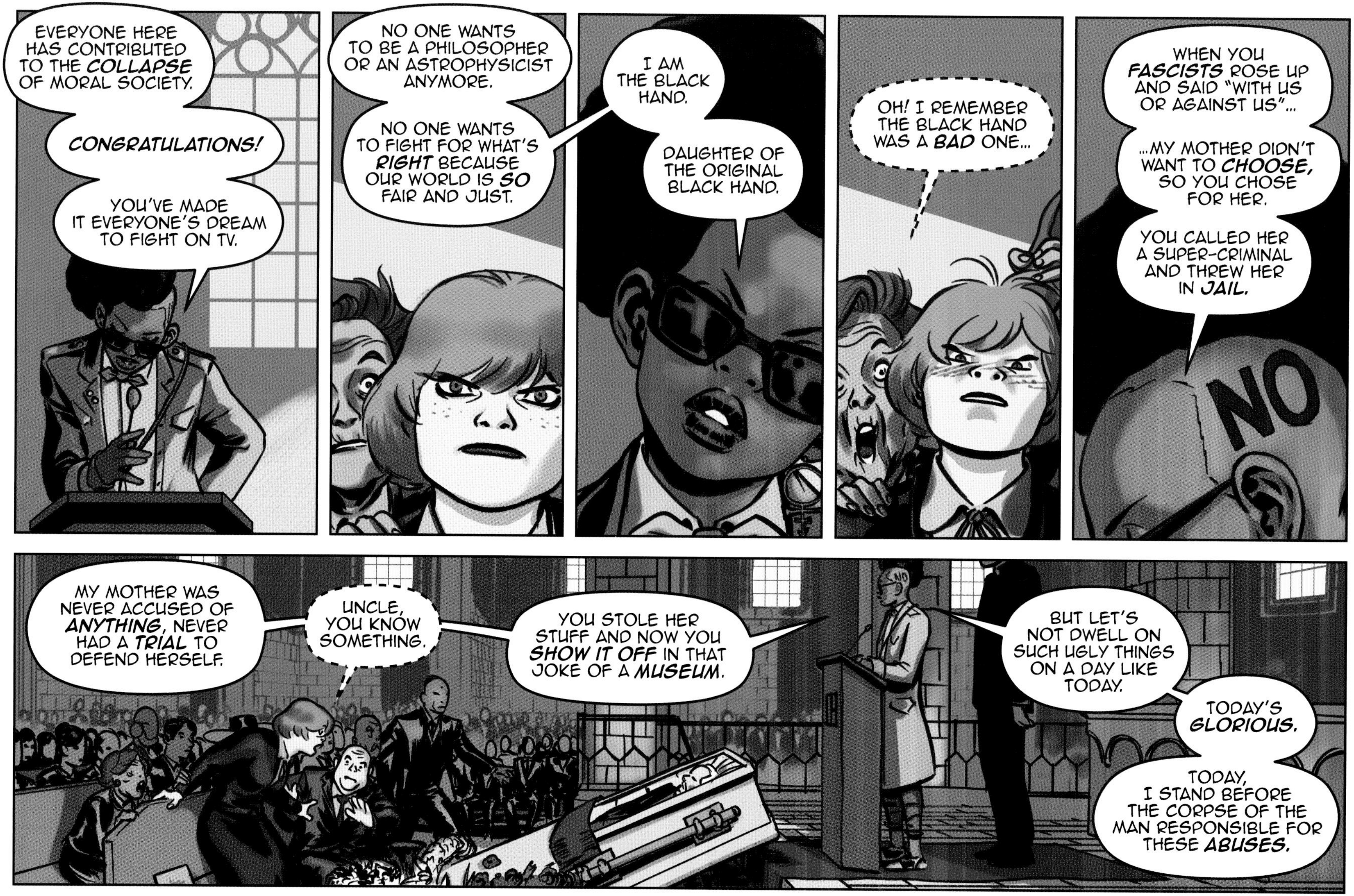
EVERYONE HERE HAS CONTRIBUTED TO THE COLLAPSE OF MORAL SOCIETY.
CONGRATULATIONS!
YOU'VE MADE IT EVERYONE'S DREAM TO FIGHT ON TV.
NO ONE WANTS TO BE A PHILOSOPHER OR AN ASTROPHYSICIST ANYMORE.
NO ONE WANTS TO FIGHT FOR WHAT'S RIGHT BECAUSE OUR WORLD IS SO FAIR AND JUST.
I AM THE BLACK HAND.
DAUGHTER OF THE ORIGINAL BLACK HAND.
OH! I REMEMBER THE BLACK HAND WAS A BAD ONE...
WHEN YOU FASCISTS ROSE UP AND SAID "WITH US OR AGAINST US"...
...MY MOTHER DIDN'T WANT TO CHOOSE, SO YOU CHOSE FOR HER.
YOU CALLED HER A SUPER-CRIMINAL AND THREW HER IN JAIL.
NO
MY MOTHER WAS NEVER ACCUSED OF ANYTHING, NEVER HAD A TRIAL TO DEFEND HERSELF.
UNCLE, YOU KNOW SOMETHING.
YOU STOLE HER STUFF AND NOW YOU SHOW IT OFF IN THAT JOKE OF A MUSEUM.
BUT LET'S NOT DWELL ON SUCH UGLY THINGS ON A DAY LIKE TODAY.
TODAY'S GLORIOUS.
TODAY, I STAND BEFORE THE CORPSE OF THE MAN RESPONSIBLE FOR THESE ABUSES.

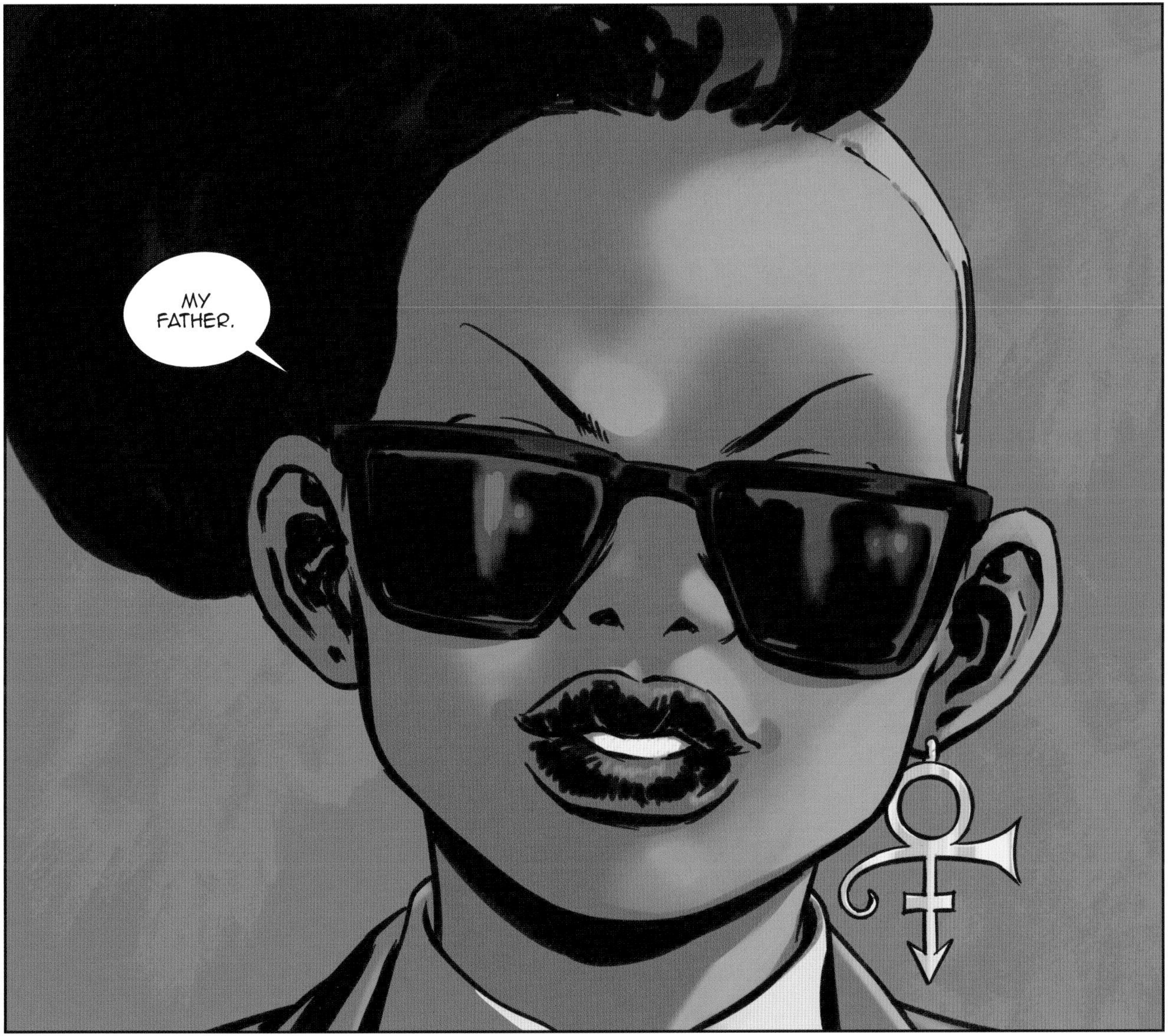
MY FATHER.
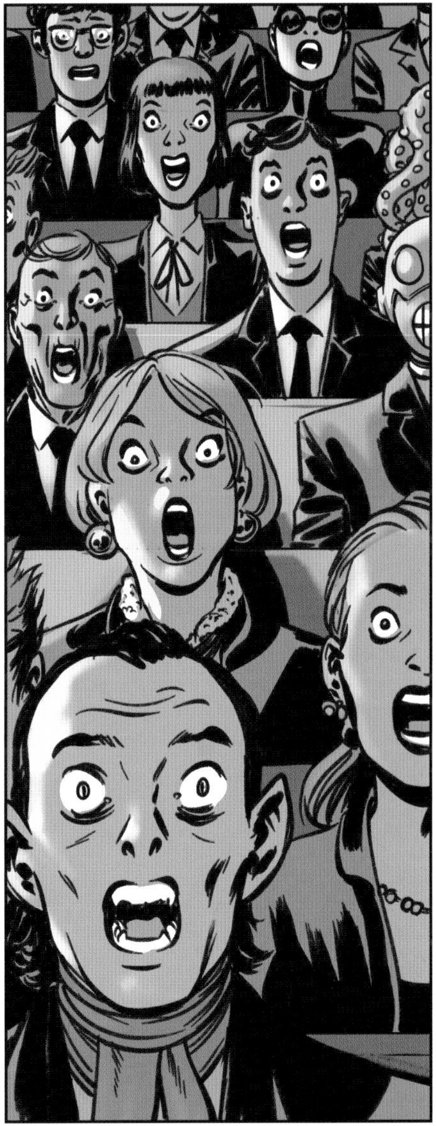

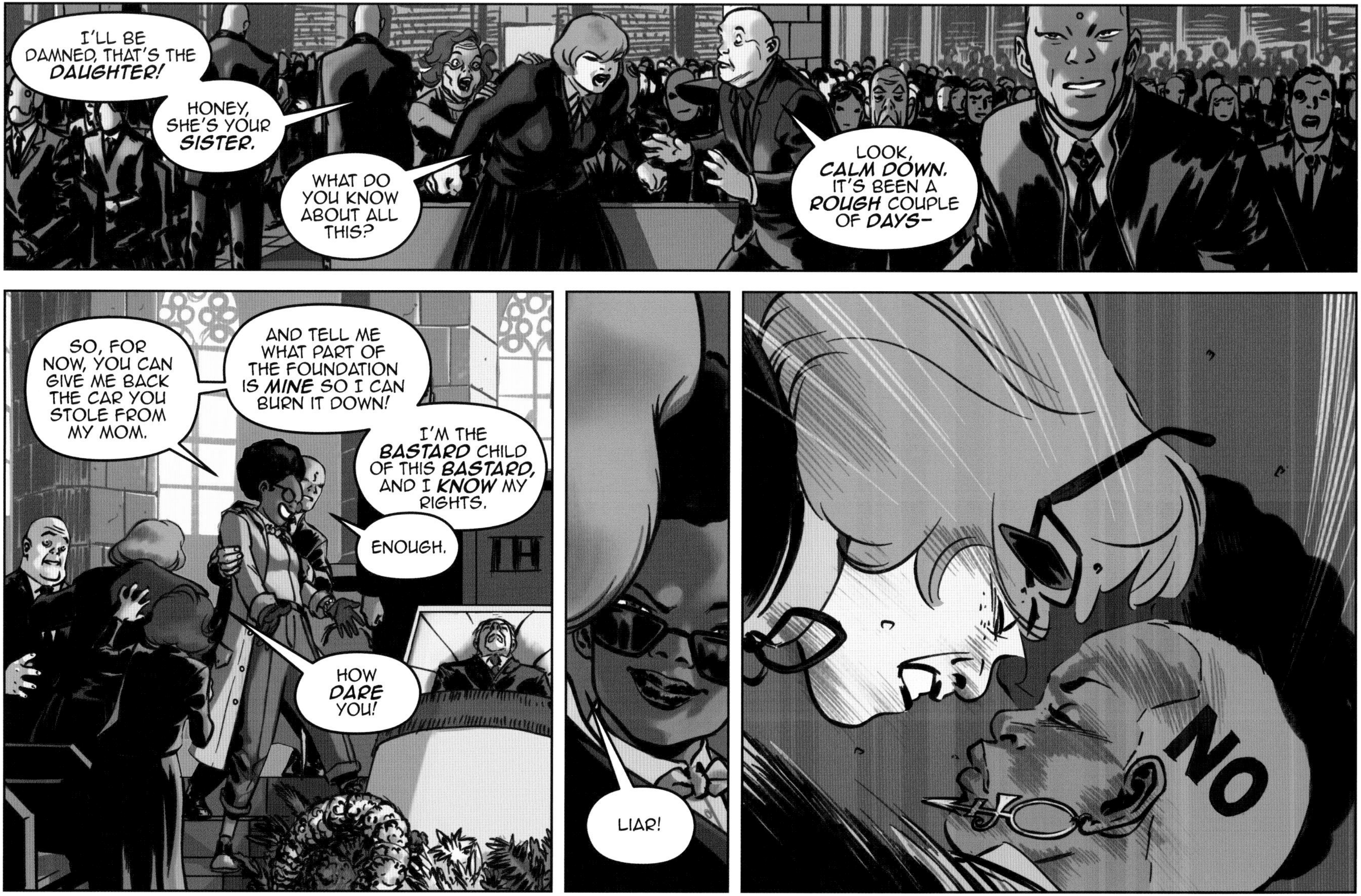
I'LL BE DAMNED, THAT'S THE DAUGHTER!
HONEY, SHE'S YOUR SISTER.
WHAT DO YOU KNOW ABOUT ALL THIS?
LOOK, CALM DOWN. IT'S BEEN A ROUGH COUPLE OF DAYS—
SO, FOR NOW, YOU CAN GIVE ME BACK THE CAR YOU STOLE FROM MY MOM.
AND TELL ME WHAT PART OF THE FOUNDATION IS MINE SO I CAN BURN IT DOWN!
I'M THE BASTARD CHILD OF THIS BASTARD, AND I KNOW MY RIGHTS.
ENOUGH.
HOW DARE YOU!
LIAR!
NO

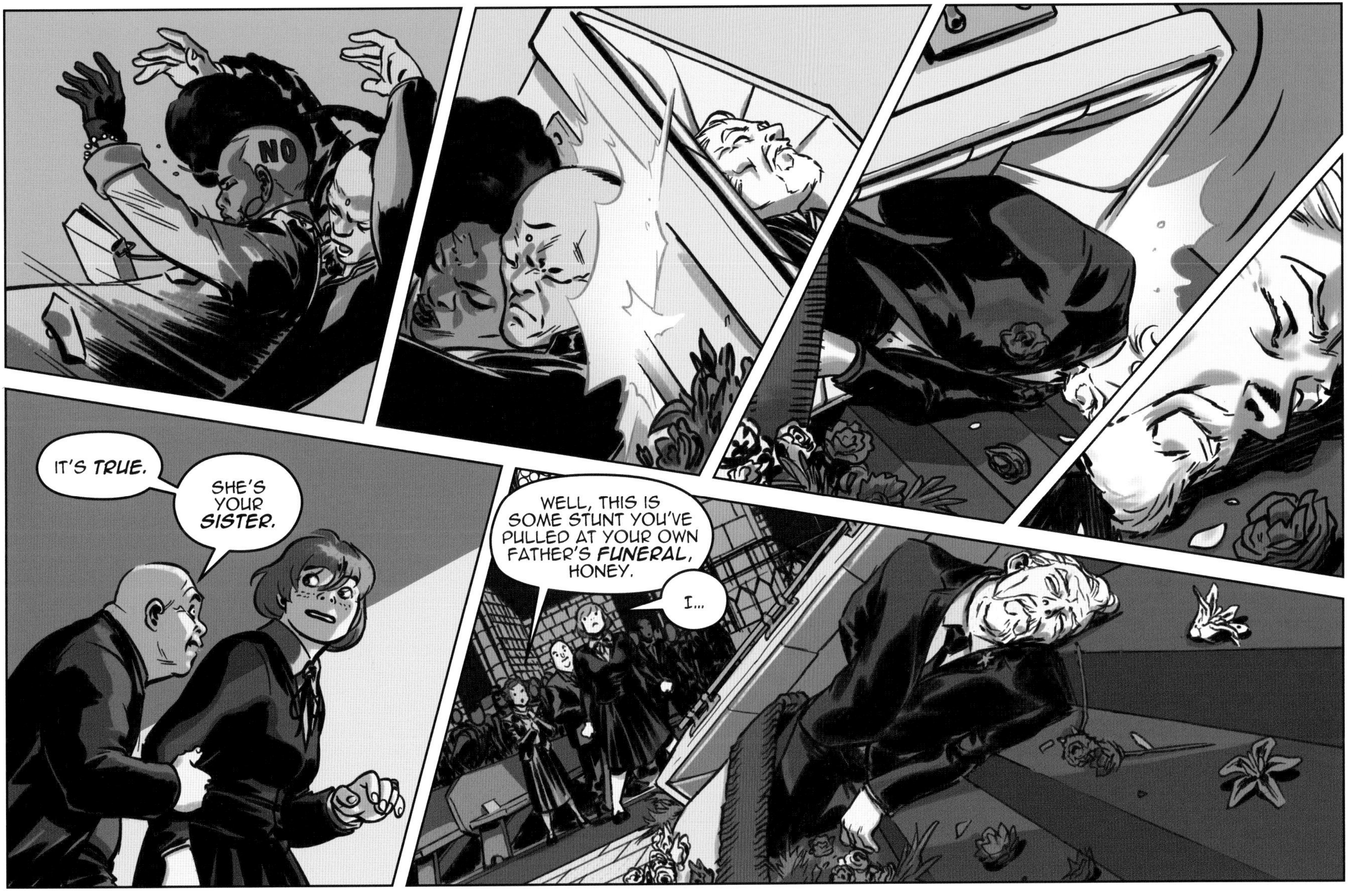
NO
IT'S **TRUE.**
SHE'S YOUR **SISTER.**
WELL, THIS IS SOME STUNT YOU'VE PULLED AT YOUR OWN FATHER'S **FUNERAL,** HONEY.
I...

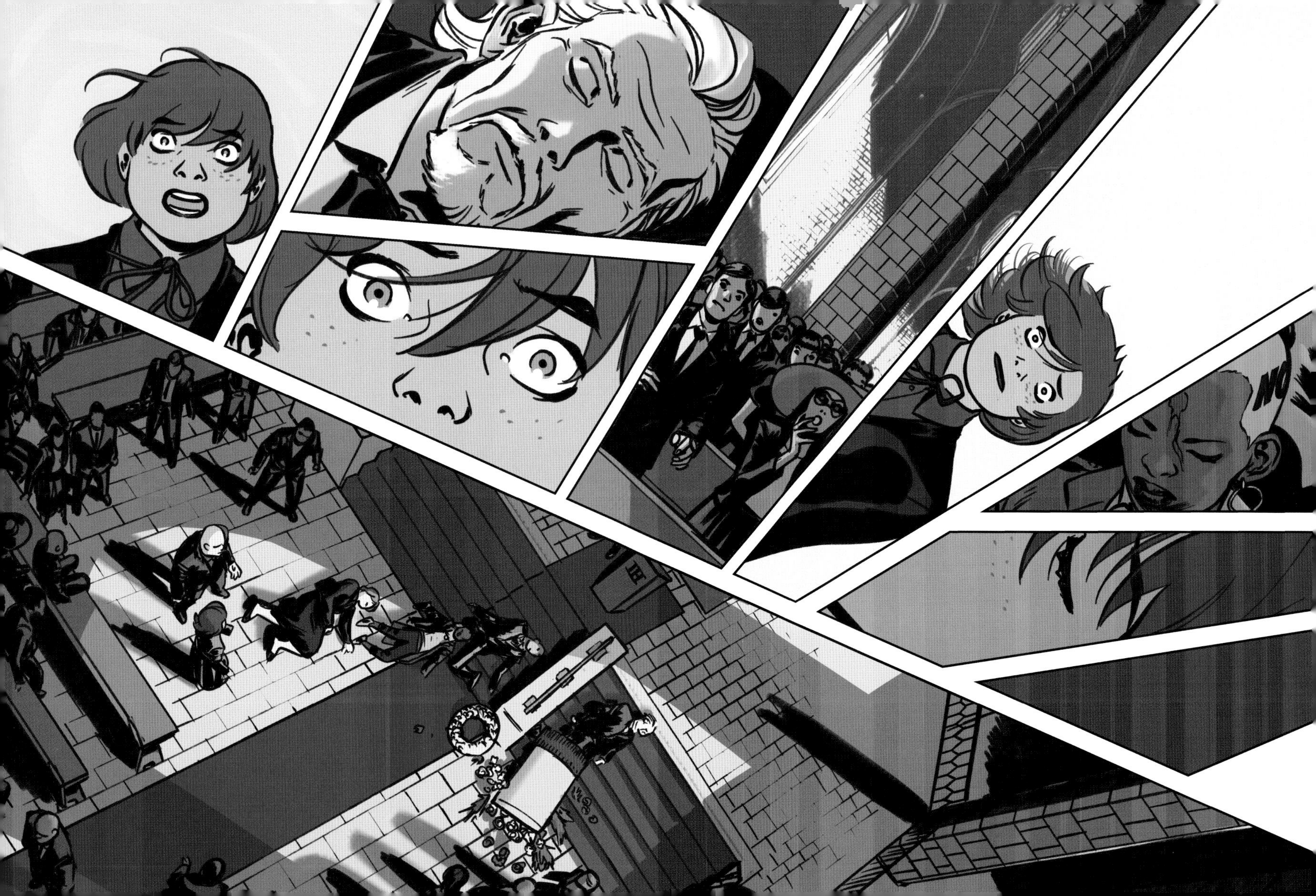
NO

BLACKHAND & IRONHEAD

Chapter Two

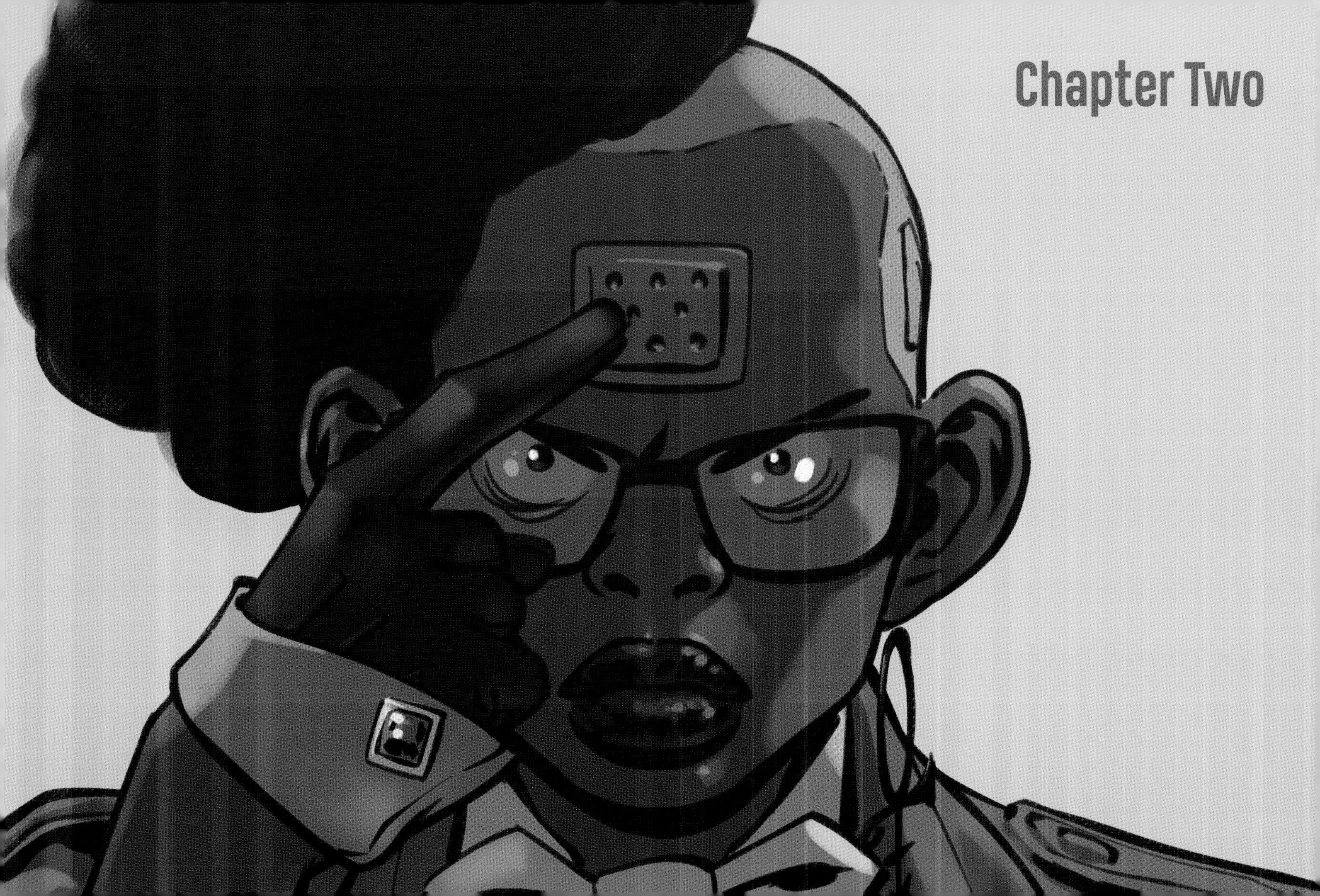

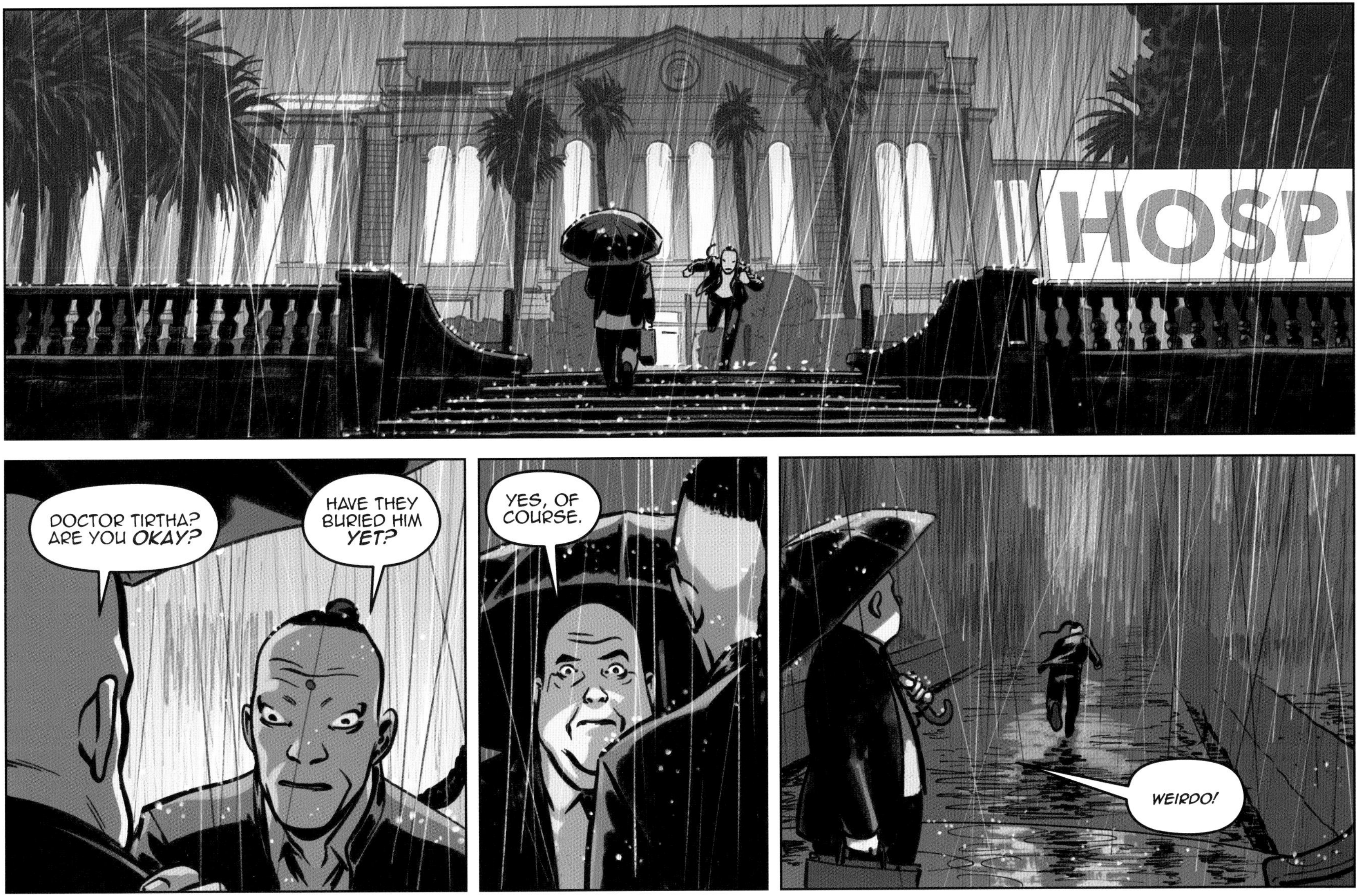
HOSP
DOCTOR TIRTHA? ARE YOU *OKAY?*
HAVE THEY BURIED HIM *YET?*
YES, OF COURSE.
WEIRDO!

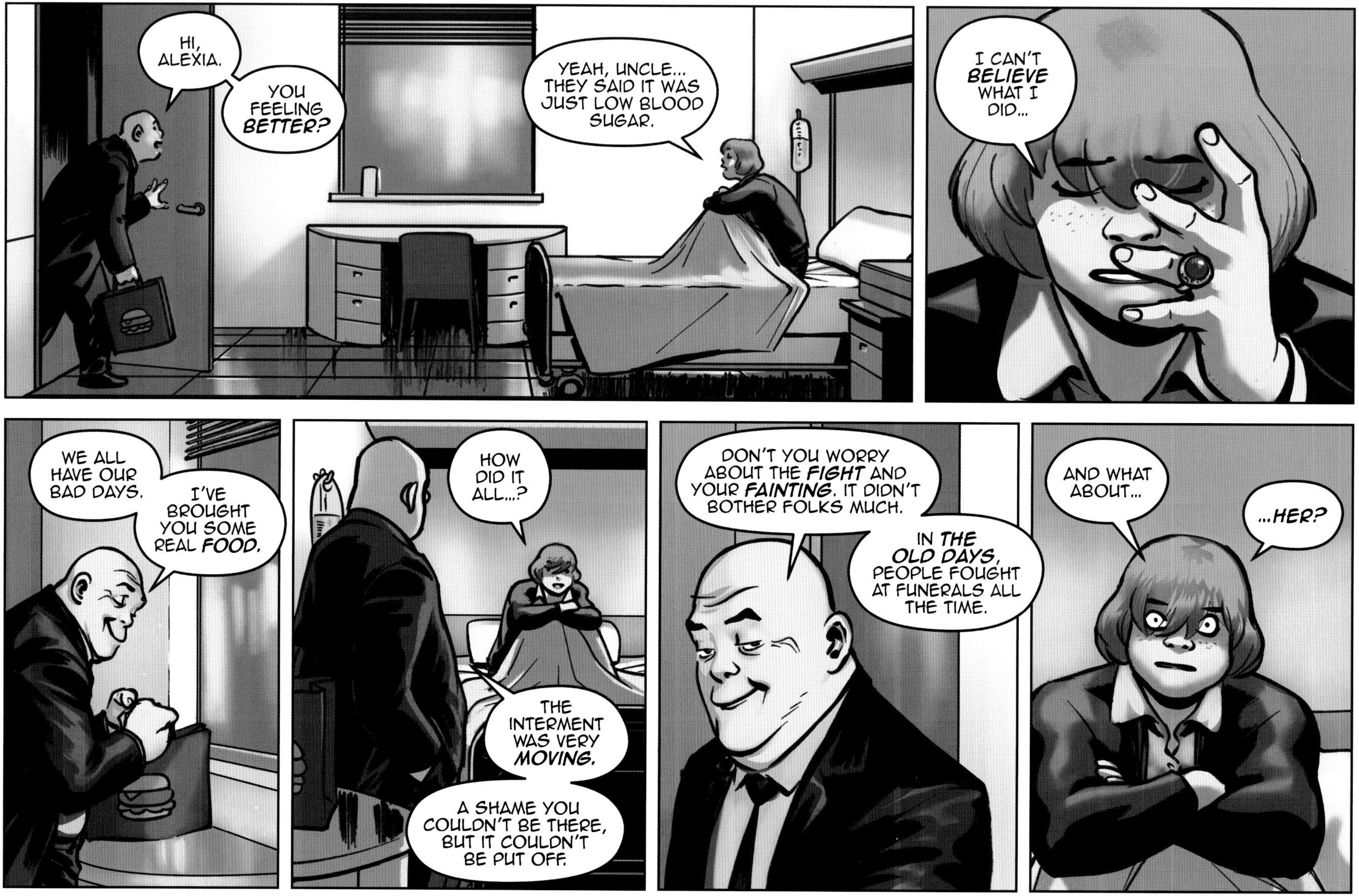
HI, ALEXIA.
YOU FEELING BETTER?
YEAH, UNCLE... THEY SAID IT WAS JUST LOW BLOOD SUGAR.
I CAN'T BELIEVE WHAT I DID...
WE ALL HAVE OUR BAD DAYS.
I'VE BROUGHT YOU SOME REAL FOOD.
HOW DID IT ALL...?
THE INTERMENT WAS VERY MOVING.
A SHAME YOU COULDN'T BE THERE, BUT IT COULDN'T BE PUT OFF.
DON'T YOU WORRY ABOUT THE FIGHT AND YOUR FAINTING. IT DIDN'T BOTHER FOLKS MUCH.
IN THE OLD DAYS, PEOPLE FOUGHT AT FUNERALS ALL THE TIME.
AND WHAT ABOUT...
...HER?

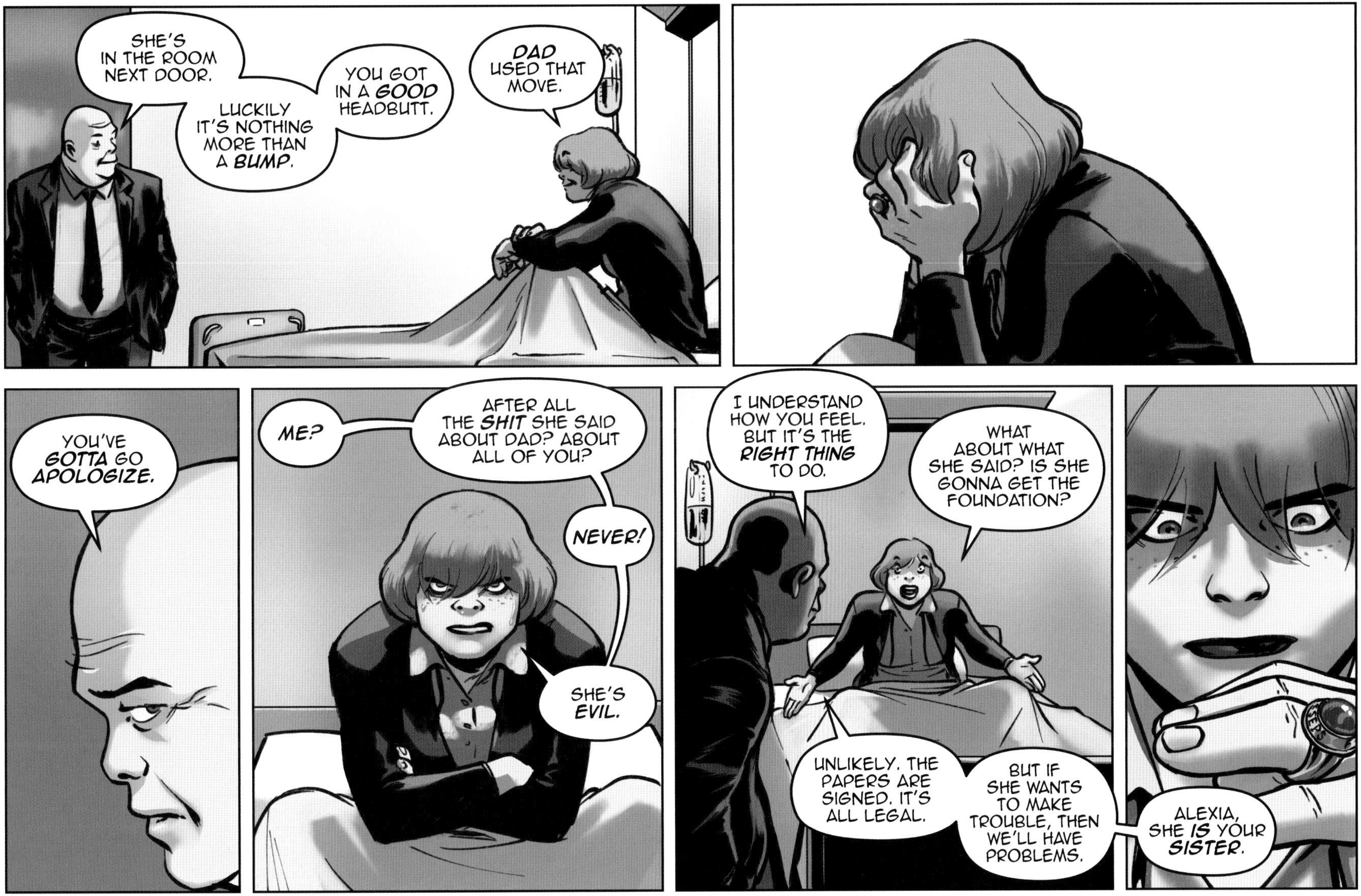

SHE'S IN THE ROOM NEXT DOOR.
LUCKILY IT'S NOTHING MORE THAN A **BUMP**.
YOU GOT IN A **GOOD** HEADBUTT.
DAD USED THAT MOVE.
YOU'VE **GOTTA** GO **APOLOGIZE.**
ME?
AFTER ALL THE **SHIT** SHE SAID ABOUT DAD? ABOUT ALL OF YOU?
NEVER!
SHE'S **EVIL.**
I UNDERSTAND HOW YOU FEEL. BUT IT'S THE **RIGHT THING** TO DO.
WHAT ABOUT WHAT SHE SAID? IS SHE GONNA GET THE FOUNDATION?
UNLIKELY. THE PAPERS ARE SIGNED. IT'S ALL LEGAL.
BUT IF SHE WANTS TO MAKE TROUBLE, THEN WE'LL HAVE PROBLEMS.
ALEXIA, SHE **IS** YOUR **SISTER**.

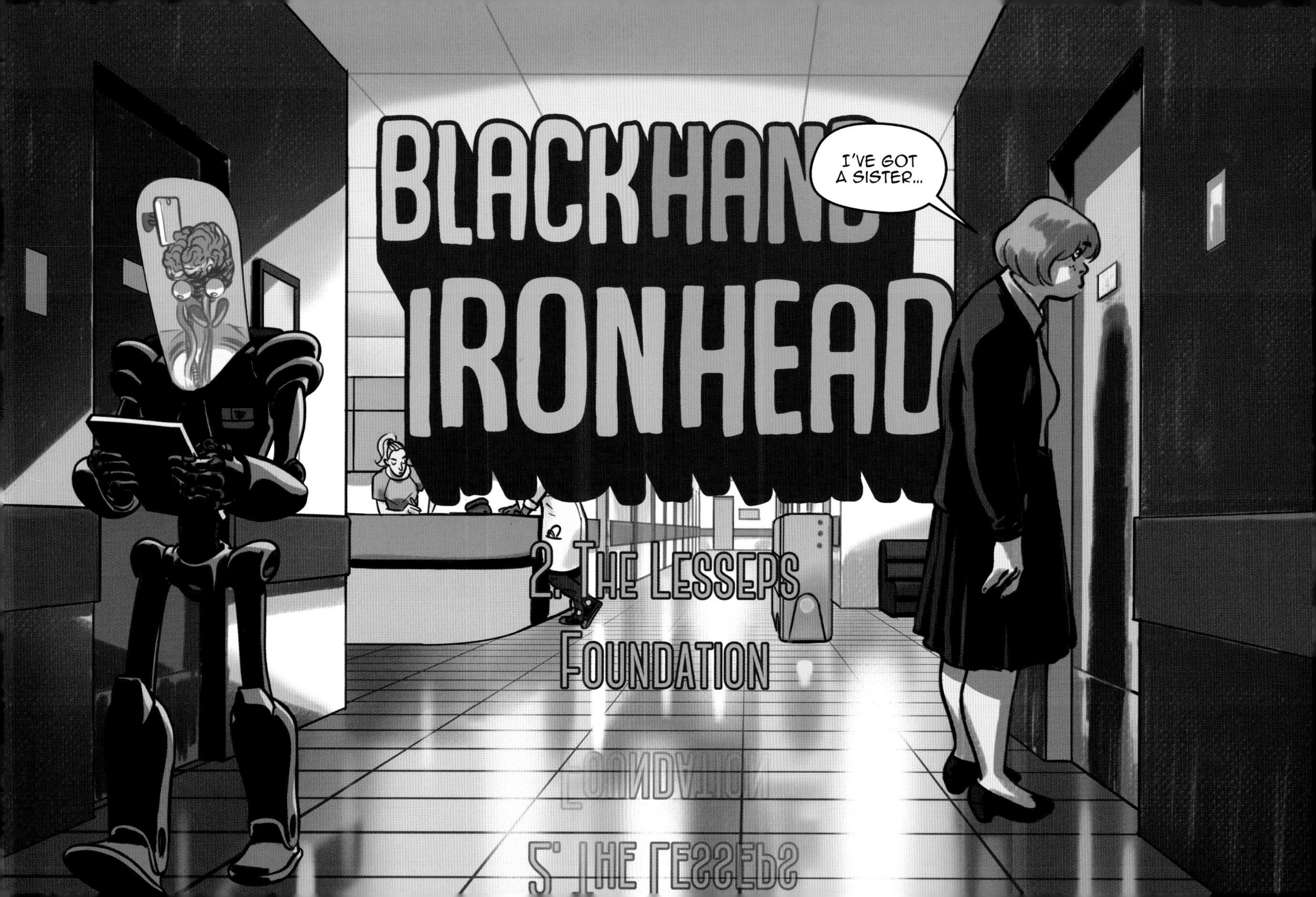
BLACKHAND
IRONHEAD
I'VE GOT A SISTER...
2. The Lesseps
Foundation

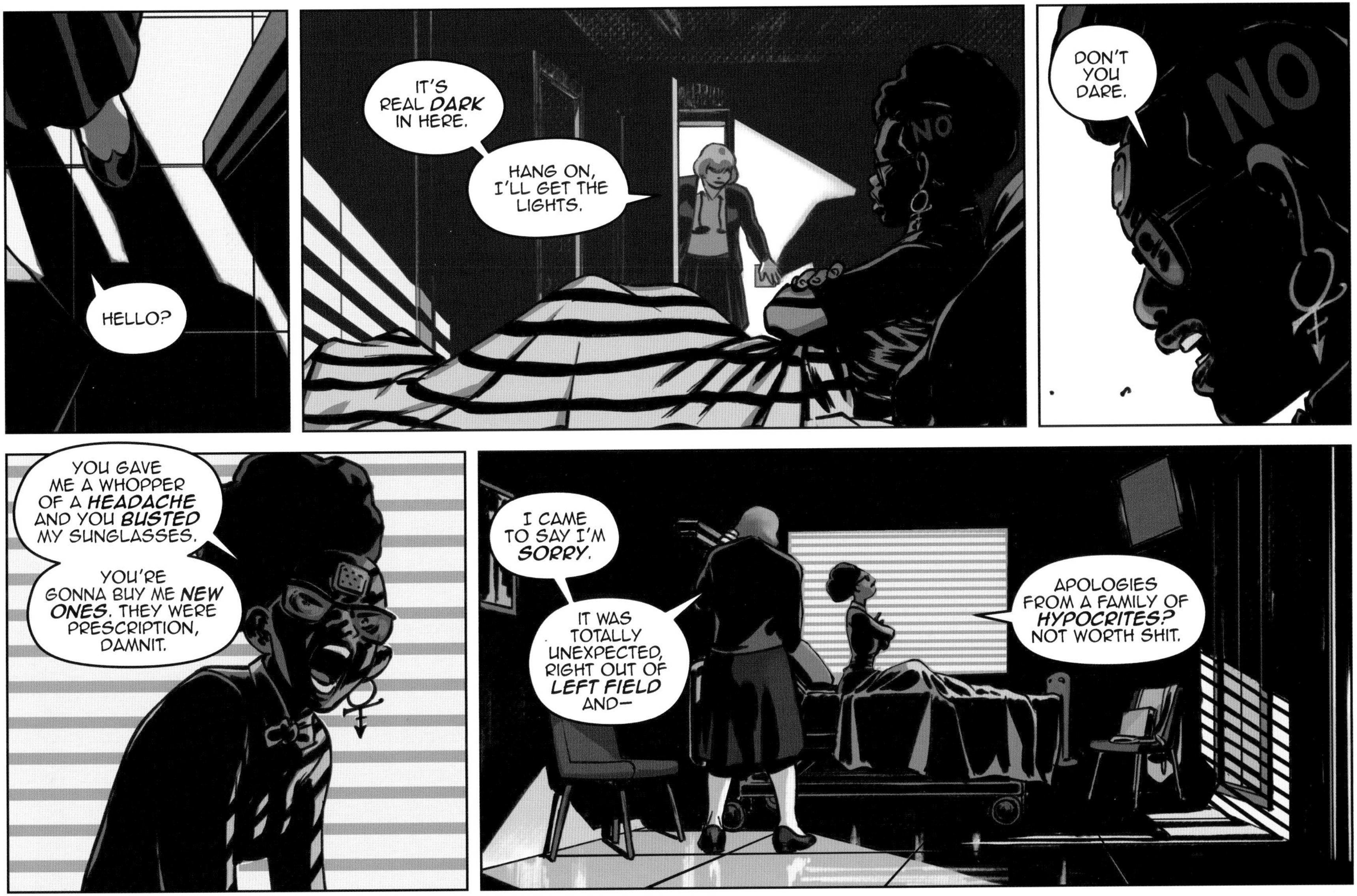
HELLO?
IT'S REAL DARK IN HERE.
HANG ON, I'LL GET THE LIGHTS.
NO
DON'T YOU DARE.
NO
YOU GAVE ME A WHOPPER OF A HEADACHE AND YOU BUSTED MY SUNGLASSES.
YOU'RE GONNA BUY ME NEW ONES. THEY WERE PRESCRIPTION, DAMNIT.
I CAME TO SAY I'M SORRY.
IT WAS TOTALLY UNEXPECTED, RIGHT OUT OF LEFT FIELD AND—
APOLOGIES FROM A FAMILY OF HYPOCRITES? NOT WORTH SHIT.

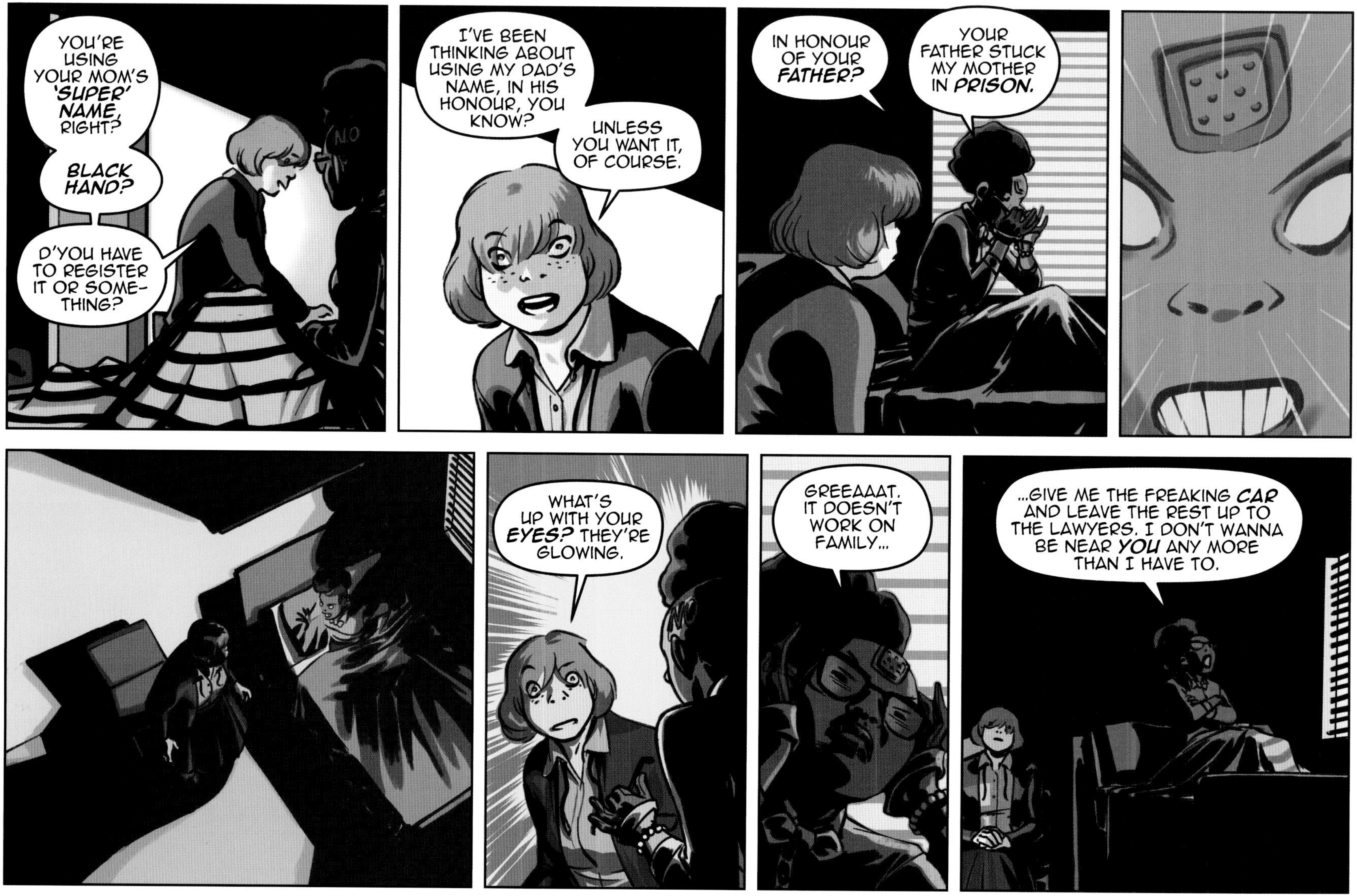
YOU'RE USING YOUR MOM'S '*SUPER*' *NAME*, RIGHT?
BLACK HAND?
D'YOU HAVE TO REGISTER IT OR SOME-THING?
I'VE BEEN THINKING ABOUT USING MY DAD'S NAME, IN HIS HONOUR, YOU KNOW?
UNLESS YOU WANT IT, OF COURSE.
IN HONOUR OF YOUR *FATHER?*
YOUR FATHER STUCK MY MOTHER IN *PRISON.*
WHAT'S UP WITH YOUR *EYES?* THEY'RE GLOWING.
GREEAAAT. IT DOESN'T WORK ON FAMILY...
...GIVE ME THE FREAKING *CAR* AND LEAVE THE REST UP TO THE LAWYERS. I DON'T WANNA BE NEAR *YOU* ANY MORE THAN I HAVE TO.

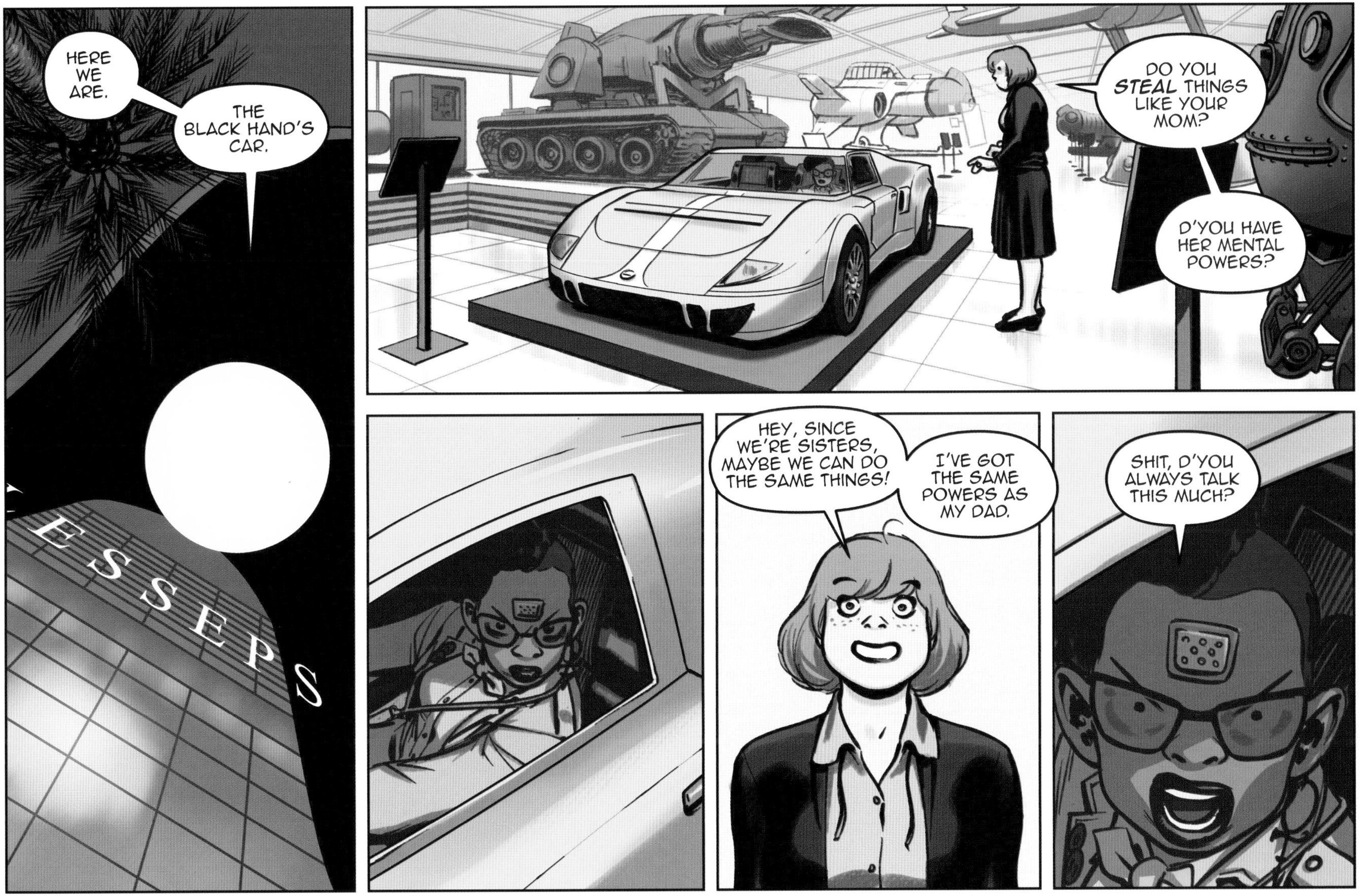
HERE WE ARE.
THE BLACK HAND'S CAR.
ESSEPS
DO YOU **STEAL** THINGS LIKE YOUR MOM?
D'YOU HAVE HER MENTAL POWERS?
HEY, SINCE WE'RE SISTERS, MAYBE WE CAN DO THE SAME THINGS!
I'VE GOT THE SAME POWERS AS MY DAD.
SHIT, D'YOU ALWAYS TALK THIS MUCH?

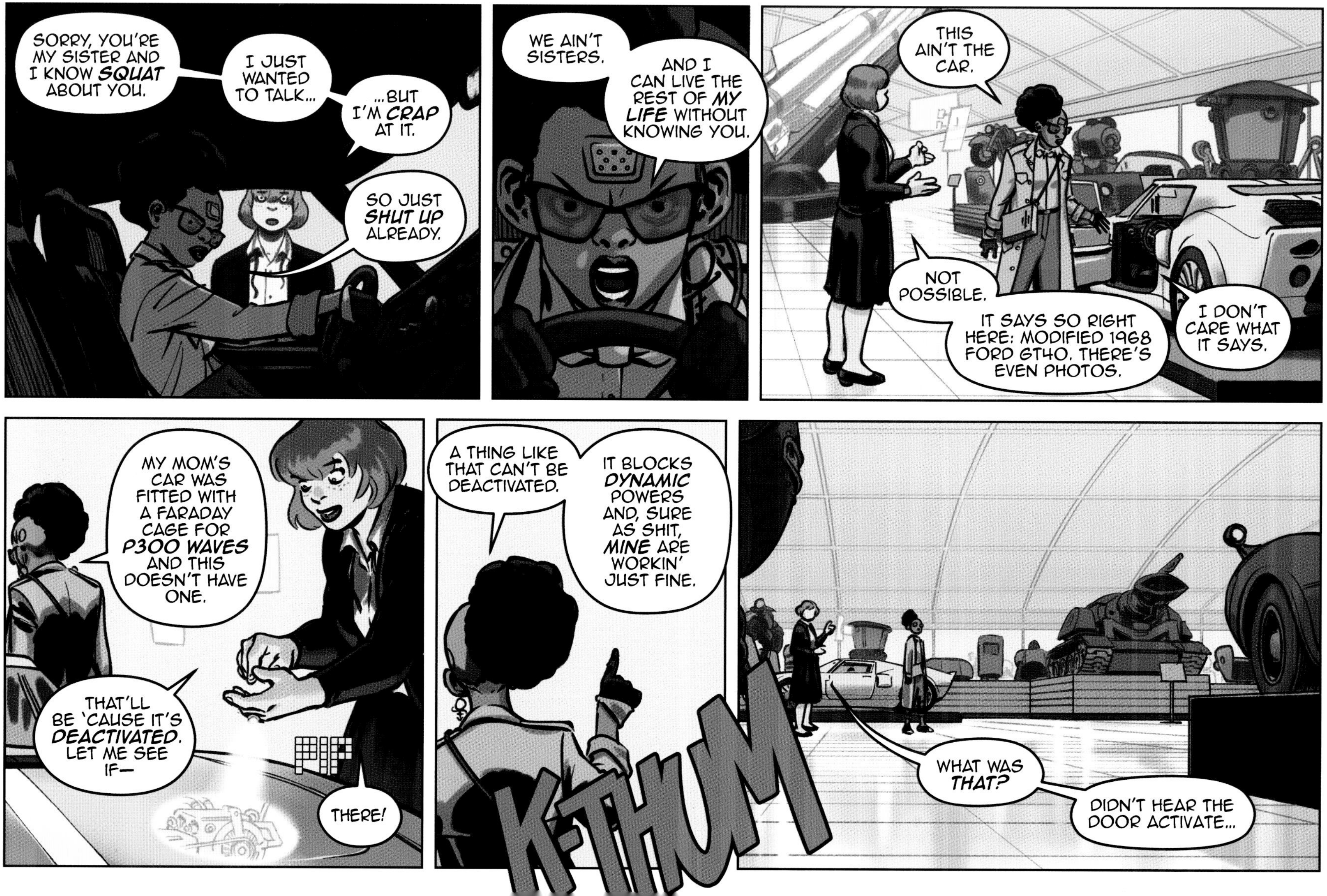
SORRY, YOU'RE MY SISTER AND I KNOW SQUAT ABOUT YOU.
I JUST WANTED TO TALK...
...BUT I'M CRAP AT IT.
SO JUST SHUT UP ALREADY.
WE AIN'T SISTERS.
AND I CAN LIVE THE REST OF MY LIFE WITHOUT KNOWING YOU.
THIS AIN'T THE CAR.
NOT POSSIBLE.
IT SAYS SO RIGHT HERE: MODIFIED 1968 FORD GT40. THERE'S EVEN PHOTOS.
I DON'T CARE WHAT IT SAYS.
MY MOM'S CAR WAS FITTED WITH A FARADAY CAGE FOR P300 WAVES AND THIS DOESN'T HAVE ONE.
THAT'LL BE 'CAUSE IT'S DEACTIVATED. LET ME SEE IF—
PIP
THERE!
A THING LIKE THAT CAN'T BE DEACTIVATED.
IT BLOCKS DYNAMIC POWERS AND, SURE AS SHIT, MINE ARE WORKIN' JUST FINE.
K-THUM
WHAT WAS THAT?
DIDN'T HEAR THE DOOR ACTIVATE...

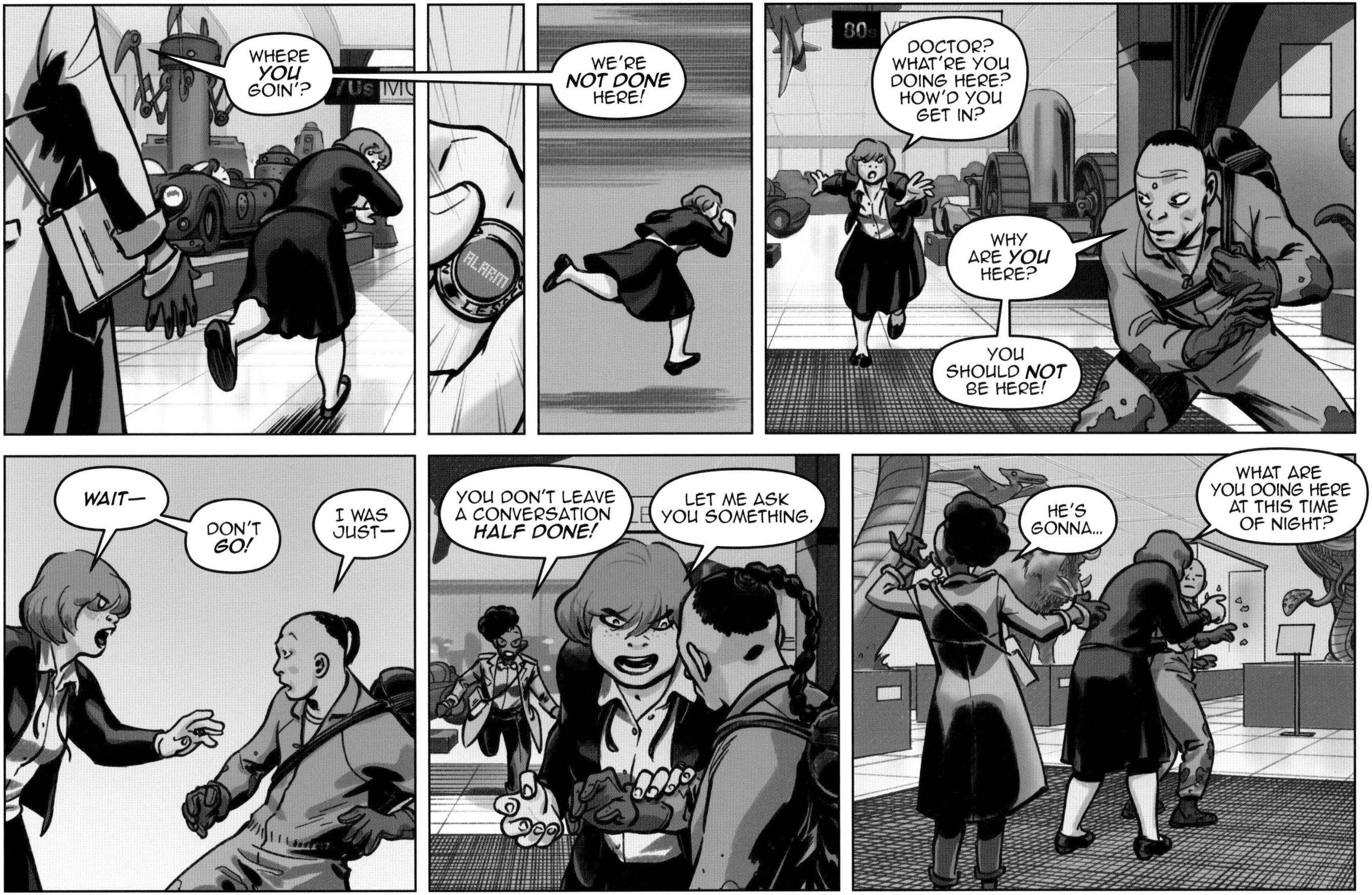
WHERE YOU GOIN'?
70s
WE'RE NOT DONE HERE!
ALARM
80s
DOCTOR? WHAT'RE YOU DOING HERE? HOW'D YOU GET IN?
WHY ARE YOU HERE?
YOU SHOULD NOT BE HERE!
WAIT—
DON'T GO!
I WAS JUST—
YOU DON'T LEAVE A CONVERSATION HALF DONE!
LET ME ASK YOU SOMETHING.
HE'S GONNA...
WHAT ARE YOU DOING HERE AT THIS TIME OF NIGHT?

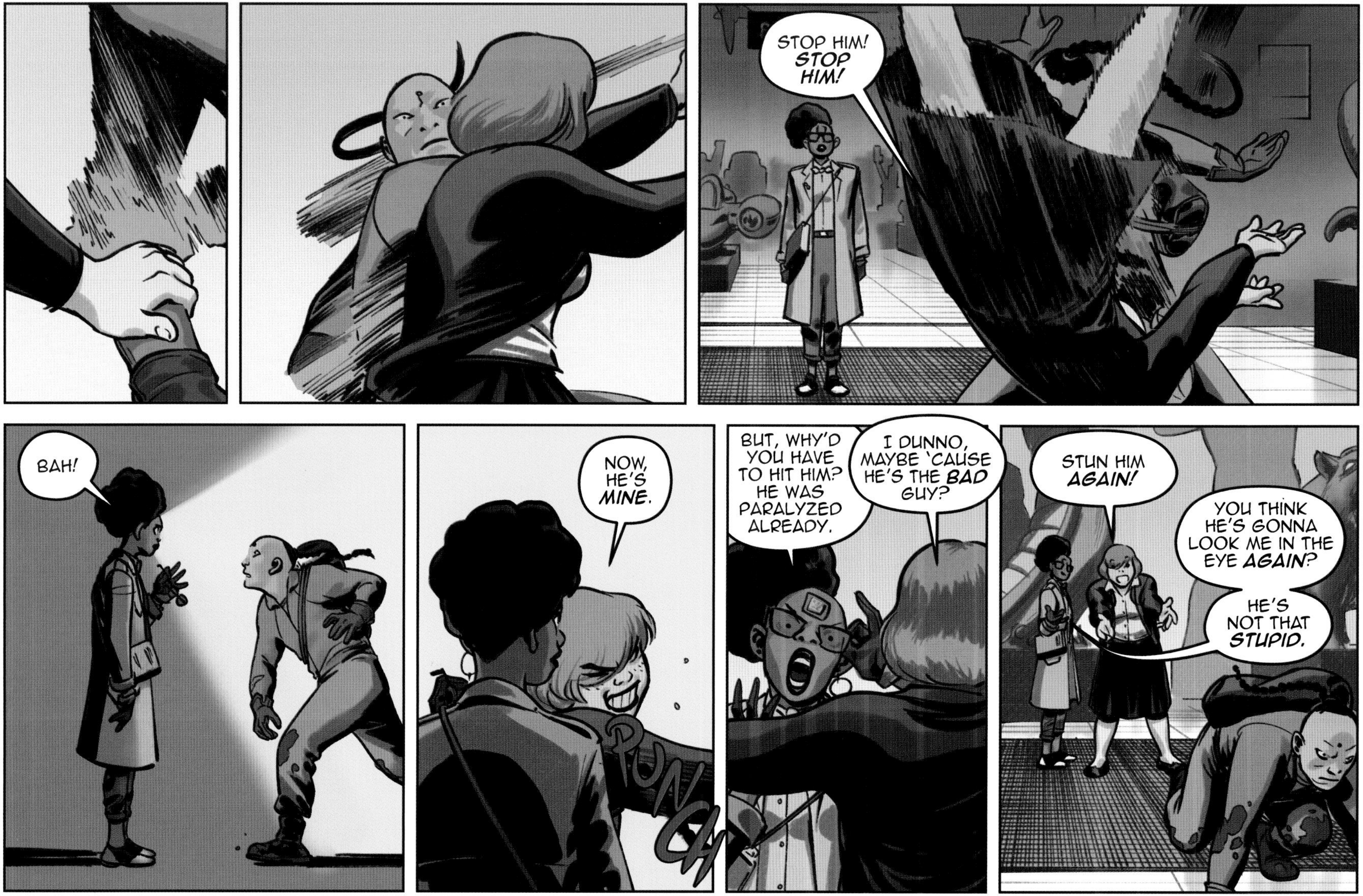
STOP HIM! STOP HIM!
BAH!
NOW, HE'S MINE.
PUNCH
BUT, WHY'D YOU HAVE TO HIT HIM? HE WAS PARALYZED ALREADY.
I DUNNO, MAYBE 'CAUSE HE'S THE BAD GUY?
STUN HIM AGAIN!
YOU THINK HE'S GONNA LOOK ME IN THE EYE AGAIN?
HE'S NOT THAT STUPID.

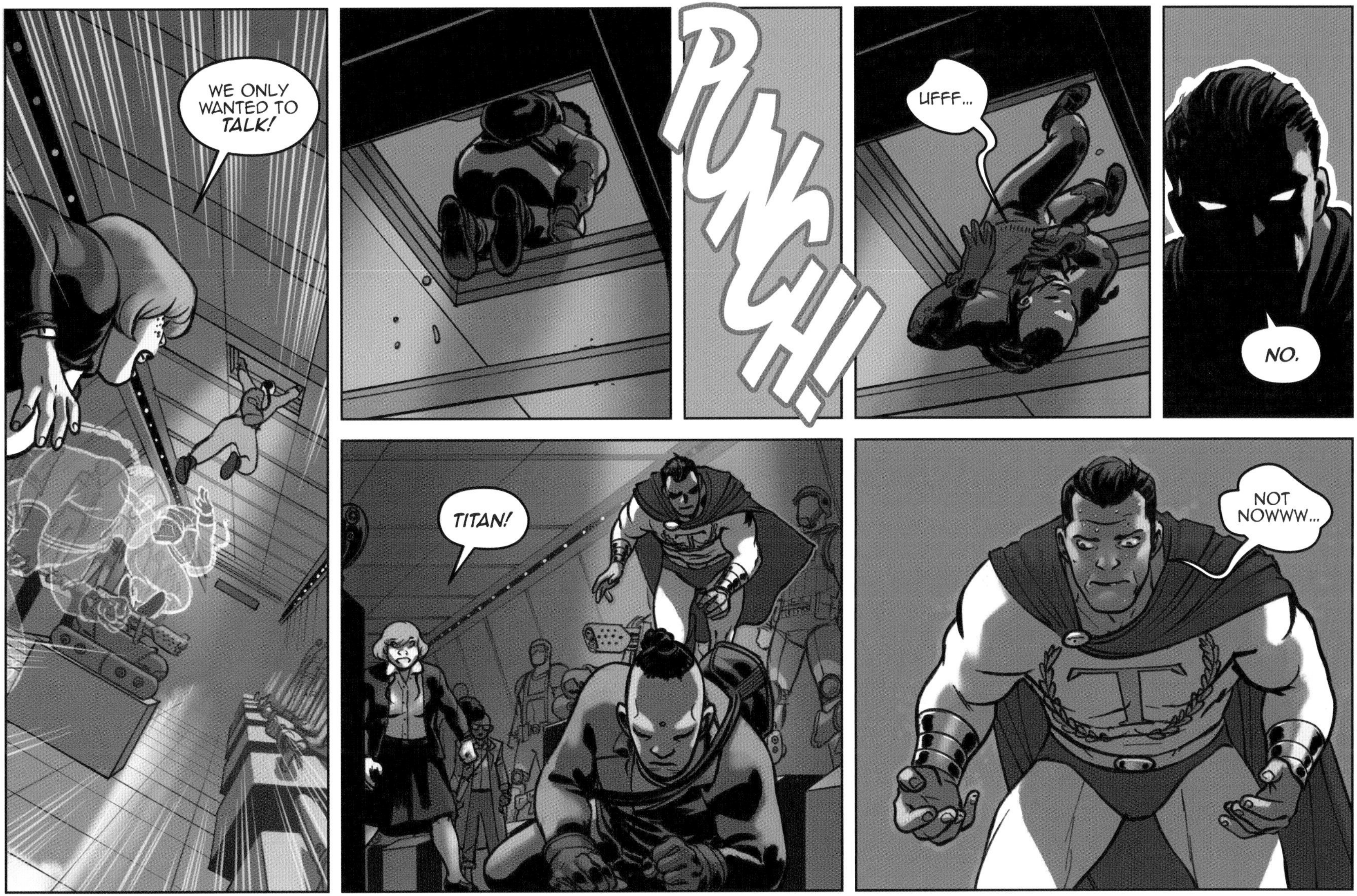
WE ONLY WANTED TO TALK!
PUNCH!
UFFF...
NO.
TITAN!
NOT NOWWW...

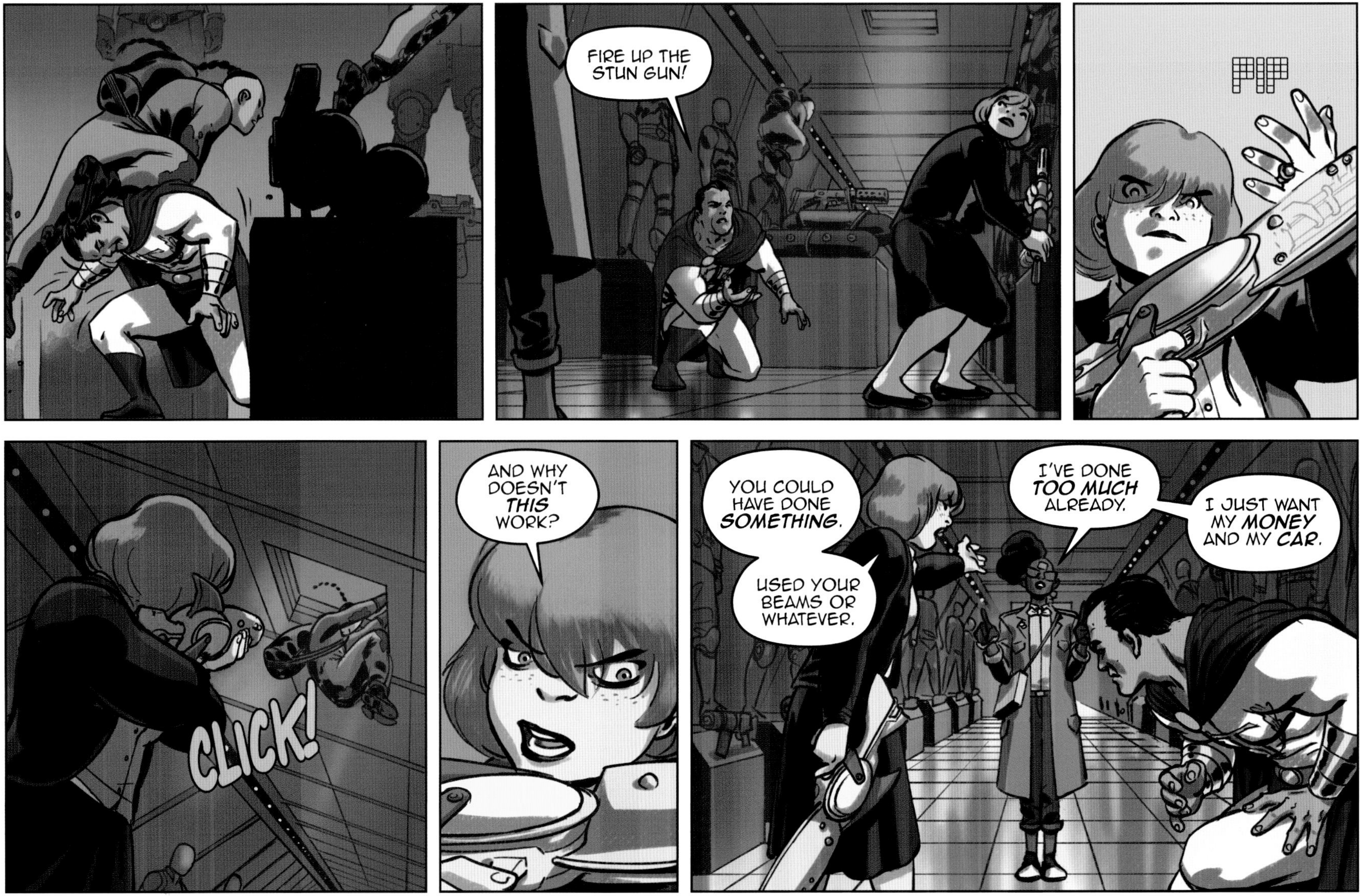
FIRE UP THE STUN GUN!
PIP
CLICK!
AND WHY DOESN'T *THIS* WORK?
YOU COULD HAVE DONE *SOMETHING*.
USED YOUR BEAMS OR WHATEVER.
I'VE DONE *TOO MUCH* ALREADY.
I JUST WANT MY *MONEY* AND MY *CAR*.

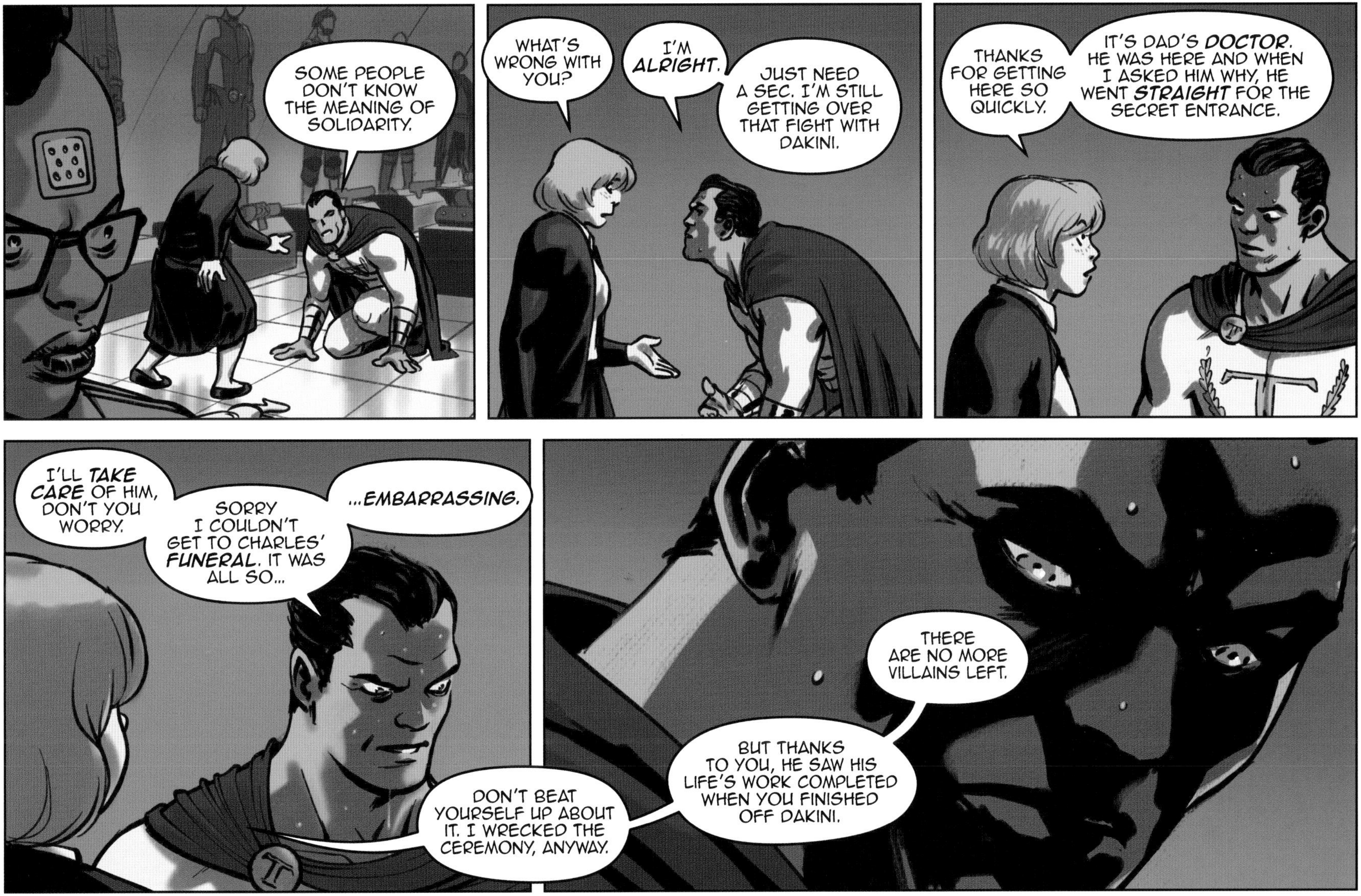
SOME PEOPLE DON'T KNOW THE MEANING OF SOLIDARITY.
WHAT'S WRONG WITH YOU?
I'M ALRIGHT.
JUST NEED A SEC. I'M STILL GETTING OVER THAT FIGHT WITH DAKINI.
THANKS FOR GETTING HERE SO QUICKLY.
IT'S DAD'S DOCTOR. HE WAS HERE AND WHEN I ASKED HIM WHY, HE WENT STRAIGHT FOR THE SECRET ENTRANCE.
I'LL TAKE CARE OF HIM, DON'T YOU WORRY.
SORRY I COULDN'T GET TO CHARLES' FUNERAL. IT WAS ALL SO...
...EMBARRASSING.
DON'T BEAT YOURSELF UP ABOUT IT. I WRECKED THE CEREMONY, ANYWAY.
BUT THANKS TO YOU, HE SAW HIS LIFE'S WORK COMPLETED WHEN YOU FINISHED OFF DAKINI.
THERE ARE NO MORE VILLAINS LEFT.

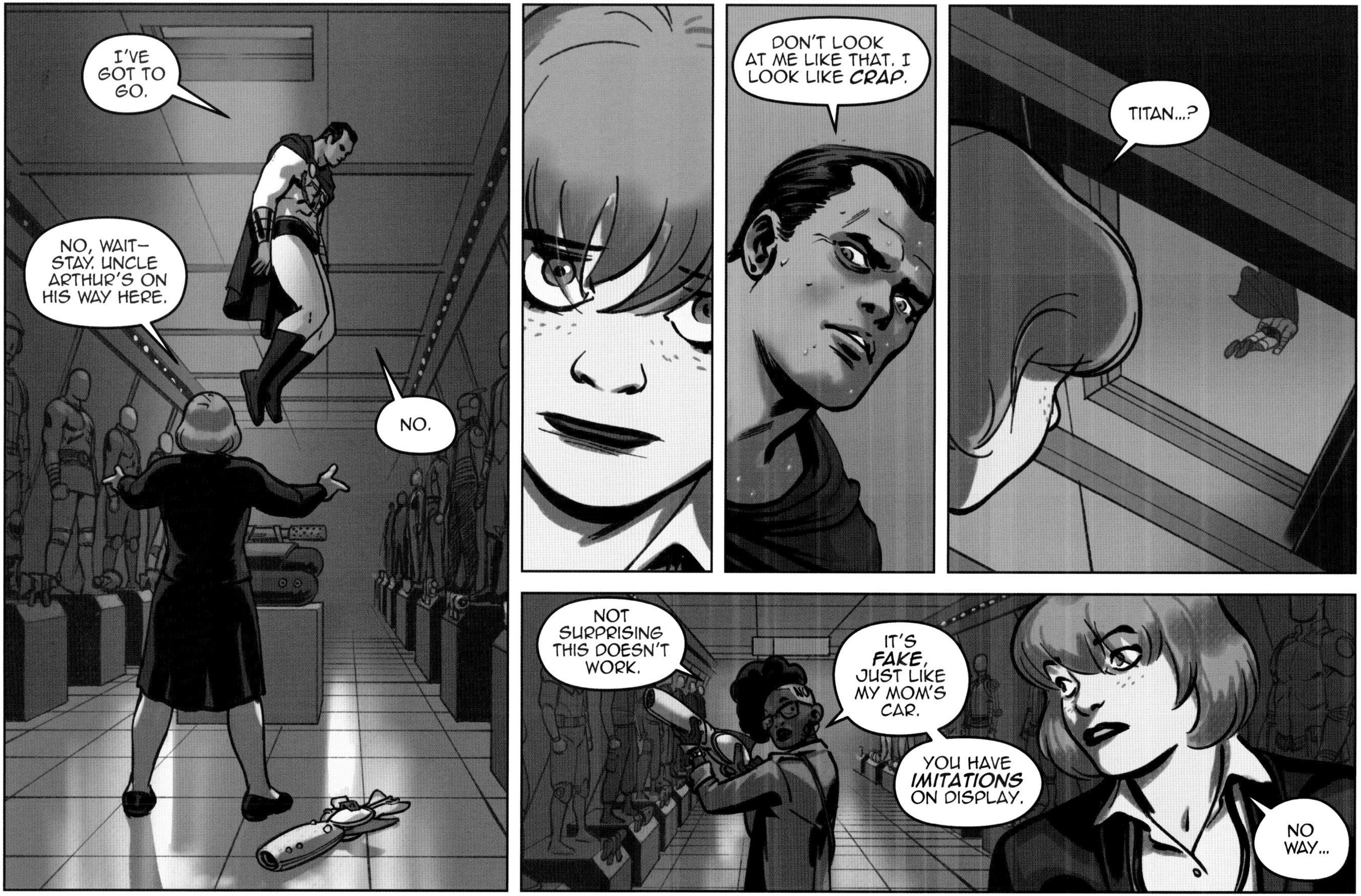
I'VE GOT TO GO.
NO, WAIT–STAY. UNCLE ARTHUR'S ON HIS WAY HERE.
NO.
DON'T LOOK AT ME LIKE THAT. I LOOK LIKE *CRAP*.
TITAN...?
NOT SURPRISING THIS DOESN'T WORK.
IT'S *FAKE*, JUST LIKE MY MOM'S CAR.
YOU HAVE *IMITATIONS* ON DISPLAY.
NO WAY...

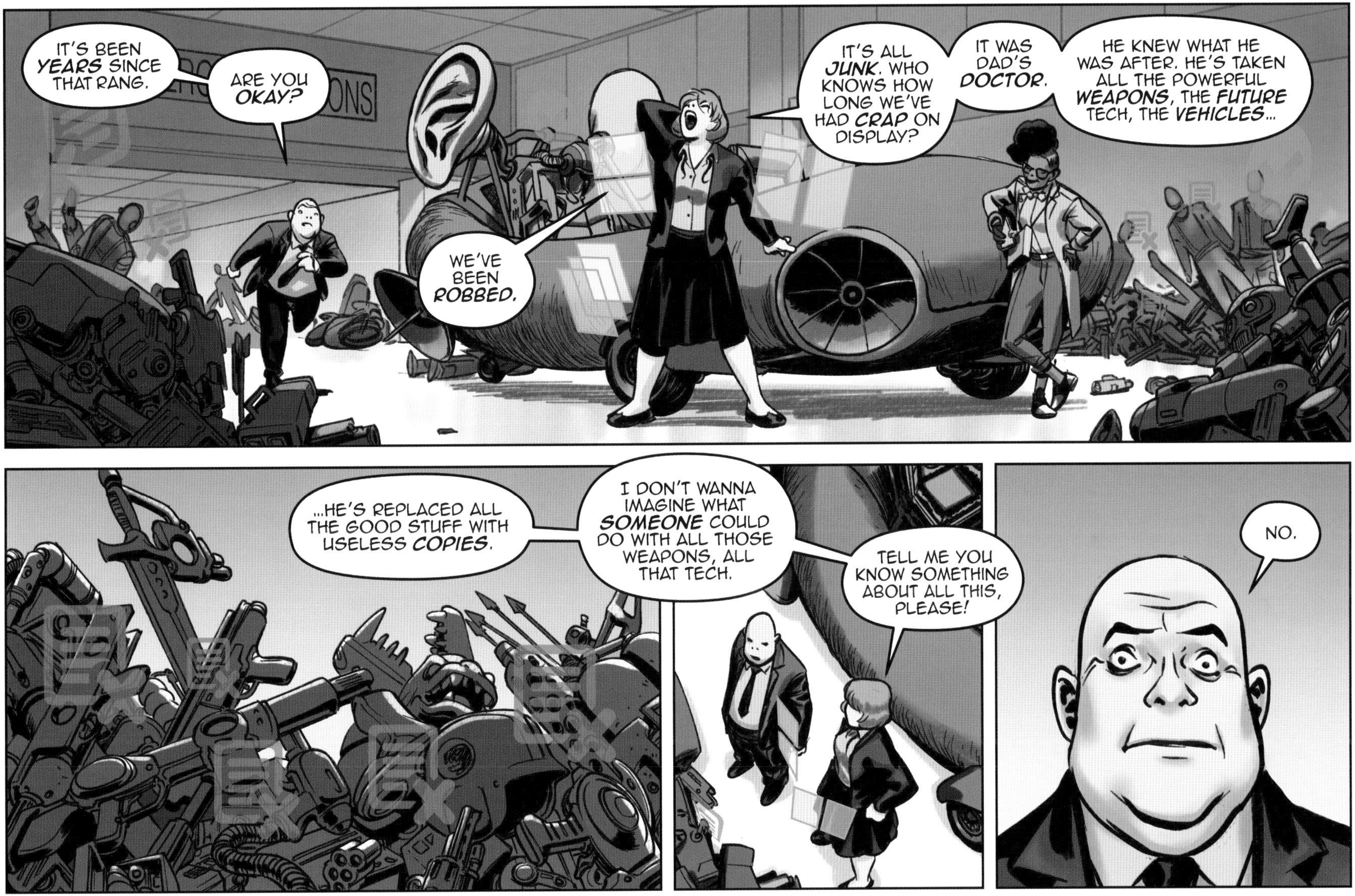
IT'S BEEN YEARS SINCE THAT RANG.
ARE YOU OKAY?
WE'VE BEEN ROBBED.
IT'S ALL JUNK. WHO KNOWS HOW LONG WE'VE HAD CRAP ON DISPLAY?
IT WAS DAD'S DOCTOR.
HE KNEW WHAT HE WAS AFTER. HE'S TAKEN ALL THE POWERFUL WEAPONS, THE FUTURE TECH, THE VEHICLES...
...HE'S REPLACED ALL THE GOOD STUFF WITH USELESS COPIES.
I DON'T WANNA IMAGINE WHAT SOMEONE COULD DO WITH ALL THOSE WEAPONS, ALL THAT TECH.
TELL ME YOU KNOW SOMETHING ABOUT ALL THIS, PLEASE!
NO.

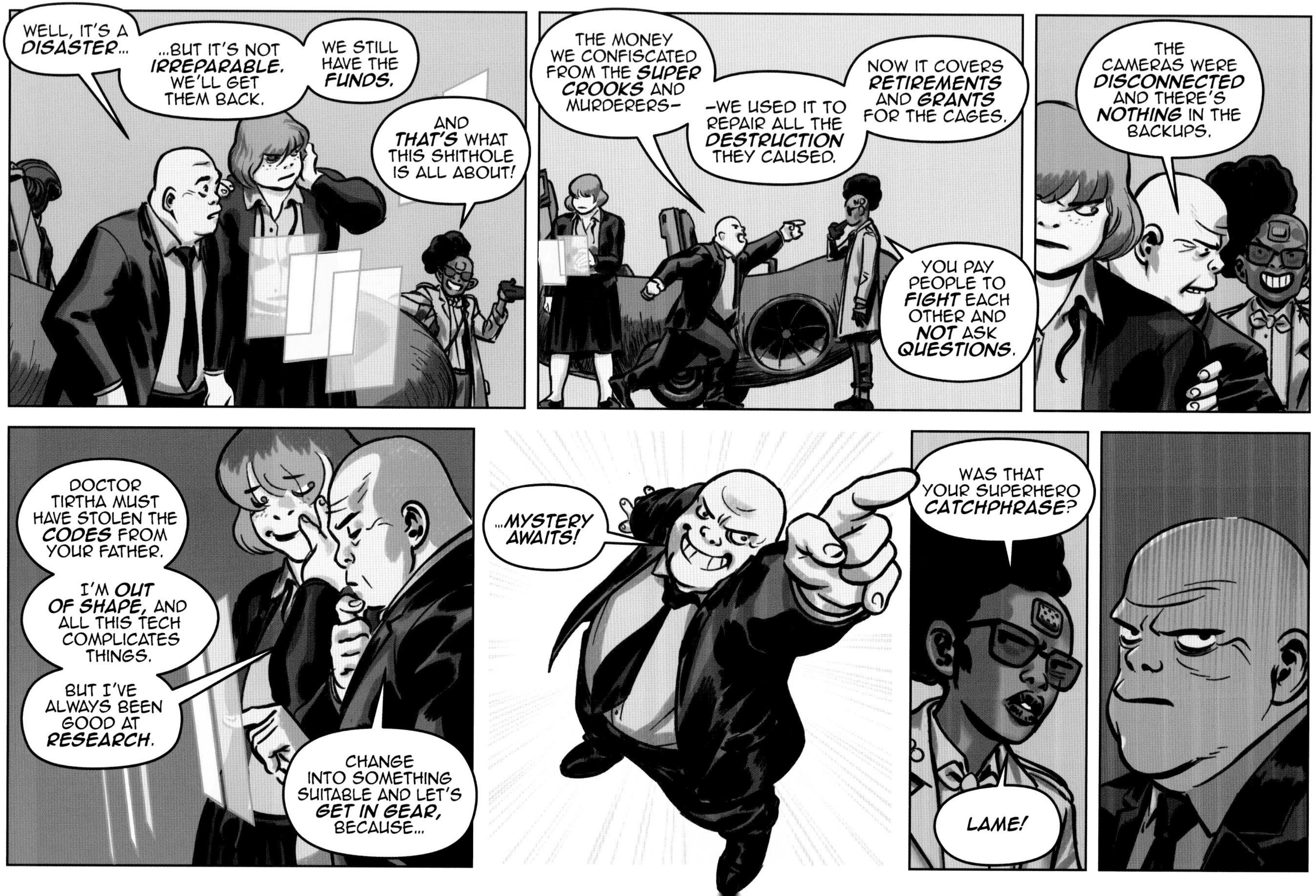

WELL, IT'S A *DISASTER*...
...BUT IT'S NOT *IRREPARABLE.* WE'LL GET THEM BACK.
WE STILL HAVE THE *FUNDS.*
AND *THAT'S* WHAT THIS SHITHOLE IS ALL ABOUT!
THE MONEY WE CONFISCATED FROM THE *SUPER CROOKS* AND MURDERERS–
–WE USED IT TO REPAIR ALL THE *DESTRUCTION* THEY CAUSED.
NOW IT COVERS *RETIREMENTS* AND *GRANTS* FOR THE CAGES.
YOU PAY PEOPLE TO *FIGHT* EACH OTHER AND *NOT* ASK *QUESTIONS*.
THE CAMERAS WERE *DISCONNECTED* AND THERE'S *NOTHING* IN THE BACKUPS.
DOCTOR TIRTHA MUST HAVE STOLEN THE *CODES* FROM YOUR FATHER.
I'M *OUT OF SHAPE,* AND ALL THIS TECH COMPLICATES THINGS.
BUT I'VE ALWAYS BEEN GOOD AT *RESEARCH*.
CHANGE INTO SOMETHING SUITABLE AND LET'S *GET IN GEAR,* BECAUSE...
...*MYSTERY AWAITS!*
WAS THAT YOUR SUPERHERO *CATCHPHRASE*?
LAME!

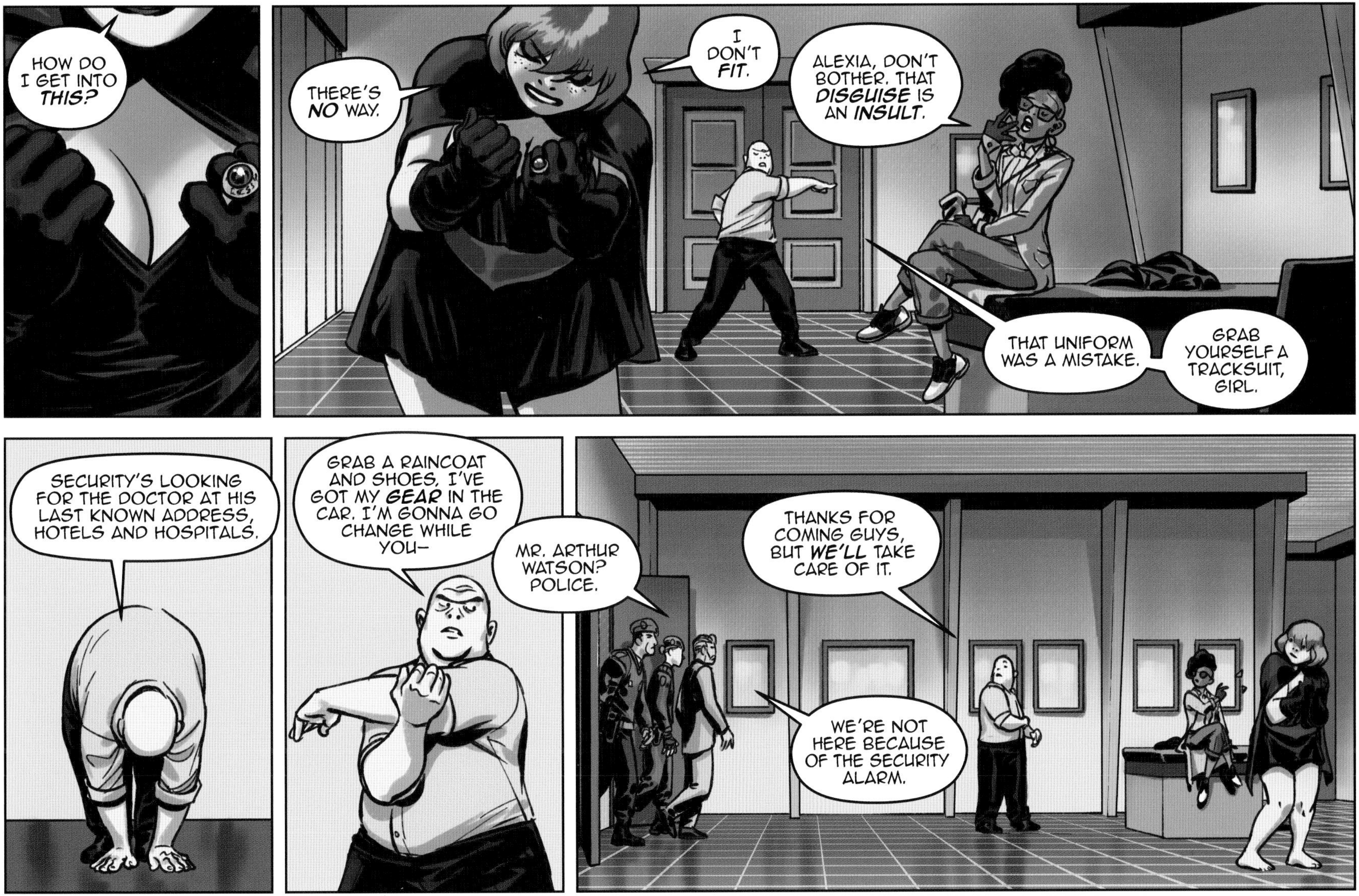
HOW DO I GET INTO *THIS?*
THERE'S *NO* WAY.
I DON'T *FIT*.
ALEXIA, DON'T BOTHER. THAT *DISGUISE* IS AN *INSULT*.
THAT UNIFORM WAS A MISTAKE.
GRAB YOURSELF A TRACKSUIT, GIRL.
SECURITY'S LOOKING FOR THE DOCTOR AT HIS LAST KNOWN ADDRESS, HOTELS AND HOSPITALS.
GRAB A RAINCOAT AND SHOES, I'VE GOT MY *GEAR* IN THE CAR. I'M GONNA GO CHANGE WHILE YOU—
MR. ARTHUR WATSON? POLICE.
THANKS FOR COMING GUYS, BUT *WE'LL* TAKE CARE OF IT.
WE'RE NOT HERE BECAUSE OF THE SECURITY ALARM.

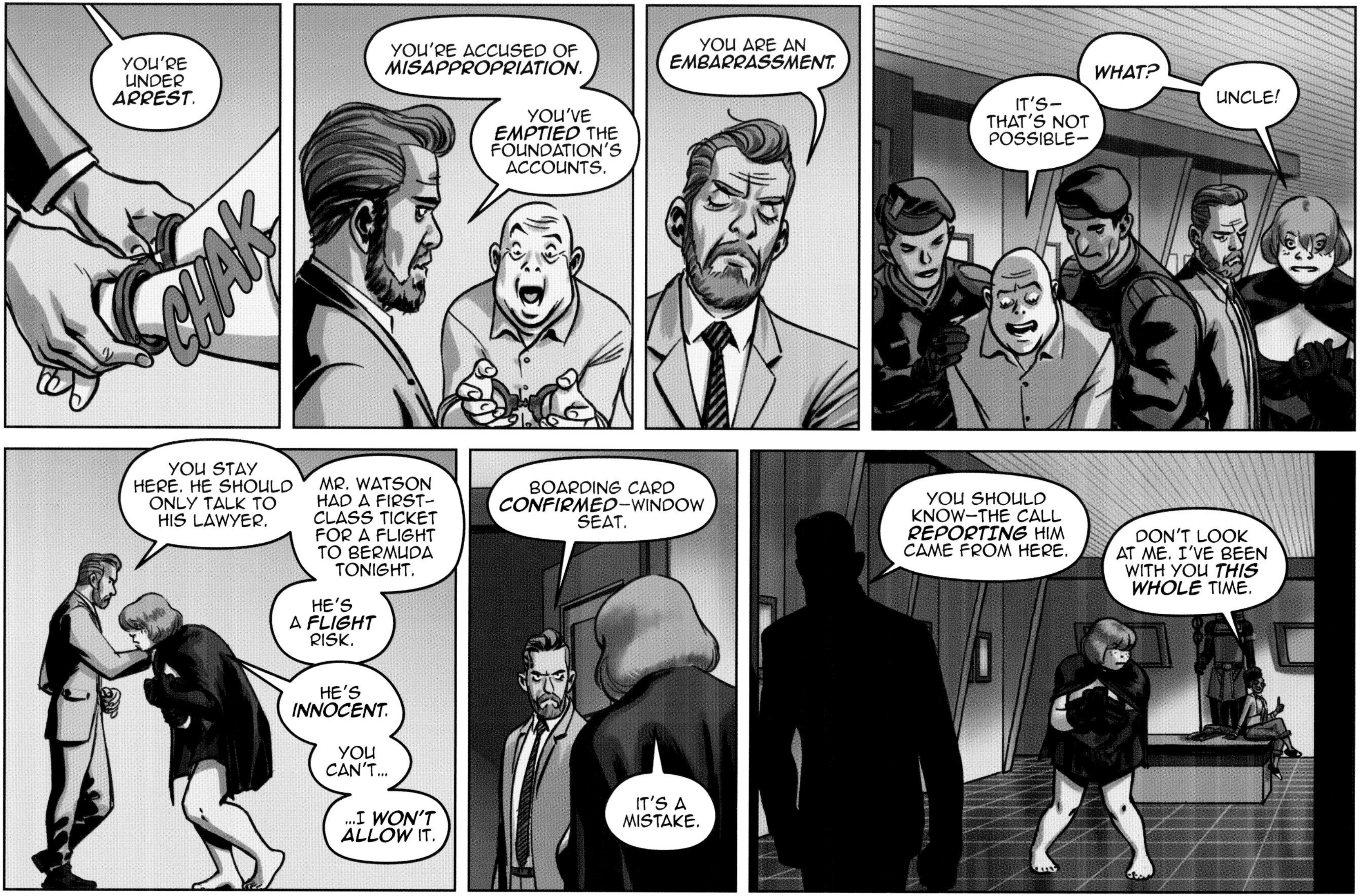
YOU'RE UNDER ARREST.
CHAK
YOU'RE ACCUSED OF MISAPPROPRIATION.
YOU'VE EMPTIED THE FOUNDATION'S ACCOUNTS.
YOU ARE AN EMBARRASSMENT.
IT'S— THAT'S NOT POSSIBLE—
WHAT?
UNCLE!
YOU STAY HERE. HE SHOULD ONLY TALK TO HIS LAWYER.
MR. WATSON HAD A FIRST-CLASS TICKET FOR A FLIGHT TO BERMUDA TONIGHT.
HE'S A FLIGHT RISK.
HE'S INNOCENT.
YOU CAN'T...
...I WON'T ALLOW IT.
BOARDING CARD CONFIRMED—WINDOW SEAT.
IT'S A MISTAKE.
YOU SHOULD KNOW—THE CALL REPORTING HIM CAME FROM HERE.
DON'T LOOK AT ME. I'VE BEEN WITH YOU THIS WHOLE TIME.

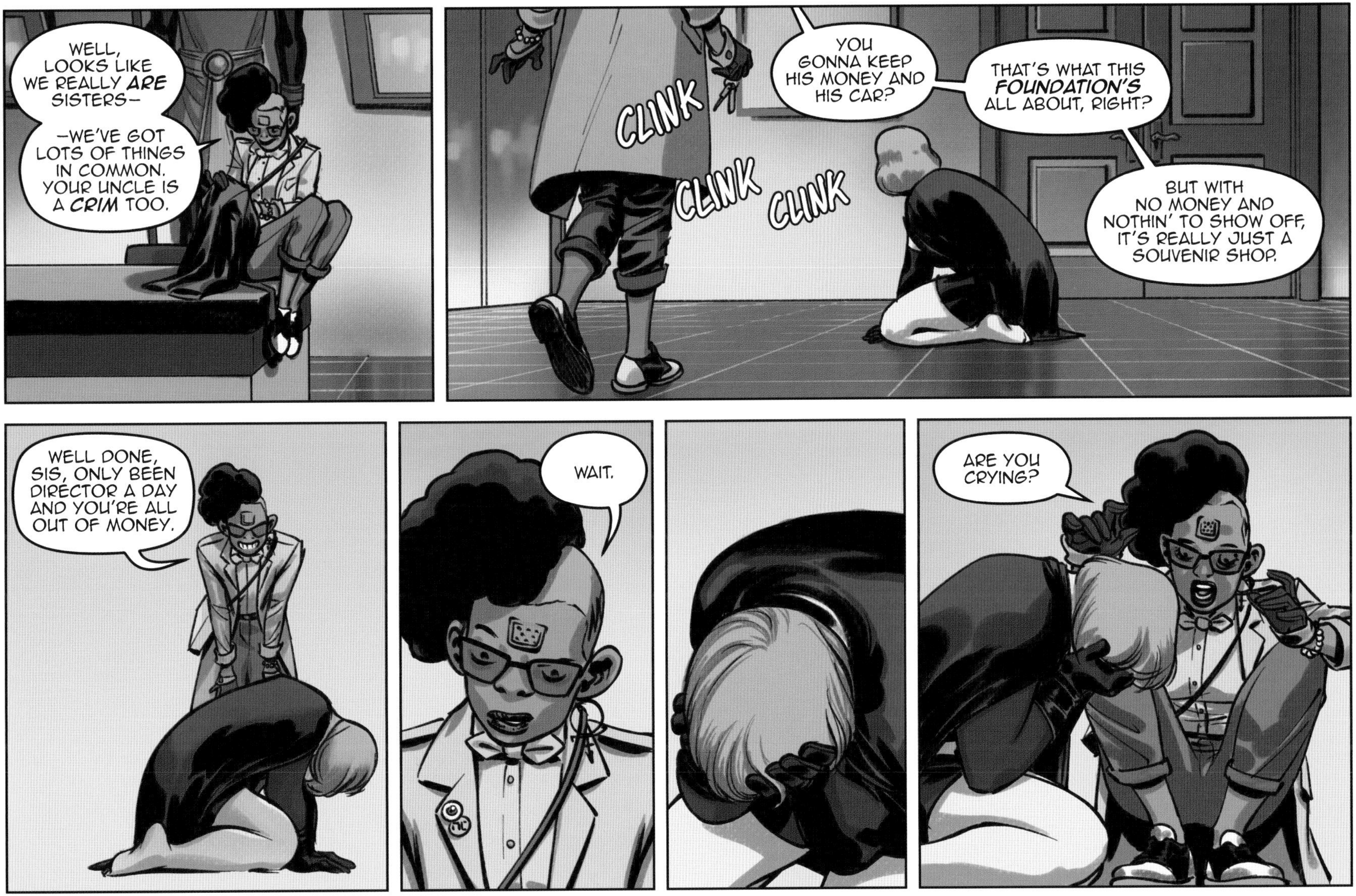
WELL, LOOKS LIKE WE REALLY ARE SISTERS–
–WE'VE GOT LOTS OF THINGS IN COMMON. YOUR UNCLE IS A CRIM TOO.
CLINK
CLINK
CLINK
YOU GONNA KEEP HIS MONEY AND HIS CAR?
THAT'S WHAT THIS FOUNDATION'S ALL ABOUT, RIGHT?
BUT WITH NO MONEY AND NOTHIN' TO SHOW OFF, IT'S REALLY JUST A SOUVENIR SHOP.
WELL DONE, SIS, ONLY BEEN DIRECTOR A DAY AND YOU'RE ALL OUT OF MONEY.
WAIT.
ARE YOU CRYING?

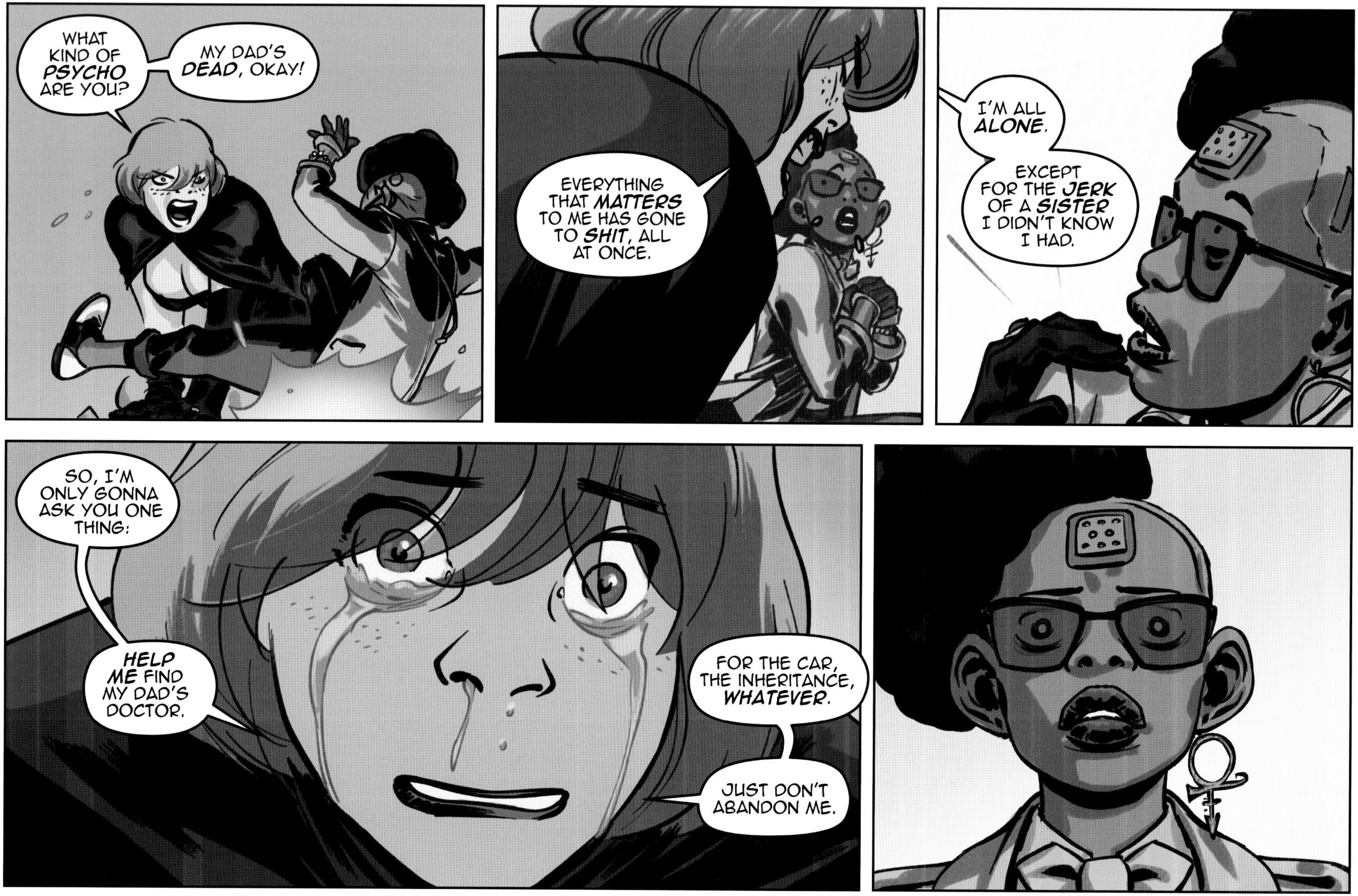
WHAT KIND OF PSYCHO ARE YOU?
MY DAD'S DEAD, OKAY!
EVERYTHING THAT MATTERS TO ME HAS GONE TO SHIT, ALL AT ONCE.
I'M ALL ALONE.
EXCEPT FOR THE JERK OF A SISTER I DIDN'T KNOW I HAD.
SO, I'M ONLY GONNA ASK YOU ONE THING:
HELP ME FIND MY DAD'S DOCTOR.
FOR THE CAR, THE INHERITANCE, WHATEVER.
JUST DON'T ABANDON ME.

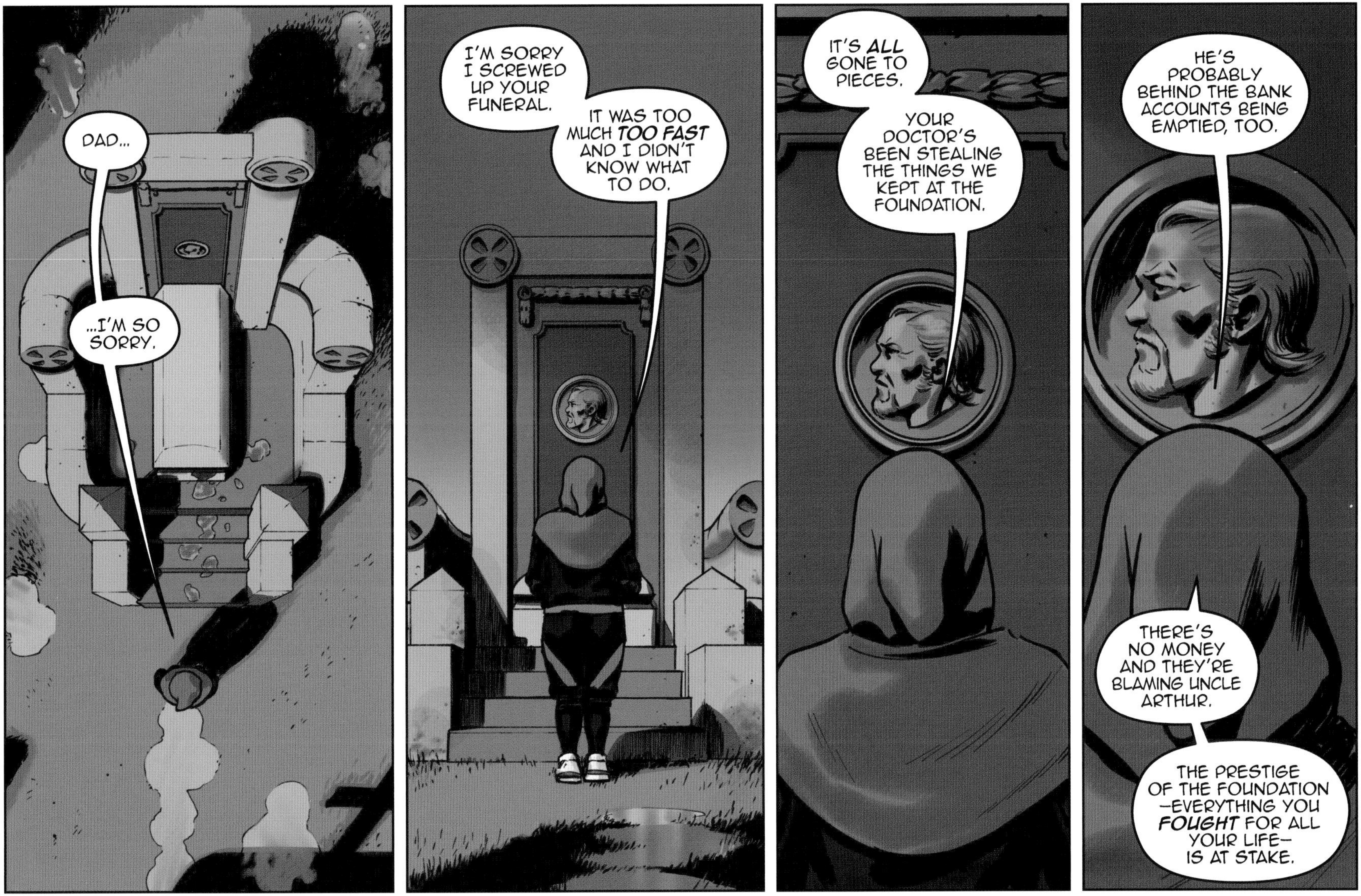
DAD...
...I'M SO SORRY.
I'M SORRY I SCREWED UP YOUR FUNERAL.
IT WAS TOO MUCH TOO FAST AND I DIDN'T KNOW WHAT TO DO.
IT'S ALL GONE TO PIECES.
YOUR DOCTOR'S BEEN STEALING THE THINGS WE KEPT AT THE FOUNDATION.
HE'S PROBABLY BEHIND THE BANK ACCOUNTS BEING EMPTIED, TOO.
THERE'S NO MONEY AND THEY'RE BLAMING UNCLE ARTHUR.
THE PRESTIGE OF THE FOUNDATION —EVERYTHING YOU FOUGHT FOR ALL YOUR LIFE— IS AT STAKE.

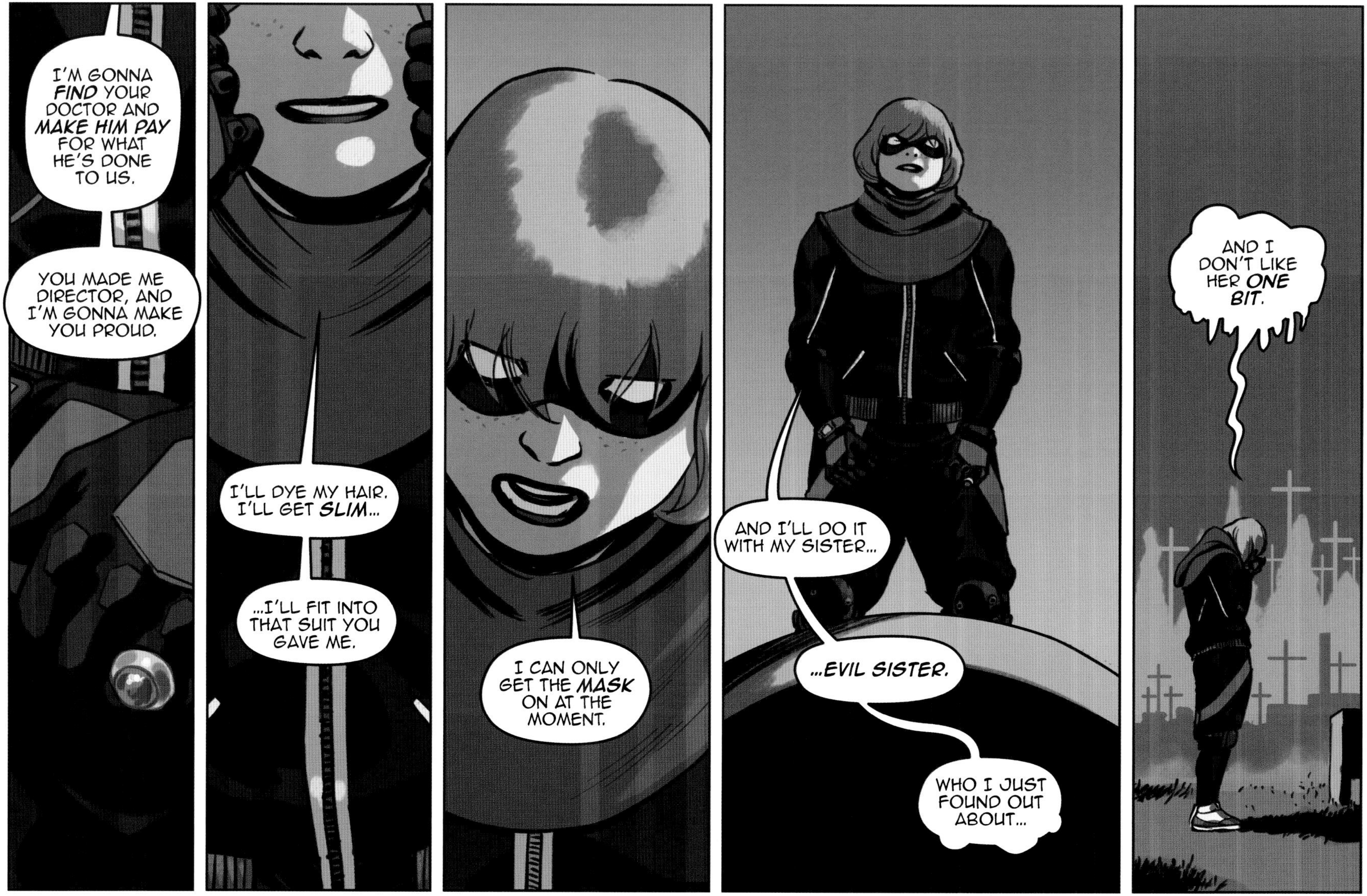
I'M GONNA **FIND** YOUR DOCTOR AND **MAKE HIM PAY** FOR WHAT HE'S DONE TO US.
YOU MADE ME DIRECTOR, AND I'M GONNA MAKE YOU PROUD.
I'LL DYE MY HAIR. I'LL GET **SLIM**...
...I'LL FIT INTO THAT SUIT YOU GAVE ME.
I CAN ONLY GET THE **MASK** ON AT THE MOMENT.
AND I'LL DO IT WITH MY SISTER...
...EVIL SISTER.
WHO I JUST FOUND OUT ABOUT...
AND I DON'T LIKE HER **ONE BIT**.

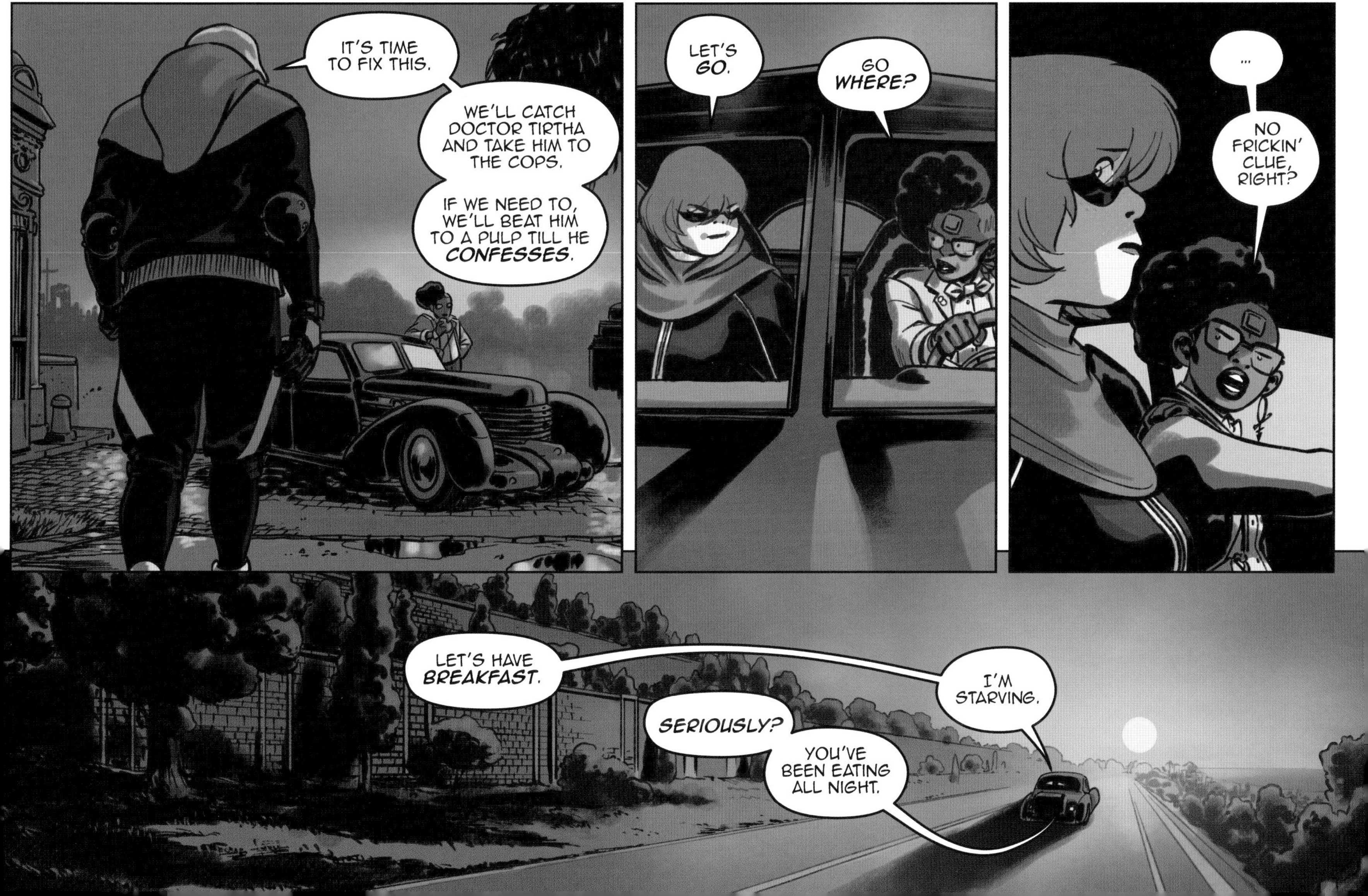

IT'S TIME TO FIX THIS.
WE'LL CATCH DOCTOR TIRTHA AND TAKE HIM TO THE COPS.
IF WE NEED TO, WE'LL BEAT HIM TO A PULP TILL HE *CONFESSES*.
LET'S *GO*.
GO *WHERE?*
...
NO FRICKIN' CLUE, RIGHT?
LET'S HAVE *BREAKFAST*.
I'M STARVING.
SERIOUSLY?
YOU'VE BEEN EATING ALL NIGHT.

Chapter Three

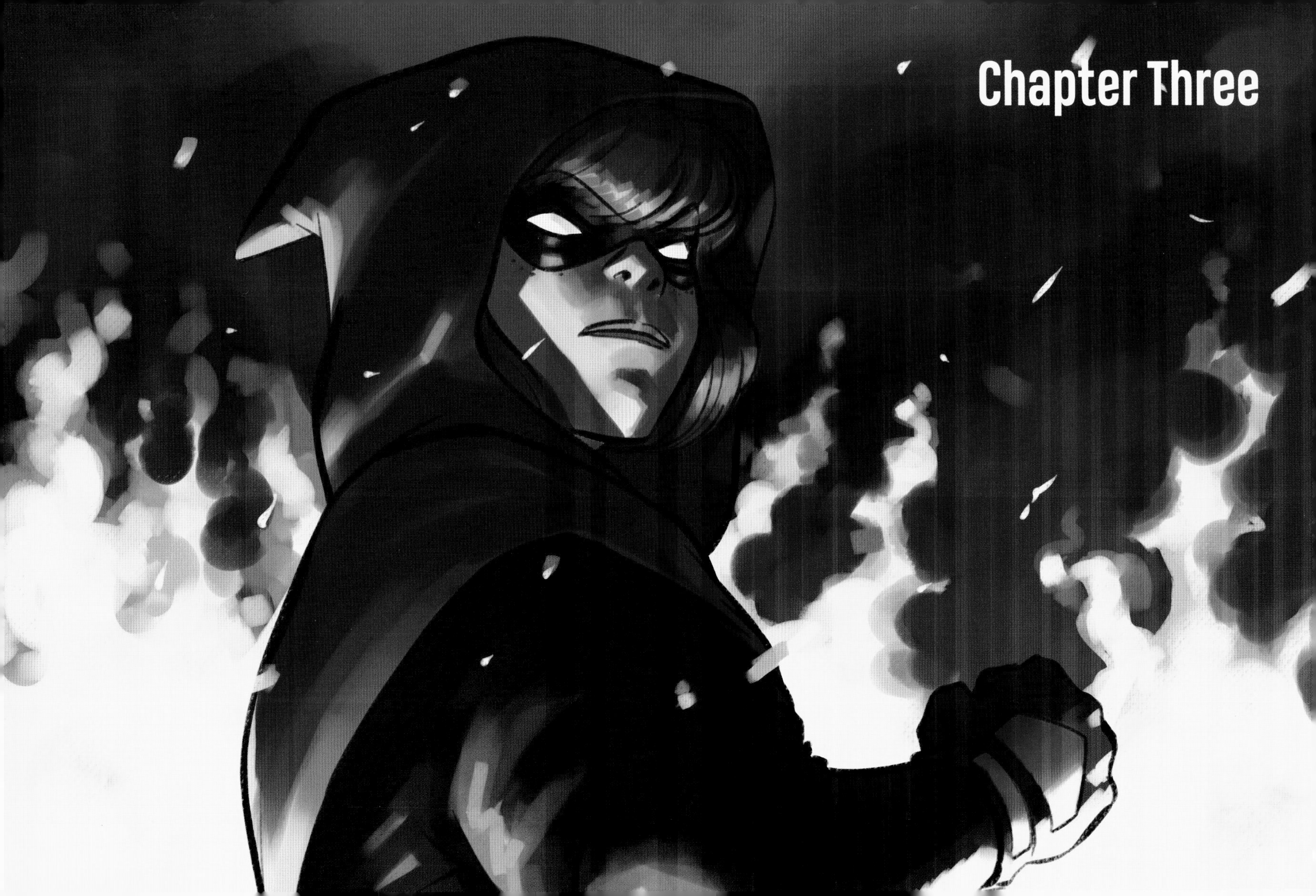

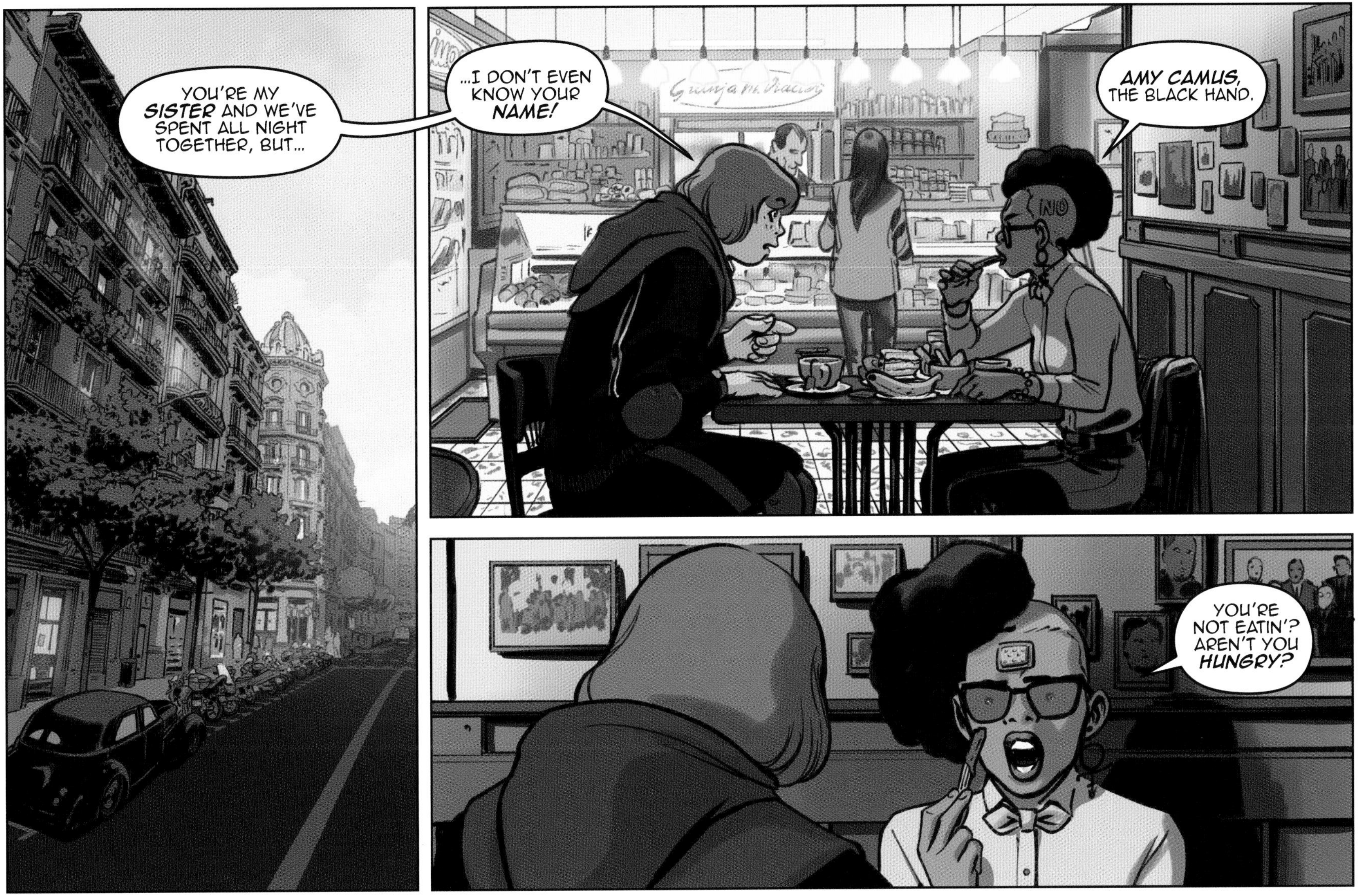

YOU'RE MY SISTER AND WE'VE SPENT ALL NIGHT TOGETHER, BUT...
...I DON'T EVEN KNOW YOUR NAME!
AMY CAMUS, THE BLACK HAND.
YOU'RE NOT EATIN'? AREN'T YOU HUNGRY?

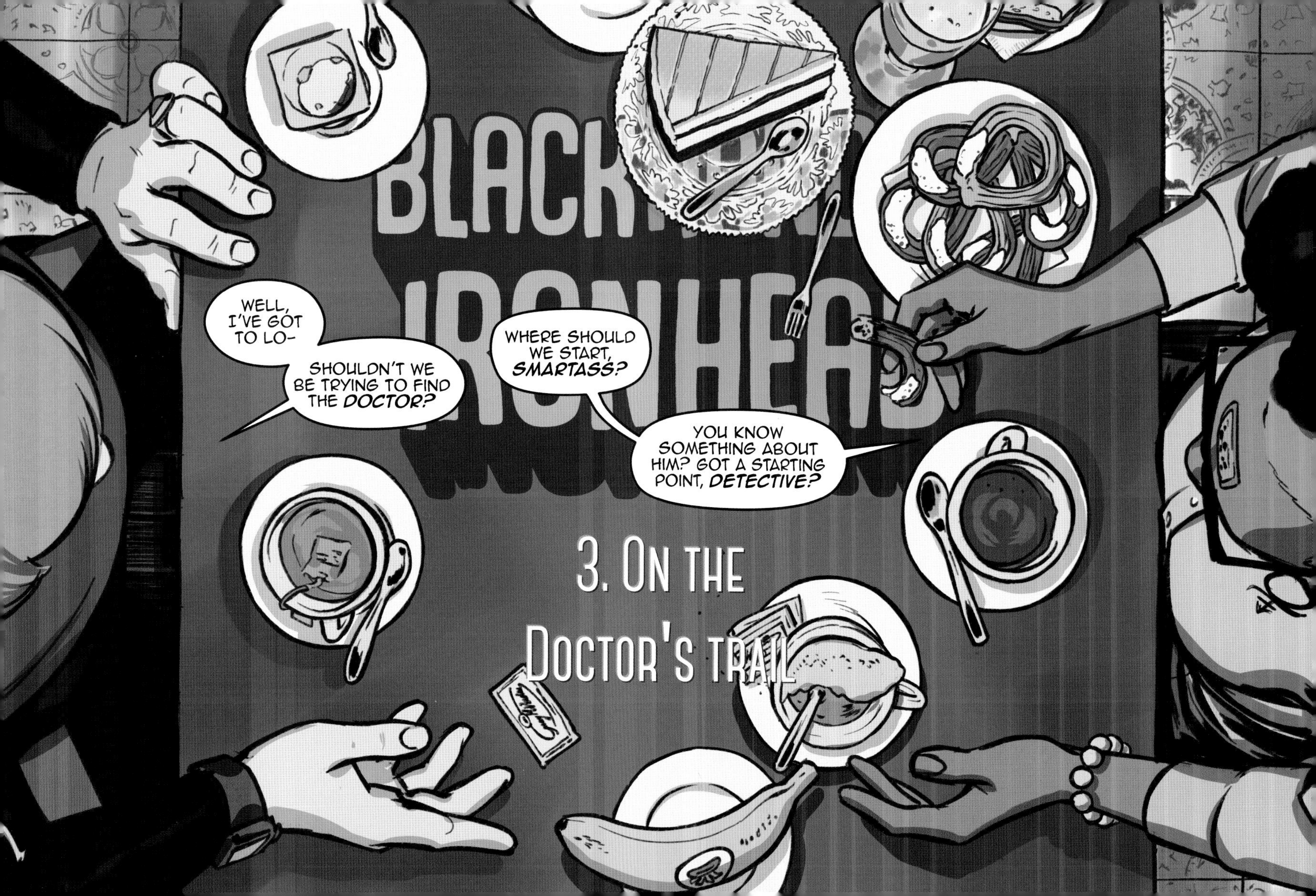
WELL, I'VE GOT TO LO-
SHOULDN'T WE BE TRYING TO FIND THE *DOCTOR?*
WHERE SHOULD WE START, *SMARTASS?*
YOU KNOW SOMETHING ABOUT HIM? GOT A STARTING POINT, *DETECTIVE?*
3. On the Doctor's trail

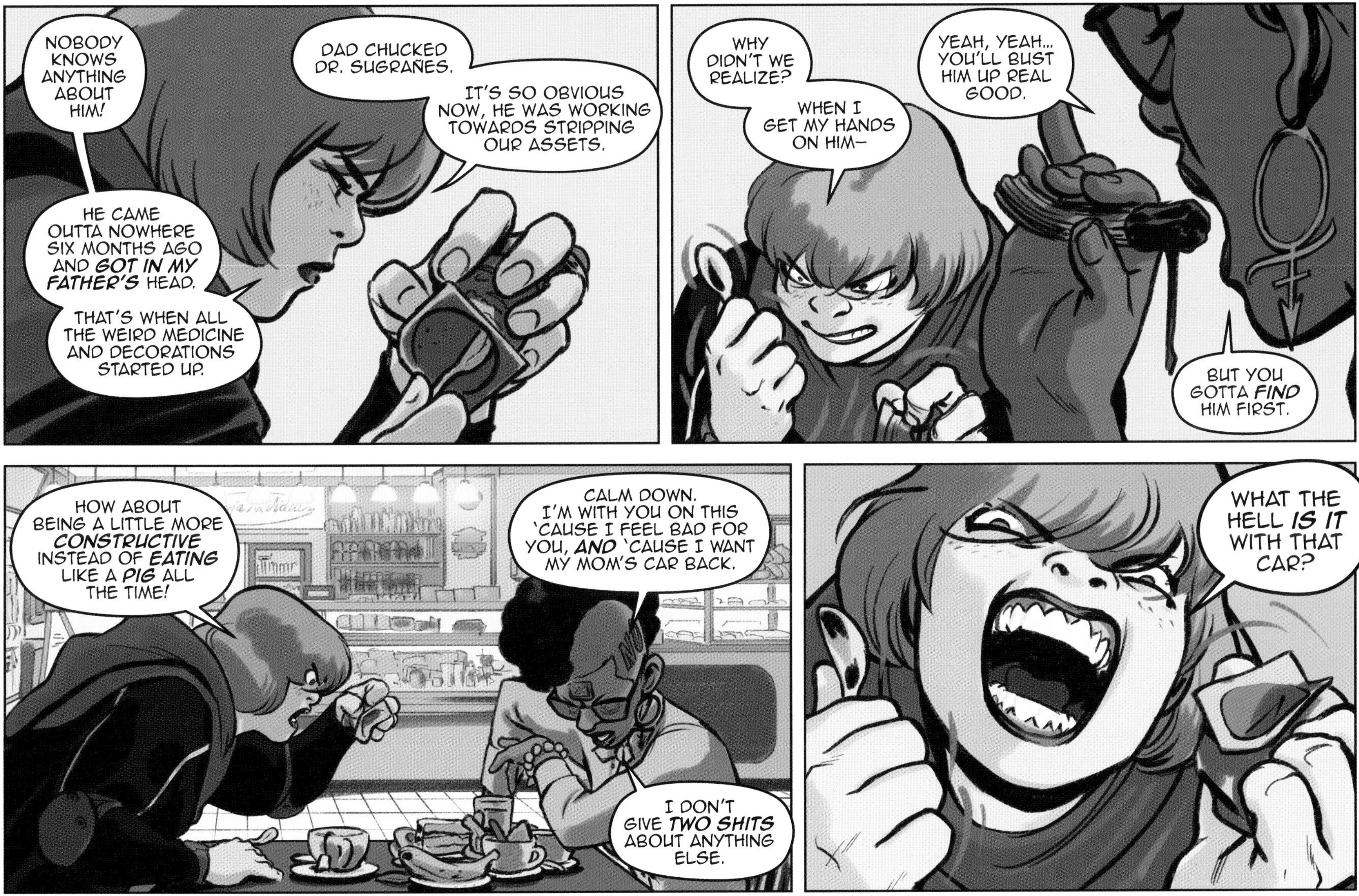
NOBODY KNOWS ANYTHING ABOUT HIM!
DAD CHUCKED DR. SUGRAÑES.
IT'S SO OBVIOUS NOW, HE WAS WORKING TOWARDS STRIPPING OUR ASSETS.
HE CAME OUTTA NOWHERE SIX MONTHS AGO AND ***GOT IN MY FATHER'S*** HEAD.
THAT'S WHEN ALL THE WEIRD MEDICINE AND DECORATIONS STARTED UP.
WHY DIDN'T WE REALIZE?
WHEN I GET MY HANDS ON HIM–
YEAH, YEAH... YOU'LL BUST HIM UP REAL GOOD.
BUT YOU GOTTA ***FIND*** HIM FIRST.
HOW ABOUT BEING A LITTLE MORE ***CONSTRUCTIVE*** INSTEAD OF ***EATING*** LIKE A ***PIG*** ALL THE TIME!
CALM DOWN. I'M WITH YOU ON THIS 'CAUSE I FEEL BAD FOR YOU, ***AND*** 'CAUSE I WANT MY MOM'S CAR BACK.
I DON'T GIVE ***TWO SHITS*** ABOUT ANYTHING ELSE.
WHAT THE HELL ***IS IT*** WITH THAT CAR?

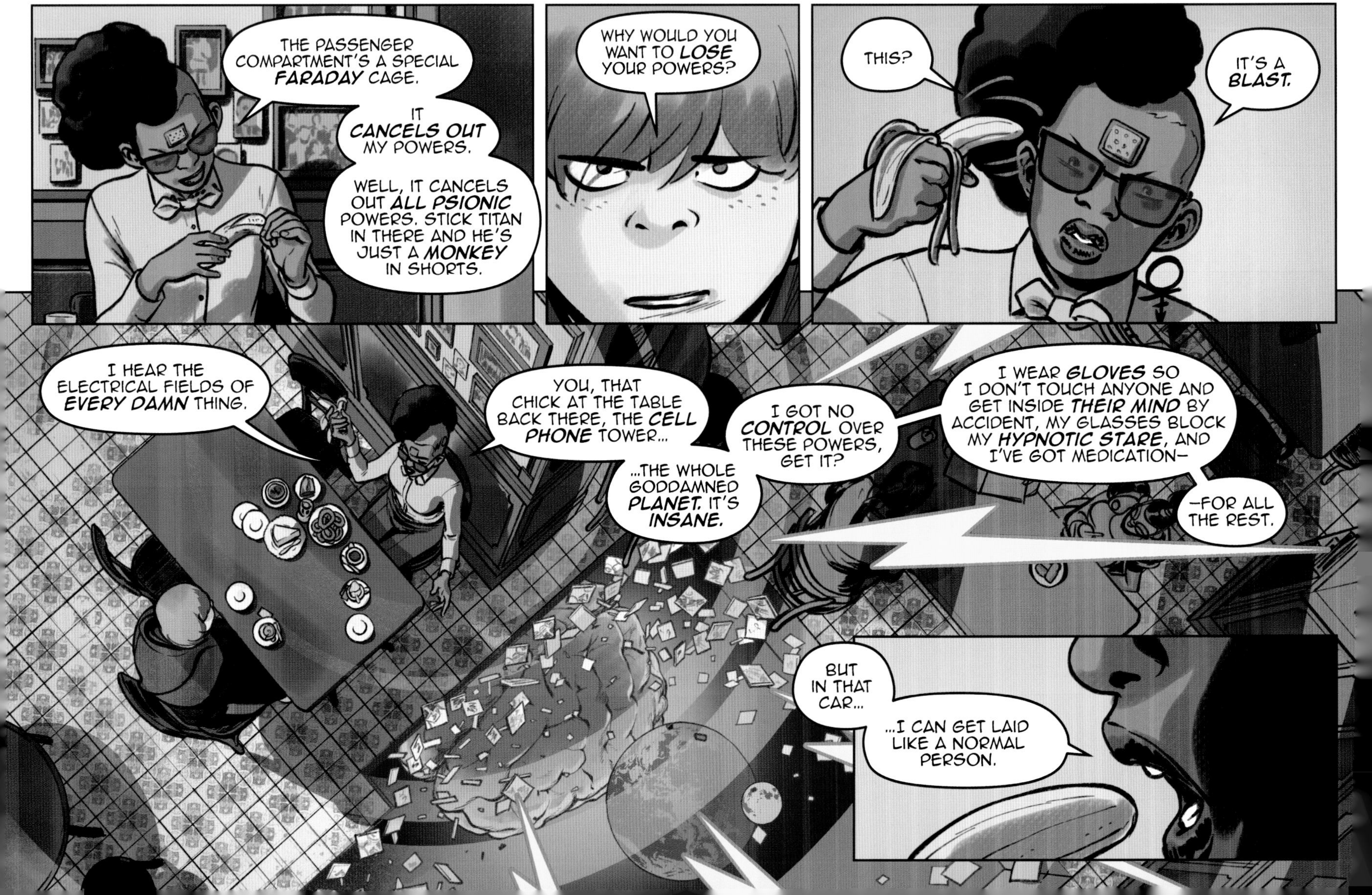
THE PASSENGER COMPARTMENT'S A SPECIAL FARADAY CAGE.
IT CANCELS OUT MY POWERS.
WELL, IT CANCELS OUT ALL PSIONIC POWERS. STICK TITAN IN THERE AND HE'S JUST A MONKEY IN SHORTS.
WHY WOULD YOU WANT TO LOSE YOUR POWERS?
THIS?
IT'S A BLAST.
I HEAR THE ELECTRICAL FIELDS OF EVERY DAMN THING.
YOU, THAT CHICK AT THE TABLE BACK THERE, THE CELL PHONE TOWER...
...THE WHOLE GODDAMNED PLANET. IT'S INSANE.
I GOT NO CONTROL OVER THESE POWERS, GET IT?
I WEAR GLOVES SO I DON'T TOUCH ANYONE AND GET INSIDE THEIR MIND BY ACCIDENT, MY GLASSES BLOCK MY HYPNOTIC STARE, AND I'VE GOT MEDICATION—
—FOR ALL THE REST.
BUT IN THAT CAR...
...I CAN GET LAID LIKE A NORMAL PERSON.

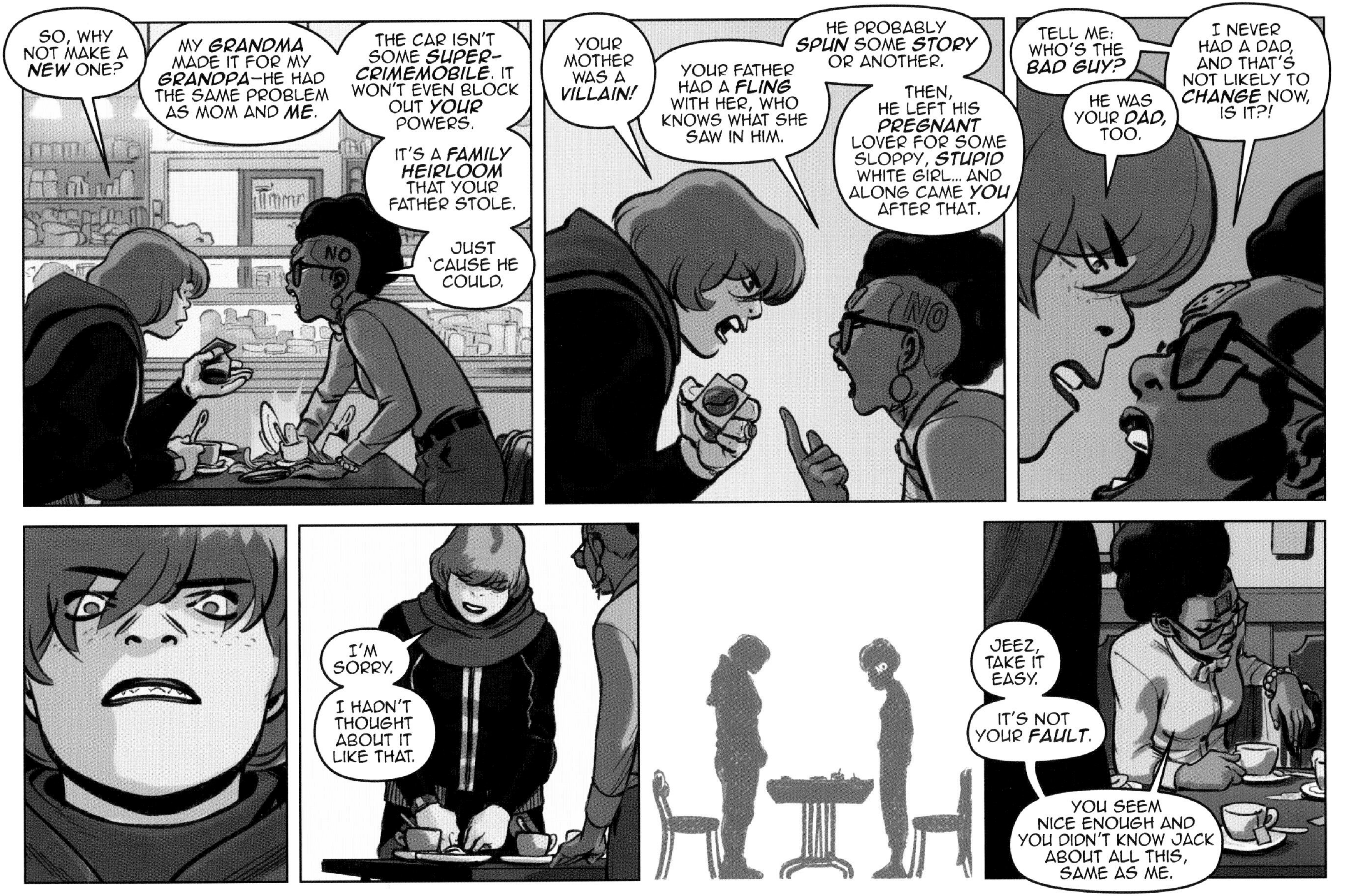
SO, WHY NOT MAKE A NEW ONE?
MY GRANDMA MADE IT FOR MY GRANDPA—HE HAD THE SAME PROBLEM AS MOM AND ME.
THE CAR ISN'T SOME SUPER-CRIMEMOBILE. IT WON'T EVEN BLOCK OUT YOUR POWERS.
IT'S A FAMILY HEIRLOOM THAT YOUR FATHER STOLE.
JUST 'CAUSE HE COULD.
YOUR MOTHER WAS A VILLAIN!
HE PROBABLY SPUN SOME STORY OR ANOTHER.
YOUR FATHER HAD A FLING WITH HER, WHO KNOWS WHAT SHE SAW IN HIM.
THEN, HE LEFT HIS PREGNANT LOVER FOR SOME SLOPPY, STUPID WHITE GIRL... AND ALONG CAME YOU AFTER THAT.
TELL ME: WHO'S THE BAD GUY?
HE WAS YOUR DAD, TOO.
I NEVER HAD A DAD, AND THAT'S NOT LIKELY TO CHANGE NOW, IS IT?!
I'M SORRY.
I HADN'T THOUGHT ABOUT IT LIKE THAT.
JEEZ, TAKE IT EASY.
IT'S NOT YOUR FAULT.
YOU SEEM NICE ENOUGH AND YOU DIDN'T KNOW JACK ABOUT ALL THIS, SAME AS ME.

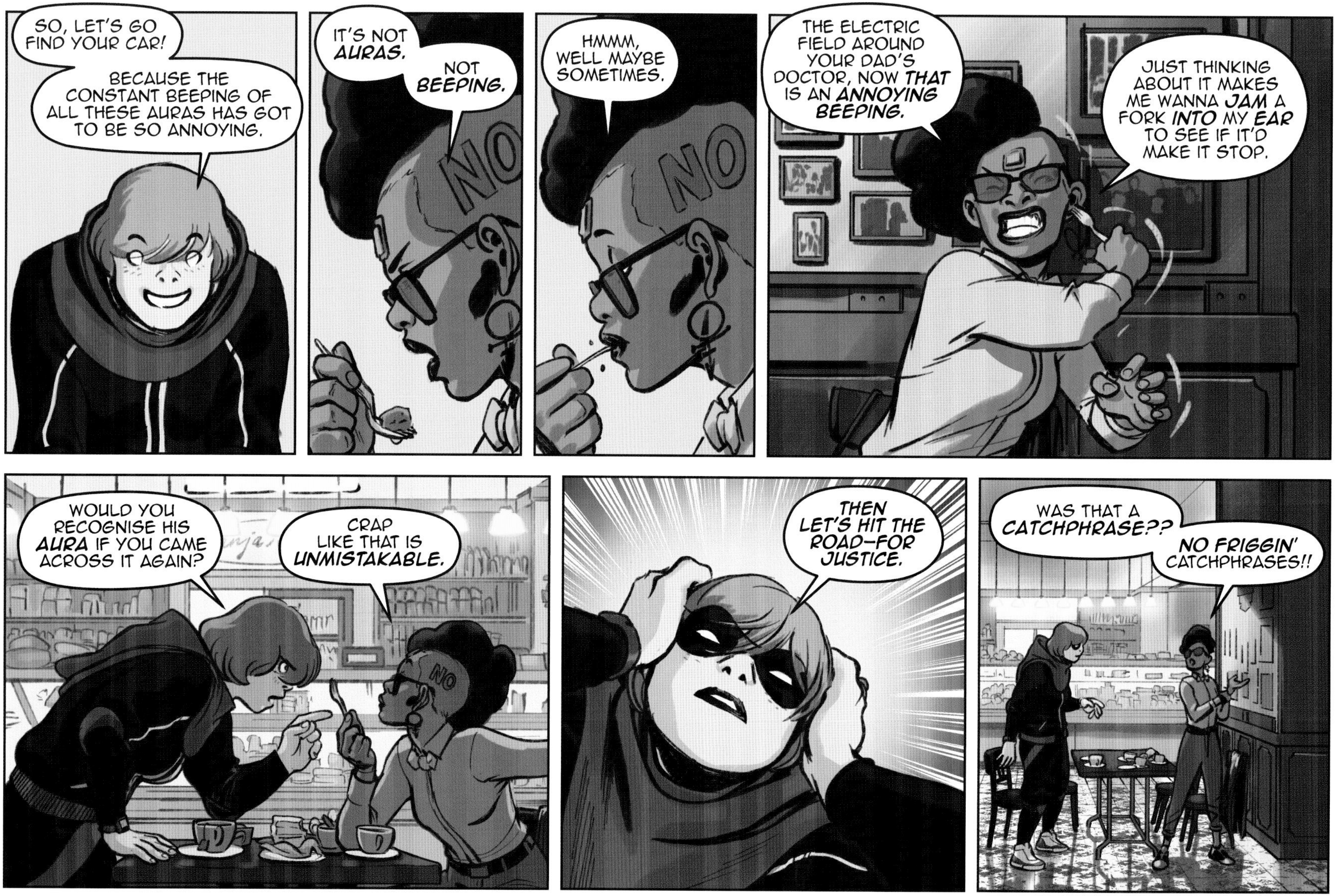
SO, LET'S GO FIND YOUR CAR!
BECAUSE THE CONSTANT BEEPING OF ALL THESE AURAS HAS GOT TO BE SO ANNOYING.
IT'S NOT AURAS.
NOT BEEPING.
NO
HMMM, WELL MAYBE SOMETIMES.
NO
THE ELECTRIC FIELD AROUND YOUR DAD'S DOCTOR, NOW THAT IS AN ANNOYING BEEPING.
JUST THINKING ABOUT IT MAKES ME WANNA JAM A FORK INTO MY EAR TO SEE IF IT'D MAKE IT STOP.
WOULD YOU RECOGNISE HIS AURA IF YOU CAME ACROSS IT AGAIN?
CRAP LIKE THAT IS UNMISTAKABLE.
NO
THEN LET'S HIT THE ROAD—FOR JUSTICE.
WAS THAT A CATCHPHRASE??
NO FRIGGIN' CATCHPHRASES!!

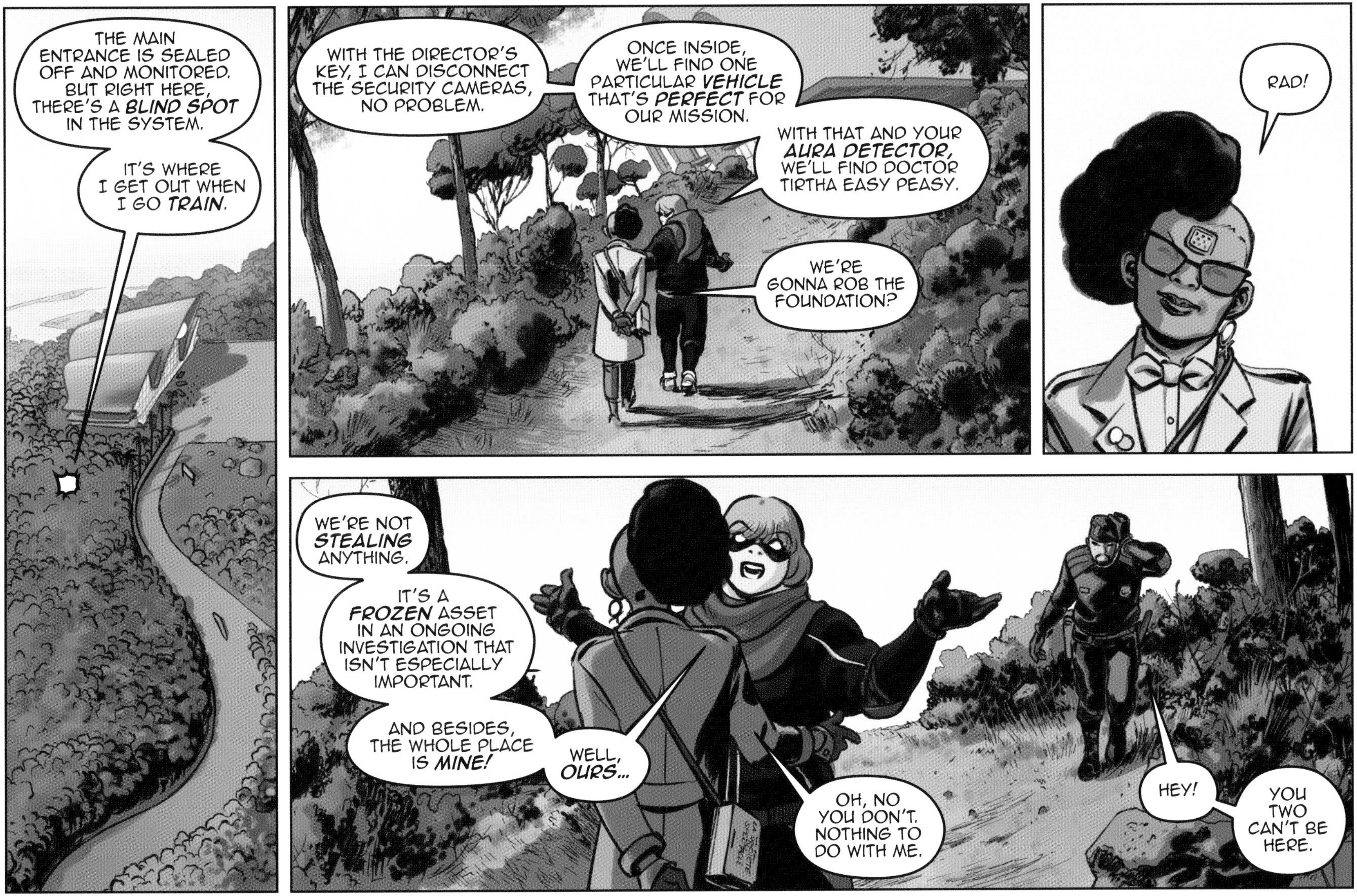

THE MAIN ENTRANCE IS SEALED OFF AND MONITORED. BUT RIGHT HERE, THERE'S A **BLIND SPOT** IN THE SYSTEM.
IT'S WHERE I GET OUT WHEN I GO **TRAIN**.
WITH THE DIRECTOR'S KEY, I CAN DISCONNECT THE SECURITY CAMERAS, NO PROBLEM.
ONCE INSIDE, WE'LL FIND ONE PARTICULAR **VEHICLE** THAT'S **PERFECT** FOR OUR MISSION.
WITH THAT AND YOUR **AURA DETECTOR,** WE'LL FIND DOCTOR TIRTHA EASY PEASY.
WE'RE GONNA ROB THE FOUNDATION?
RAD!
WE'RE NOT **STEALING** ANYTHING.
IT'S A **FROZEN** ASSET IN AN ONGOING INVESTIGATION THAT ISN'T ESPECIALLY IMPORTANT.
AND BESIDES, THE WHOLE PLACE IS **MINE!**
WELL, **OURS...**
OH, NO YOU DON'T. NOTHING TO DO WITH ME.
HEY!
YOU TWO CAN'T BE HERE.

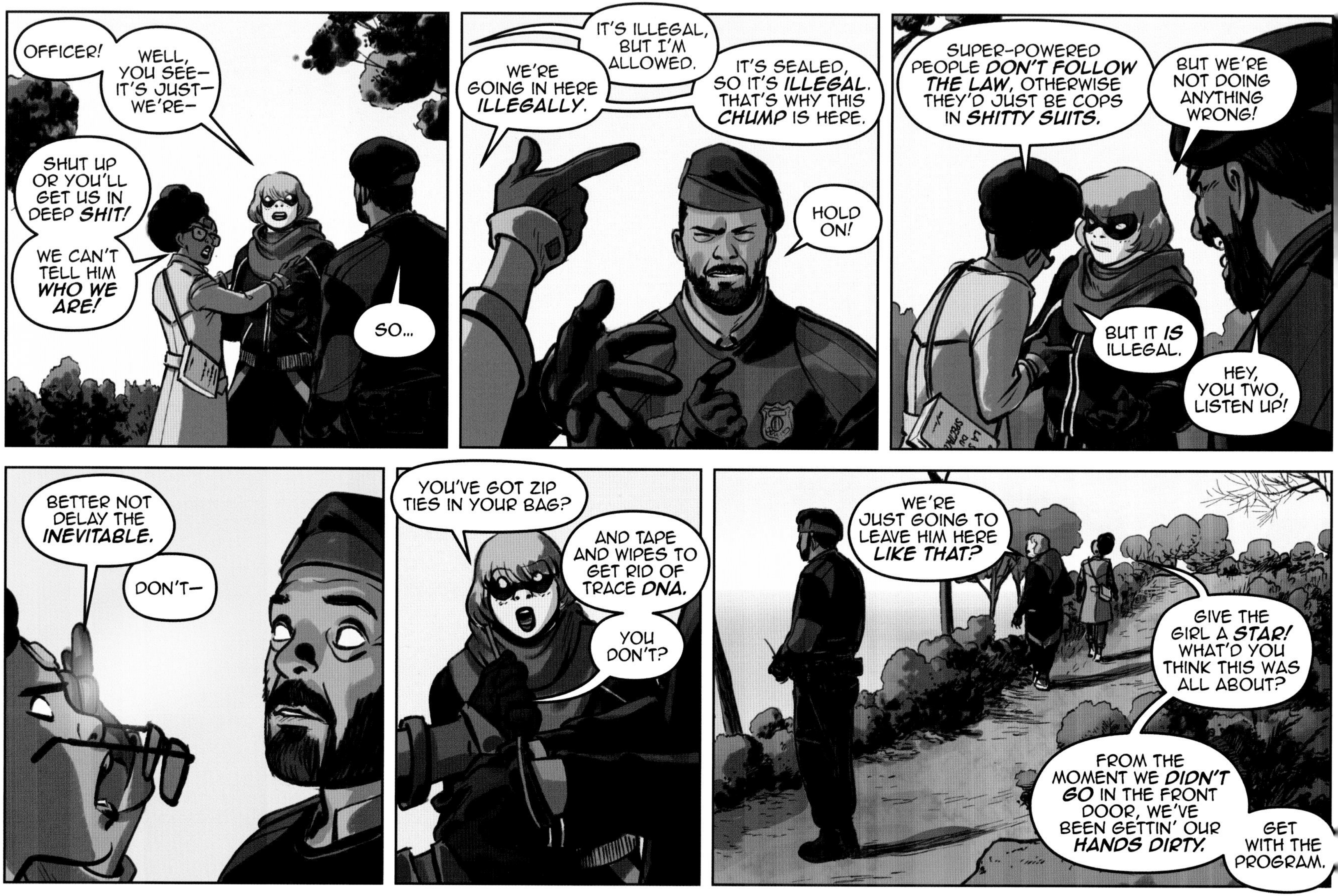

OFFICER!
WELL, YOU SEE— IT'S JUST— WE'RE—
SHUT UP OR YOU'LL GET US IN DEEP SHIT!
WE CAN'T TELL HIM WHO WE ARE!
SO...
WE'RE GOING IN HERE ILLEGALLY.
IT'S ILLEGAL, BUT I'M ALLOWED.
IT'S SEALED, SO IT'S ILLEGAL. THAT'S WHY THIS CHUMP IS HERE.
HOLD ON!
SUPER-POWERED PEOPLE DON'T FOLLOW THE LAW, OTHERWISE THEY'D JUST BE COPS IN SHITTY SUITS.
BUT WE'RE NOT DOING ANYTHING WRONG!
BUT IT IS ILLEGAL.
HEY, YOU TWO, LISTEN UP!
BETTER NOT DELAY THE INEVITABLE.
DON'T—
YOU'VE GOT ZIP TIES IN YOUR BAG?
AND TAPE AND WIPES TO GET RID OF TRACE DNA.
YOU DON'T?
WE'RE JUST GOING TO LEAVE HIM HERE LIKE THAT?
GIVE THE GIRL A STAR! WHAT'D YOU THINK THIS WAS ALL ABOUT?
FROM THE MOMENT WE DIDN'T GO IN THE FRONT DOOR, WE'VE BEEN GETTIN' OUR HANDS DIRTY.
GET WITH THE PROGRAM.

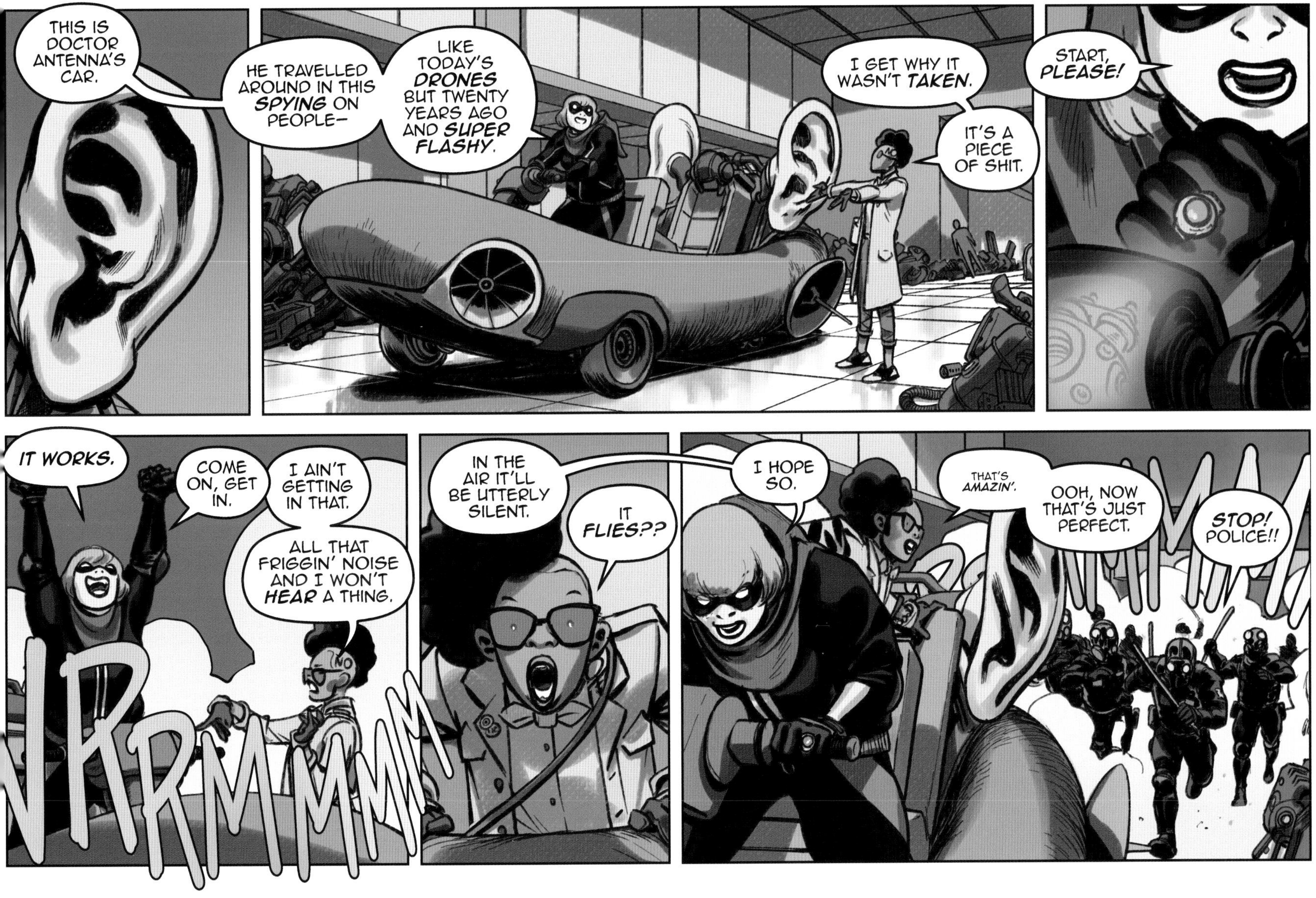
THIS IS DOCTOR ANTENNA'S CAR.
HE TRAVELLED AROUND IN THIS *SPYING* ON PEOPLE–
LIKE TODAY'S ***DRONES*** BUT TWENTY YEARS AGO AND ***SUPER FLASHY***.
I GET WHY IT WASN'T ***TAKEN***.
IT'S A PIECE OF SHIT.
START, ***PLEASE!***
IT WORKS.
COME ON, GET IN.
I AIN'T GETTING IN THAT.
ALL THAT FRIGGIN' NOISE AND I WON'T ***HEAR*** A THING.
NO
VRRMMMMM
IN THE AIR IT'LL BE UTTERLY SILENT.
IT ***FLIES??***
I HOPE SO.
THAT'S *AMAZIN'*.
OOH, NOW THAT'S JUST PERFECT.
STOP! POLICE!!

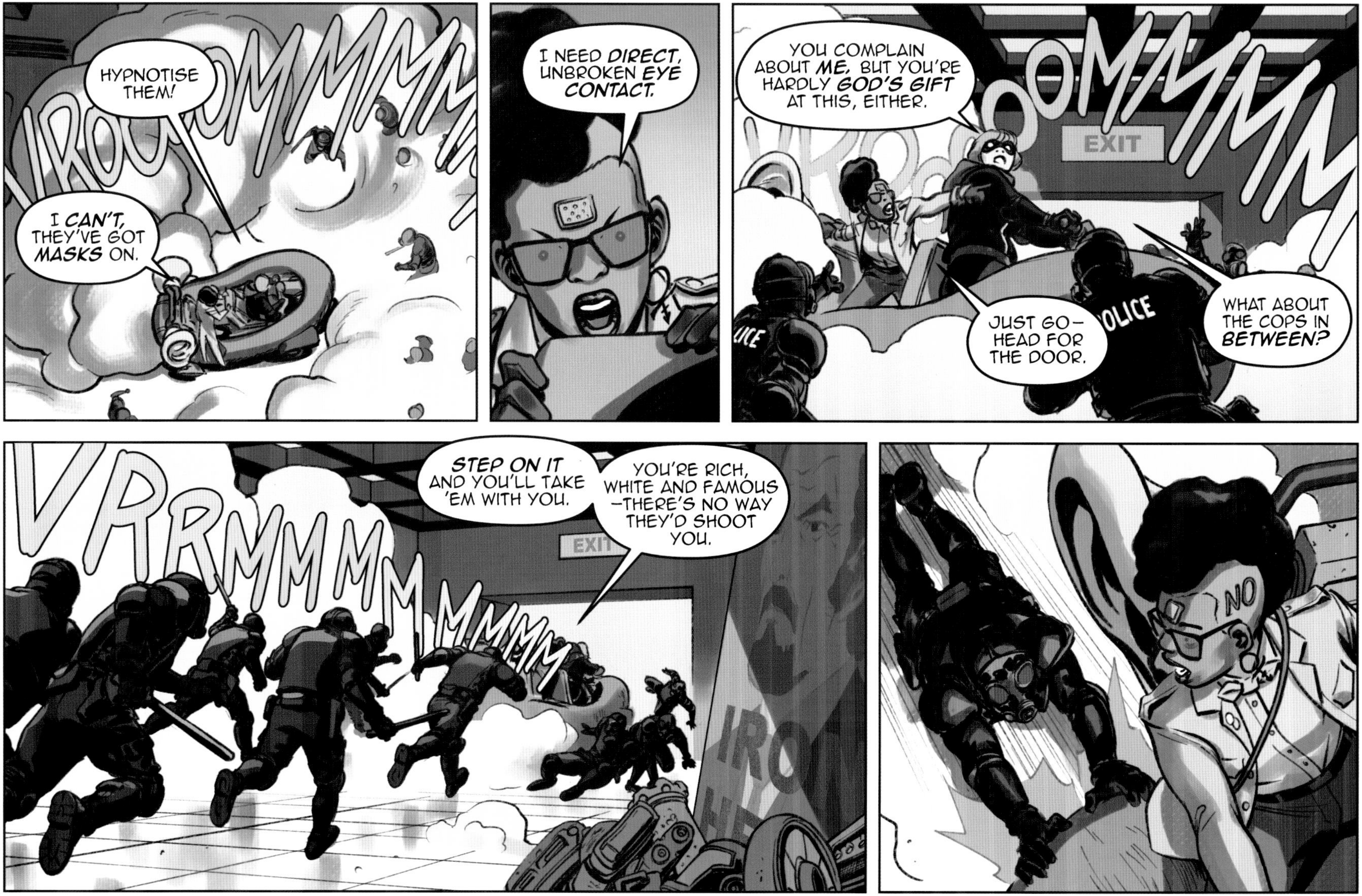
HYPNOTISE THEM!
I CAN'T, THEY'VE GOT MASKS ON.
I NEED DIRECT, UNBROKEN EYE CONTACT.
YOU COMPLAIN ABOUT ME, BUT YOU'RE HARDLY GOD'S GIFT AT THIS, EITHER.
EXIT
JUST GO—HEAD FOR THE DOOR.
POLICE
WHAT ABOUT THE COPS IN BETWEEN?
STEP ON IT AND YOU'LL TAKE 'EM WITH YOU.
YOU'RE RICH, WHITE AND FAMOUS —THERE'S NO WAY THEY'D SHOOT YOU.
EXIT
NO

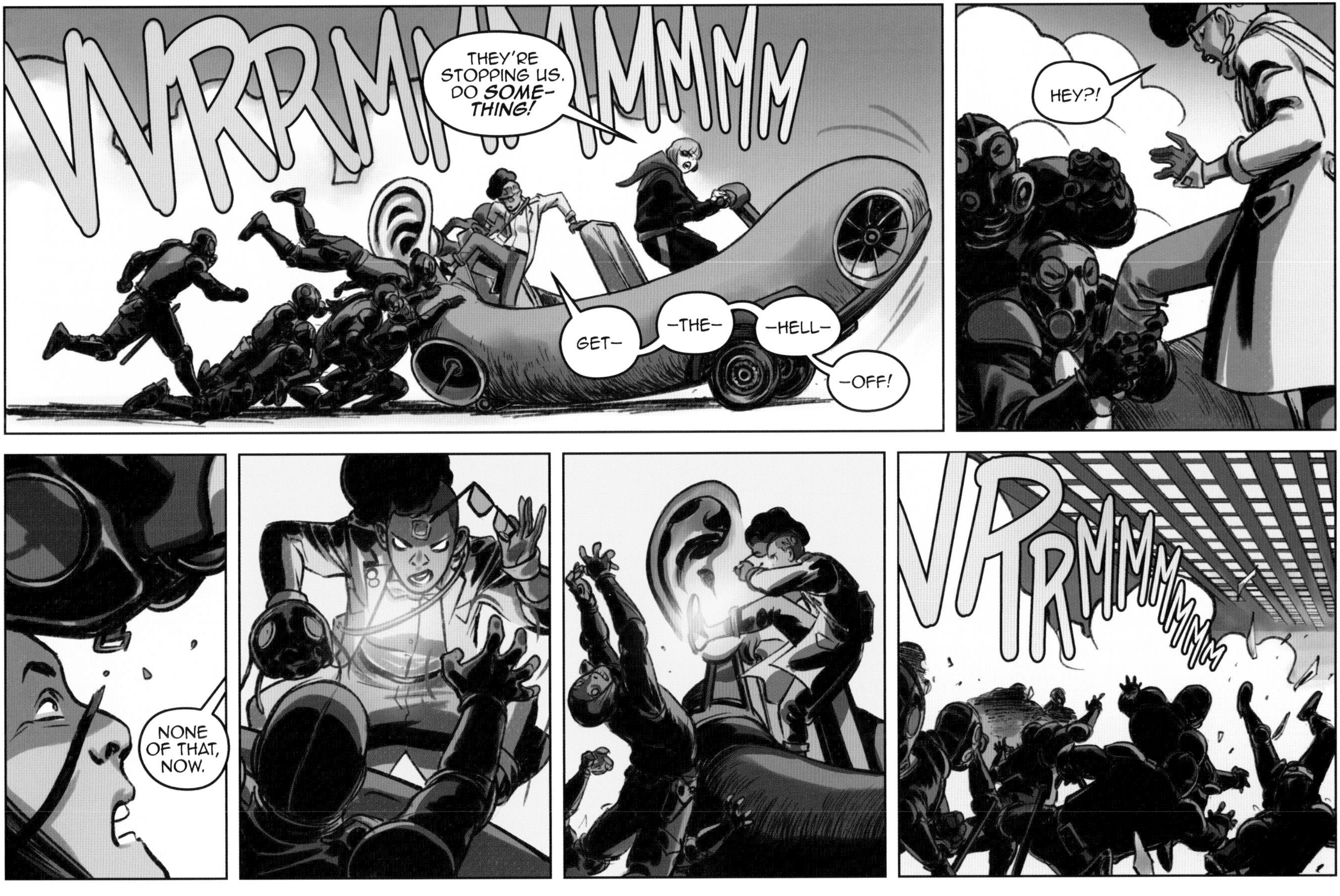

WRRMMMMMMMM
THEY'RE STOPPING US. DO *SOME-THING!*
GET—
—THE—
—HELL—
—OFF!
HEY?!
NONE OF THAT, NOW.
VRRMMMMMMMM

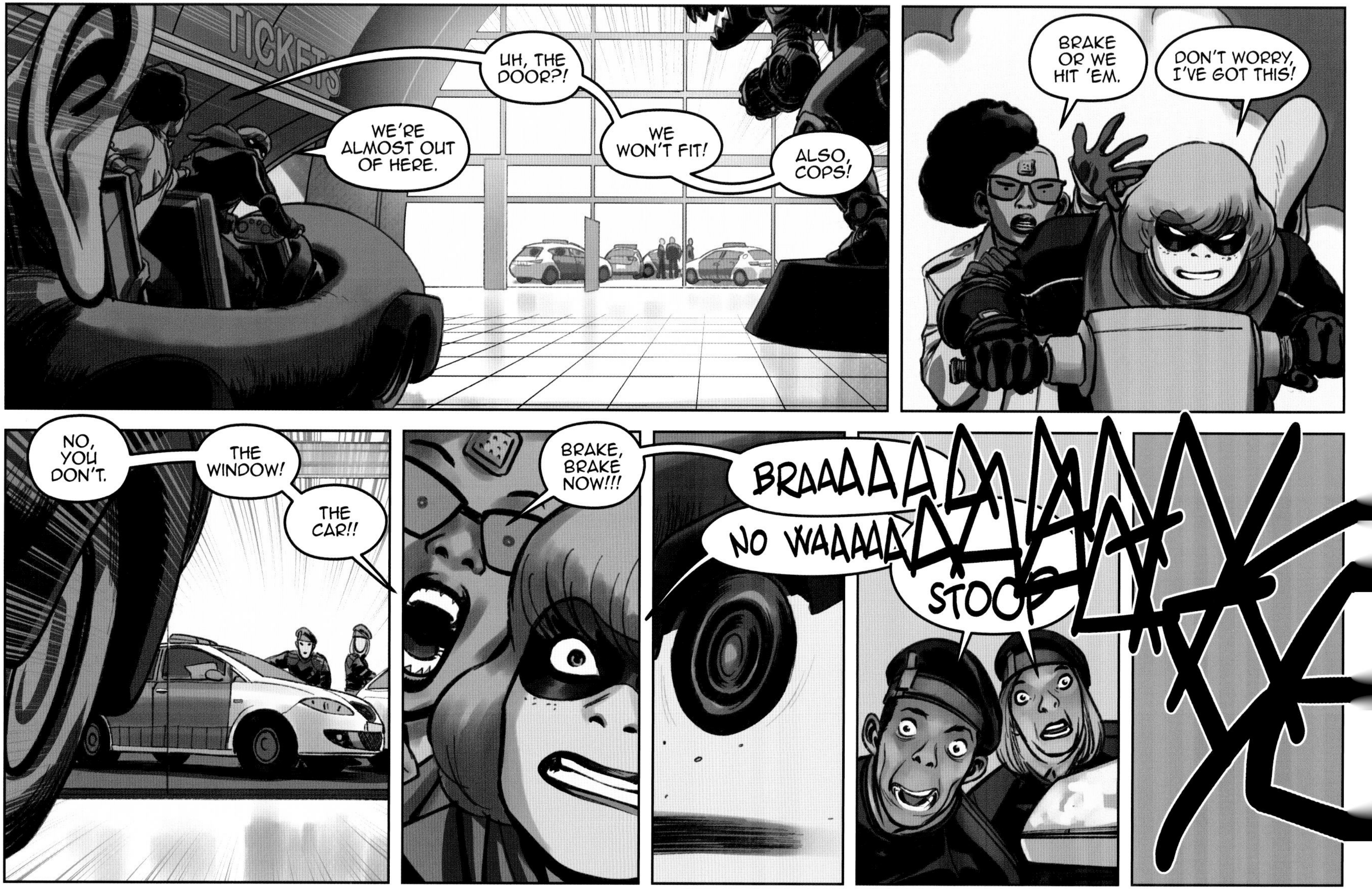
WE'RE ALMOST OUT OF HERE.
UH, THE DOOR?!
WE WON'T FIT!
ALSO, COPS!
BRAKE OR WE HIT 'EM.
DON'T WORRY, I'VE GOT THIS!
NO, YOU DON'T.
THE WINDOW!
THE CAR!!
BRAKE, BRAKE NOW!!!
BRAAAAAAAAAAAAAAAAAK
NO WAAAAAAAAAAAAAA
STOOP

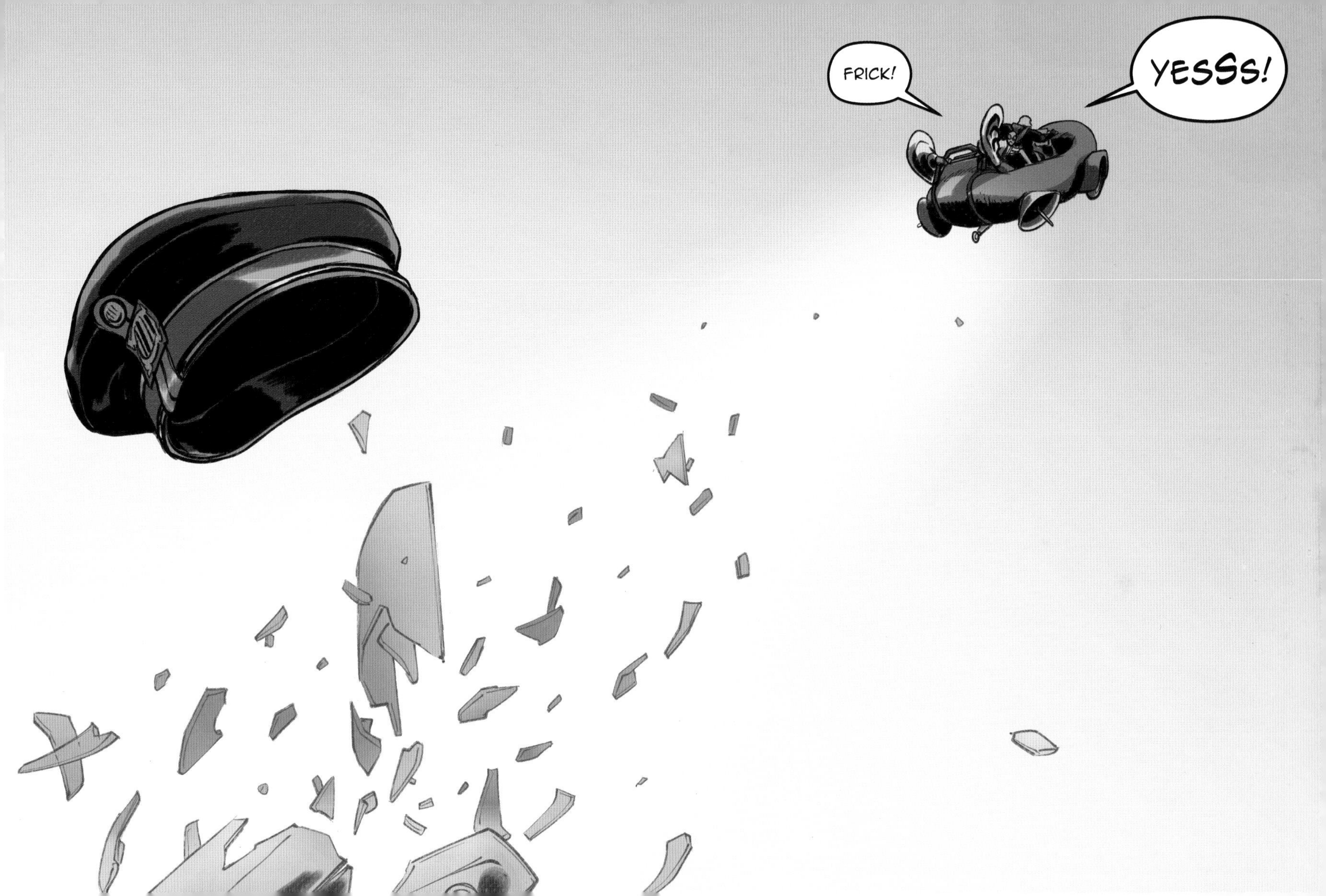
FRICK!
YESSS!

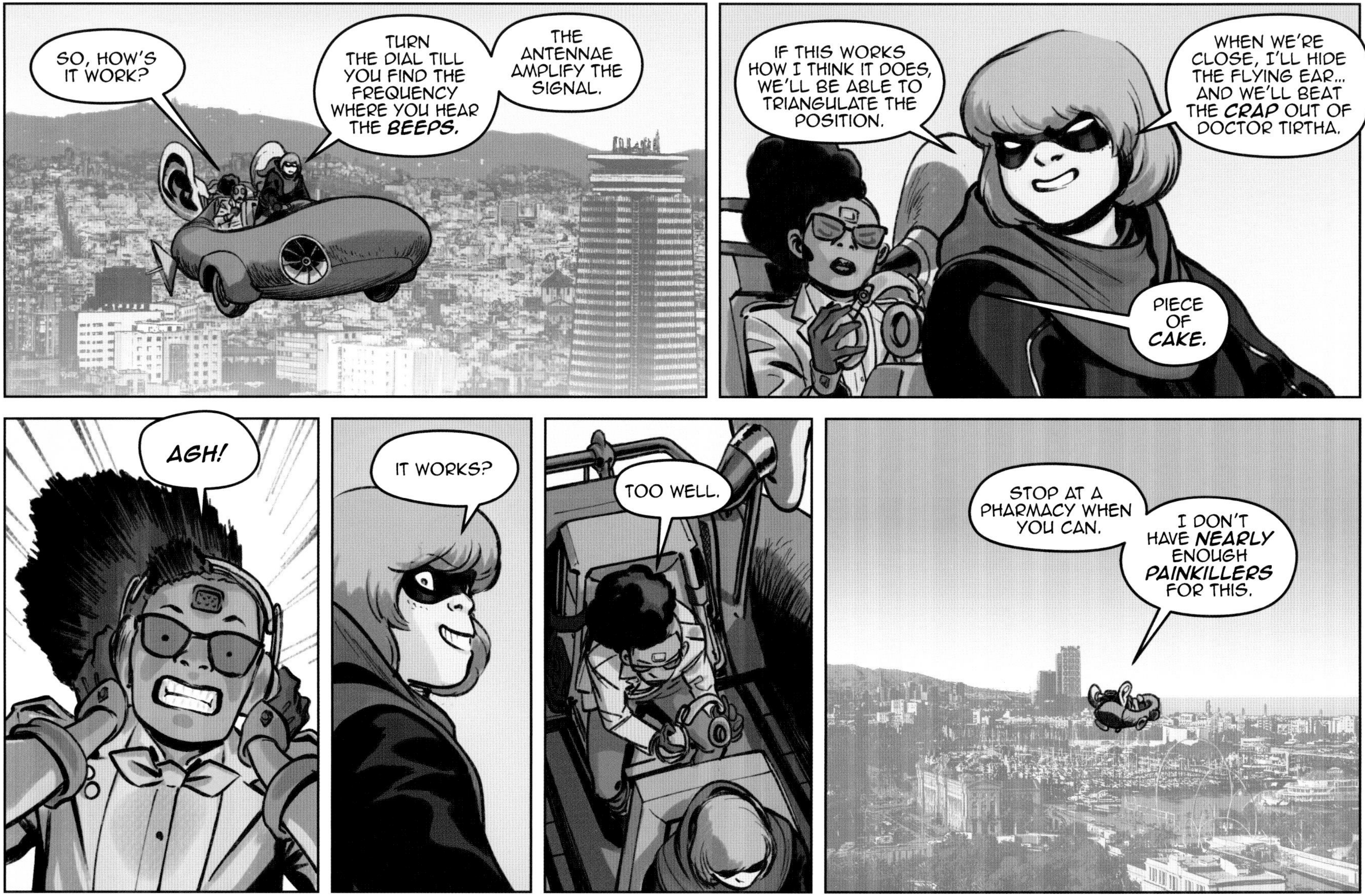
SO, HOW'S IT WORK?
TURN THE DIAL TILL YOU FIND THE FREQUENCY WHERE YOU HEAR THE *BEEPS.*
THE ANTENNAE AMPLIFY THE SIGNAL.
IF THIS WORKS HOW I THINK IT DOES, WE'LL BE ABLE TO TRIANGULATE THE POSITION.
WHEN WE'RE CLOSE, I'LL HIDE THE FLYING EAR... AND WE'LL BEAT THE *CRAP* OUT OF DOCTOR TIRTHA.
PIECE OF *CAKE.*
AGH!
IT WORKS?
TOO WELL.
STOP AT A PHARMACY WHEN YOU CAN.
I DON'T HAVE *NEARLY* ENOUGH *PAINKILLERS* FOR THIS.

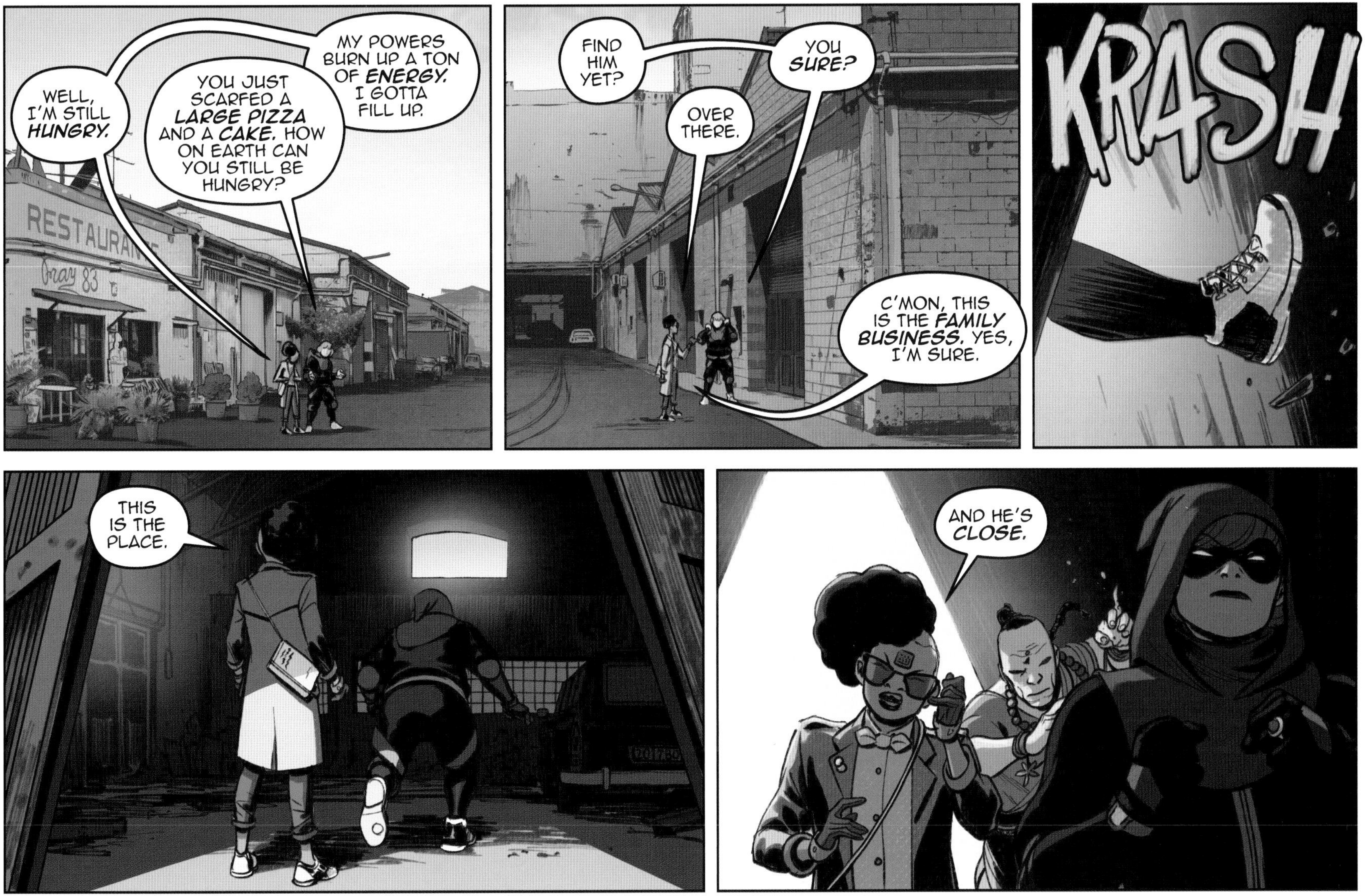
WELL, I'M STILL HUNGRY.
MY POWERS BURN UP A TON OF ENERGY. I GOTTA FILL UP.
YOU JUST SCARFED A LARGE PIZZA AND A CAKE. HOW ON EARTH CAN YOU STILL BE HUNGRY?
RESTAURANT
FIND HIM YET?
YOU SURE?
OVER THERE.
C'MON, THIS IS THE FAMILY BUSINESS. YES, I'M SURE.
KRASH
THIS IS THE PLACE.
AND HE'S CLOSE.

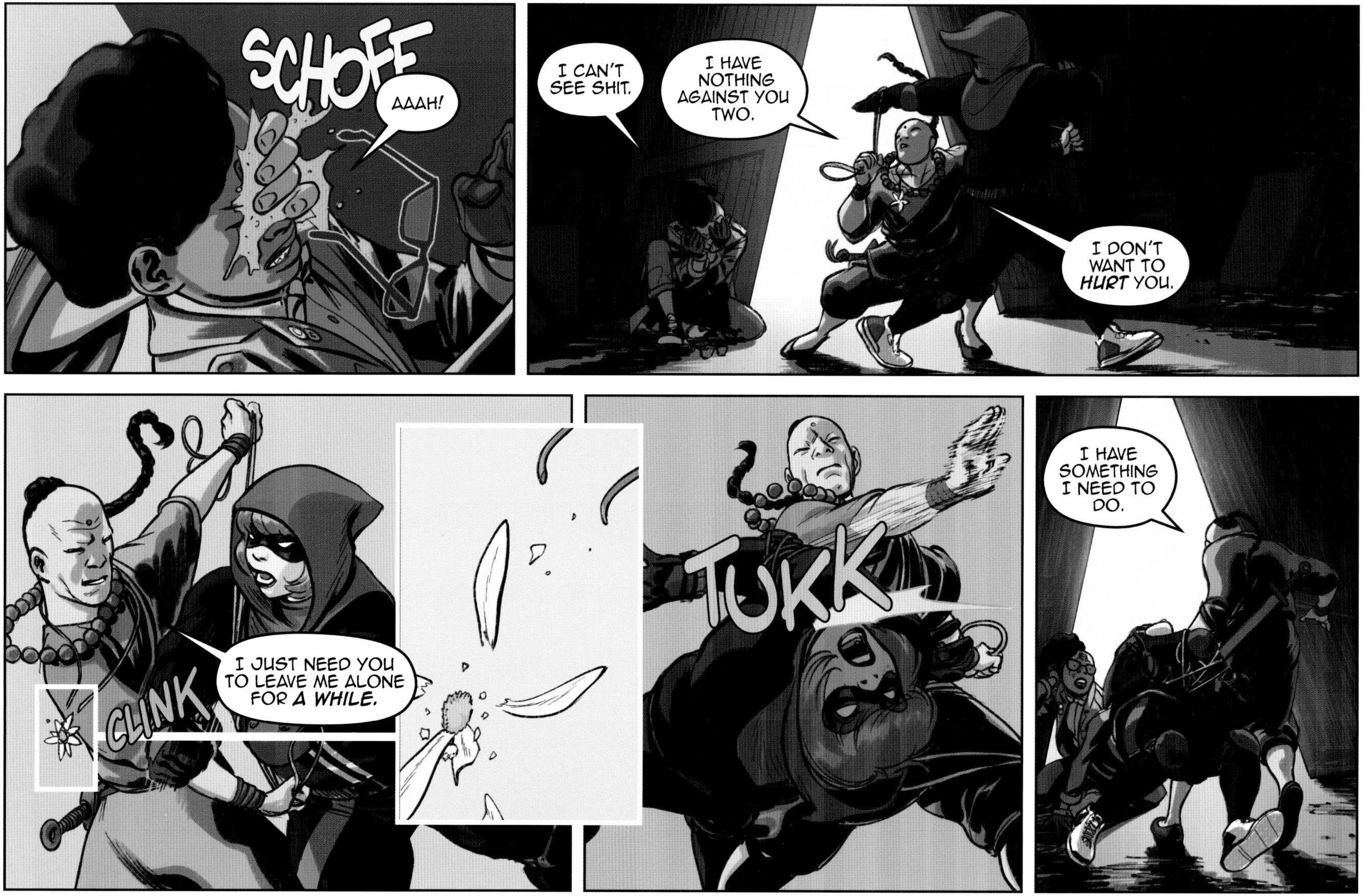
SCHOFF
AAAH!
I CAN'T SEE SHIT.
I HAVE NOTHING AGAINST YOU TWO.
I DON'T WANT TO HURT YOU.
I JUST NEED YOU TO LEAVE ME ALONE FOR A WHILE.
CLINK
TUKK
I HAVE SOMETHING I NEED TO DO.

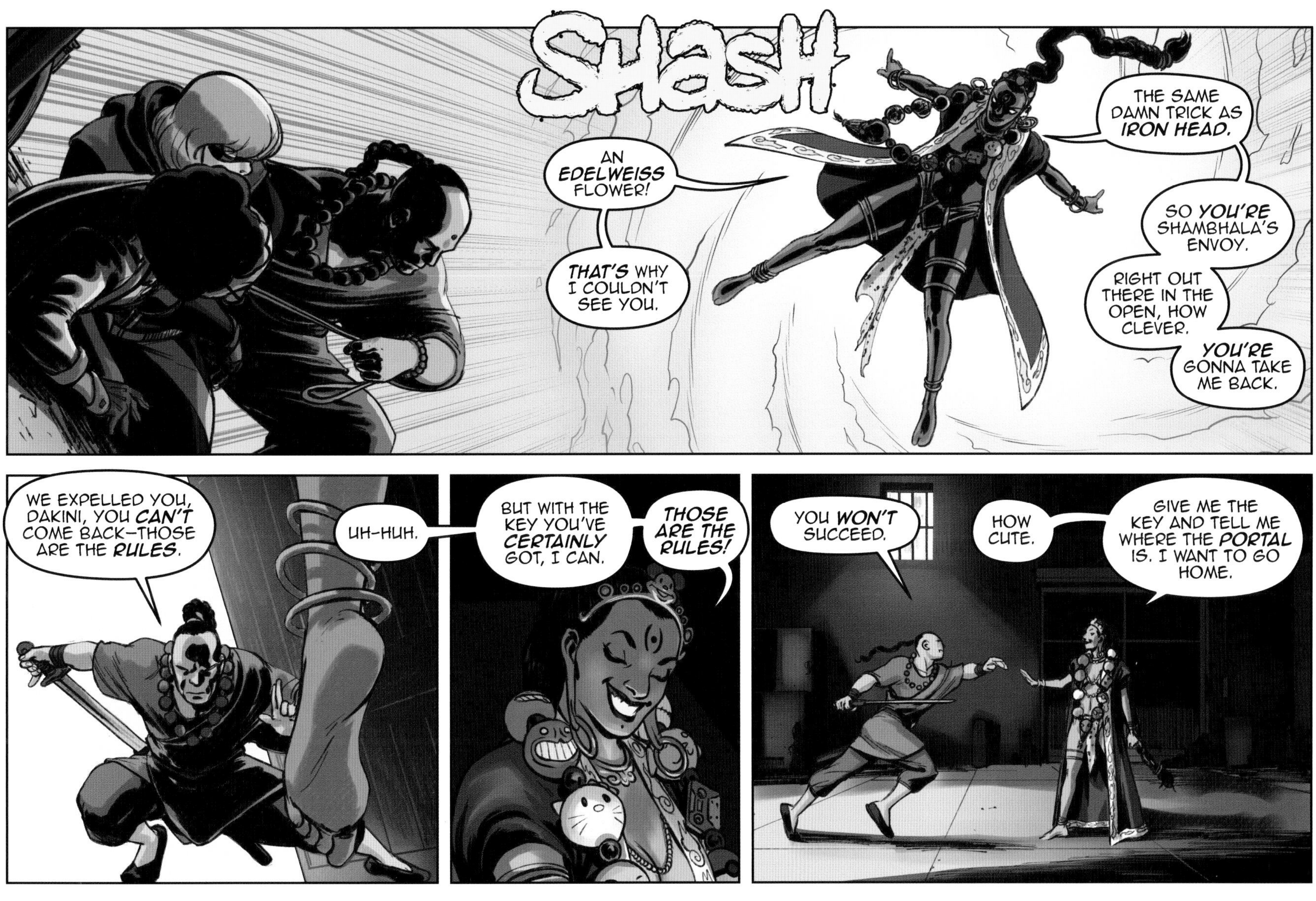
SHASH
AN EDELWEISS FLOWER!
THAT'S WHY I COULDN'T SEE YOU.
THE SAME DAMN TRICK AS IRON HEAD.
SO YOU'RE SHAMBHALA'S ENVOY.
RIGHT OUT THERE IN THE OPEN, HOW CLEVER.
YOU'RE GONNA TAKE ME BACK.
WE EXPELLED YOU, DAKINI, YOU CAN'T COME BACK—THOSE ARE THE RULES.
UH-HUH.
BUT WITH THE KEY YOU'VE CERTAINLY GOT, I CAN.
THOSE ARE THE RULES!
YOU WON'T SUCCEED.
HOW CUTE.
GIVE ME THE KEY AND TELL ME WHERE THE PORTAL IS. I WANT TO GO HOME.

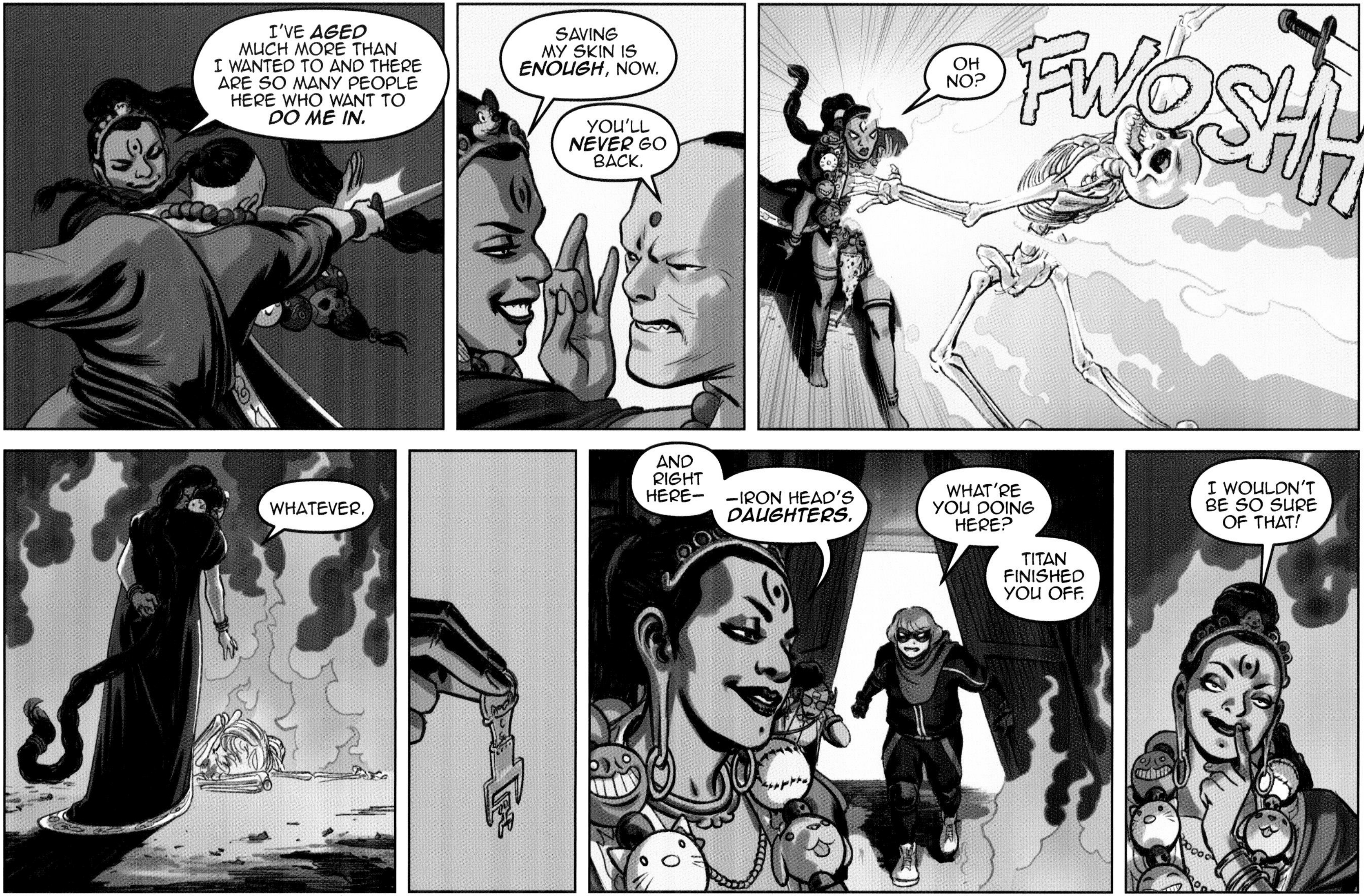
I'VE AGED MUCH MORE THAN I WANTED TO AND THERE ARE SO MANY PEOPLE HERE WHO WANT TO DO ME IN.
SAVING MY SKIN IS ENOUGH, NOW.
YOU'LL NEVER GO BACK.
OH NO?
FWOSHH
WHATEVER.
AND RIGHT HERE—
—IRON HEAD'S DAUGHTERS.
WHAT'RE YOU DOING HERE?
TITAN FINISHED YOU OFF.
I WOULDN'T BE SO SURE OF THAT!

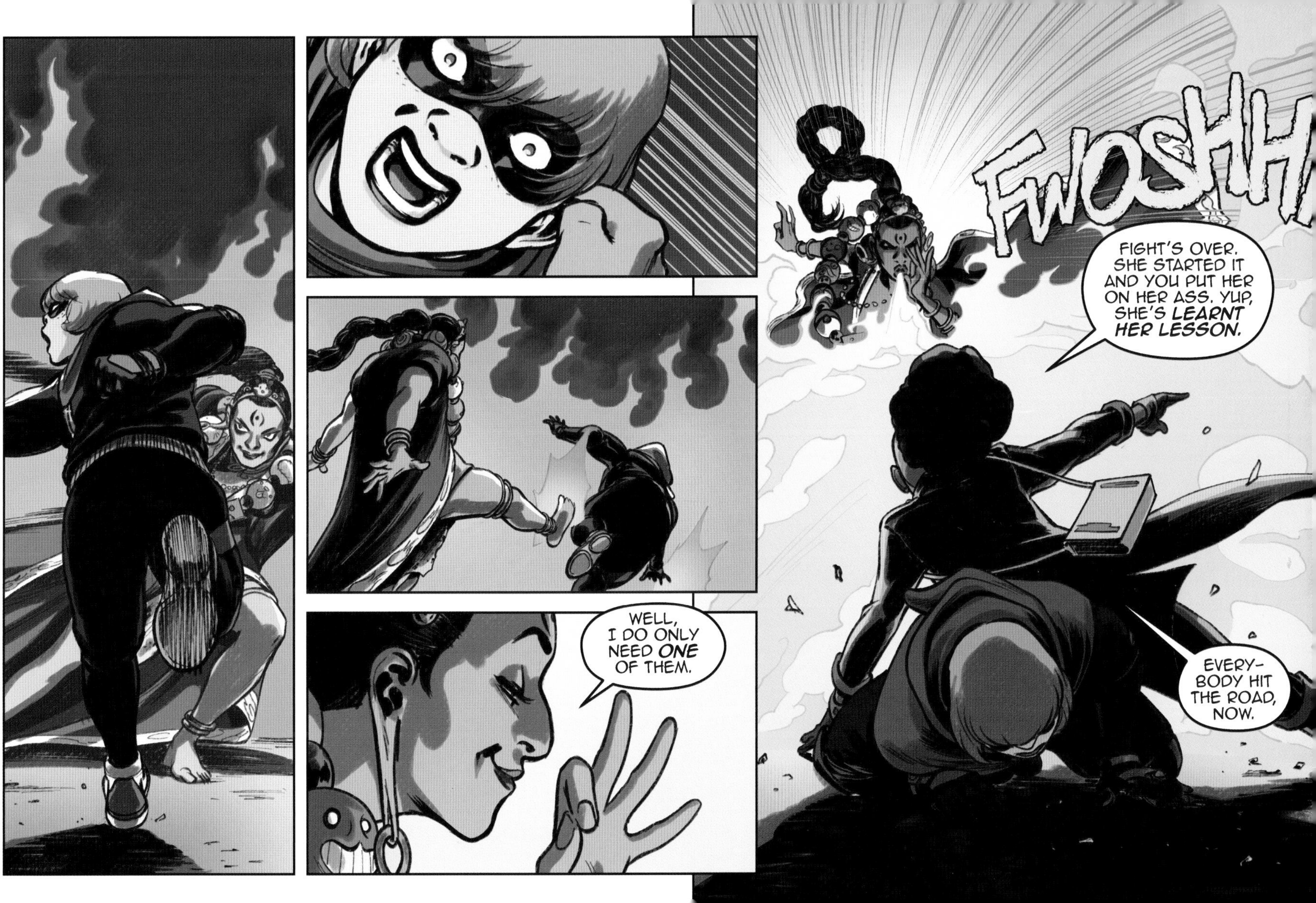
WELL, I DO ONLY NEED **ONE** OF THEM.
FWOSHH
FIGHT'S OVER. SHE STARTED IT AND YOU PUT HER ON HER ASS. YUP, SHE'S ***LEARNT HER LESSON.***
EVERY-BODY HIT THE ROAD, NOW.

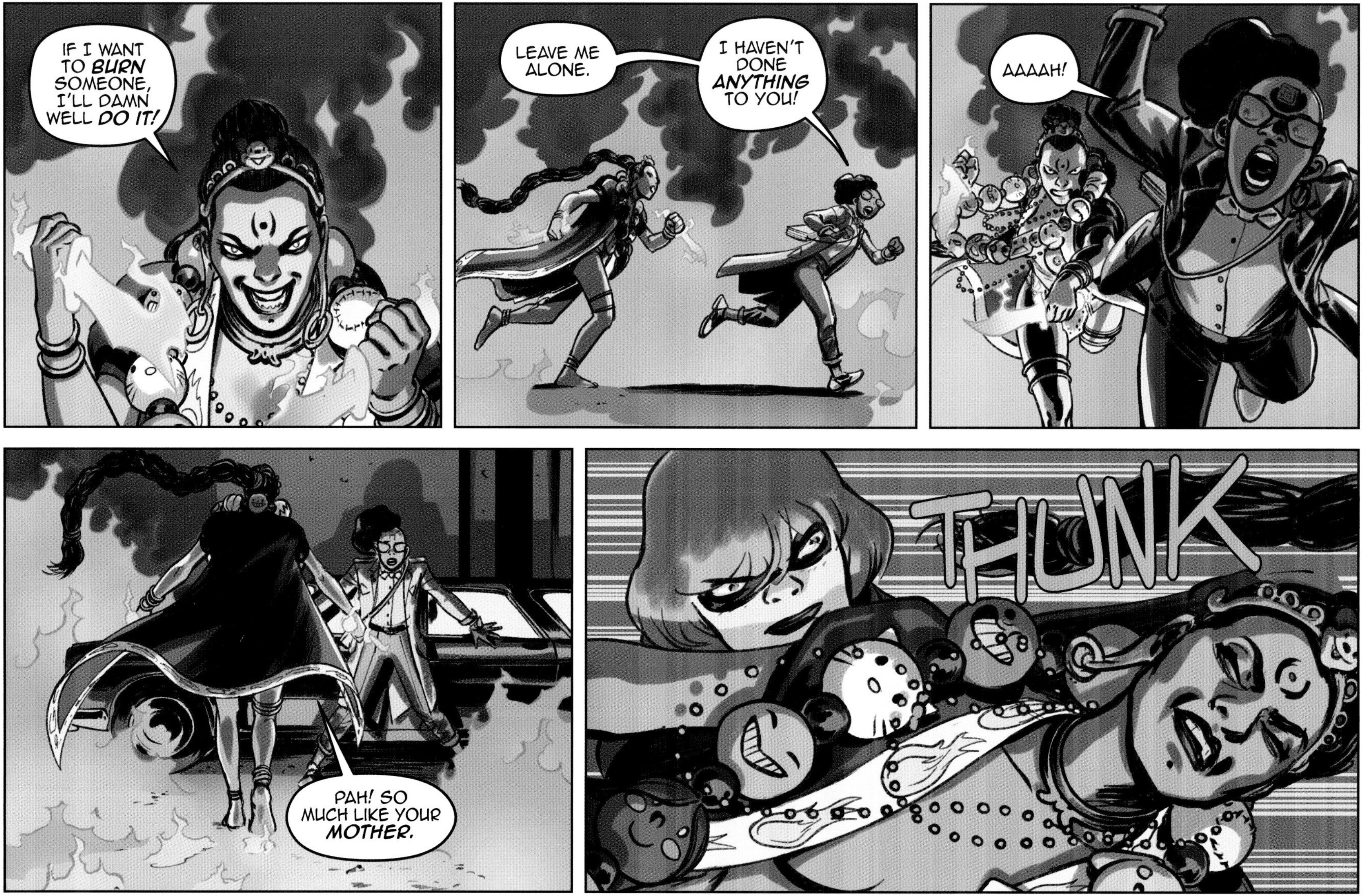
IF I WANT TO **BURN** SOMEONE, I'LL DAMN WELL ***DO IT!***
LEAVE ME ALONE.
I HAVEN'T DONE ***ANYTHING*** TO YOU!
AAAAH!
PAH! SO MUCH LIKE YOUR ***MOTHER.***
THUNK

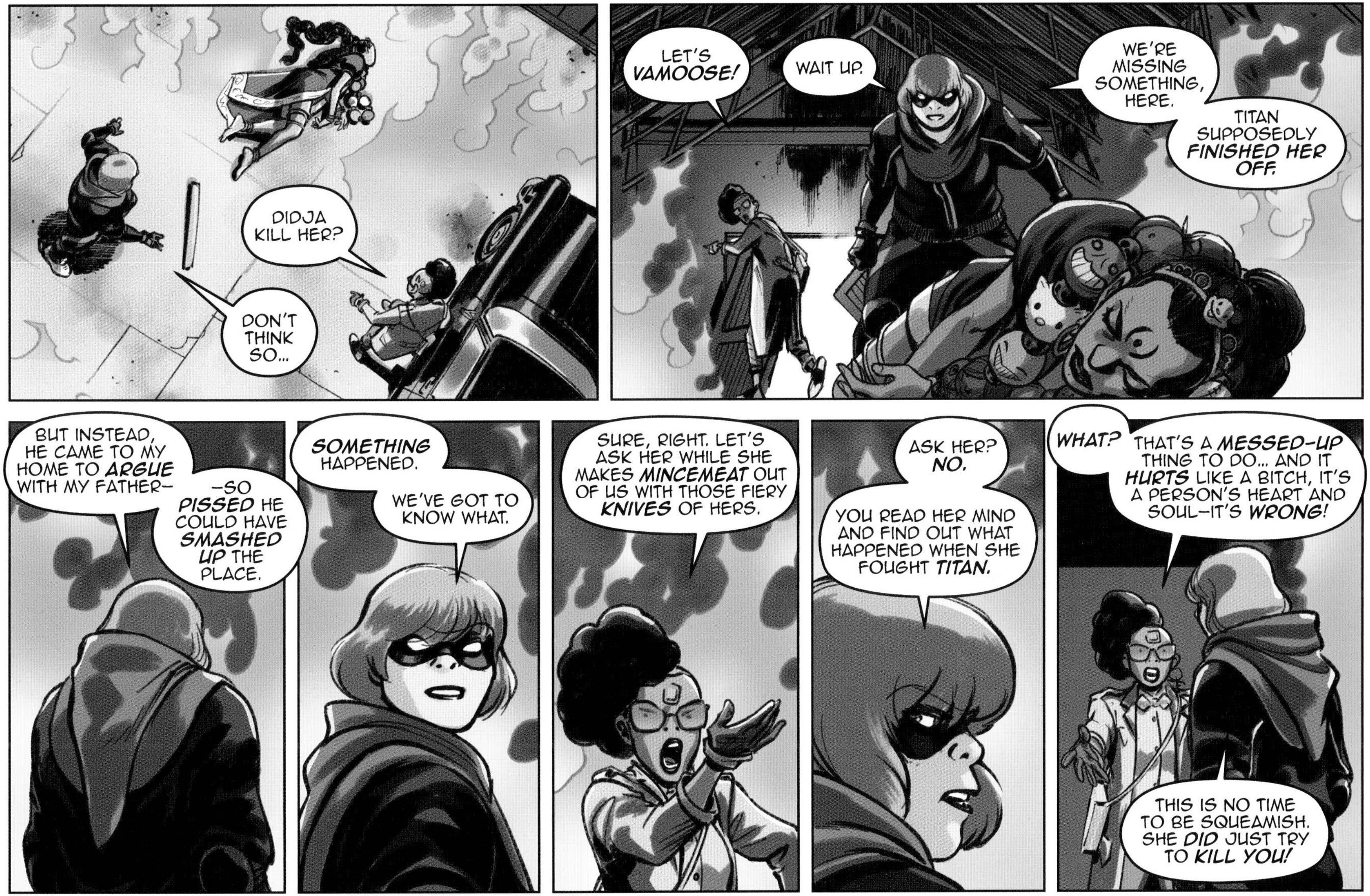
DIDJA KILL HER?
DON'T THINK SO...
LET'S VAMOOSE!
WAIT UP.
WE'RE MISSING SOMETHING, HERE.
TITAN SUPPOSEDLY FINISHED HER OFF.
BUT INSTEAD, HE CAME TO MY HOME TO ARGUE WITH MY FATHER—
—SO PISSED HE COULD HAVE SMASHED UP THE PLACE.
SOMETHING HAPPENED.
WE'VE GOT TO KNOW WHAT.
SURE, RIGHT. LET'S ASK HER WHILE SHE MAKES MINCEMEAT OUT OF US WITH THOSE FIERY KNIVES OF HERS.
ASK HER? NO.
YOU READ HER MIND AND FIND OUT WHAT HAPPENED WHEN SHE FOUGHT TITAN.
WHAT?
THAT'S A MESSED-UP THING TO DO... AND IT HURTS LIKE A BITCH, IT'S A PERSON'S HEART AND SOUL—IT'S WRONG!
THIS IS NO TIME TO BE SQUEAMISH. SHE DID JUST TRY TO KILL YOU!

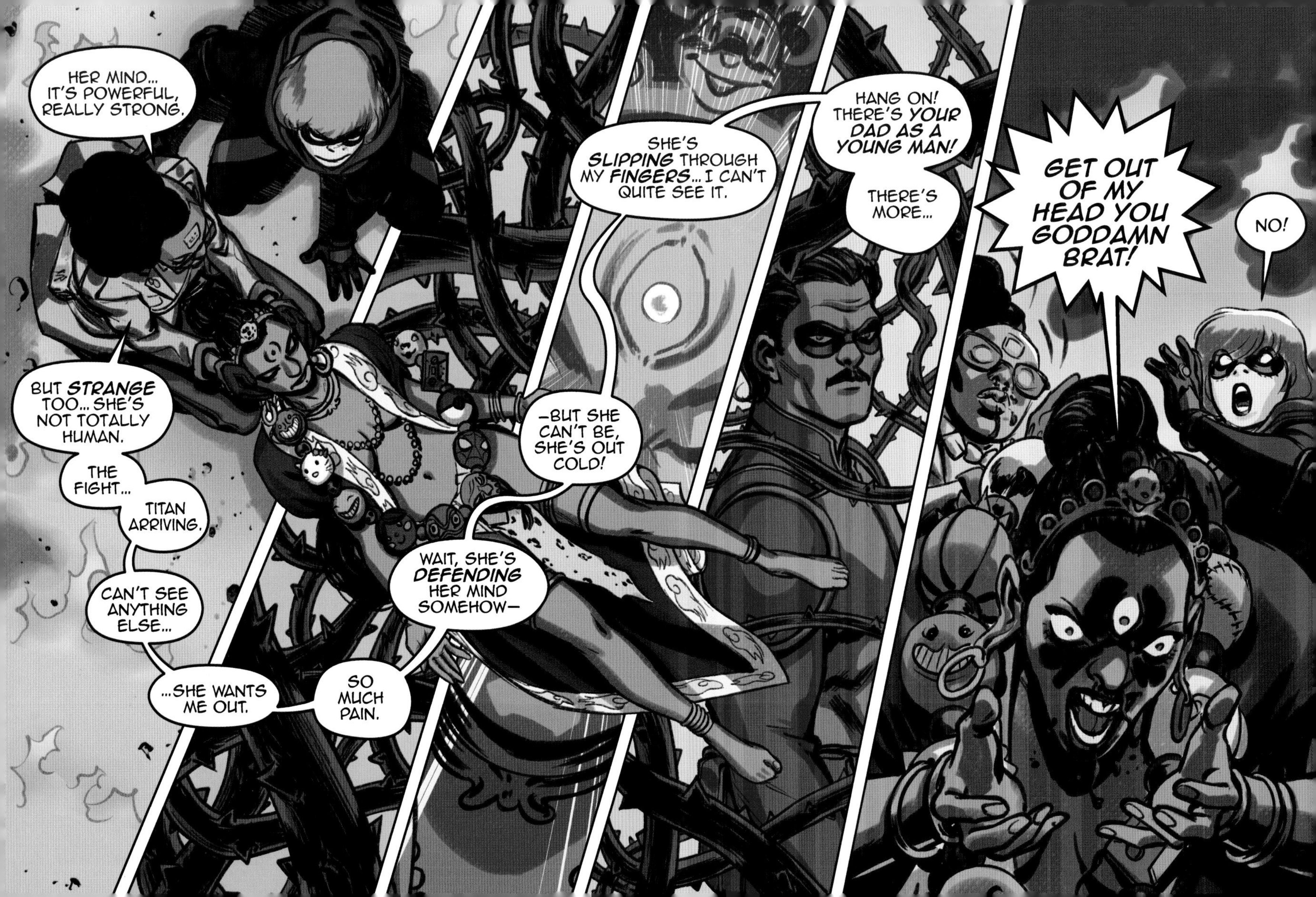
HER MIND... IT'S POWERFUL, REALLY STRONG.
BUT STRANGE TOO... SHE'S NOT TOTALLY HUMAN.
THE FIGHT...
TITAN ARRIVING.
CAN'T SEE ANYTHING ELSE...
...SHE WANTS ME OUT.
SO MUCH PAIN.
WAIT, SHE'S DEFENDING HER MIND SOMEHOW—
—BUT SHE CAN'T BE, SHE'S OUT COLD!
SHE'S SLIPPING THROUGH MY FINGERS... I CAN'T QUITE SEE IT.
HANG ON! THERE'S YOUR DAD AS A YOUNG MAN!
THERE'S MORE...
GET OUT OF MY HEAD YOU GODDAMN BRAT!
NO!

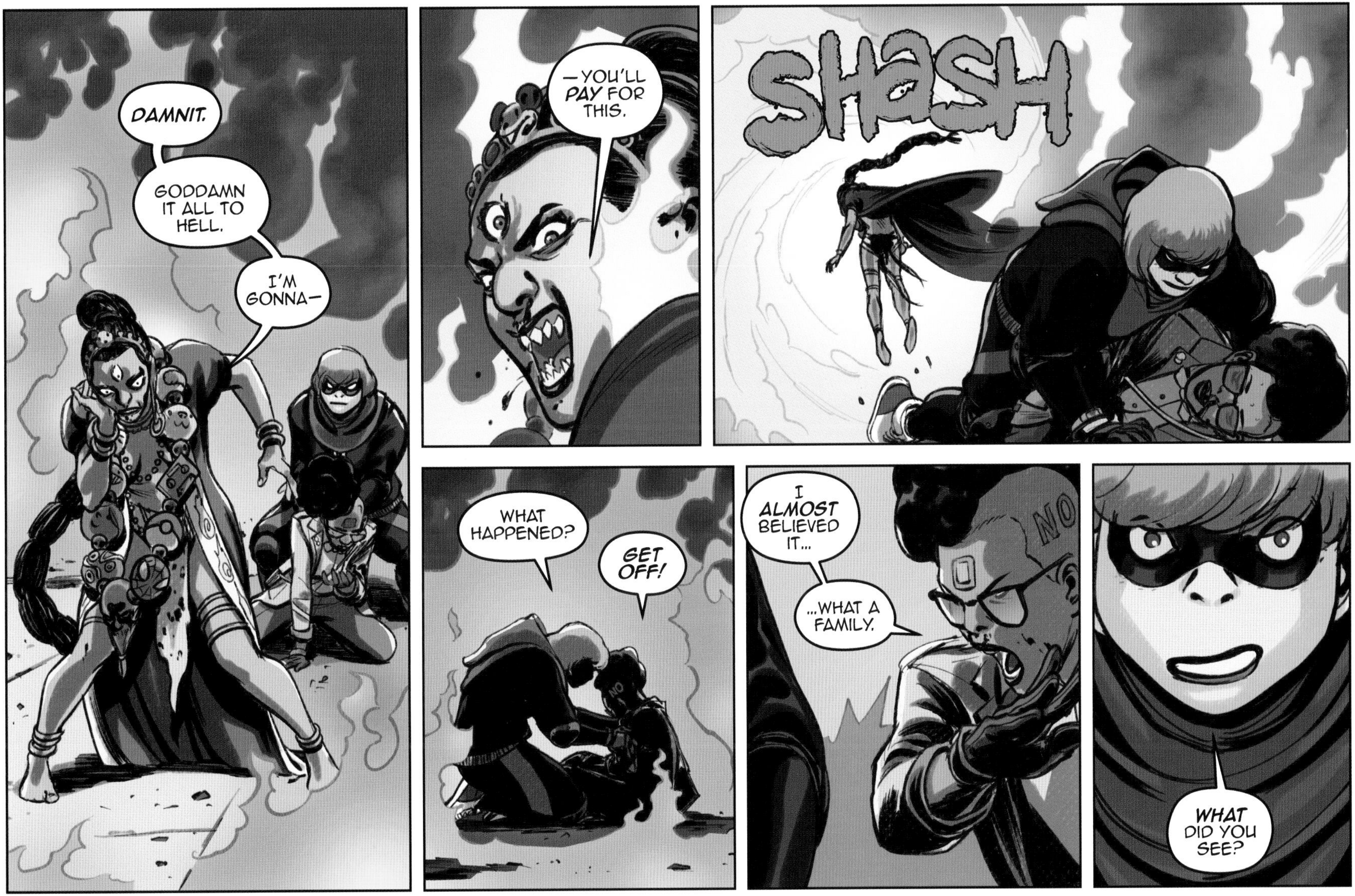
DAMNIT.
GODDAMN IT ALL TO HELL.
I'M GONNA—
—YOU'LL PAY FOR THIS.
SHASH
WHAT HAPPENED?
GET OFF!
I ALMOST BELIEVED IT...
...WHAT A FAMILY.
WHAT DID YOU SEE?

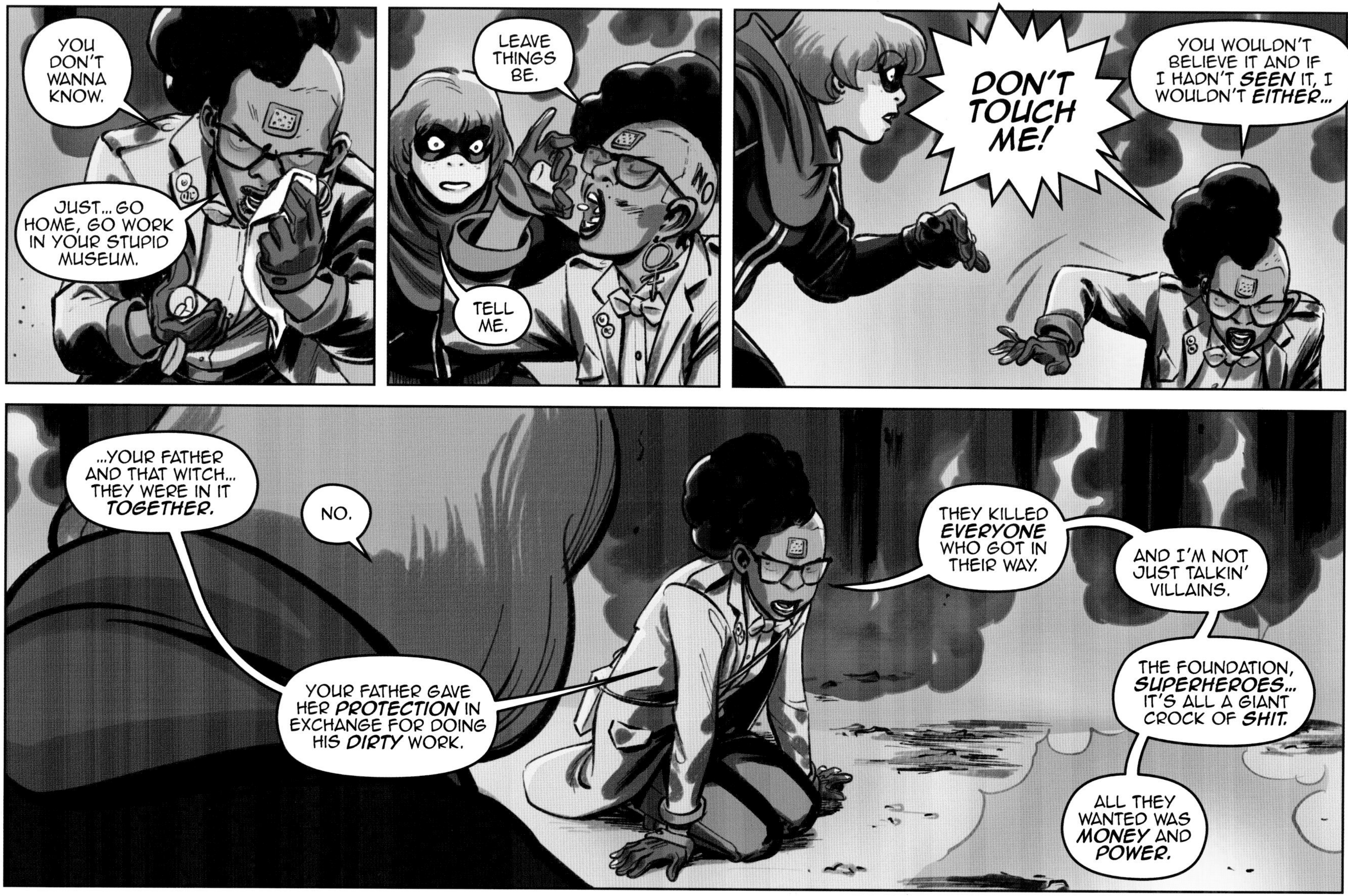

YOU DON'T WANNA KNOW.
JUST... GO HOME, GO WORK IN YOUR STUPID MUSEUM.
LEAVE THINGS BE.
TELL ME.
DON'T TOUCH ME!
YOU WOULDN'T BELIEVE IT AND IF I HADN'T SEEN IT, I WOULDN'T EITHER...
...YOUR FATHER AND THAT WITCH... THEY WERE IN IT TOGETHER.
NO.
YOUR FATHER GAVE HER PROTECTION IN EXCHANGE FOR DOING HIS DIRTY WORK.
THEY KILLED EVERYONE WHO GOT IN THEIR WAY.
AND I'M NOT JUST TALKIN' VILLAINS.
THE FOUNDATION, SUPERHEROES... IT'S ALL A GIANT CROCK OF SHIT.
ALL THEY WANTED WAS MONEY AND POWER.

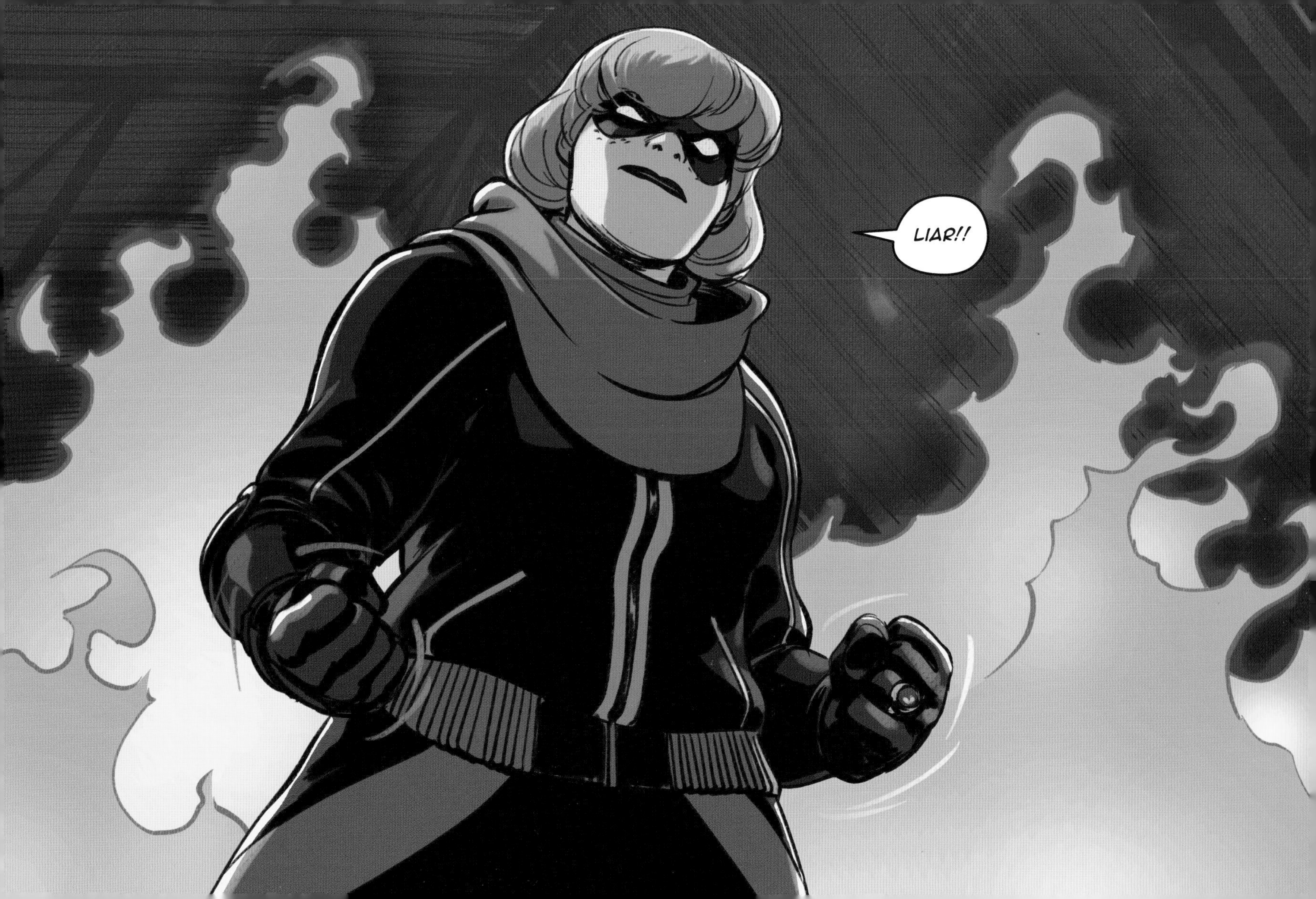
LIAR!!

Chapter Four

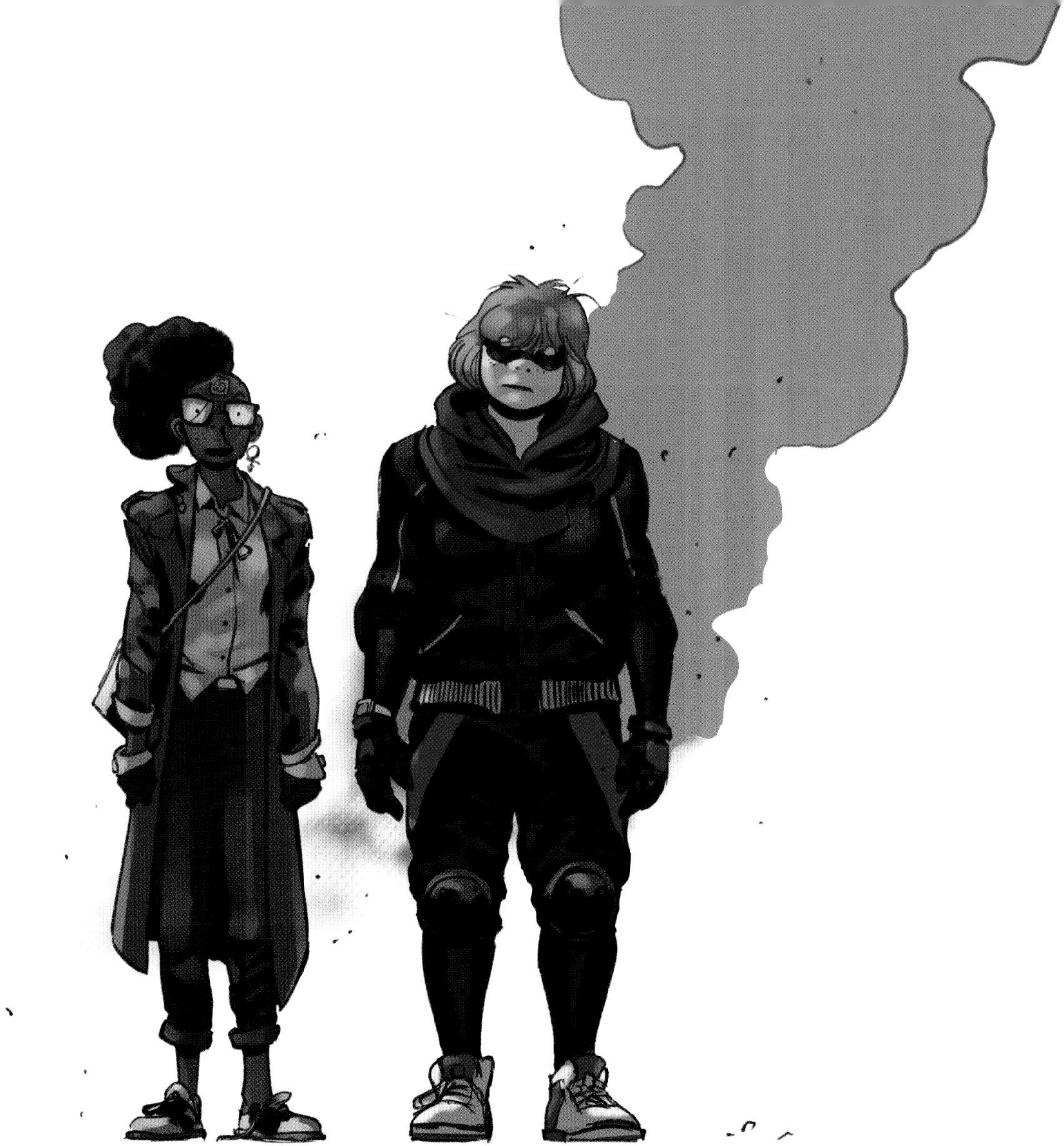

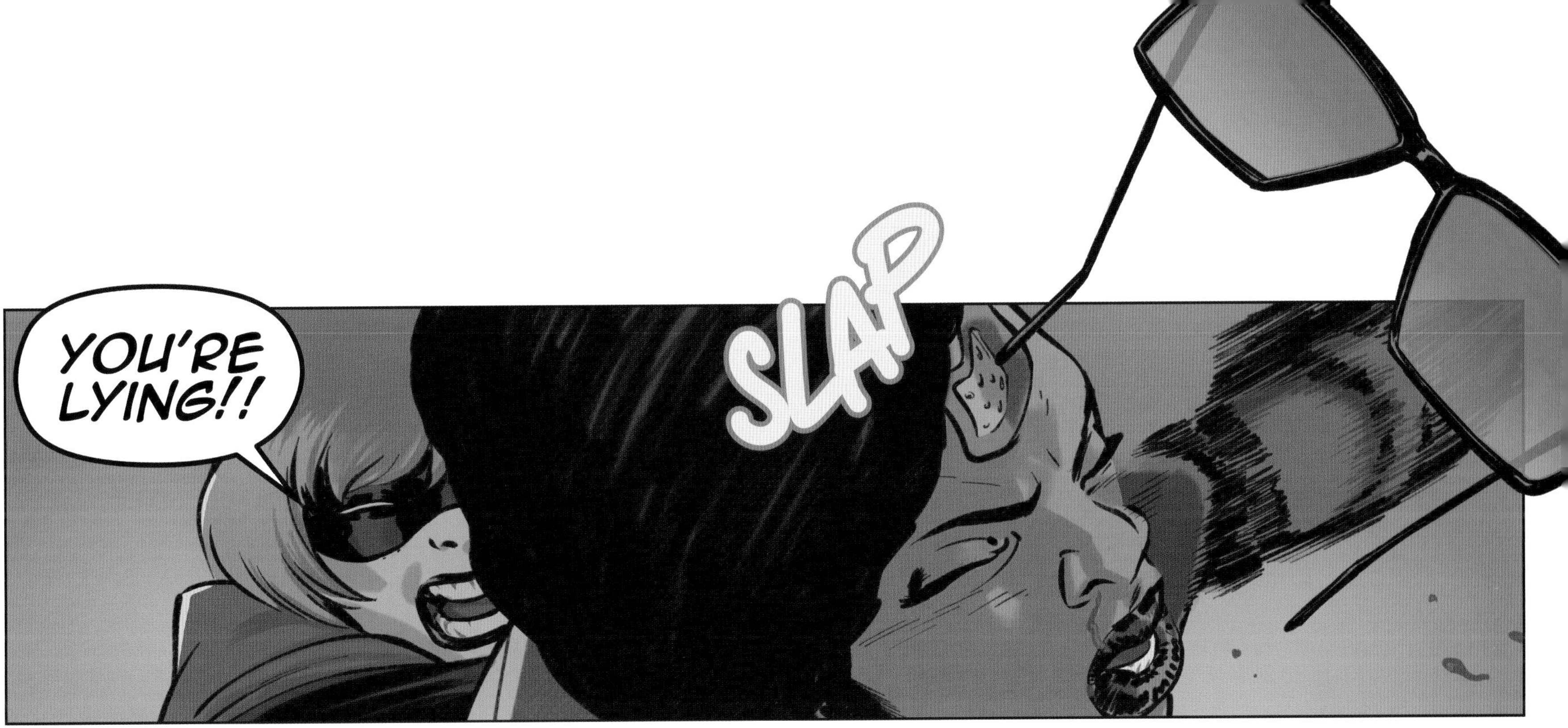
YOU'RE LYING!!
SLAP

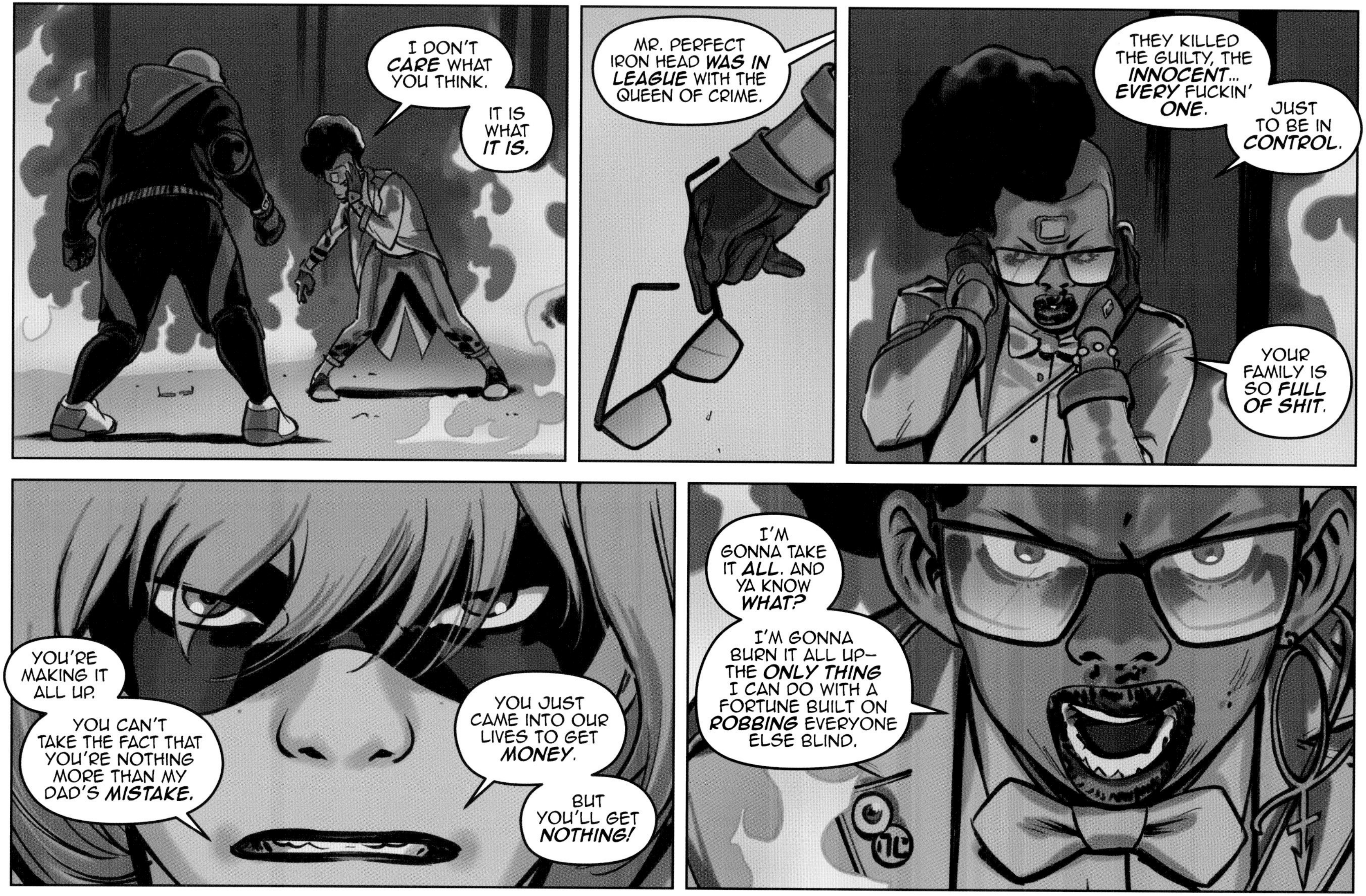

I DON'T CARE WHAT YOU THINK.
IT IS WHAT IT IS.
MR. PERFECT IRON HEAD WAS IN LEAGUE WITH THE QUEEN OF CRIME.
THEY KILLED THE GUILTY, THE INNOCENT... EVERY FUCKIN' ONE.
JUST TO BE IN CONTROL.
YOUR FAMILY IS SO FULL OF SHIT.
YOU'RE MAKING IT ALL UP.
YOU CAN'T TAKE THE FACT THAT YOU'RE NOTHING MORE THAN MY DAD'S MISTAKE.
YOU JUST CAME INTO OUR LIVES TO GET MONEY.
BUT YOU'LL GET NOTHING!
I'M GONNA TAKE IT ALL. AND YA KNOW WHAT?
I'M GONNA BURN IT ALL UP—THE ONLY THING I CAN DO WITH A FORTUNE BUILT ON ROBBING EVERYONE ELSE BLIND.

4. Heroes that never were

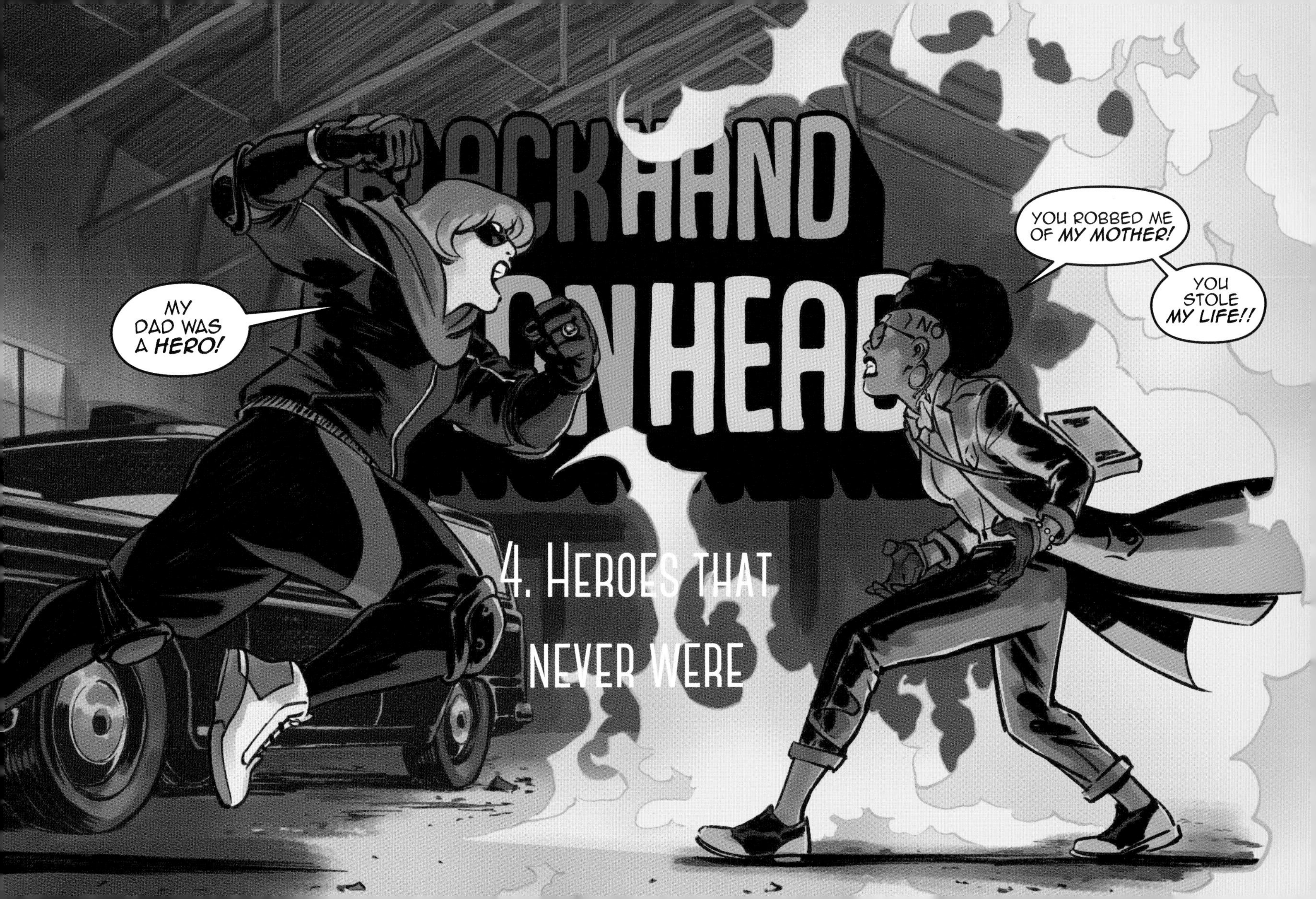
MY DAD WAS A HERO!
YOU ROBBED ME OF MY MOTHER!
YOU STOLE MY LIFE!!

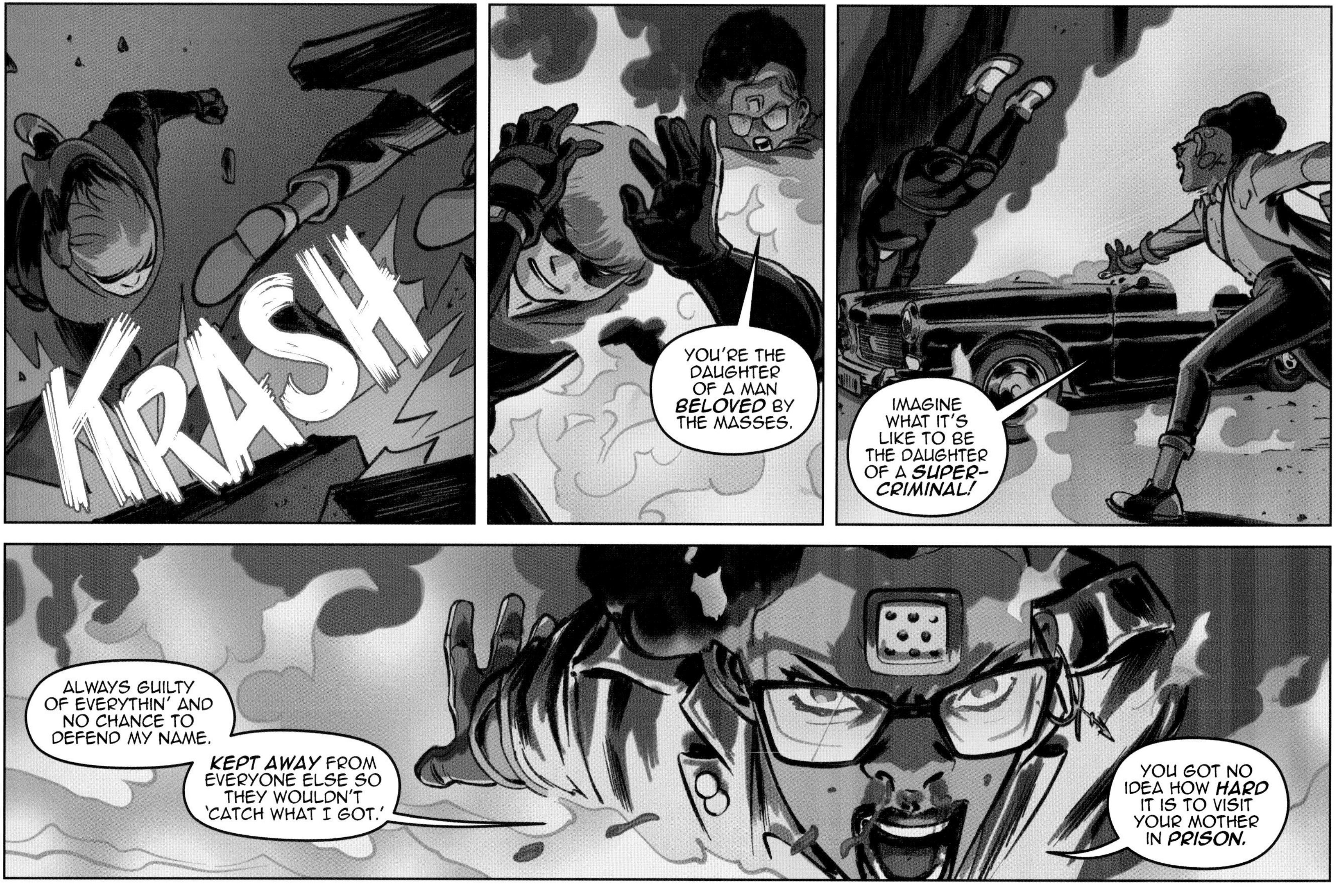
KRASH
YOU'RE THE DAUGHTER OF A MAN BELOVED BY THE MASSES.
IMAGINE WHAT IT'S LIKE TO BE THE DAUGHTER OF A SUPER-CRIMINAL!
ALWAYS GUILTY OF EVERYTHIN' AND NO CHANCE TO DEFEND MY NAME.
KEPT AWAY FROM EVERYONE ELSE SO THEY WOULDN'T 'CATCH WHAT I GOT.'
YOU GOT NO IDEA HOW HARD IT IS TO VISIT YOUR MOTHER IN PRISON.

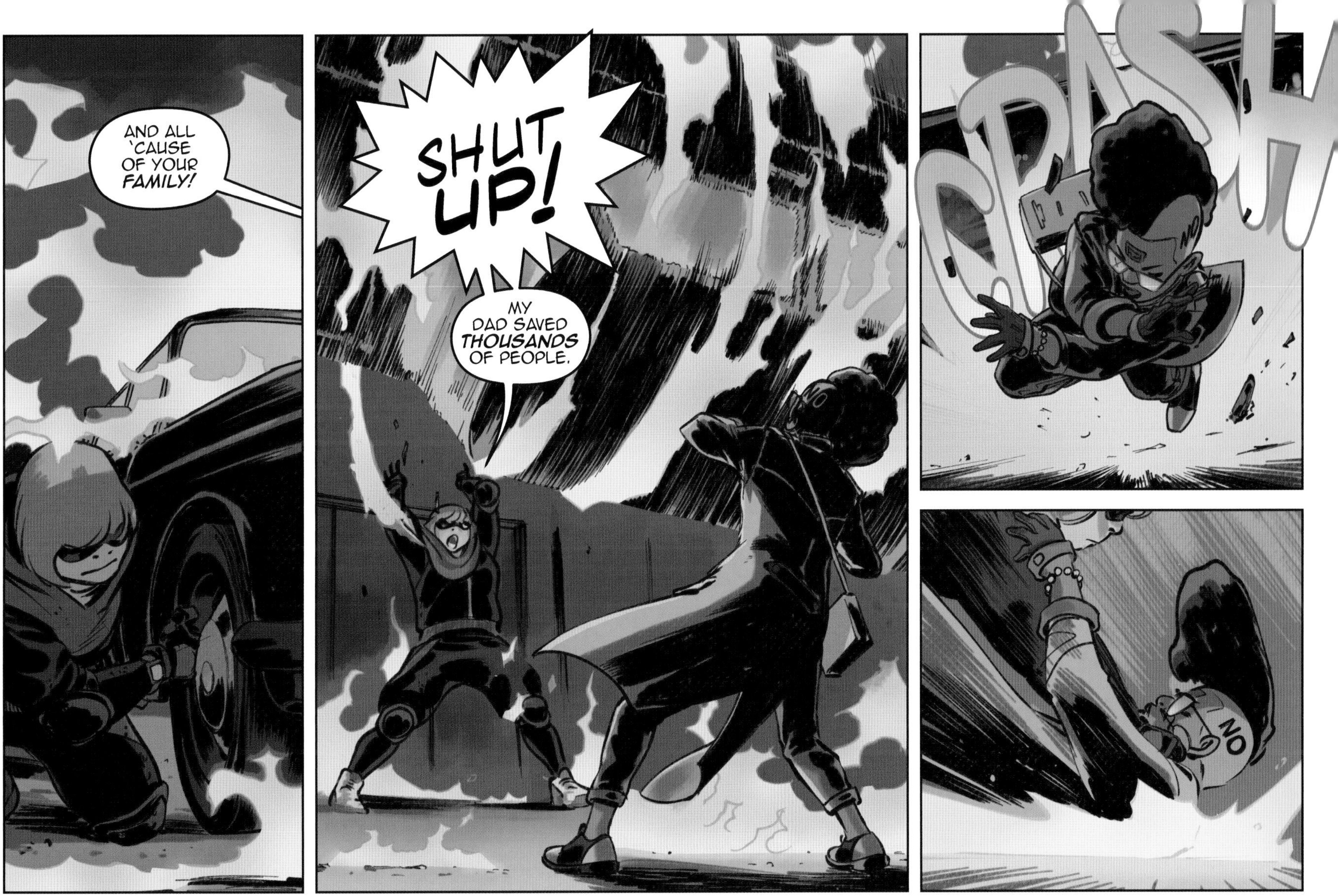
AND ALL 'CAUSE OF YOUR *FAMILY!*
SHUT UP!
MY DAD SAVED *THOUSANDS* OF PEOPLE.
CRASH
NO
NO

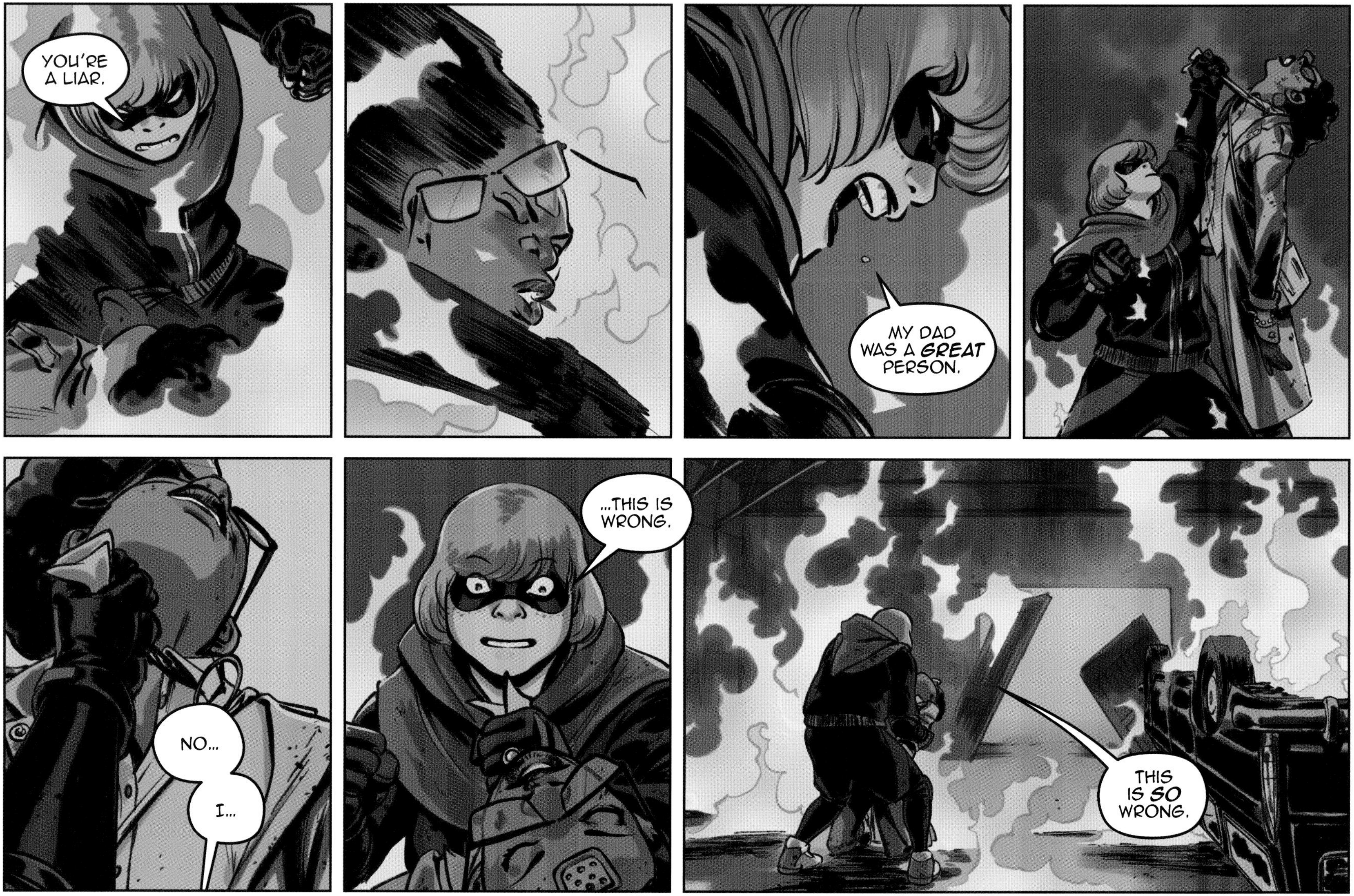
YOU'RE A LIAR.
MY DAD WAS A GREAT PERSON.
NO...
I...
...THIS IS WRONG.
THIS IS SO WRONG.

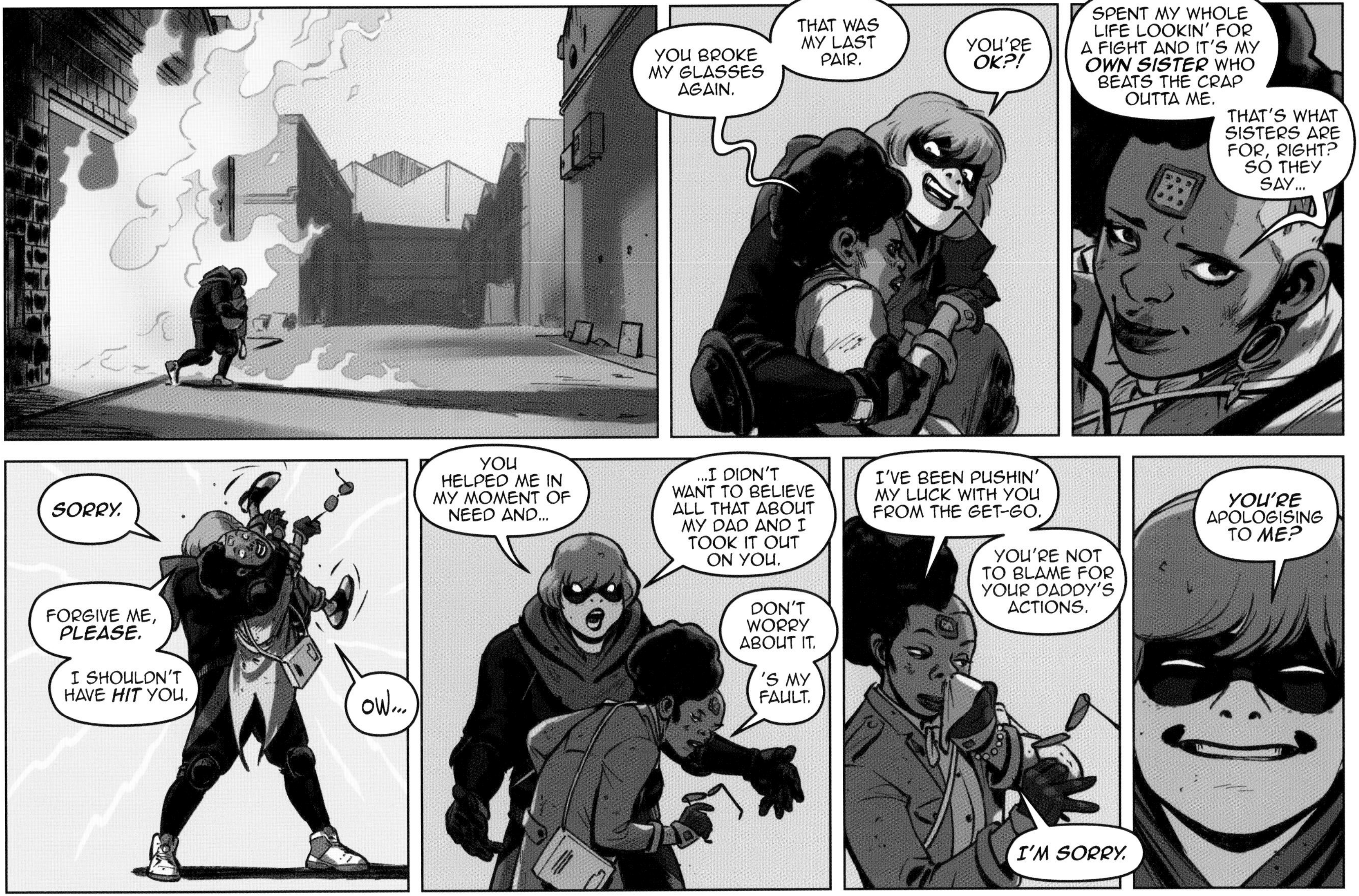

YOU BROKE MY GLASSES AGAIN.
THAT WAS MY LAST PAIR.
YOU'RE *OK?!*
SPENT MY WHOLE LIFE LOOKIN' FOR A FIGHT AND IT'S MY ***OWN SISTER*** WHO BEATS THE CRAP OUTTA ME.
THAT'S WHAT SISTERS ARE FOR, RIGHT? SO THEY SAY...
SORRY.
FORGIVE ME, ***PLEASE.***
I SHOULDN'T HAVE ***HIT*** YOU.
OW...
YOU HELPED ME IN MY MOMENT OF NEED AND...
...I DIDN'T WANT TO BELIEVE ALL THAT ABOUT MY DAD AND I TOOK IT OUT ON YOU.
DON'T WORRY ABOUT IT.
'S MY FAULT.
I'VE BEEN PUSHIN' MY LUCK WITH YOU FROM THE GET-GO.
YOU'RE NOT TO BLAME FOR YOUR DADDY'S ACTIONS.
I'M SORRY.
YOU'RE APOLOGISING TO ***ME?***

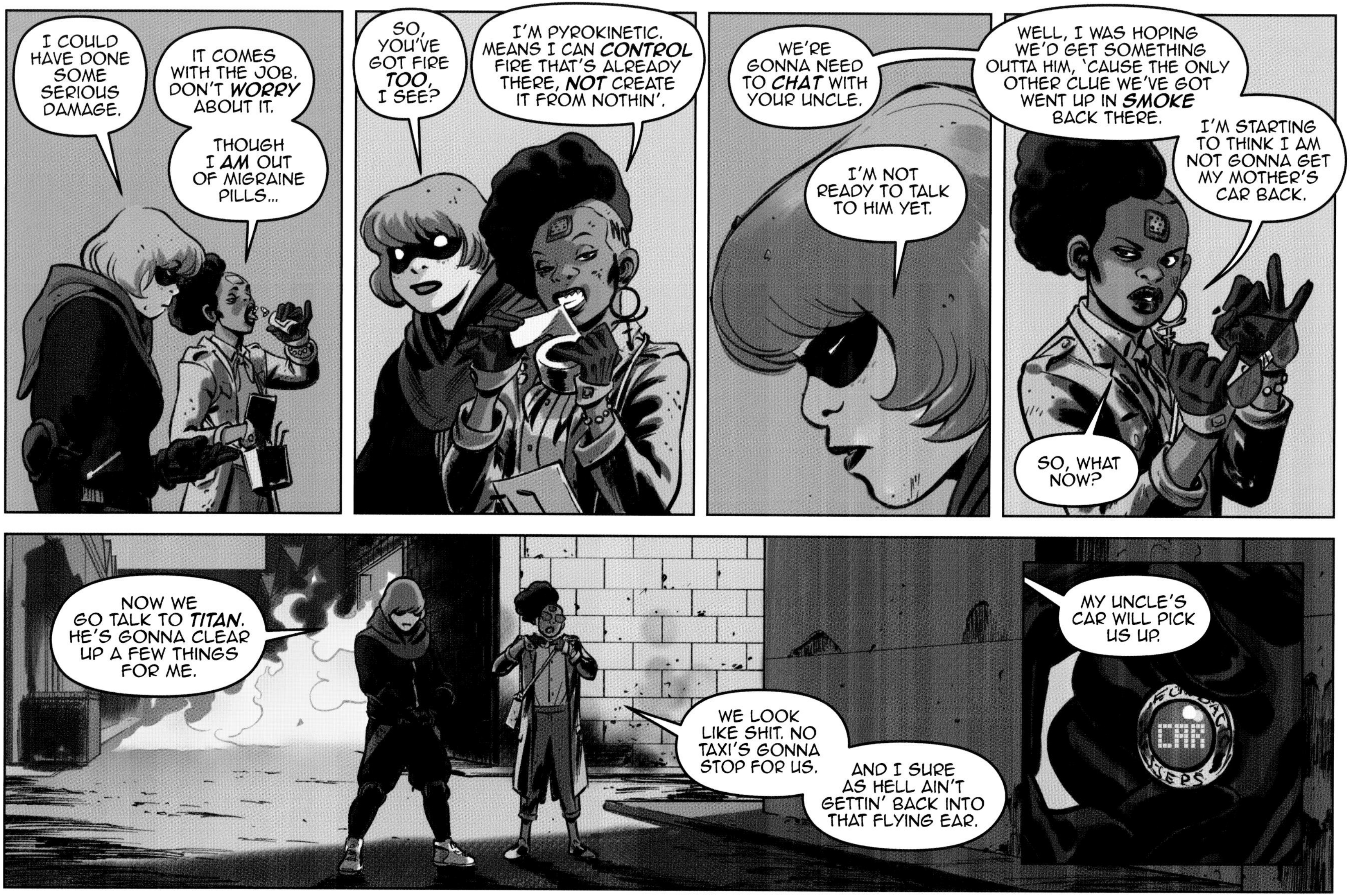

I COULD HAVE DONE SOME SERIOUS DAMAGE.
IT COMES WITH THE JOB. DON'T WORRY ABOUT IT.
THOUGH I AM OUT OF MIGRAINE PILLS...
SO, YOU'VE GOT FIRE TOO, I SEE?
I'M PYROKINETIC. MEANS I CAN CONTROL FIRE THAT'S ALREADY THERE, NOT CREATE IT FROM NOTHIN'.
WE'RE GONNA NEED TO CHAT WITH YOUR UNCLE.
I'M NOT READY TO TALK TO HIM YET.
WELL, I WAS HOPING WE'D GET SOMETHING OUTTA HIM, 'CAUSE THE ONLY OTHER CLUE WE'VE GOT WENT UP IN SMOKE BACK THERE.
I'M STARTING TO THINK I AM NOT GONNA GET MY MOTHER'S CAR BACK.
SO, WHAT NOW?
NOW WE GO TALK TO TITAN. HE'S GONNA CLEAR UP A FEW THINGS FOR ME.
WE LOOK LIKE SHIT. NO TAXI'S GONNA STOP FOR US.
AND I SURE AS HELL AIN'T GETTIN' BACK INTO THAT FLYING EAR.
MY UNCLE'S CAR WILL PICK US UP.
CAR

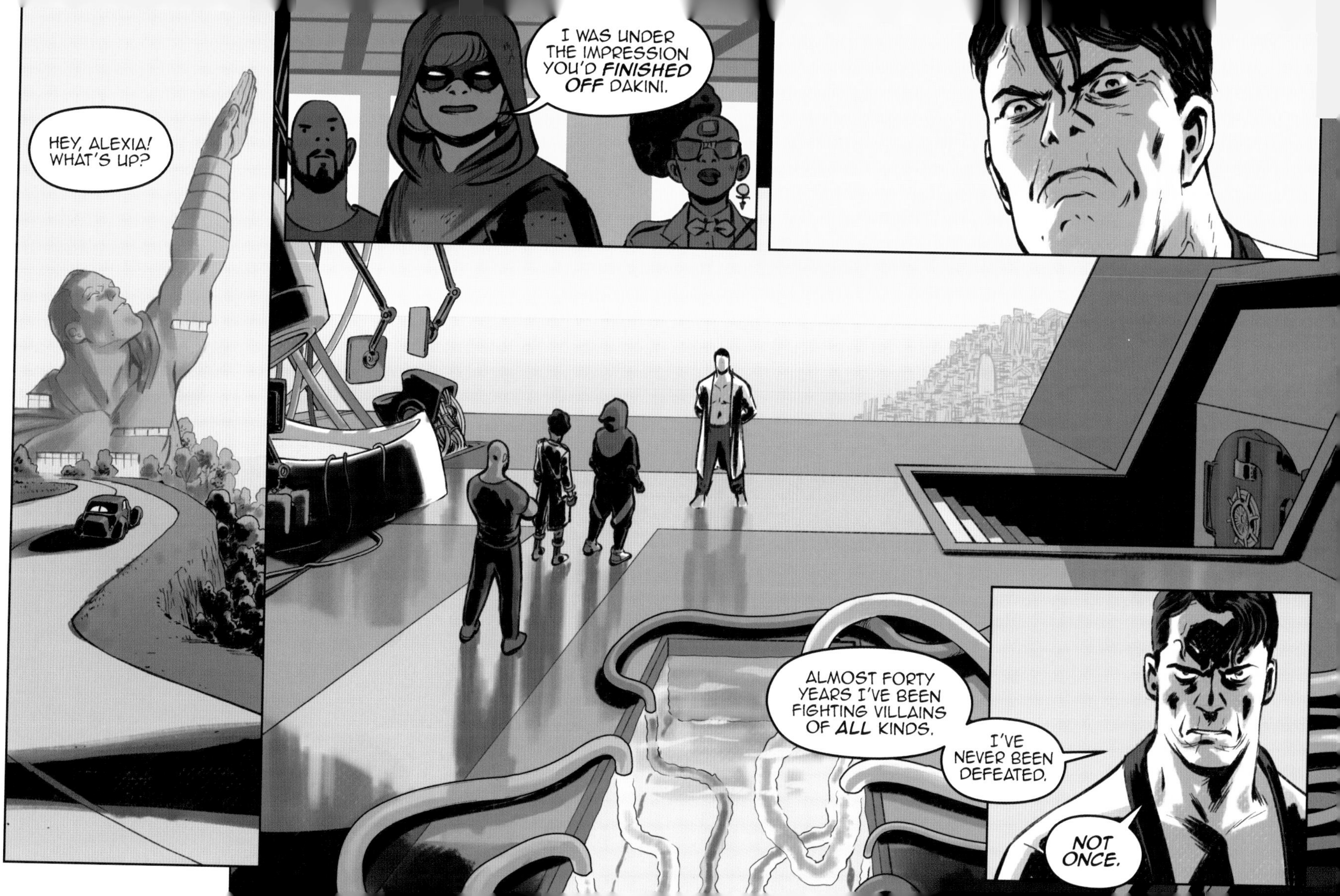
HEY, ALEXIA! WHAT'S UP?
I WAS UNDER THE IMPRESSION YOU'D **FINISHED OFF** DAKINI.
ALMOST FORTY YEARS I'VE BEEN FIGHTING VILLAINS OF **ALL** KINDS.
I'VE NEVER BEEN DEFEATED.
NOT ONCE.

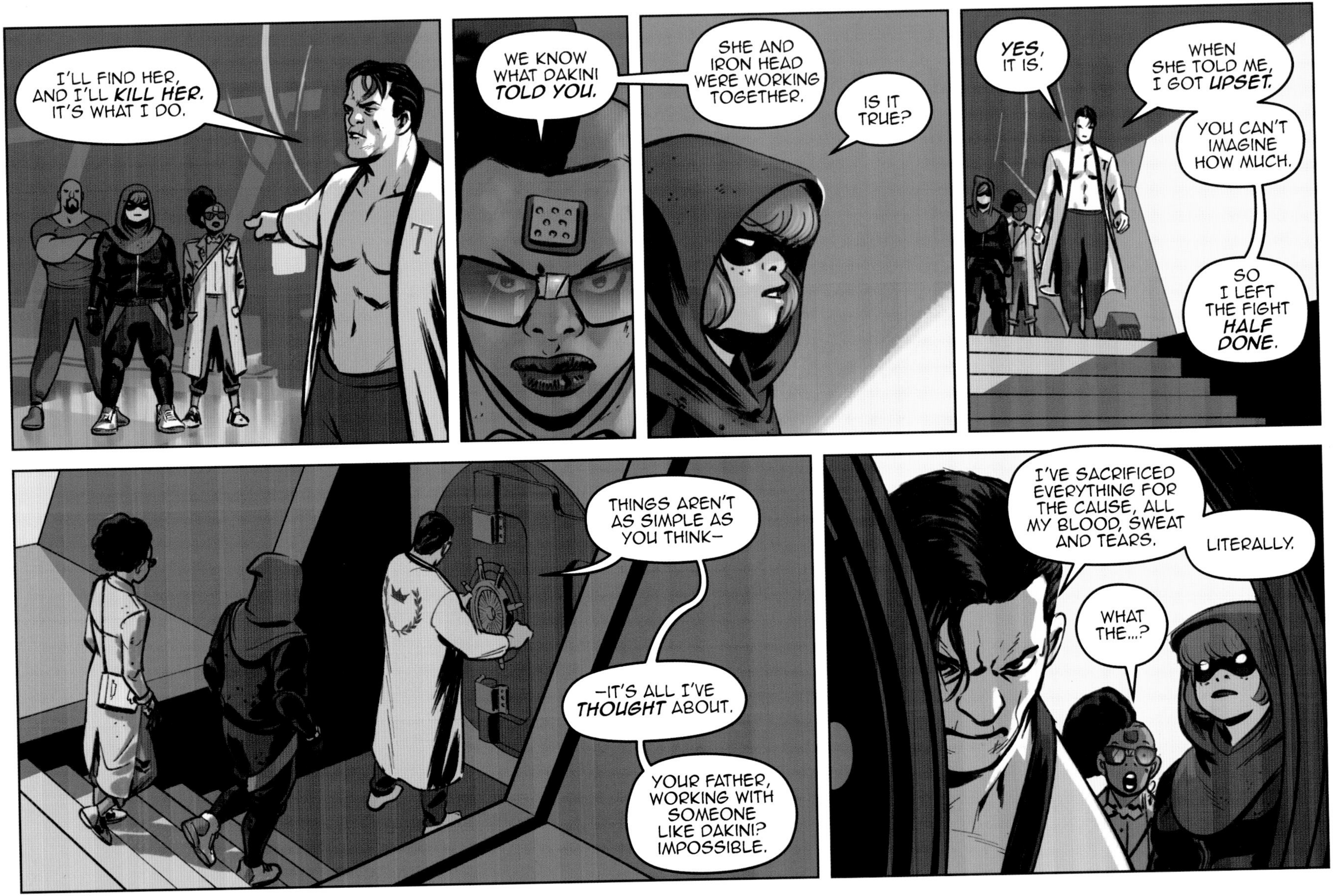
I'LL FIND HER, AND I'LL KILL HER. IT'S WHAT I DO.
WE KNOW WHAT DAKINI TOLD YOU.
SHE AND IRON HEAD WERE WORKING TOGETHER.
IS IT TRUE?
YES, IT IS.
WHEN SHE TOLD ME, I GOT UPSET.
YOU CAN'T IMAGINE HOW MUCH.
SO I LEFT THE FIGHT HALF DONE.
THINGS AREN'T AS SIMPLE AS YOU THINK—
—IT'S ALL I'VE THOUGHT ABOUT.
YOUR FATHER, WORKING WITH SOMEONE LIKE DAKINI? IMPOSSIBLE.
I'VE SACRIFICED EVERYTHING FOR THE CAUSE, ALL MY BLOOD, SWEAT AND TEARS.
LITERALLY.
WHAT THE...?

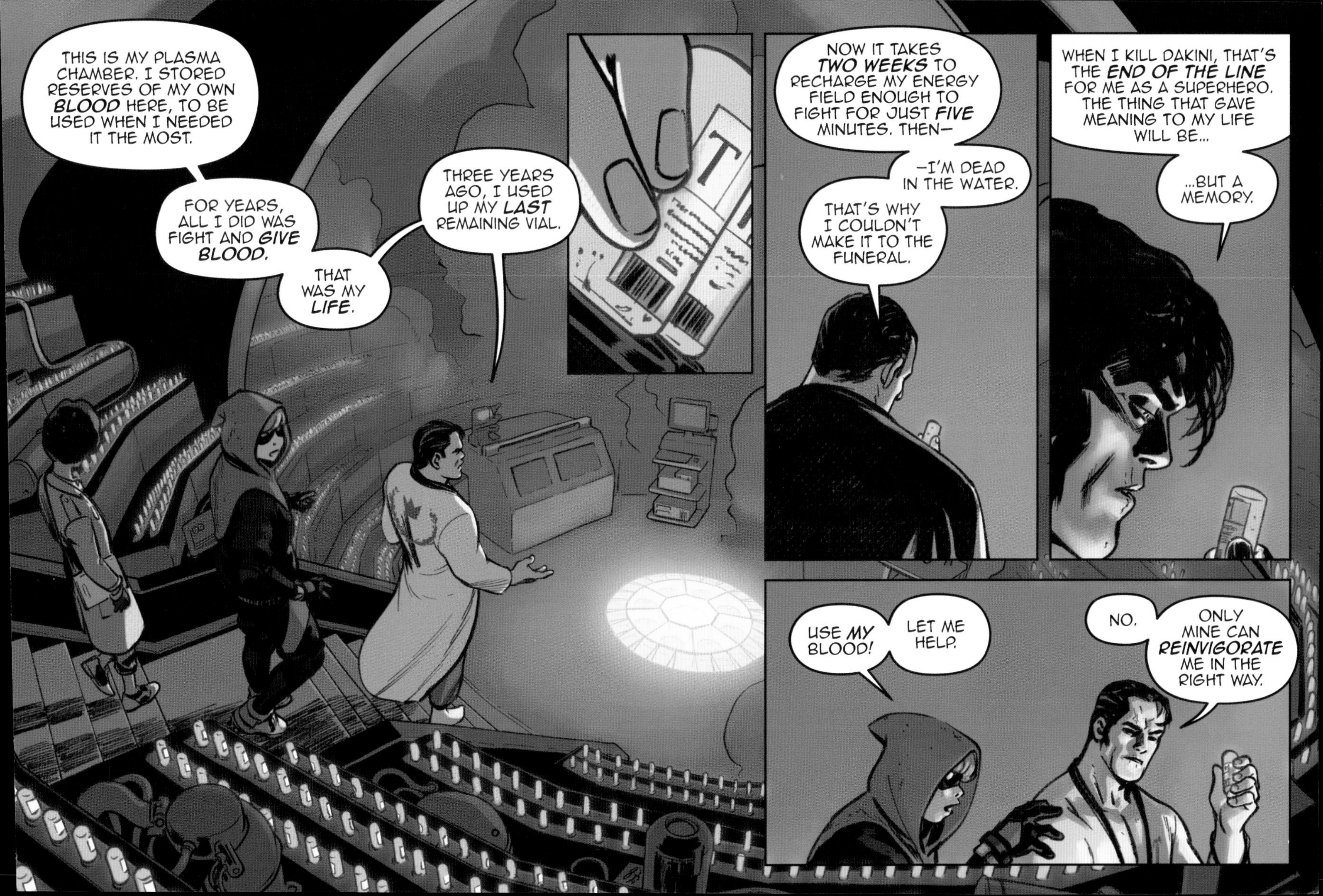
THIS IS MY PLASMA CHAMBER. I STORED RESERVES OF MY OWN **BLOOD** HERE, TO BE USED WHEN I NEEDED IT THE MOST.
FOR YEARS, ALL I DID WAS FIGHT AND **GIVE BLOOD.**
THAT WAS MY **LIFE**.
THREE YEARS AGO, I USED UP MY **LAST** REMAINING VIAL.
NOW IT TAKES **TWO WEEKS** TO RECHARGE MY ENERGY FIELD ENOUGH TO FIGHT FOR JUST **FIVE** MINUTES. THEN—
—I'M DEAD IN THE WATER.
THAT'S WHY I COULDN'T MAKE IT TO THE FUNERAL.
WHEN I KILL DAKINI, THAT'S THE **END OF THE LINE** FOR ME AS A SUPERHERO. THE THING THAT GAVE MEANING TO MY LIFE WILL BE...
...BUT A MEMORY.
USE **MY** BLOOD!
LET ME HELP.
NO.
ONLY MINE CAN **REINVIGORATE** ME IN THE RIGHT WAY.

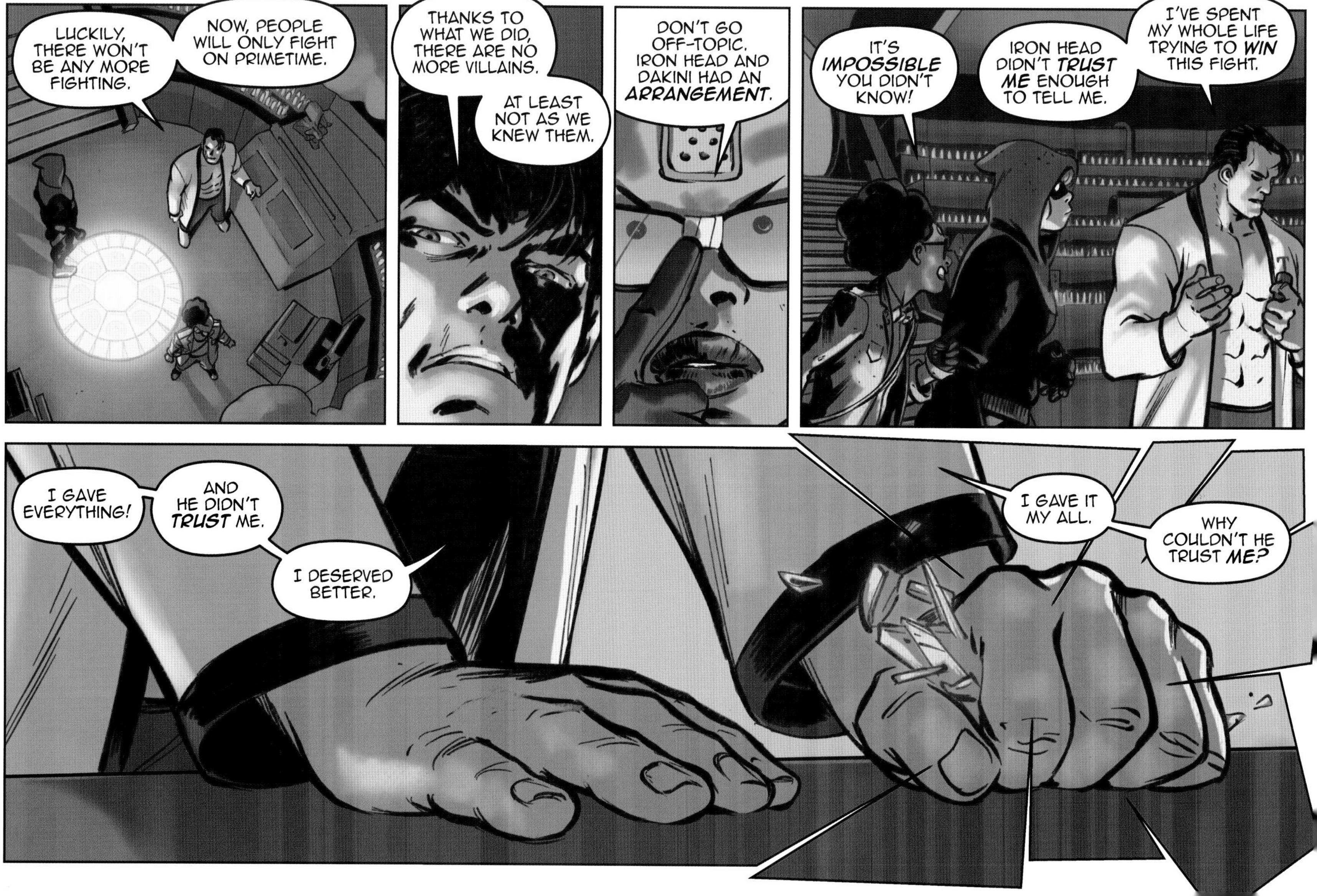
LUCKILY, THERE WON'T BE ANY MORE FIGHTING.
NOW, PEOPLE WILL ONLY FIGHT ON PRIMETIME.
THANKS TO WHAT WE DID, THERE ARE NO MORE VILLAINS.
AT LEAST NOT AS WE KNEW THEM.
DON'T GO OFF-TOPIC. IRON HEAD AND DAKINI HAD AN ARRANGEMENT.
IT'S IMPOSSIBLE YOU DIDN'T KNOW!
IRON HEAD DIDN'T TRUST ME ENOUGH TO TELL ME.
I'VE SPENT MY WHOLE LIFE TRYING TO WIN THIS FIGHT.
I GAVE EVERYTHING!
AND HE DIDN'T TRUST ME.
I DESERVED BETTER.
I GAVE IT MY ALL.
WHY COULDN'T HE TRUST ME?

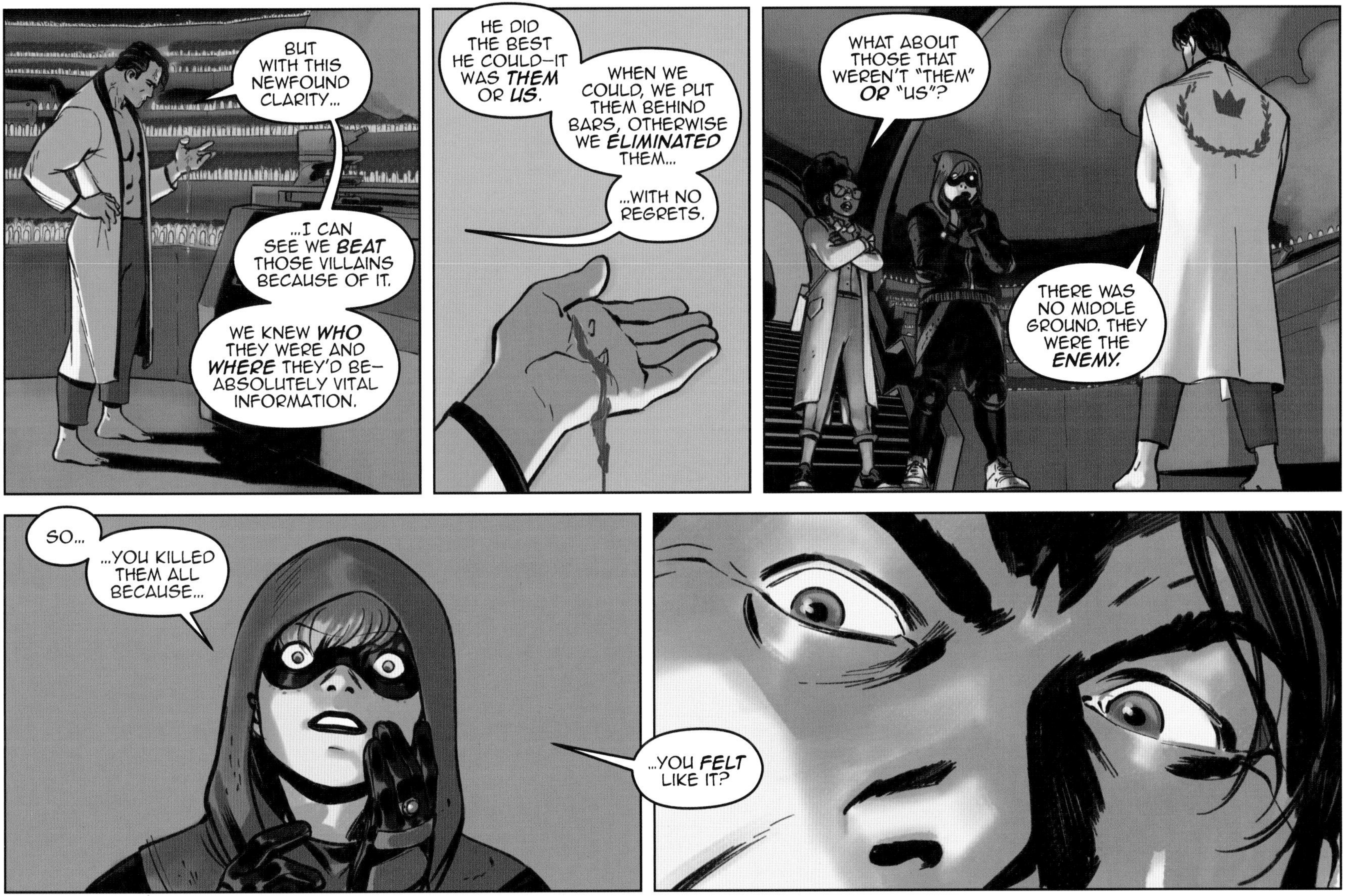
BUT WITH THIS NEWFOUND CLARITY...
...I CAN SEE WE BEAT THOSE VILLAINS BECAUSE OF IT.
WE KNEW WHO THEY WERE AND WHERE THEY'D BE—ABSOLUTELY VITAL INFORMATION.
HE DID THE BEST HE COULD—IT WAS THEM OR US.
WHEN WE COULD, WE PUT THEM BEHIND BARS, OTHERWISE WE ELIMINATED THEM...
...WITH NO REGRETS.
WHAT ABOUT THOSE THAT WEREN'T "THEM" OR "US"?
THERE WAS NO MIDDLE GROUND. THEY WERE THE ENEMY.
SO...
...YOU KILLED THEM ALL BECAUSE...
...YOU FELT LIKE IT?

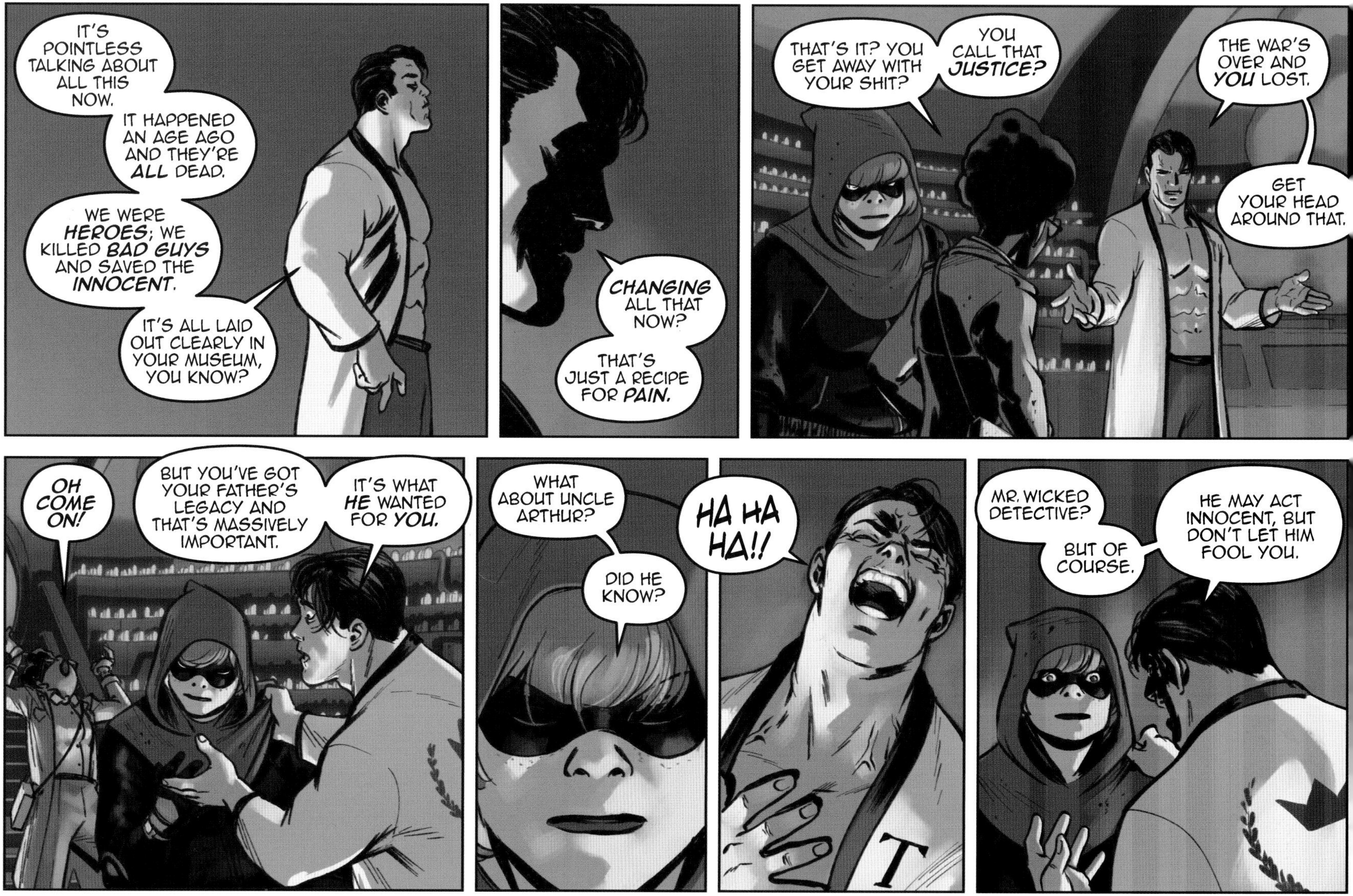

IT'S POINTLESS TALKING ABOUT ALL THIS NOW.
IT HAPPENED AN AGE AGO AND THEY'RE *ALL* DEAD.
WE WERE *HEROES*; WE KILLED *BAD GUYS* AND SAVED THE *INNOCENT*.
IT'S ALL LAID OUT CLEARLY IN YOUR MUSEUM, YOU KNOW?
CHANGING ALL THAT NOW?
THAT'S JUST A RECIPE FOR *PAIN.*
THAT'S IT? YOU GET AWAY WITH YOUR SHIT?
YOU CALL THAT *JUSTICE?*
THE WAR'S OVER AND *YOU* LOST.
GET YOUR HEAD AROUND THAT.
OH COME ON!
BUT YOU'VE GOT YOUR FATHER'S LEGACY AND THAT'S MASSIVELY IMPORTANT.
IT'S WHAT *HE* WANTED FOR *YOU.*
WHAT ABOUT UNCLE ARTHUR?
DID HE KNOW?
HA HA HA!!
MR. WICKED DETECTIVE?
BUT OF COURSE.
HE MAY ACT INNOCENT, BUT DON'T LET HIM FOOL YOU.

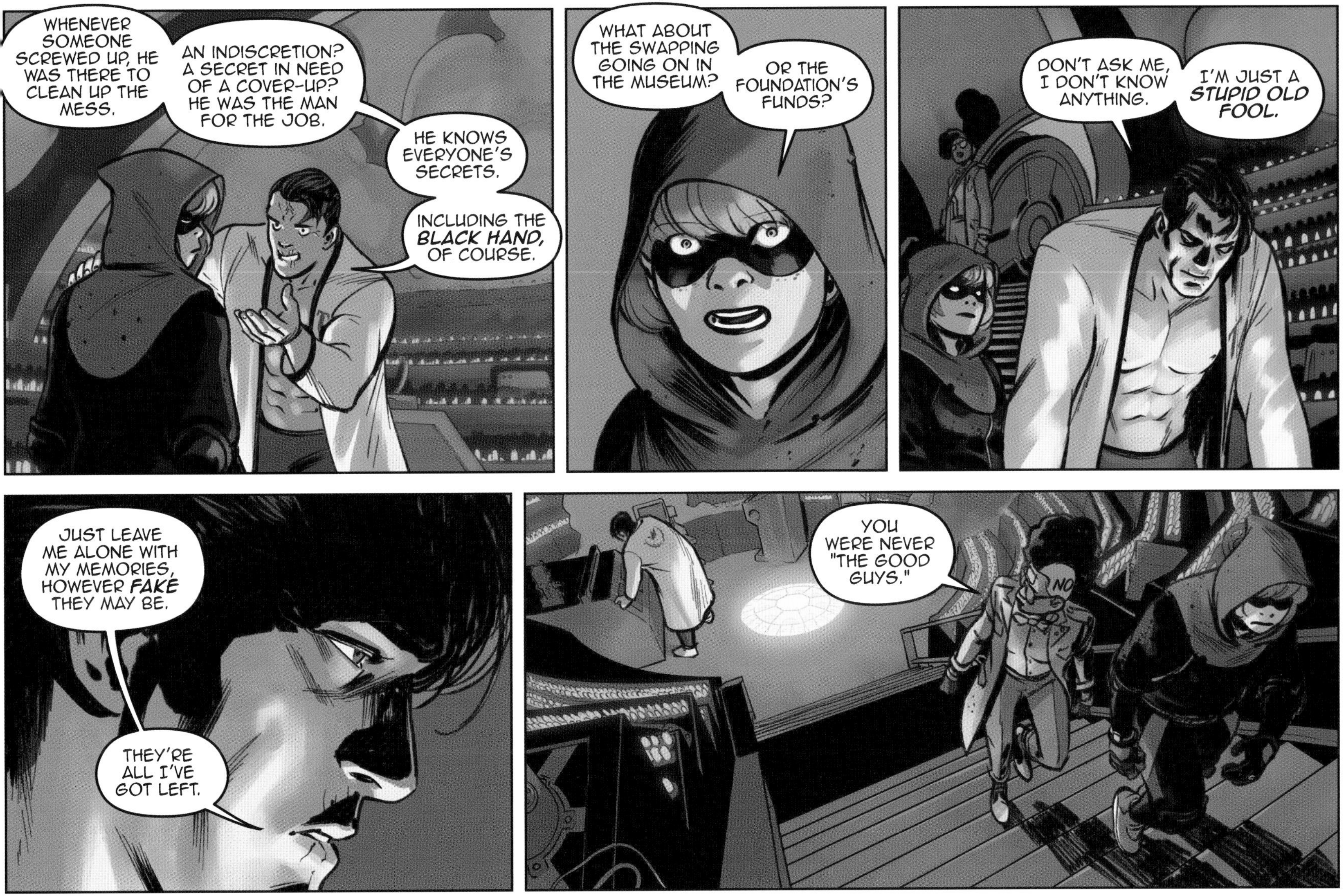
WHENEVER SOMEONE SCREWED UP, HE WAS THERE TO CLEAN UP THE MESS.
AN INDISCRETION? A SECRET IN NEED OF A COVER-UP? HE WAS THE MAN FOR THE JOB.
HE KNOWS EVERYONE'S SECRETS.
INCLUDING THE ***BLACK HAND,*** OF COURSE.
WHAT ABOUT THE SWAPPING GOING ON IN THE MUSEUM?
OR THE FOUNDATION'S FUNDS?
DON'T ASK ME, I DON'T KNOW ANYTHING.
I'M JUST A ***STUPID OLD FOOL.***
JUST LEAVE ME ALONE WITH MY MEMORIES, HOWEVER ***FAKE*** THEY MAY BE.
THEY'RE ALL I'VE GOT LEFT.
YOU WERE NEVER "THE GOOD GUYS."

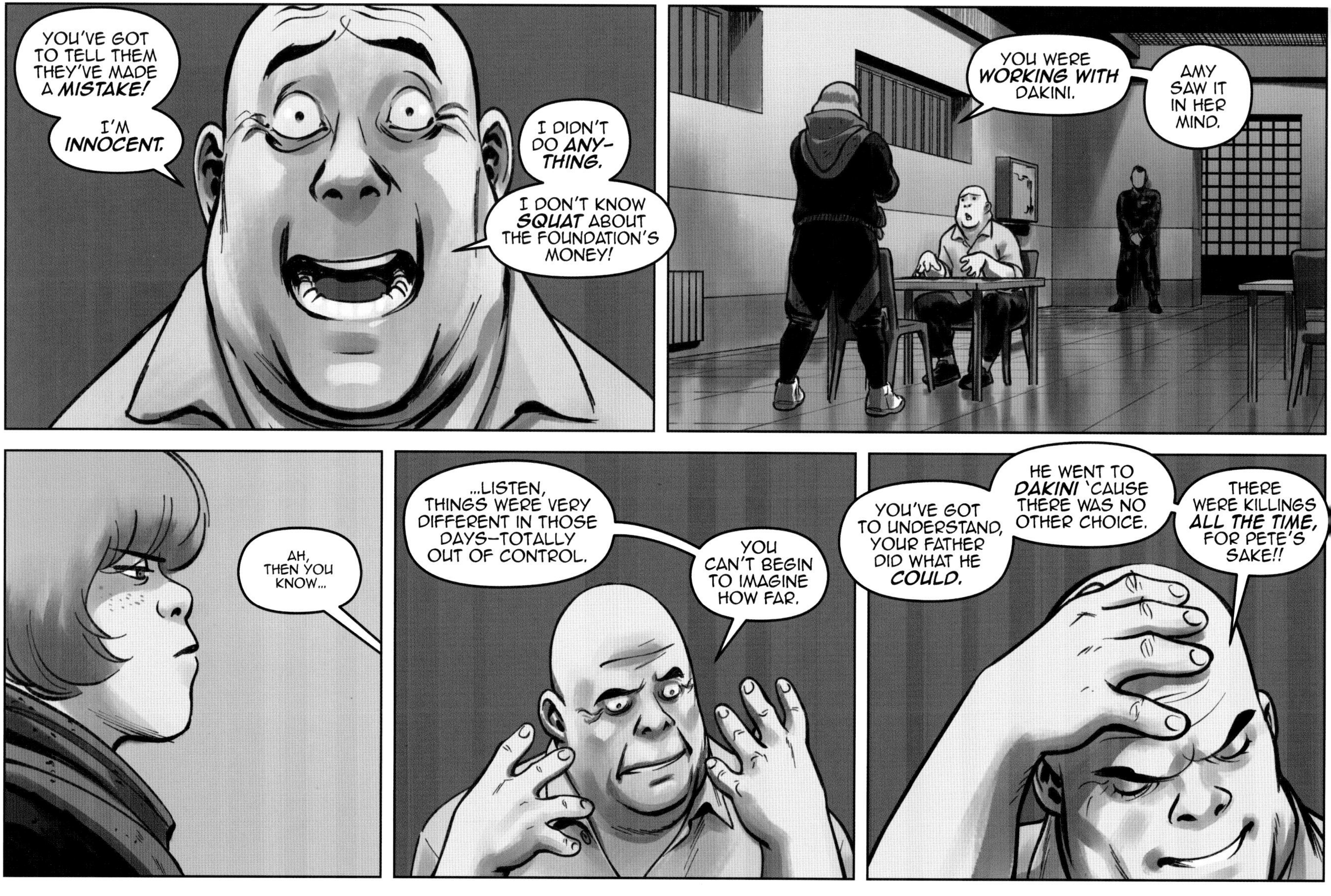
YOU'VE GOT TO TELL THEM THEY'VE MADE A *MISTAKE!*
I'M *INNOCENT.*
I DIDN'T DO *ANY-THING.*
I DON'T KNOW *SQUAT* ABOUT THE FOUNDATION'S MONEY!
YOU WERE *WORKING WITH* DAKINI.
AMY SAW IT IN HER MIND.
AH, THEN YOU KNOW...
...LISTEN, THINGS WERE VERY DIFFERENT IN THOSE DAYS—TOTALLY OUT OF CONTROL.
YOU CAN'T BEGIN TO IMAGINE HOW FAR.
YOU'VE GOT TO UNDERSTAND, YOUR FATHER DID WHAT HE *COULD.*
HE WENT TO *DAKINI* 'CAUSE THERE WAS NO OTHER CHOICE.
THERE WERE KILLINGS *ALL THE TIME,* FOR PETE'S SAKE!!

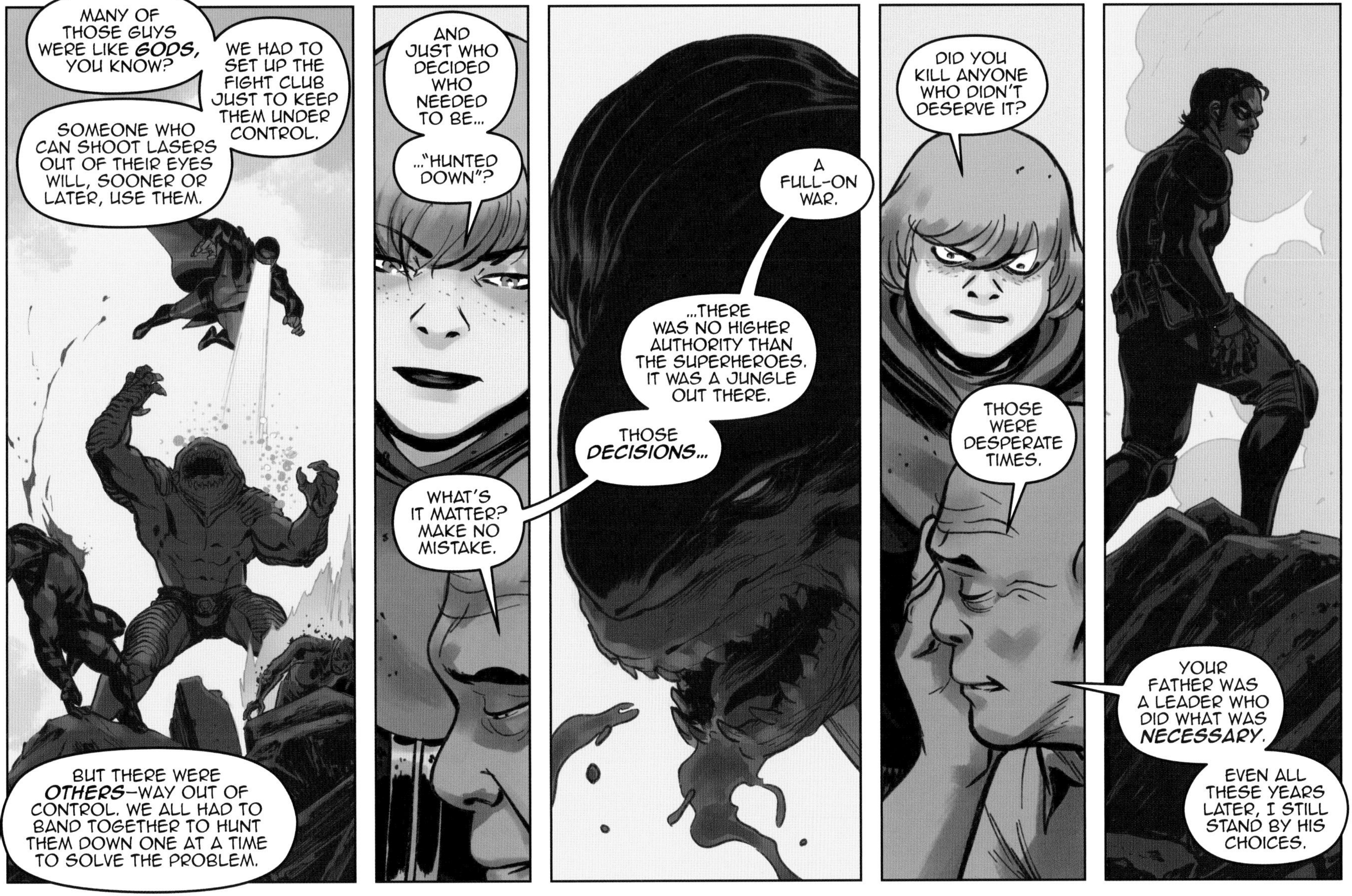
MANY OF THOSE GUYS WERE LIKE *GODS*, YOU KNOW?
WE HAD TO SET UP THE FIGHT CLUB JUST TO KEEP THEM UNDER CONTROL.
SOMEONE WHO CAN SHOOT LASERS OUT OF THEIR EYES WILL, SOONER OR LATER, USE THEM.
BUT THERE WERE *OTHERS*—WAY OUT OF CONTROL. WE ALL HAD TO BAND TOGETHER TO HUNT THEM DOWN ONE AT A TIME TO SOLVE THE PROBLEM.
AND JUST WHO DECIDED WHO NEEDED TO BE...
..."HUNTED DOWN"?
WHAT'S IT MATTER? MAKE NO MISTAKE.
A FULL-ON WAR.
...THERE WAS NO HIGHER AUTHORITY THAN THE SUPERHEROES. IT WAS A JUNGLE OUT THERE.
THOSE *DECISIONS*...
DID YOU KILL ANYONE WHO DIDN'T DESERVE IT?
THOSE WERE DESPERATE TIMES.
YOUR FATHER WAS A LEADER WHO DID WHAT WAS *NECESSARY*.
EVEN ALL THESE YEARS LATER, I STILL STAND BY HIS CHOICES.

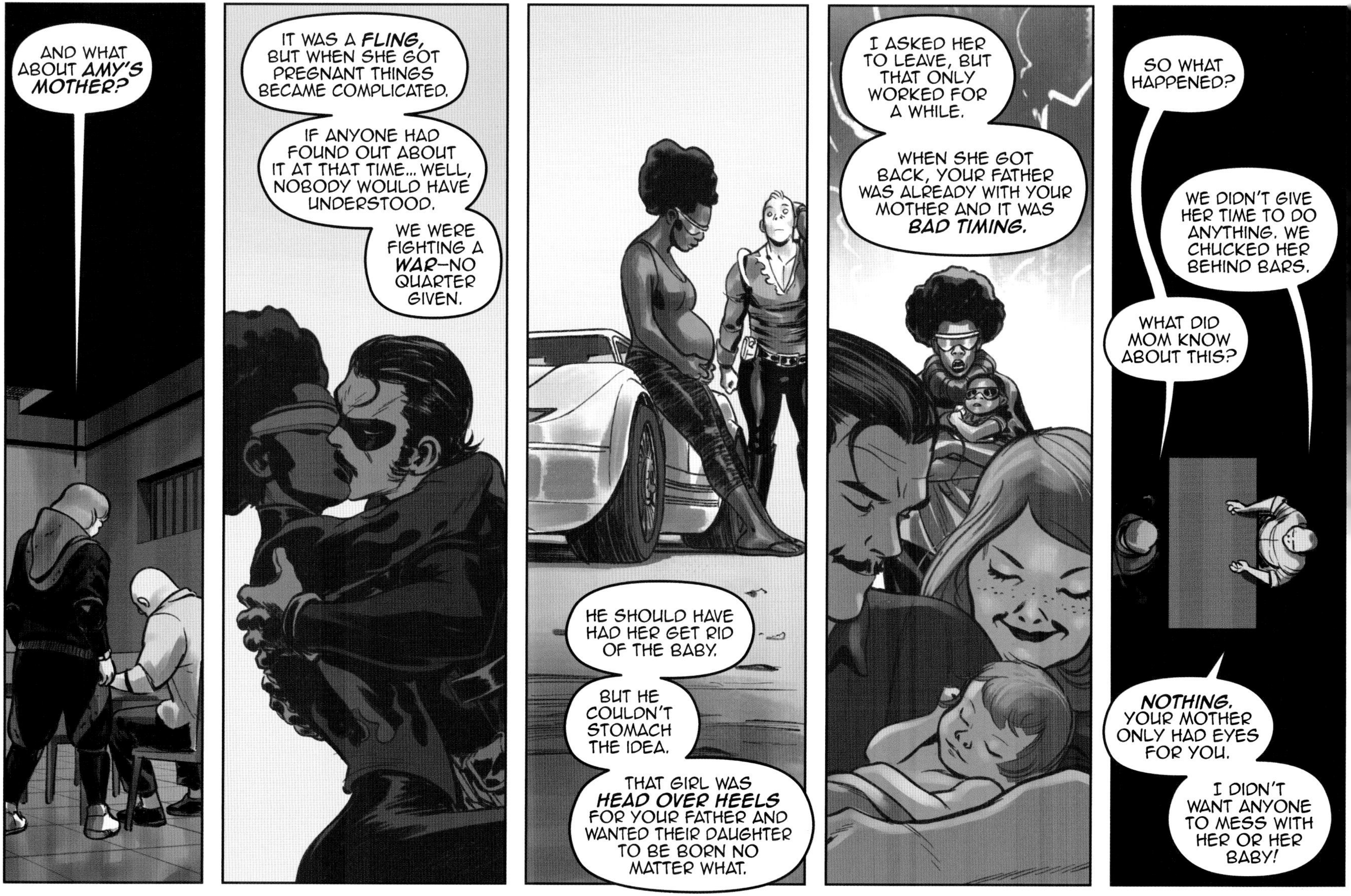
AND WHAT ABOUT AMY'S MOTHER?
IT WAS A FLING, BUT WHEN SHE GOT PREGNANT THINGS BECAME COMPLICATED.
IF ANYONE HAD FOUND OUT ABOUT IT AT THAT TIME... WELL, NOBODY WOULD HAVE UNDERSTOOD.
WE WERE FIGHTING A WAR—NO QUARTER GIVEN.
HE SHOULD HAVE HAD HER GET RID OF THE BABY.
BUT HE COULDN'T STOMACH THE IDEA.
THAT GIRL WAS HEAD OVER HEELS FOR YOUR FATHER AND WANTED THEIR DAUGHTER TO BE BORN NO MATTER WHAT.
I ASKED HER TO LEAVE, BUT THAT ONLY WORKED FOR A WHILE.
WHEN SHE GOT BACK, YOUR FATHER WAS ALREADY WITH YOUR MOTHER AND IT WAS BAD TIMING.
SO WHAT HAPPENED?
WE DIDN'T GIVE HER TIME TO DO ANYTHING. WE CHUCKED HER BEHIND BARS.
WHAT DID MOM KNOW ABOUT THIS?
NOTHING. YOUR MOTHER ONLY HAD EYES FOR YOU.
I DIDN'T WANT ANYONE TO MESS WITH HER OR HER BABY!

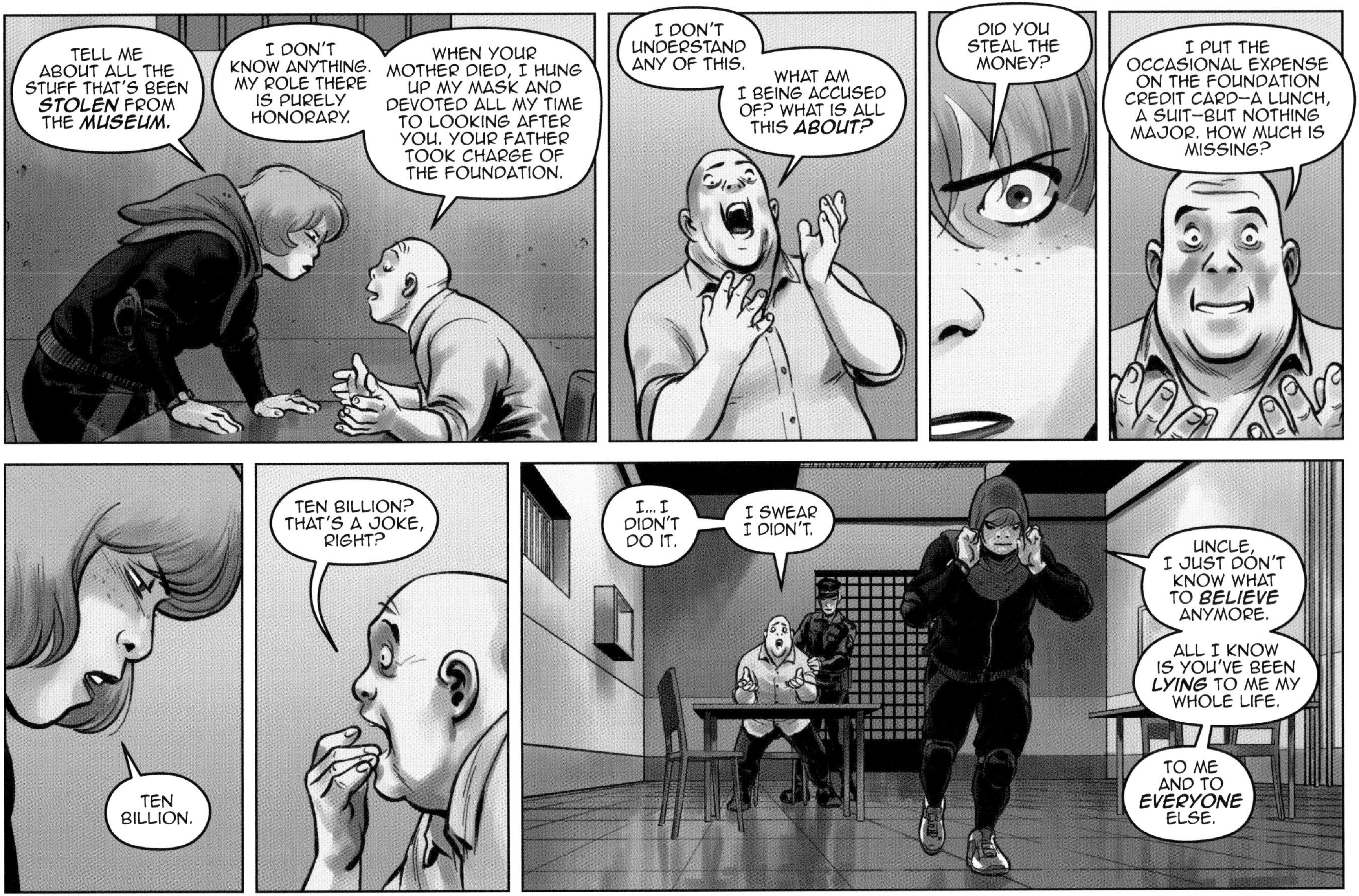
TELL ME ABOUT ALL THE STUFF THAT'S BEEN **STOLEN** FROM THE **MUSEUM.**
I DON'T KNOW ANYTHING. MY ROLE THERE IS PURELY HONORARY.
WHEN YOUR MOTHER DIED, I HUNG UP MY MASK AND DEVOTED ALL MY TIME TO LOOKING AFTER YOU. YOUR FATHER TOOK CHARGE OF THE FOUNDATION.
I DON'T UNDERSTAND ANY OF THIS.
WHAT AM I BEING ACCUSED OF? WHAT IS ALL THIS **ABOUT?**
DID YOU STEAL THE MONEY?
I PUT THE OCCASIONAL EXPENSE ON THE FOUNDATION CREDIT CARD—A LUNCH, A SUIT—BUT NOTHING MAJOR. HOW MUCH IS MISSING?
TEN BILLION.
TEN BILLION? THAT'S A JOKE, RIGHT?
I... I DIDN'T DO IT.
I SWEAR I DIDN'T.
UNCLE, I JUST DON'T KNOW WHAT TO **BELIEVE** ANYMORE.
ALL I KNOW IS YOU'VE BEEN **LYING** TO ME MY WHOLE LIFE.
TO ME AND TO **EVERYONE** ELSE.

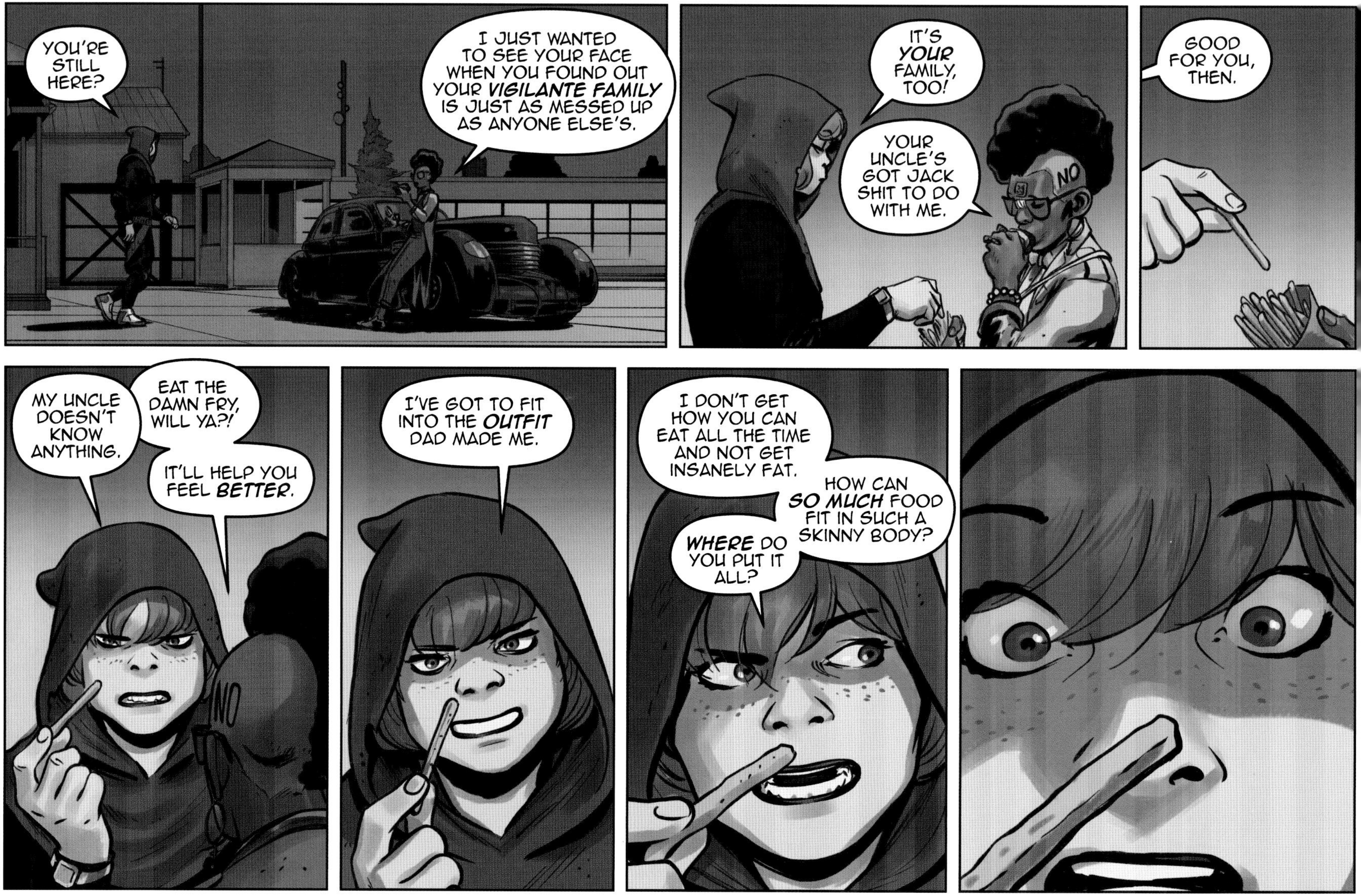
YOU'RE STILL HERE?
I JUST WANTED TO SEE YOUR FACE WHEN YOU FOUND OUT YOUR VIGILANTE FAMILY IS JUST AS MESSED UP AS ANYONE ELSE'S.
IT'S YOUR FAMILY, TOO!
YOUR UNCLE'S GOT JACK SHIT TO DO WITH ME.
NO
GOOD FOR YOU, THEN.
MY UNCLE DOESN'T KNOW ANYTHING.
EAT THE DAMN FRY, WILL YA?!
IT'LL HELP YOU FEEL BETTER.
NO
I'VE GOT TO FIT INTO THE OUTFIT DAD MADE ME.
I DON'T GET HOW YOU CAN EAT ALL THE TIME AND NOT GET INSANELY FAT.
HOW CAN SO MUCH FOOD FIT IN SUCH A SKINNY BODY?
WHERE DO YOU PUT IT ALL?

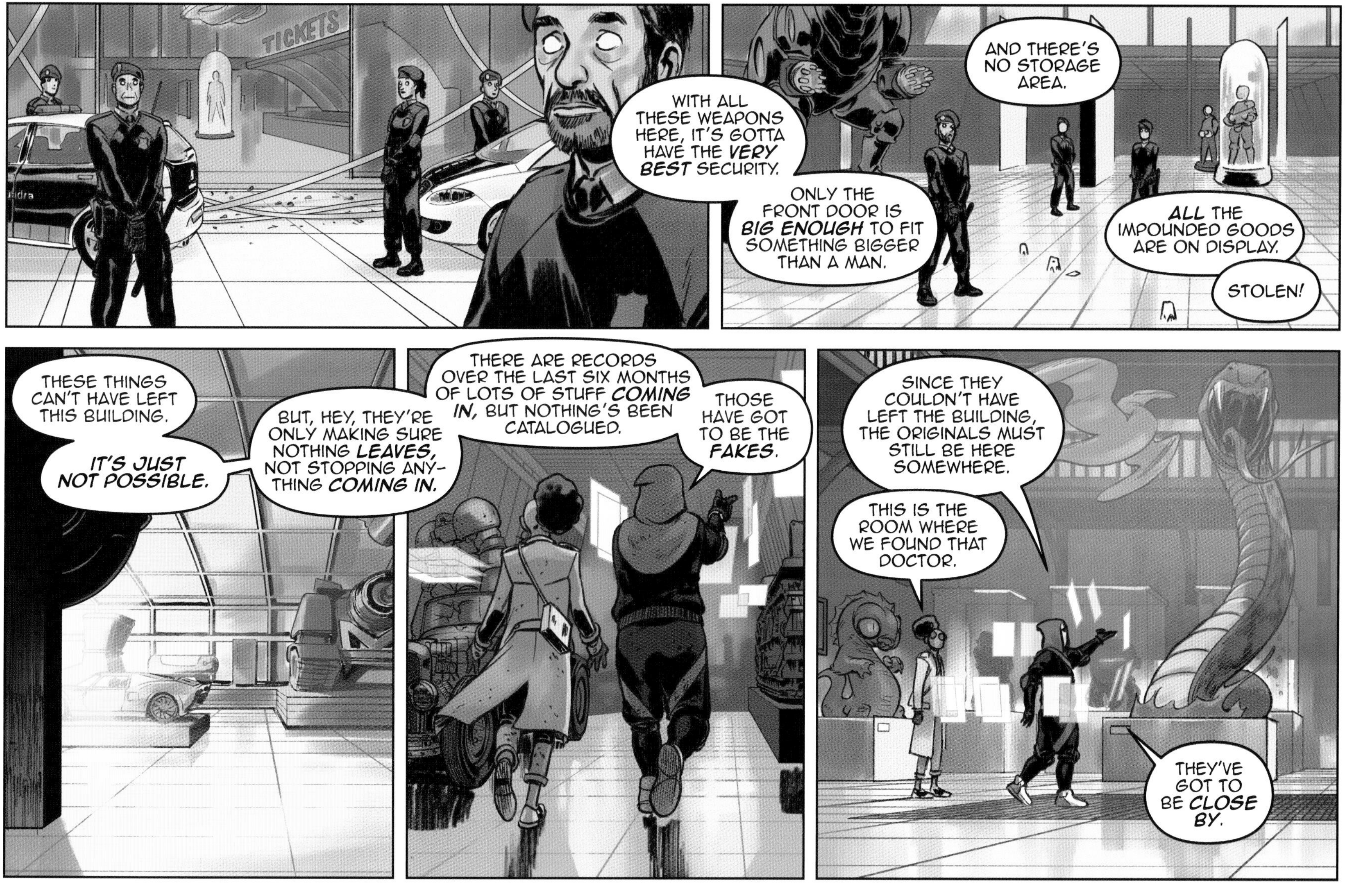
WITH ALL THESE WEAPONS HERE, IT'S GOTTA HAVE THE VERY BEST SECURITY.
ONLY THE FRONT DOOR IS BIG ENOUGH TO FIT SOMETHING BIGGER THAN A MAN.
AND THERE'S NO STORAGE AREA.
ALL THE IMPOUNDED GOODS ARE ON DISPLAY.
STOLEN!
THESE THINGS CAN'T HAVE LEFT THIS BUILDING.
IT'S JUST NOT POSSIBLE.
BUT, HEY, THEY'RE ONLY MAKING SURE NOTHING LEAVES, NOT STOPPING ANYTHING COMING IN.
THERE ARE RECORDS OVER THE LAST SIX MONTHS OF LOTS OF STUFF COMING IN, BUT NOTHING'S BEEN CATALOGUED.
THOSE HAVE GOT TO BE THE FAKES.
SINCE THEY COULDN'T HAVE LEFT THE BUILDING, THE ORIGINALS MUST STILL BE HERE SOMEWHERE.
THIS IS THE ROOM WHERE WE FOUND THAT DOCTOR.
THEY'VE GOT TO BE CLOSE BY.

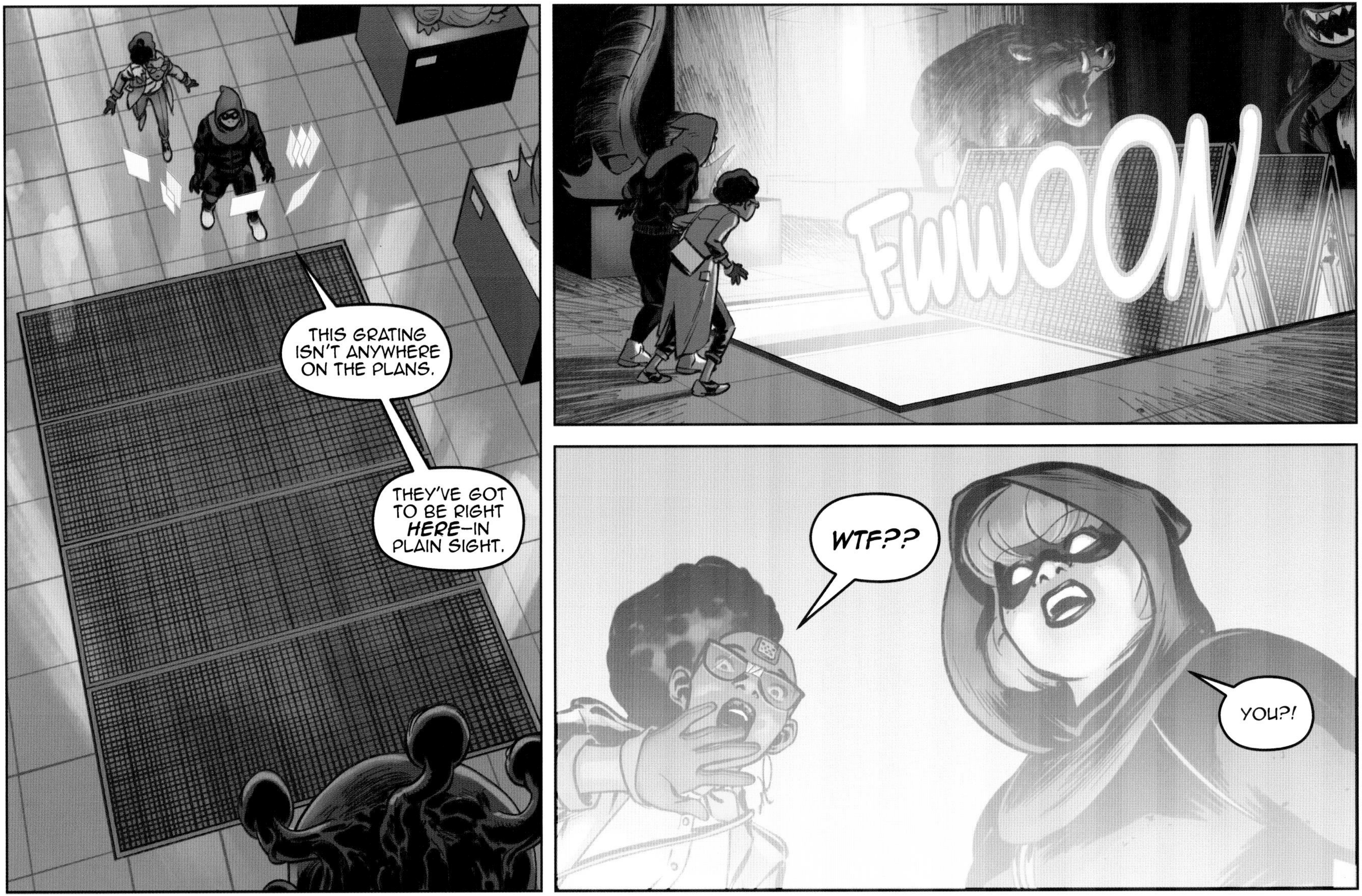
THIS GRATING ISN'T ANYWHERE ON THE PLANS.
THEY'VE GOT TO BE RIGHT *HERE*—IN PLAIN SIGHT.
FWWOON
WTF??
YOU?!

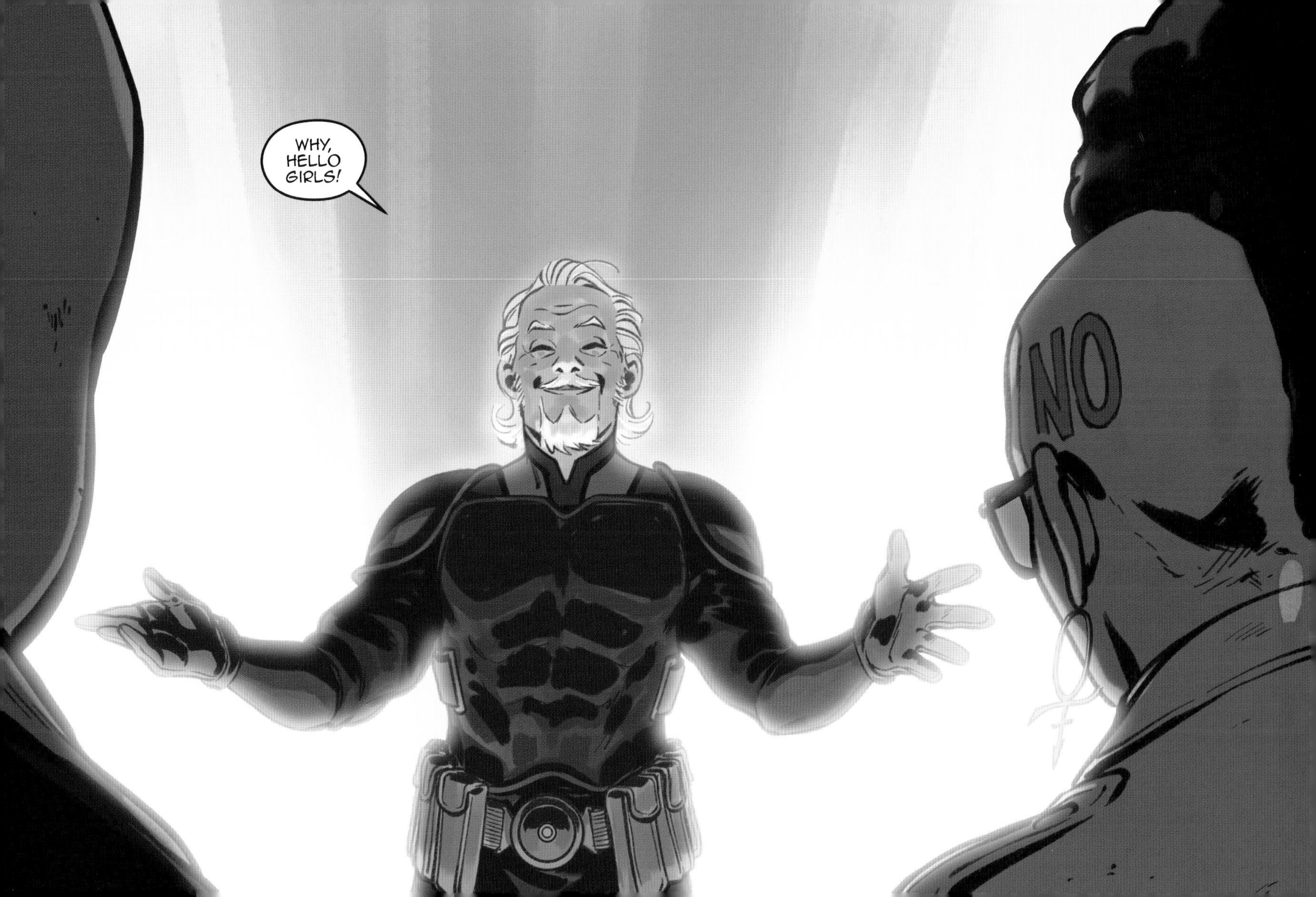
WHY, HELLO GIRLS!
NO

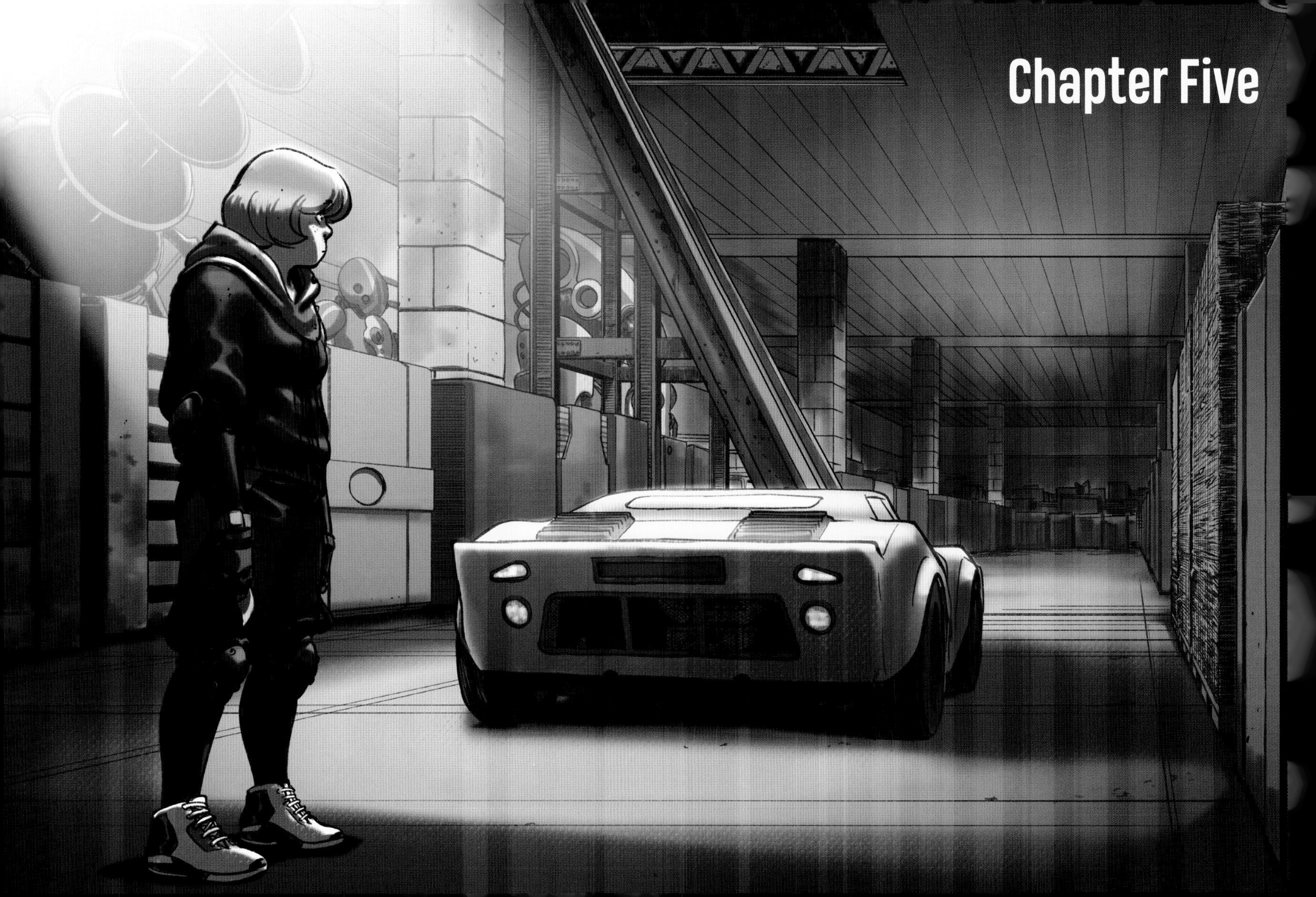
Chapter Five

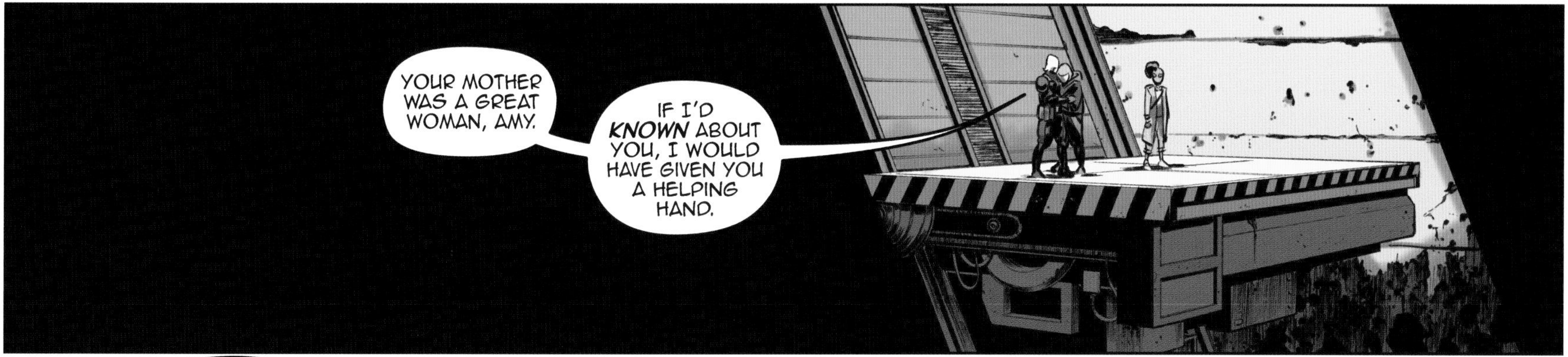
YOUR MOTHER WAS A GREAT WOMAN, AMY.
IF I'D **KNOWN** ABOUT YOU, I WOULD HAVE GIVEN YOU A HELPING HAND.

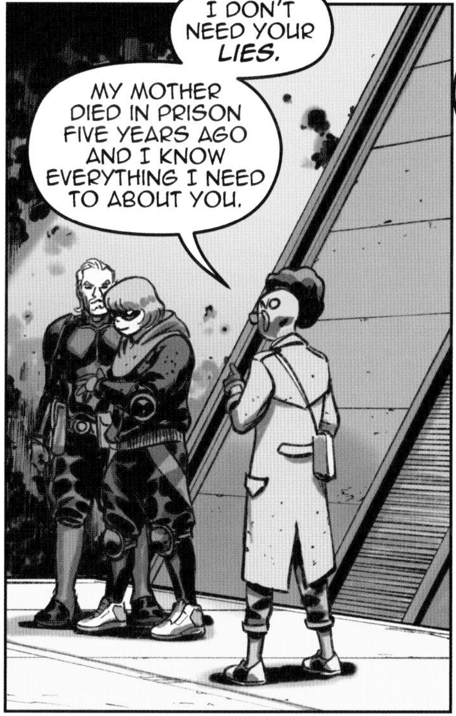
I DON'T NEED YOUR **LIES.**
MY MOTHER DIED IN PRISON FIVE YEARS AGO AND I KNOW EVERYTHING I NEED TO ABOUT YOU.

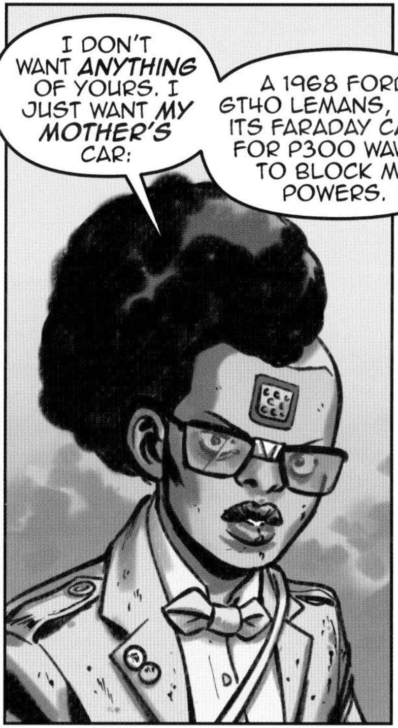
I DON'T WANT **ANYTHING** OF YOURS. I JUST WANT **MY MOTHER'S** CAR:
A 1968 FORD GT40 LEMANS, WITH ITS FARADAY CAGE FOR P300 WAVES TO BLOCK MY POWERS.

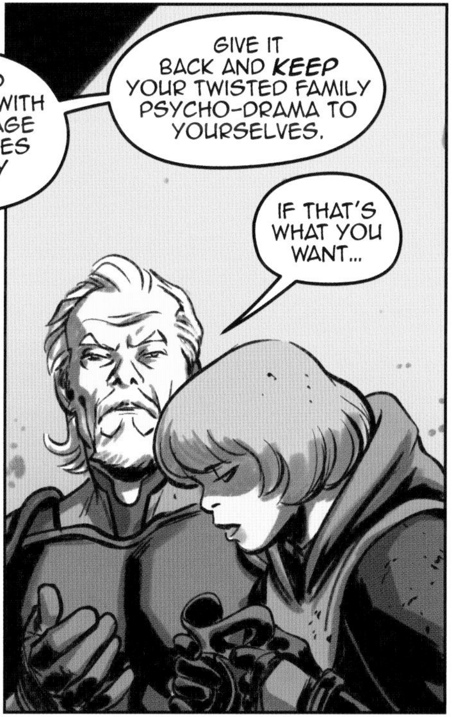
GIVE IT BACK AND **KEEP** YOUR TWISTED FAMILY PSYCHO-DRAMA TO YOURSELVES.
IF THAT'S WHAT YOU WANT...

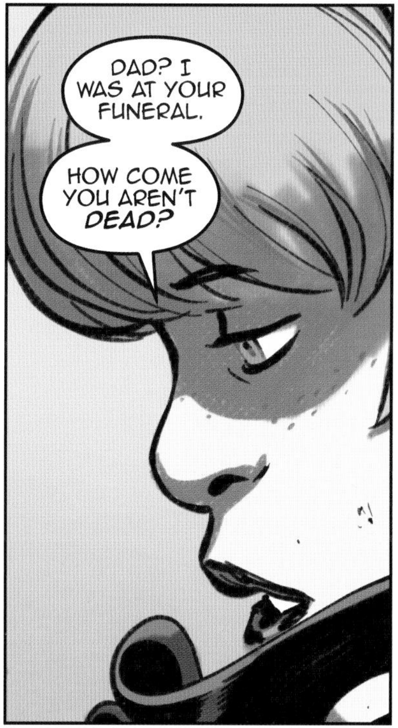
DAD? I WAS AT YOUR FUNERAL.
HOW COME YOU AREN'T **DEAD?**

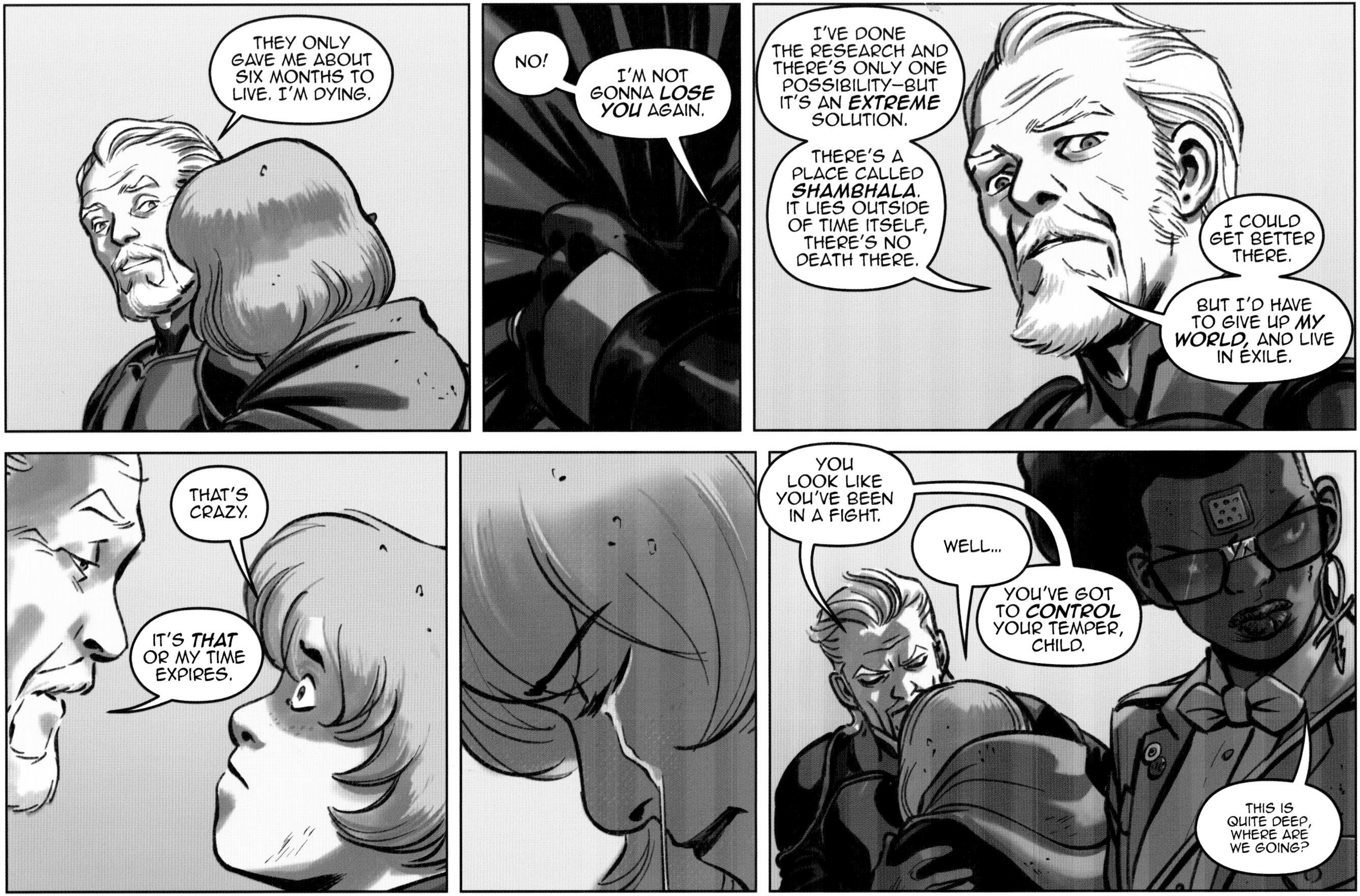
THEY ONLY GAVE ME ABOUT SIX MONTHS TO LIVE. I'M DYING.
NO!
I'M NOT GONNA **LOSE YOU** AGAIN.
I'VE DONE THE RESEARCH AND THERE'S ONLY ONE POSSIBILITY—BUT IT'S AN **EXTREME** SOLUTION.
THERE'S A PLACE CALLED **SHAMBHALA**. IT LIES OUTSIDE OF TIME ITSELF, THERE'S NO DEATH THERE.
I COULD GET BETTER THERE.
BUT I'D HAVE TO GIVE UP **MY WORLD,** AND LIVE IN EXILE.
THAT'S CRAZY.
IT'S **THAT** OR MY TIME EXPIRES.
YOU LOOK LIKE YOU'VE BEEN IN A FIGHT.
WELL...
YOU'VE GOT TO **CONTROL** YOUR TEMPER, CHILD.
THIS IS QUITE DEEP, WHERE ARE WE GOING?

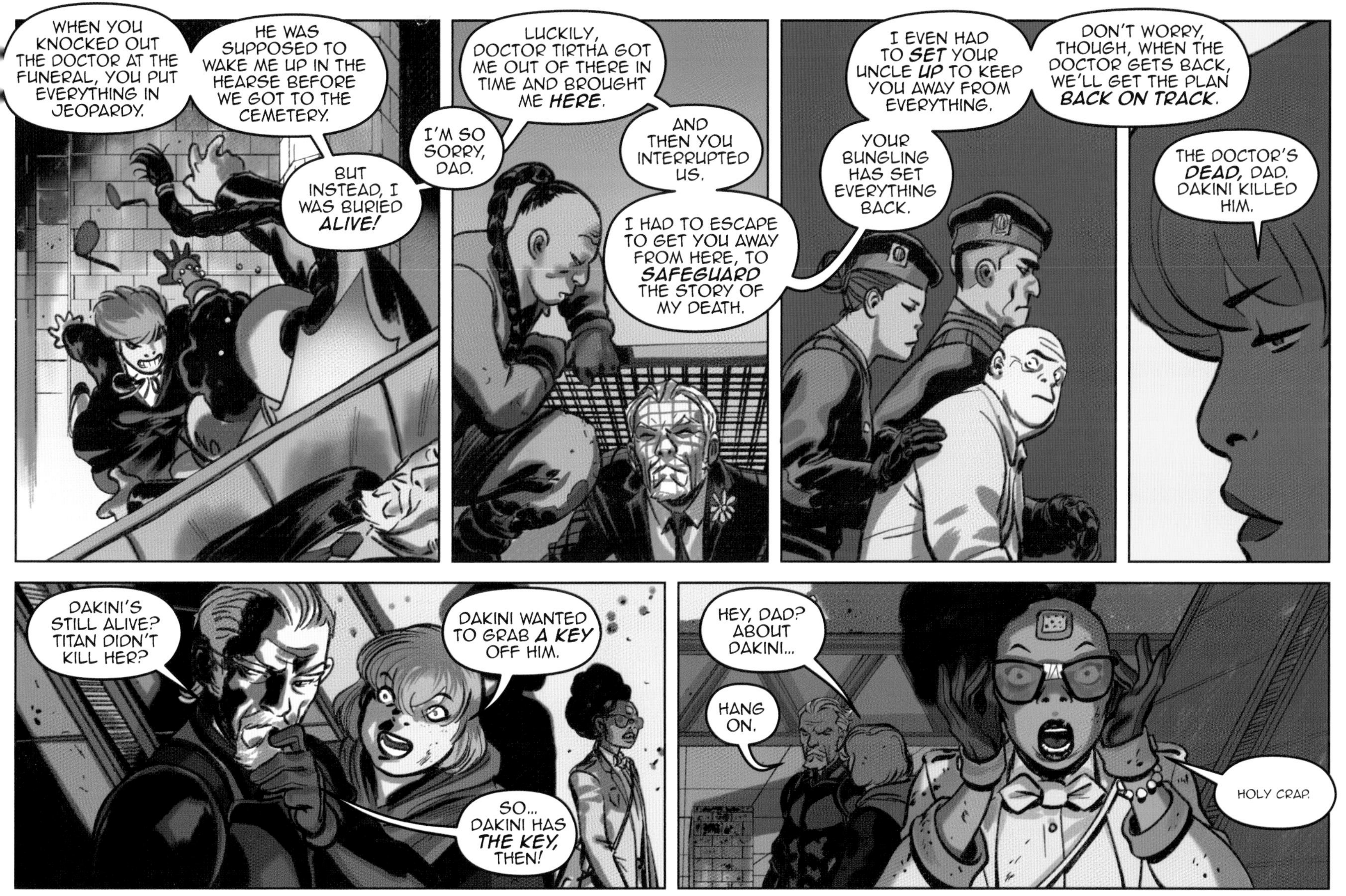

WHEN YOU KNOCKED OUT THE DOCTOR AT THE FUNERAL, YOU PUT EVERYTHING IN JEOPARDY.
HE WAS SUPPOSED TO WAKE ME UP IN THE HEARSE BEFORE WE GOT TO THE CEMETERY.
BUT INSTEAD, I WAS BURIED ALIVE!
I'M SO SORRY, DAD.
LUCKILY, DOCTOR TIRTHA GOT ME OUT OF THERE IN TIME AND BROUGHT ME HERE.
AND THEN YOU INTERRUPTED US.
I HAD TO ESCAPE TO GET YOU AWAY FROM HERE, TO SAFEGUARD THE STORY OF MY DEATH.
I EVEN HAD TO SET YOUR UNCLE UP TO KEEP YOU AWAY FROM EVERYTHING.
YOUR BUNGLING HAS SET EVERYTHING BACK.
DON'T WORRY, THOUGH, WHEN THE DOCTOR GETS BACK, WE'LL GET THE PLAN BACK ON TRACK.
THE DOCTOR'S DEAD, DAD. DAKINI KILLED HIM.
DAKINI'S STILL ALIVE? TITAN DIDN'T KILL HER?
DAKINI WANTED TO GRAB A KEY OFF HIM.
SO... DAKINI HAS THE KEY, THEN!
HEY, DAD? ABOUT DAKINI...
HANG ON.
HOLY CRAP.

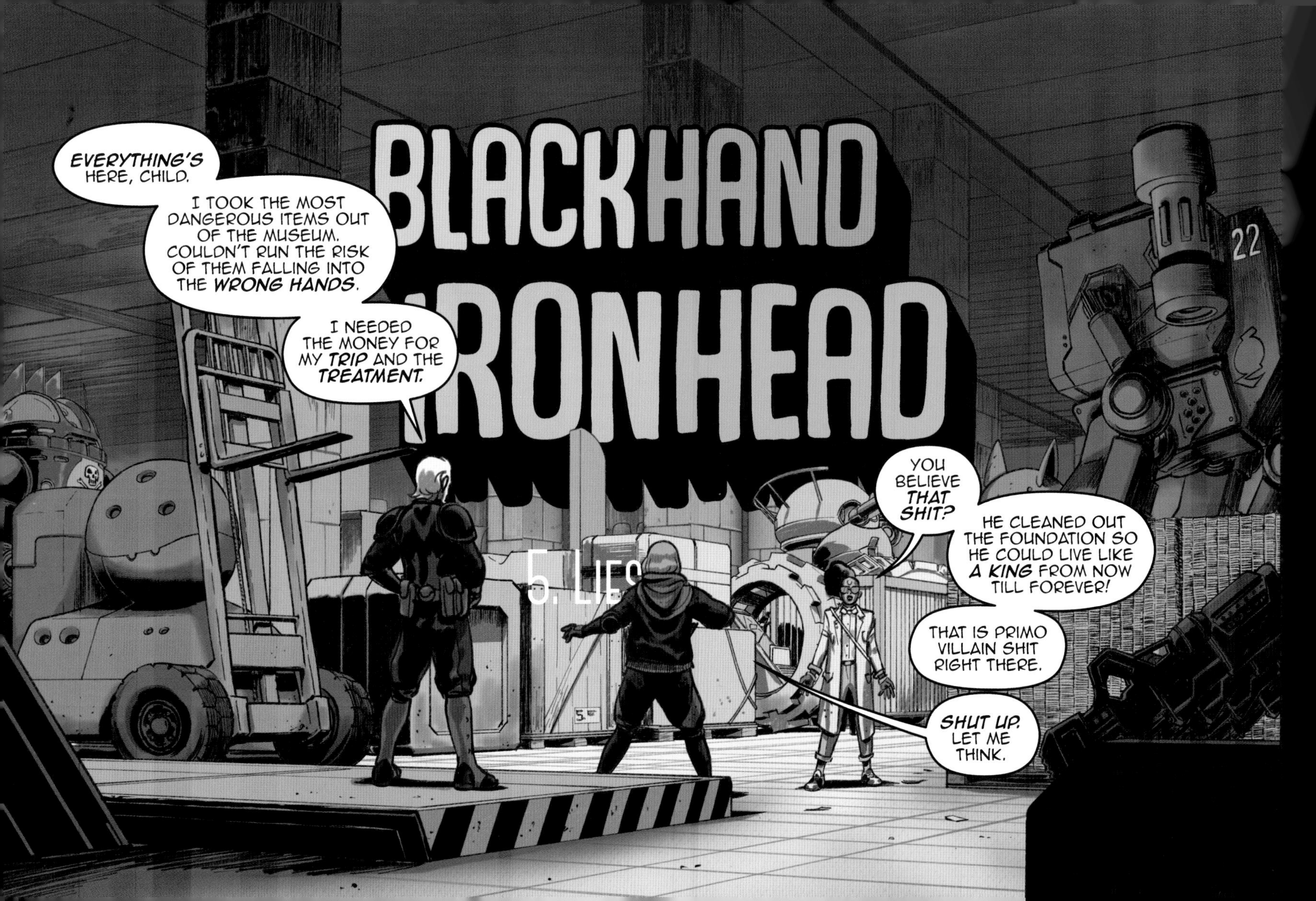
BLACKHAND IRONHEAD
5. LIES
EVERYTHING'S HERE, CHILD.
I TOOK THE MOST DANGEROUS ITEMS OUT OF THE MUSEUM. COULDN'T RUN THE RISK OF THEM FALLING INTO THE WRONG HANDS.
I NEEDED THE MONEY FOR MY TRIP AND THE TREATMENT.
YOU BELIEVE THAT SHIT?
HE CLEANED OUT THE FOUNDATION SO HE COULD LIVE LIKE A KING FROM NOW TILL FOREVER!
THAT IS PRIMO VILLAIN SHIT RIGHT THERE.
SHUT UP. LET ME THINK.

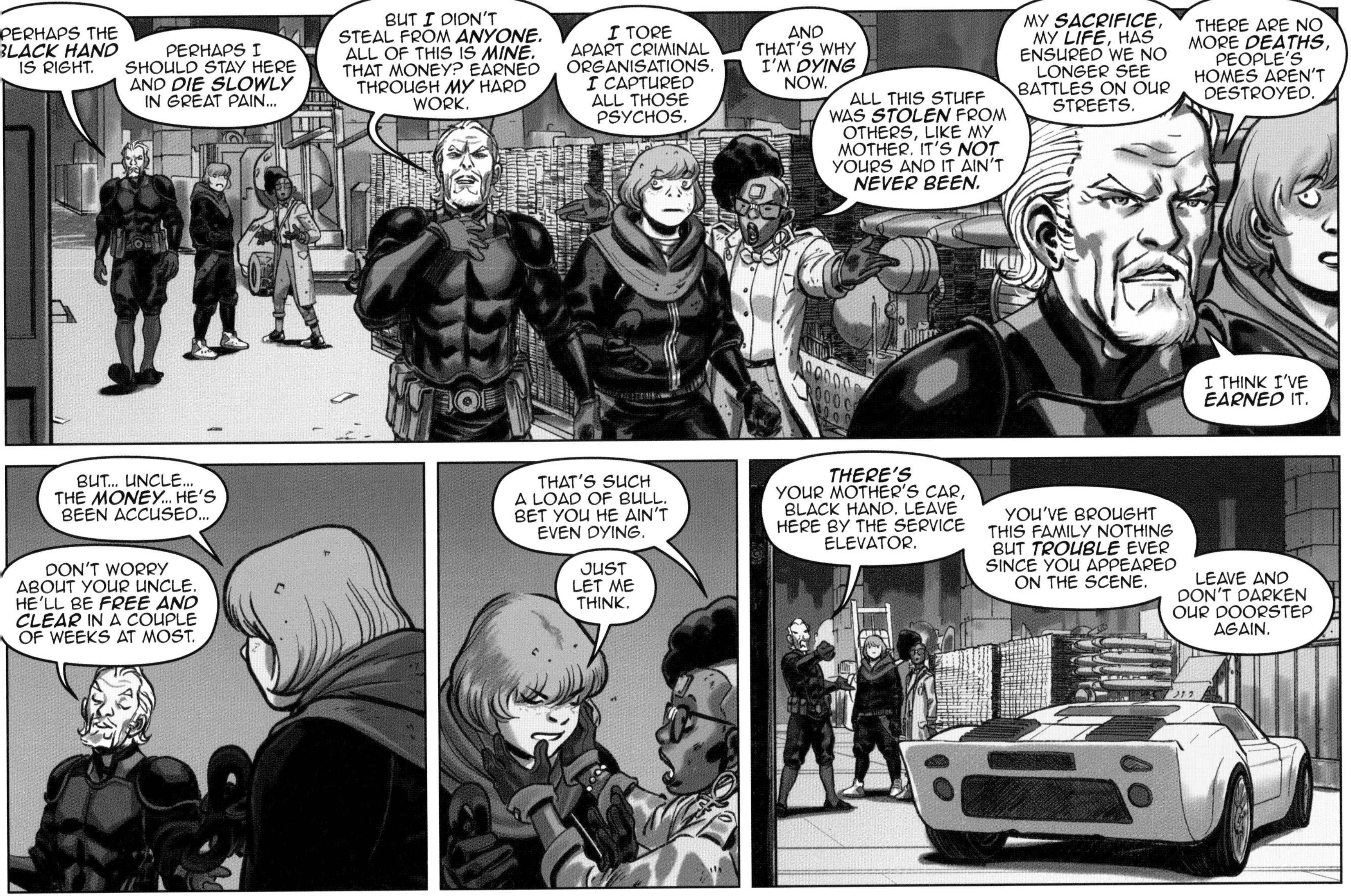
PERHAPS THE BLACK HAND IS RIGHT.
PERHAPS I SHOULD STAY HERE AND DIE SLOWLY IN GREAT PAIN...
BUT I DIDN'T STEAL FROM ANYONE. ALL OF THIS IS MINE. THAT MONEY? EARNED THROUGH MY HARD WORK.
I TORE APART CRIMINAL ORGANISATIONS. I CAPTURED ALL THOSE PSYCHOS.
AND THAT'S WHY I'M DYING NOW.
ALL THIS STUFF WAS STOLEN FROM OTHERS, LIKE MY MOTHER. IT'S NOT YOURS AND IT AIN'T NEVER BEEN.
MY SACRIFICE, MY LIFE, HAS ENSURED WE NO LONGER SEE BATTLES ON OUR STREETS.
THERE ARE NO MORE DEATHS, PEOPLE'S HOMES AREN'T DESTROYED.
I THINK I'VE EARNED IT.
BUT... UNCLE... THE MONEY... HE'S BEEN ACCUSED...
DON'T WORRY ABOUT YOUR UNCLE. HE'LL BE FREE AND CLEAR IN A COUPLE OF WEEKS AT MOST.
THAT'S SUCH A LOAD OF BULL. BET YOU HE AIN'T EVEN DYING.
JUST LET ME THINK.
THERE'S YOUR MOTHER'S CAR, BLACK HAND. LEAVE HERE BY THE SERVICE ELEVATOR.
YOU'VE BROUGHT THIS FAMILY NOTHING BUT TROUBLE EVER SINCE YOU APPEARED ON THE SCENE.
LEAVE AND DON'T DARKEN OUR DOORSTEP AGAIN.

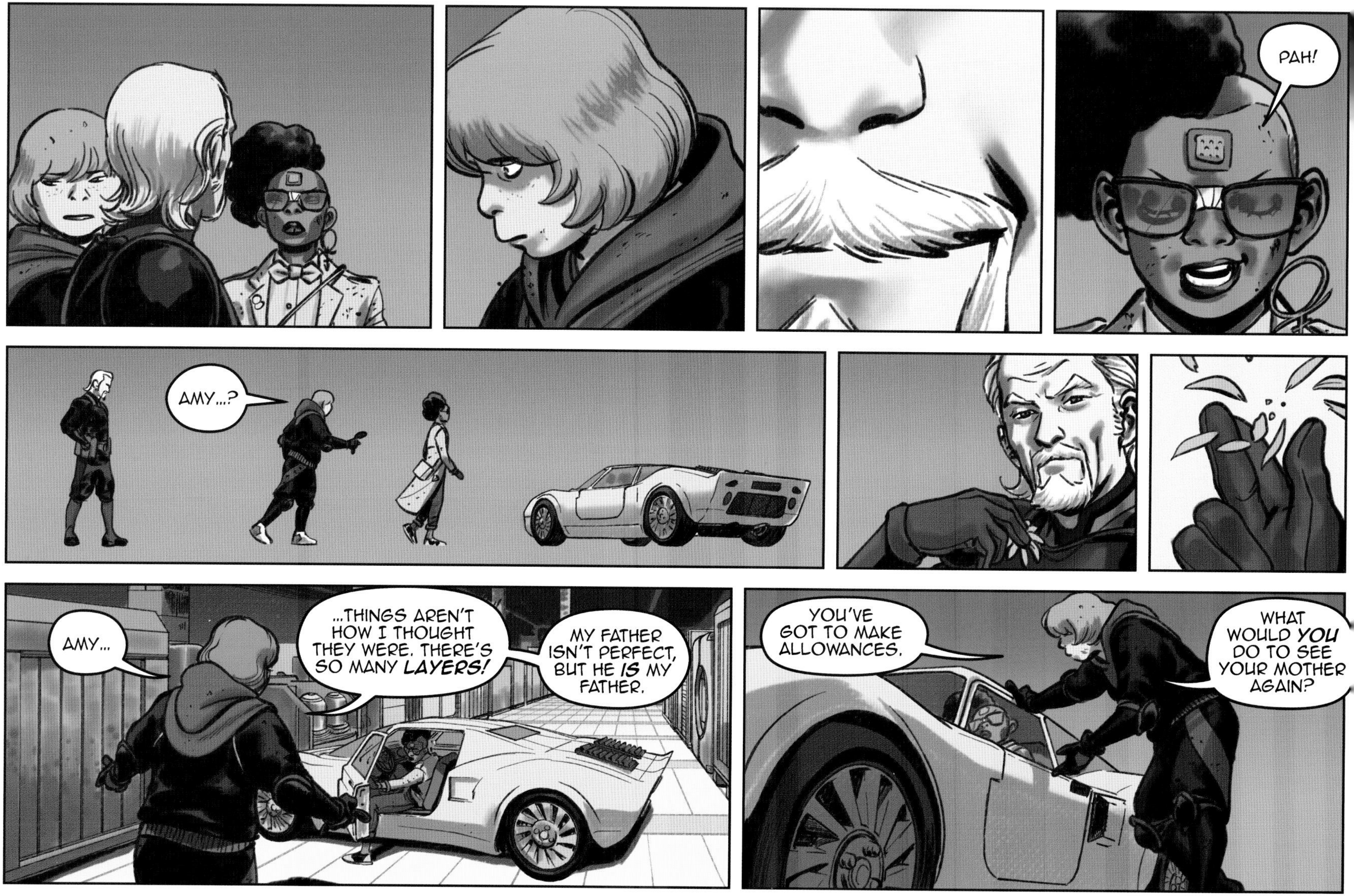
PAH!
AMY...?
AMY...
...THINGS AREN'T HOW I THOUGHT THEY WERE. THERE'S SO MANY LAYERS!
MY FATHER ISN'T PERFECT, BUT HE IS MY FATHER.
YOU'VE GOT TO MAKE ALLOWANCES.
WHAT WOULD YOU DO TO SEE YOUR MOTHER AGAIN?

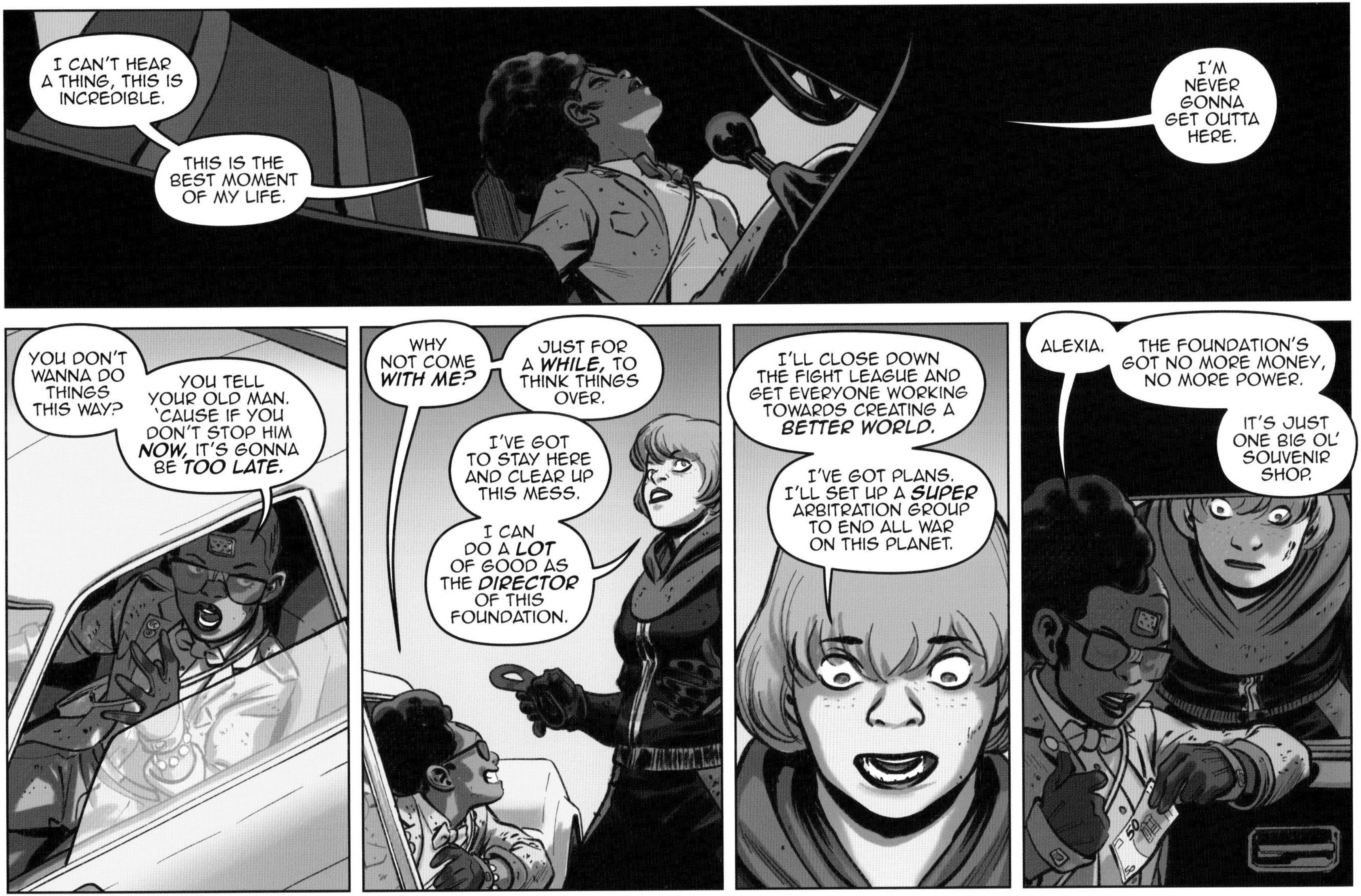
I CAN'T HEAR A THING, THIS IS INCREDIBLE.
THIS IS THE BEST MOMENT OF MY LIFE.
I'M NEVER GONNA GET OUTTA HERE.
YOU DON'T WANNA DO THINGS THIS WAY?
YOU TELL YOUR OLD MAN. 'CAUSE IF YOU DON'T STOP HIM NOW, IT'S GONNA BE TOO LATE.
WHY NOT COME WITH ME?
JUST FOR A WHILE, TO THINK THINGS OVER.
I'VE GOT TO STAY HERE AND CLEAR UP THIS MESS.
I CAN DO A LOT OF GOOD AS THE DIRECTOR OF THIS FOUNDATION.
I'LL CLOSE DOWN THE FIGHT LEAGUE AND GET EVERYONE WORKING TOWARDS CREATING A BETTER WORLD.
I'VE GOT PLANS. I'LL SET UP A SUPER ARBITRATION GROUP TO END ALL WAR ON THIS PLANET.
ALEXIA.
THE FOUNDATION'S GOT NO MORE MONEY, NO MORE POWER.
IT'S JUST ONE BIG OL' SOUVENIR SHOP.

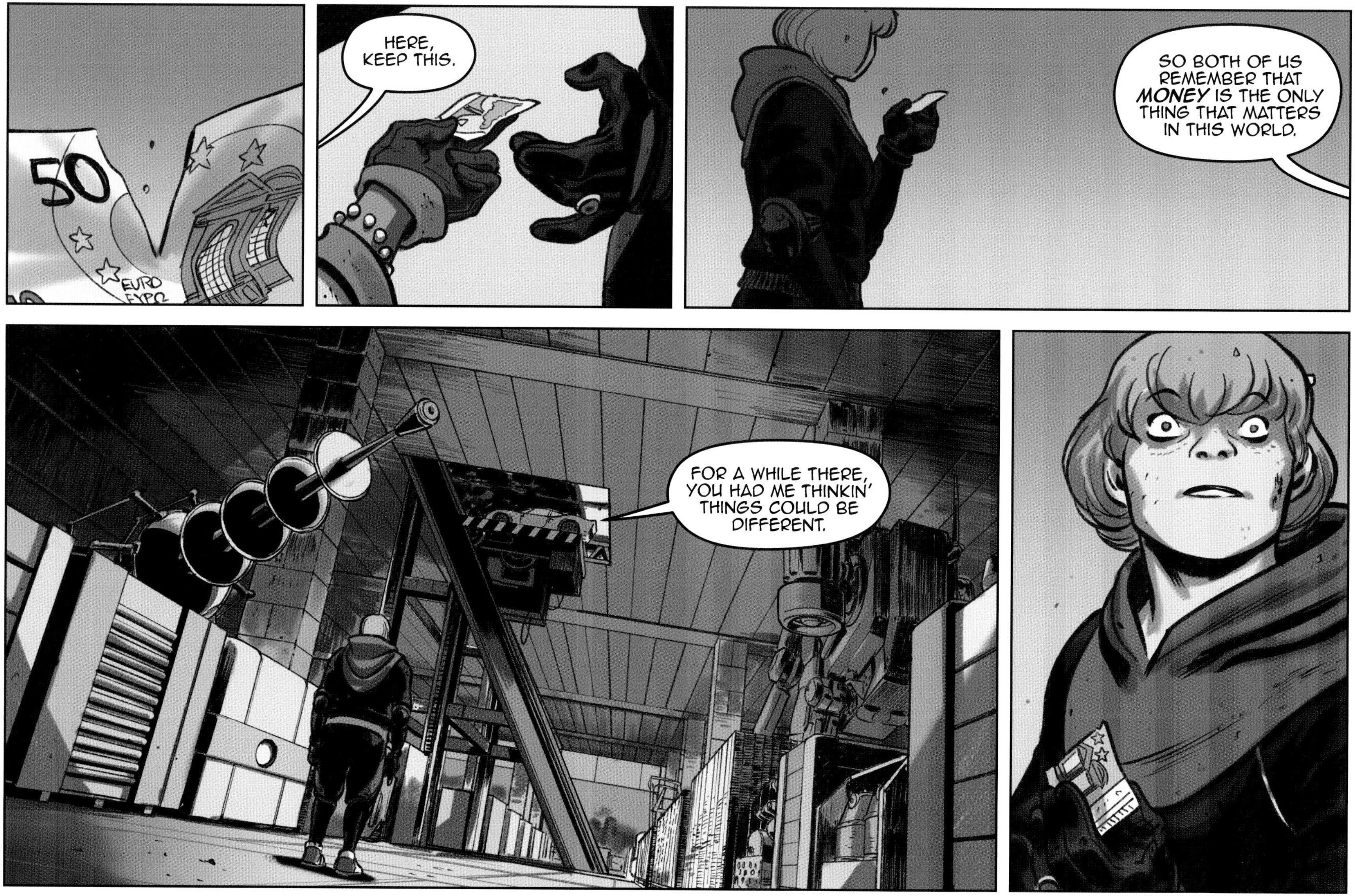
50
EURO
HERE, KEEP THIS.
SO BOTH OF US REMEMBER THAT *MONEY* IS THE ONLY THING THAT MATTERS IN THIS WORLD.
FOR A WHILE THERE, YOU HAD ME THINKIN' THINGS COULD BE DIFFERENT.

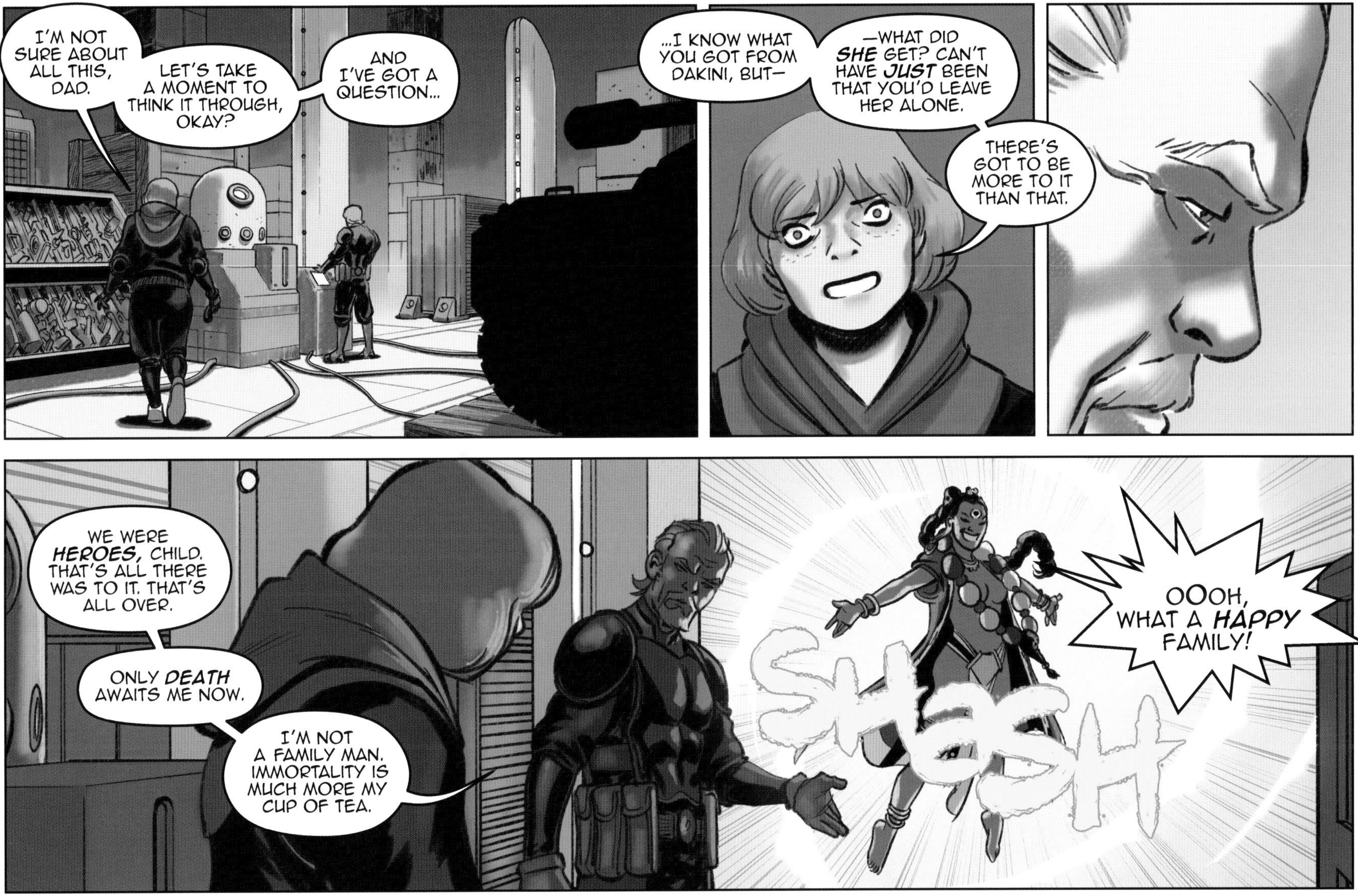
I'M NOT SURE ABOUT ALL THIS, DAD.
LET'S TAKE A MOMENT TO THINK IT THROUGH, OKAY?
AND I'VE GOT A QUESTION...
...I KNOW WHAT YOU GOT FROM DAKINI, BUT—
—WHAT DID SHE GET? CAN'T HAVE JUST BEEN THAT YOU'D LEAVE HER ALONE.
THERE'S GOT TO BE MORE TO IT THAN THAT.
WE WERE HEROES, CHILD. THAT'S ALL THERE WAS TO IT. THAT'S ALL OVER.
ONLY DEATH AWAITS ME NOW.
I'M NOT A FAMILY MAN. IMMORTALITY IS MUCH MORE MY CUP OF TEA.
SHASH
OOOH, WHAT A HAPPY FAMILY!

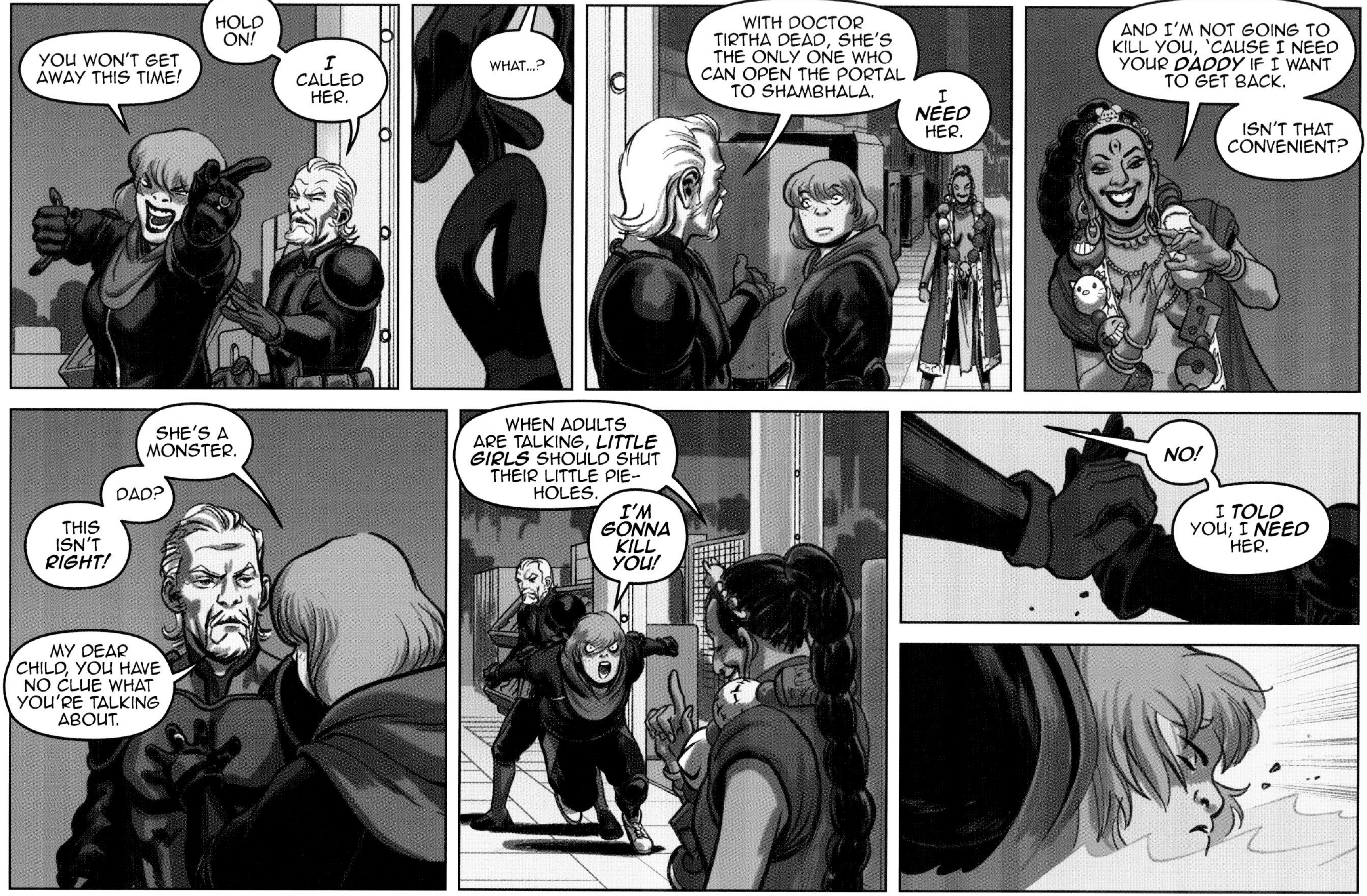
YOU WON'T GET AWAY THIS TIME!
HOLD ON!
I CALLED HER.
WHAT...?
WITH DOCTOR TIRTHA DEAD, SHE'S THE ONLY ONE WHO CAN OPEN THE PORTAL TO SHAMBHALA.
I NEED HER.
AND I'M NOT GOING TO KILL YOU, 'CAUSE I NEED YOUR DADDY IF I WANT TO GET BACK.
ISN'T THAT CONVENIENT?
SHE'S A MONSTER.
DAD?
THIS ISN'T RIGHT!
MY DEAR CHILD, YOU HAVE NO CLUE WHAT YOU'RE TALKING ABOUT.
WHEN ADULTS ARE TALKING, LITTLE GIRLS SHOULD SHUT THEIR LITTLE PIE-HOLES.
I'M GONNA KILL YOU!
NO!
I TOLD YOU; I NEED HER.

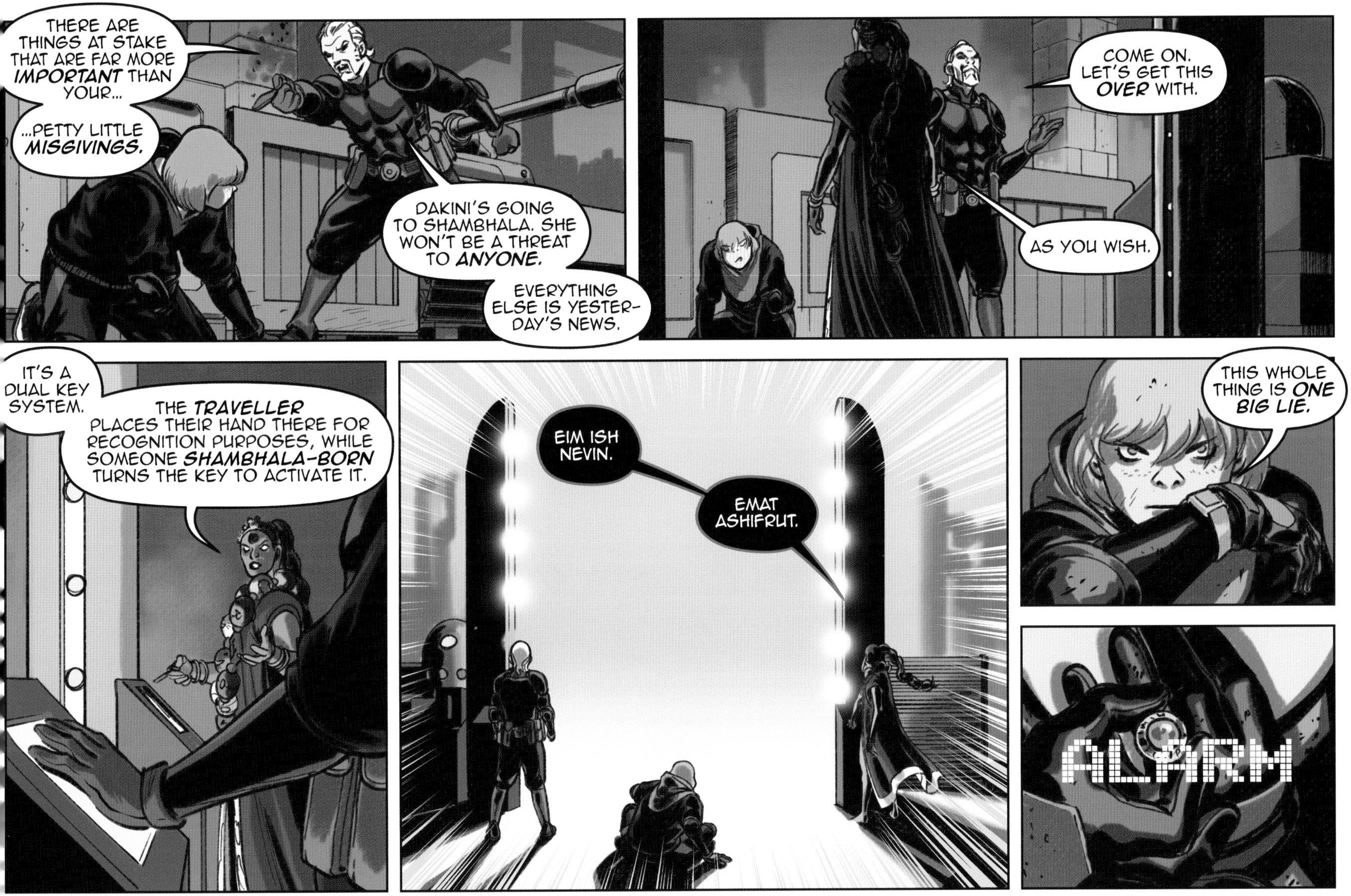
THERE ARE THINGS AT STAKE THAT ARE FAR MORE IMPORTANT THAN YOUR...
...PETTY LITTLE MISGIVINGS.
DAKINI'S GOING TO SHAMBHALA. SHE WON'T BE A THREAT TO ANYONE.
EVERYTHING ELSE IS YESTER-DAY'S NEWS.
COME ON. LET'S GET THIS OVER WITH.
AS YOU WISH.
IT'S A DUAL KEY SYSTEM.
THE TRAVELLER PLACES THEIR HAND THERE FOR RECOGNITION PURPOSES, WHILE SOMEONE SHAMBHALA-BORN TURNS THE KEY TO ACTIVATE IT.
EIM ISH NEVIN.
EMAT ASHIFRUT.
THIS WHOLE THING IS ONE BIG LIE.
ALARM

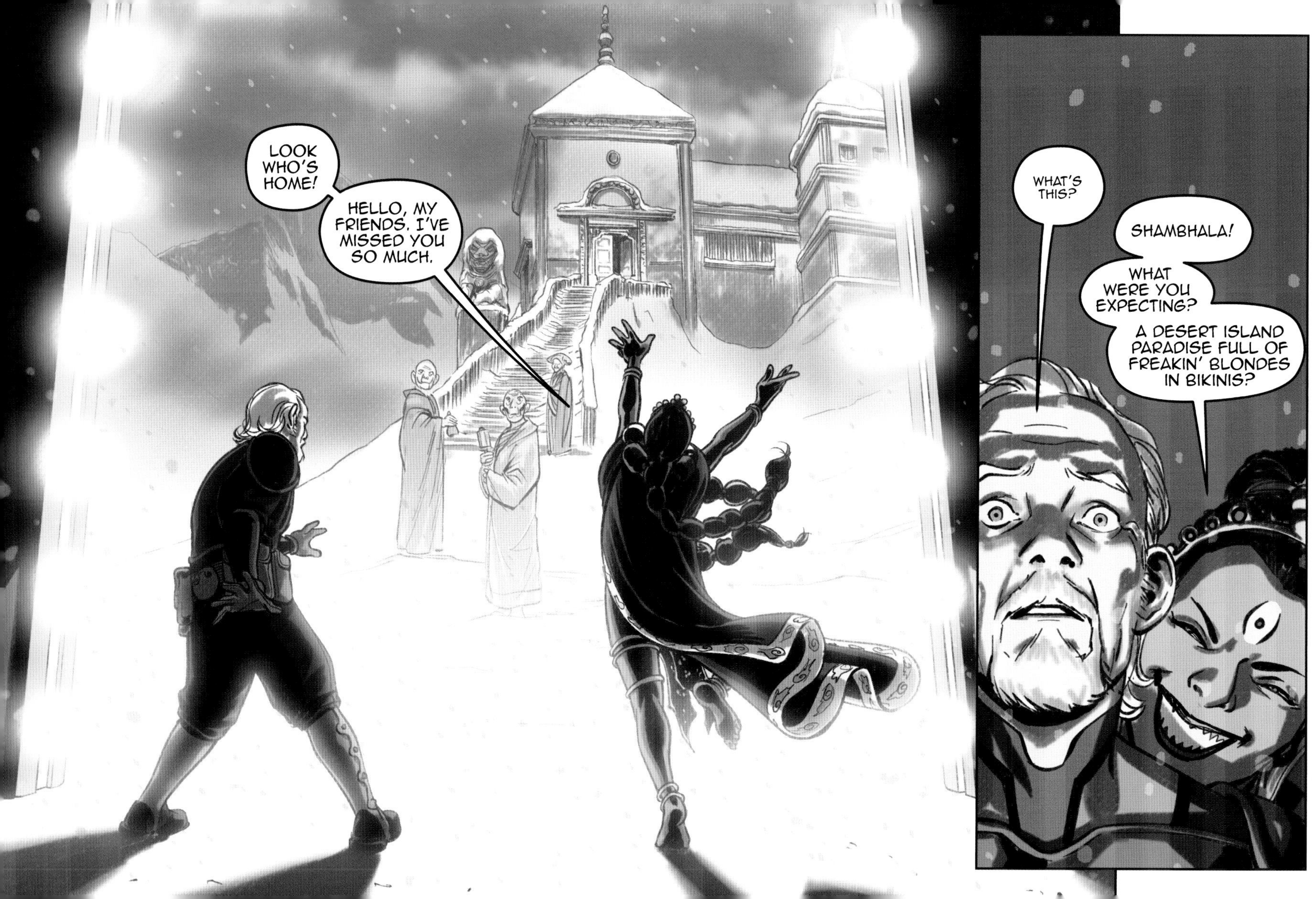
LOOK WHO'S HOME!
HELLO, MY FRIENDS. I'VE MISSED YOU SO MUCH.
WHAT'S THIS?
SHAMBHALA!
WHAT WERE YOU EXPECTING?
A DESERT ISLAND PARADISE FULL OF FREAKIN' BLONDES IN BIKINIS?

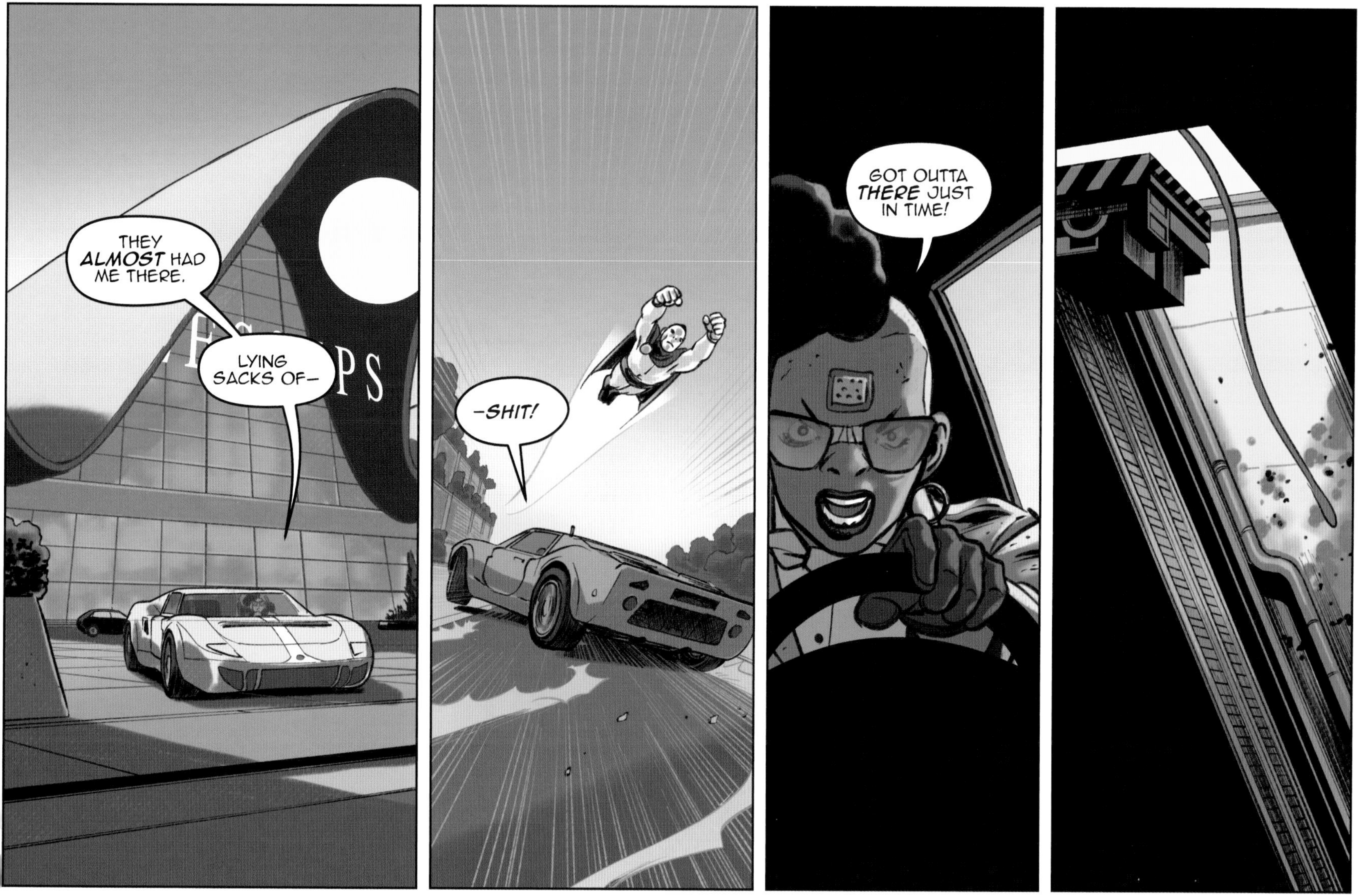
THEY ALMOST HAD ME THERE.
LYING SACKS OF—
—SHIT!
GOT OUTTA THERE JUST IN TIME!

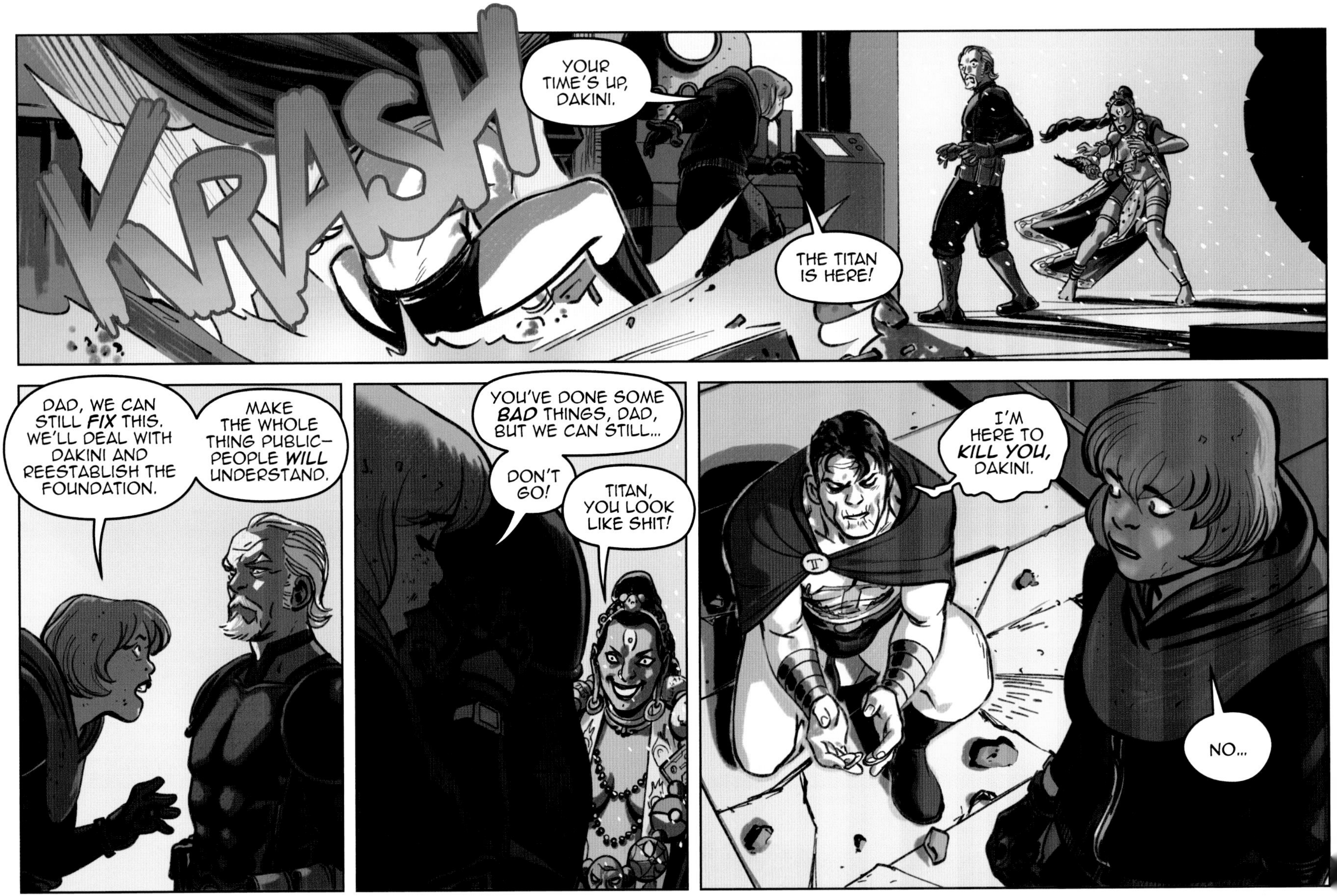
KRASH
YOUR TIME'S UP, DAKINI.
THE TITAN IS HERE!
DAD, WE CAN STILL FIX THIS. WE'LL DEAL WITH DAKINI AND REESTABLISH THE FOUNDATION.
MAKE THE WHOLE THING PUBLIC— PEOPLE WILL UNDERSTAND.
YOU'VE DONE SOME BAD THINGS, DAD, BUT WE CAN STILL...
DON'T GO!
TITAN, YOU LOOK LIKE SHIT!
I'M HERE TO KILL YOU, DAKINI.
NO...

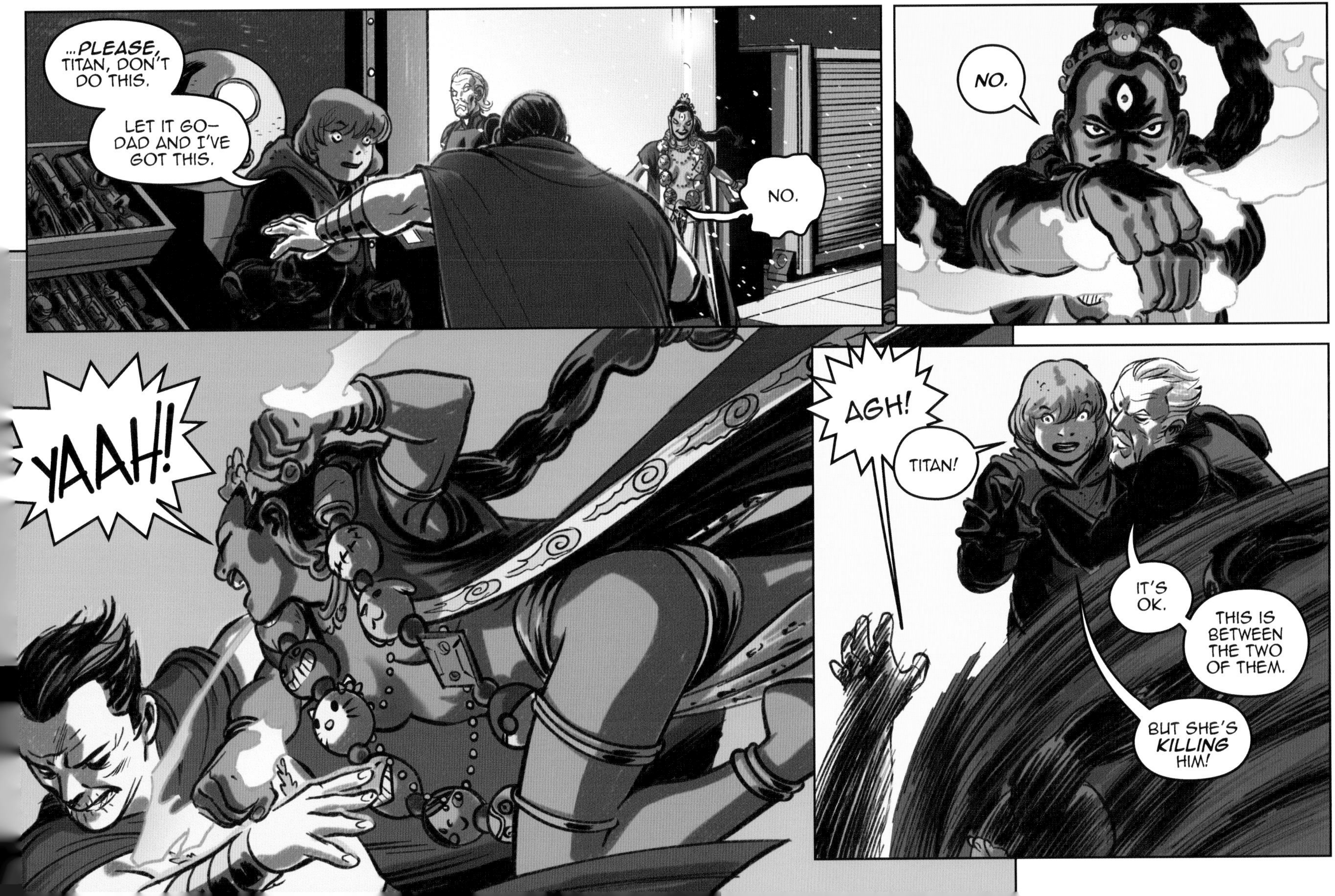
...PLEASE, TITAN, DON'T DO THIS.
LET IT GO— DAD AND I'VE GOT THIS.
NO.
NO.
YAAH!
AGH!
TITAN!
IT'S OK.
THIS IS BETWEEN THE TWO OF THEM.
BUT SHE'S KILLING HIM!

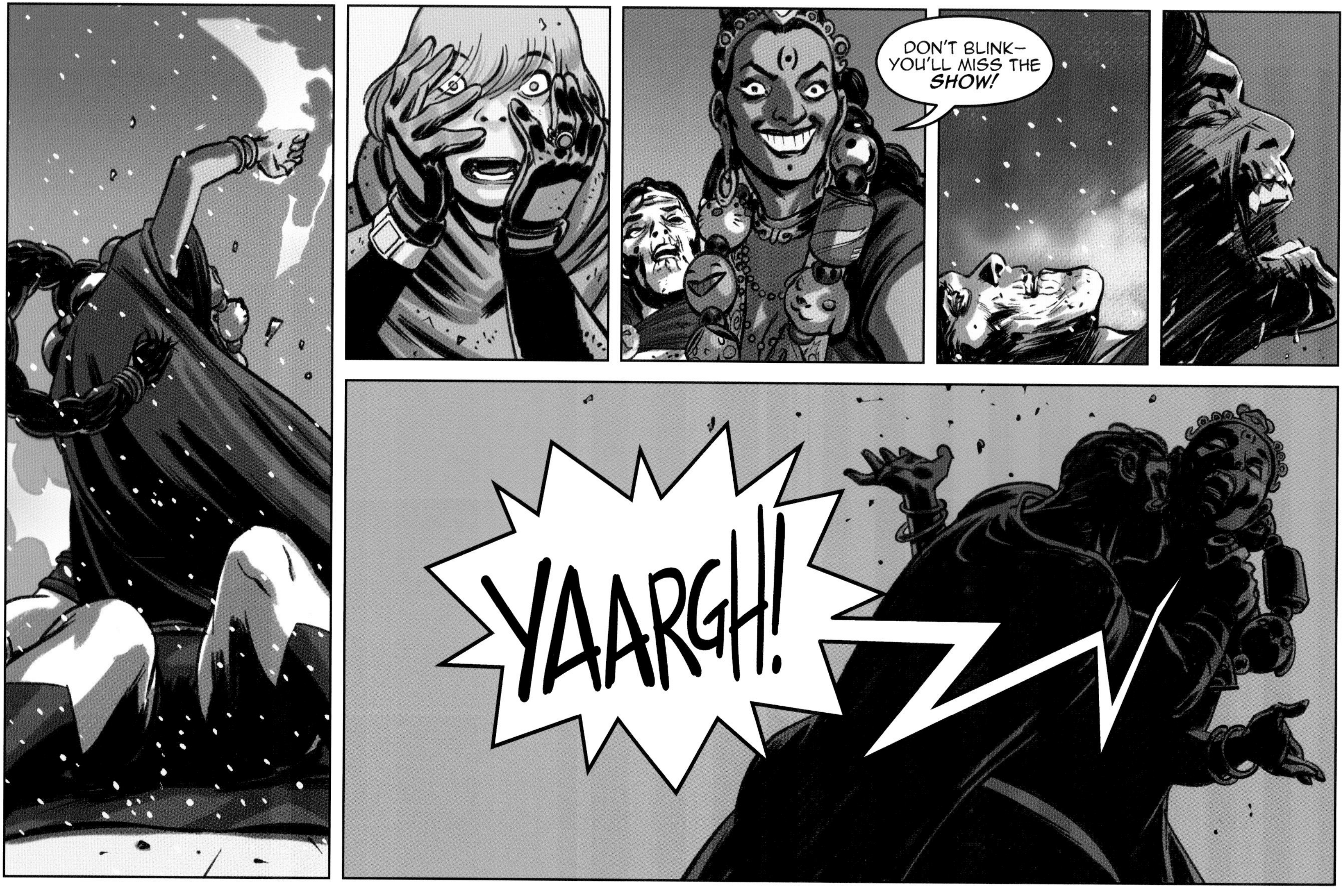
DON'T BLINK—
YOU'LL MISS THE
SHOW!
YAARGH!

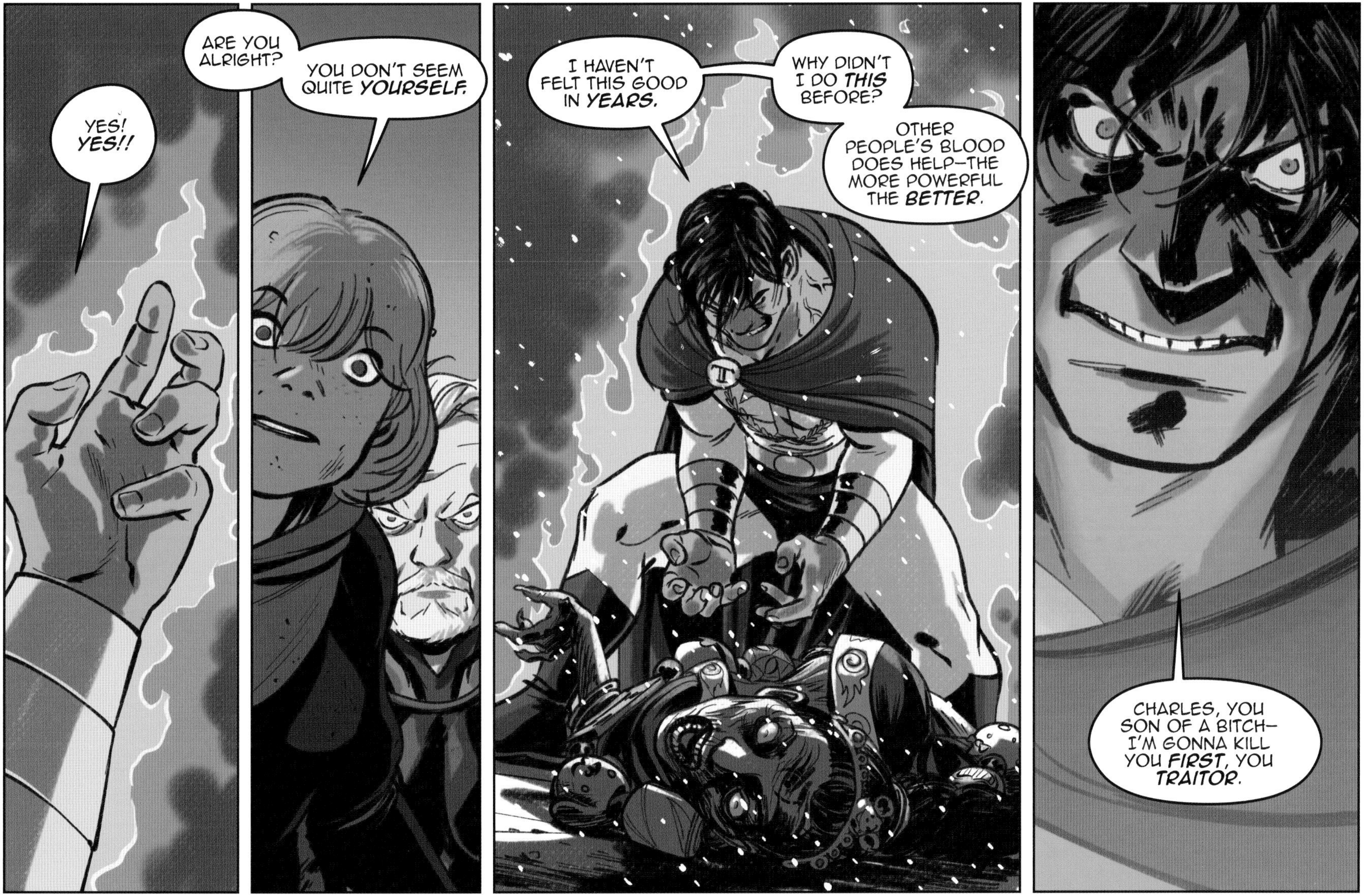
YES! YES!!
ARE YOU ALRIGHT?
YOU DON'T SEEM QUITE YOURSELF.
I HAVEN'T FELT THIS GOOD IN YEARS.
WHY DIDN'T I DO THIS BEFORE?
OTHER PEOPLE'S BLOOD DOES HELP—THE MORE POWERFUL THE BETTER.
CHARLES, YOU SON OF A BITCH— I'M GONNA KILL YOU FIRST, YOU TRAITOR.

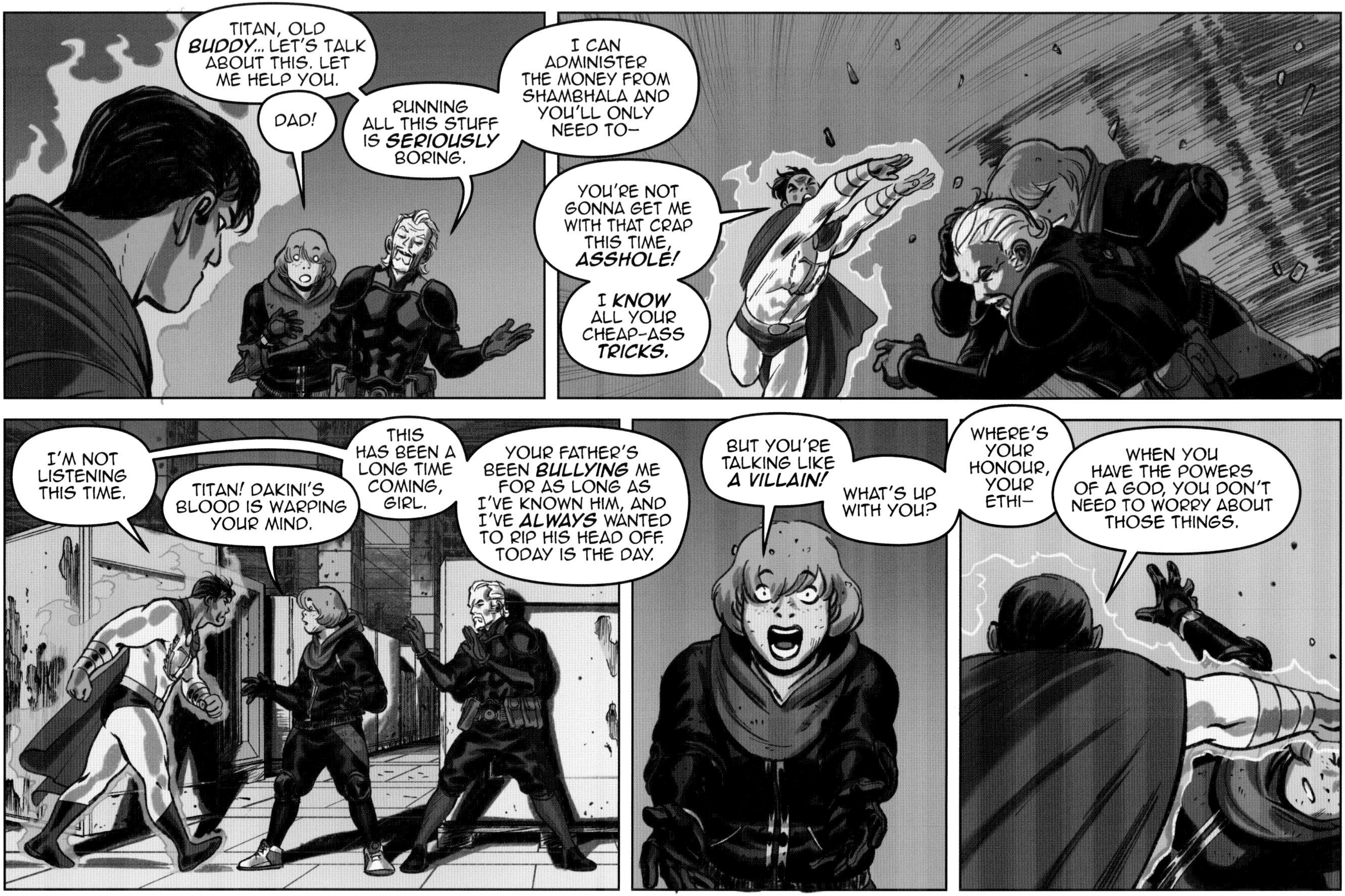
TITAN, OLD BUDDY... LET'S TALK ABOUT THIS. LET ME HELP YOU.
DAD!
RUNNING ALL THIS STUFF IS SERIOUSLY BORING.
I CAN ADMINISTER THE MONEY FROM SHAMBHALA AND YOU'LL ONLY NEED TO–
YOU'RE NOT GONNA GET ME WITH THAT CRAP THIS TIME, ASSHOLE!
I KNOW ALL YOUR CHEAP-ASS TRICKS.
I'M NOT LISTENING THIS TIME.
TITAN! DAKINI'S BLOOD IS WARPING YOUR MIND.
THIS HAS BEEN A LONG TIME COMING, GIRL.
YOUR FATHER'S BEEN BULLYING ME FOR AS LONG AS I'VE KNOWN HIM, AND I'VE ALWAYS WANTED TO RIP HIS HEAD OFF. TODAY IS THE DAY.
BUT YOU'RE TALKING LIKE A VILLAIN!
WHAT'S UP WITH YOU?
WHERE'S YOUR HONOUR, YOUR ETHI–
WHEN YOU HAVE THE POWERS OF A GOD, YOU DON'T NEED TO WORRY ABOUT THOSE THINGS.

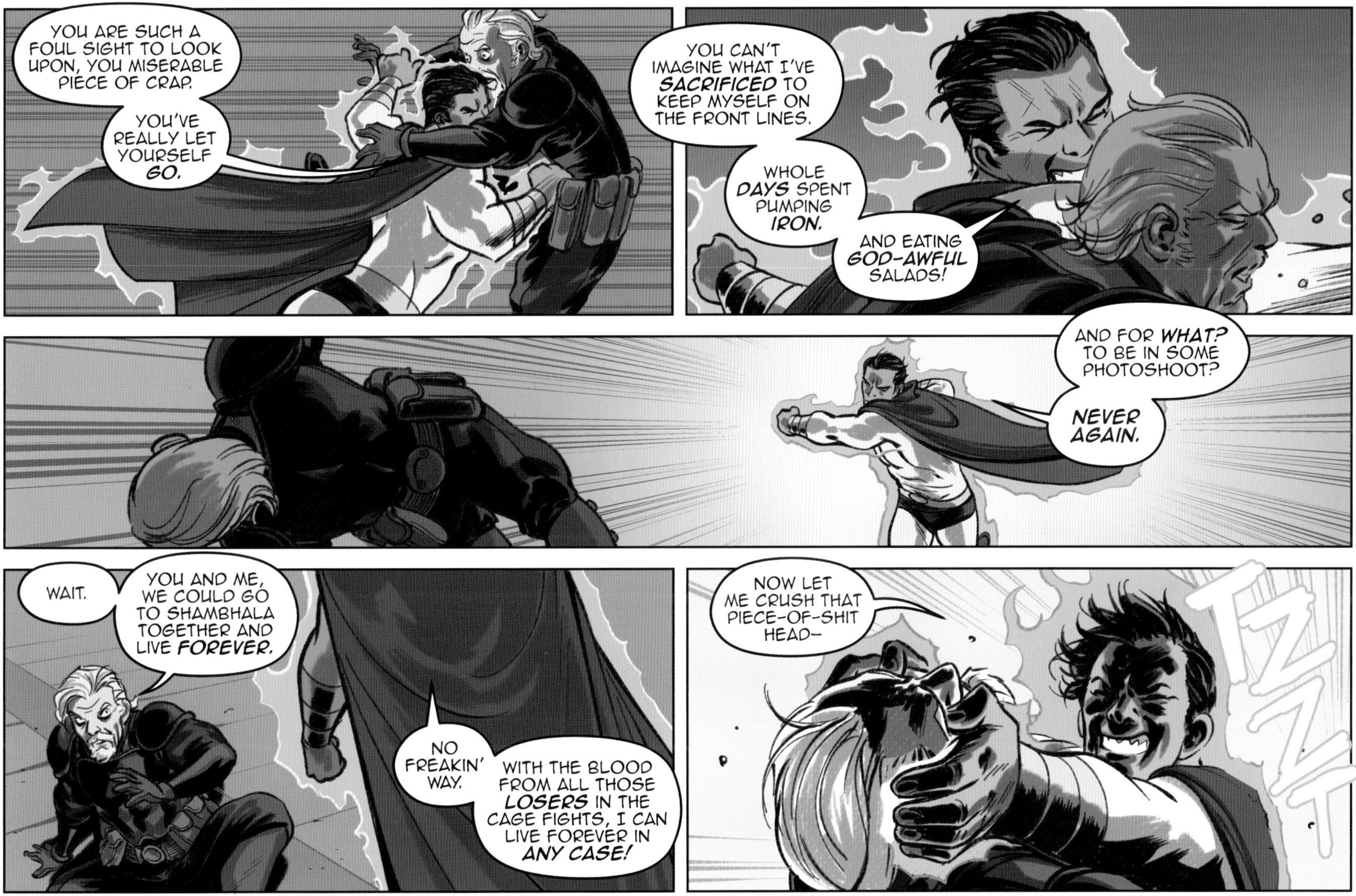
YOU ARE SUCH A FOUL SIGHT TO LOOK UPON, YOU MISERABLE PIECE OF CRAP.
YOU'VE REALLY LET YOURSELF GO.
YOU CAN'T IMAGINE WHAT I'VE SACRIFICED TO KEEP MYSELF ON THE FRONT LINES.
WHOLE DAYS SPENT PUMPING IRON.
AND EATING GOD-AWFUL SALADS!
AND FOR WHAT? TO BE IN SOME PHOTOSHOOT?
NEVER AGAIN.
WAIT.
YOU AND ME, WE COULD GO TO SHAMBHALA TOGETHER AND LIVE FOREVER.
NO FREAKIN' WAY.
WITH THE BLOOD FROM ALL THOSE LOSERS IN THE CAGE FIGHTS, I CAN LIVE FOREVER IN ANY CASE!
NOW LET ME CRUSH THAT PIECE-OF-SHIT HEAD–
TZZT

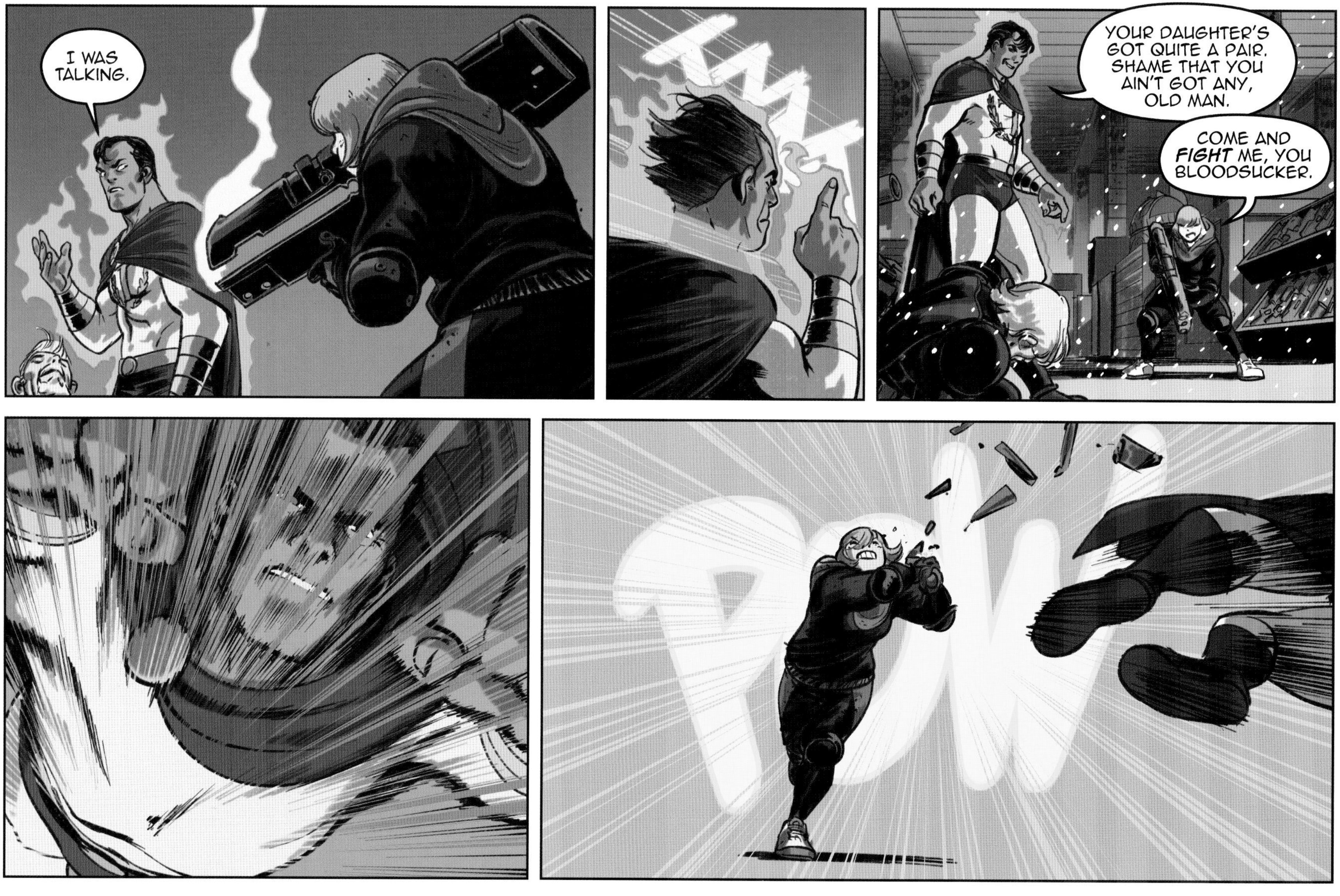
I WAS TALKING.
TZZT
YOUR DAUGHTER'S GOT QUITE A PAIR. SHAME THAT YOU AIN'T GOT ANY, OLD MAN.
COME AND **FIGHT** ME, YOU BLOODSUCKER.
POW

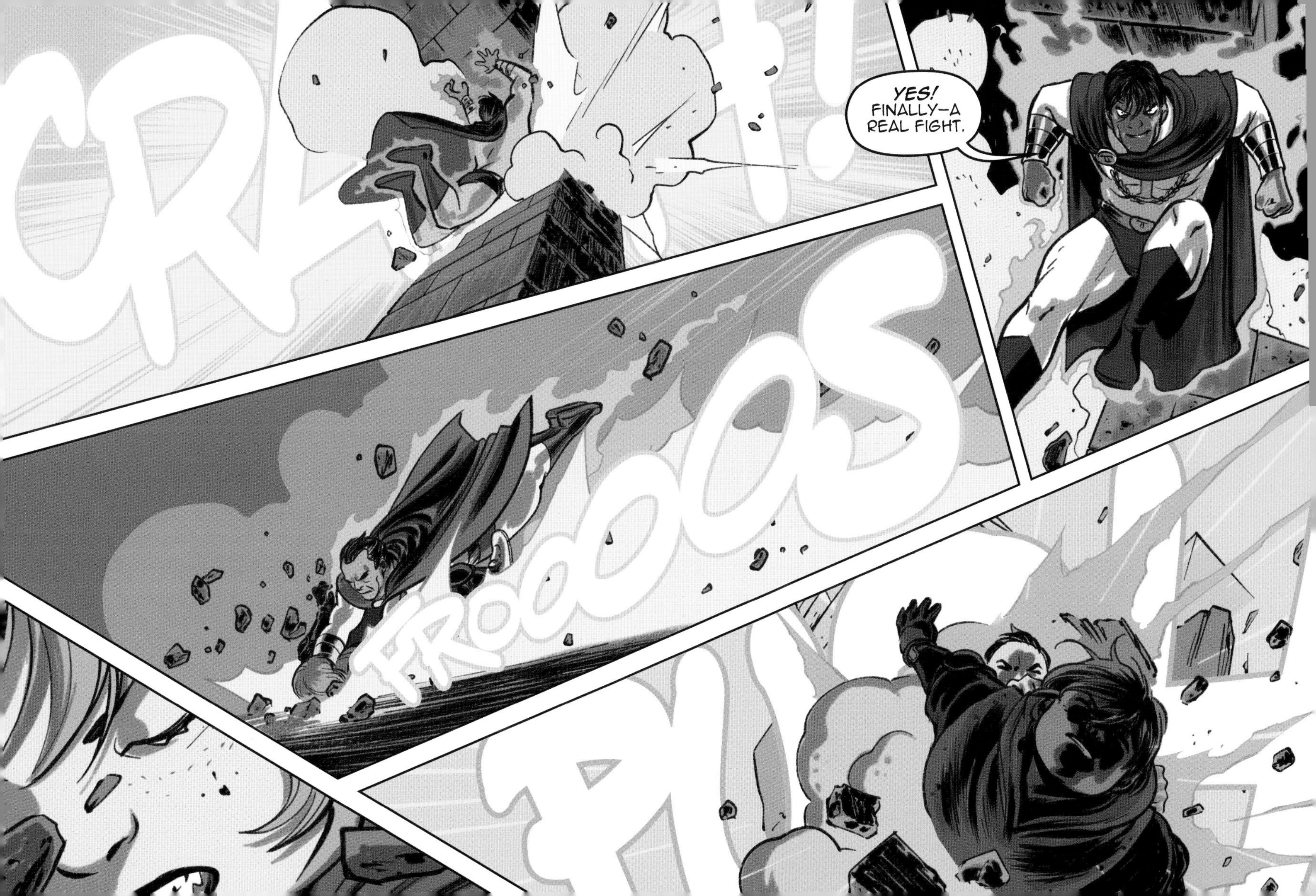
YES! FINALLY—A REAL FIGHT.

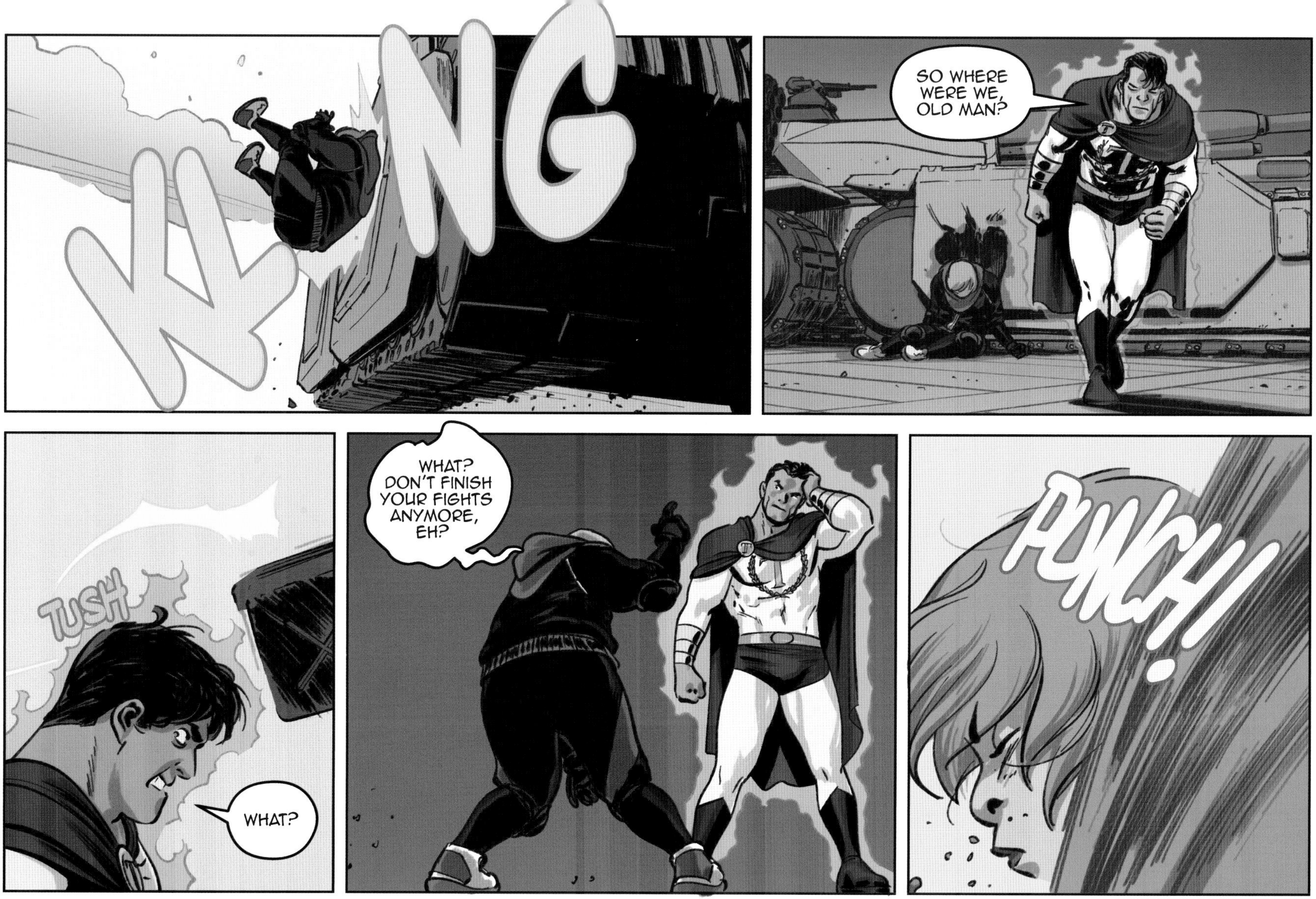
KLANG
SO WHERE WERE WE, OLD MAN?
TUSH
WHAT?
WHAT? DON'T FINISH YOUR FIGHTS ANYMORE, EH?
PUNCH!

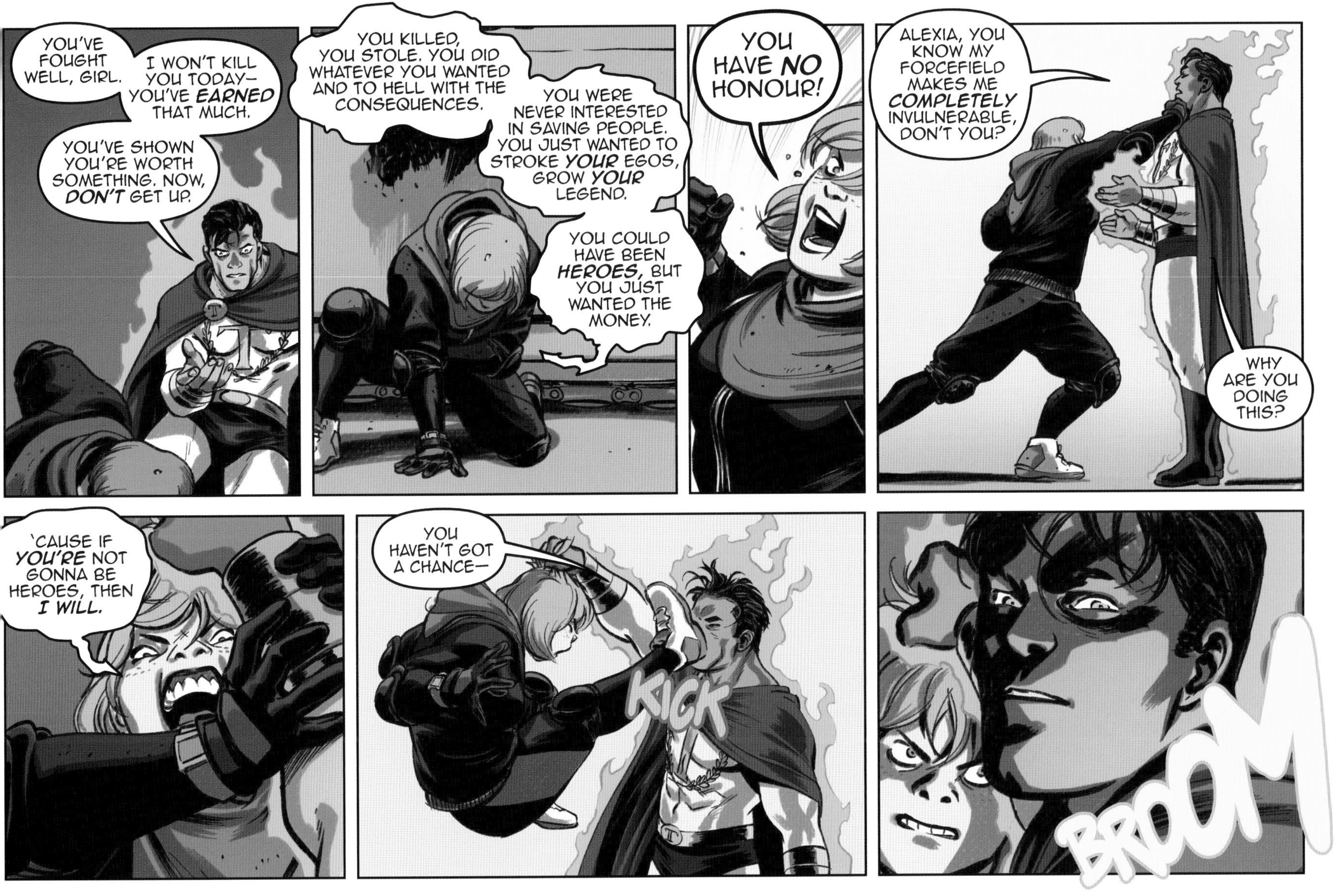
YOU'VE FOUGHT WELL, GIRL.
I WON'T KILL YOU TODAY—YOU'VE EARNED THAT MUCH.
YOU'VE SHOWN YOU'RE WORTH SOMETHING. NOW, DON'T GET UP.
YOU KILLED, YOU STOLE. YOU DID WHATEVER YOU WANTED AND TO HELL WITH THE CONSEQUENCES.
YOU WERE NEVER INTERESTED IN SAVING PEOPLE. YOU JUST WANTED TO STROKE YOUR EGOS, GROW YOUR LEGEND.
YOU COULD HAVE BEEN HEROES, BUT YOU JUST WANTED THE MONEY.
YOU HAVE NO HONOUR!
ALEXIA, YOU KNOW MY FORCEFIELD MAKES ME COMPLETELY INVULNERABLE, DON'T YOU?
WHY ARE YOU DOING THIS?
'CAUSE IF YOU'RE NOT GONNA BE HEROES, THEN I WILL.
YOU HAVEN'T GOT A CHANCE—
KICK
BROOM

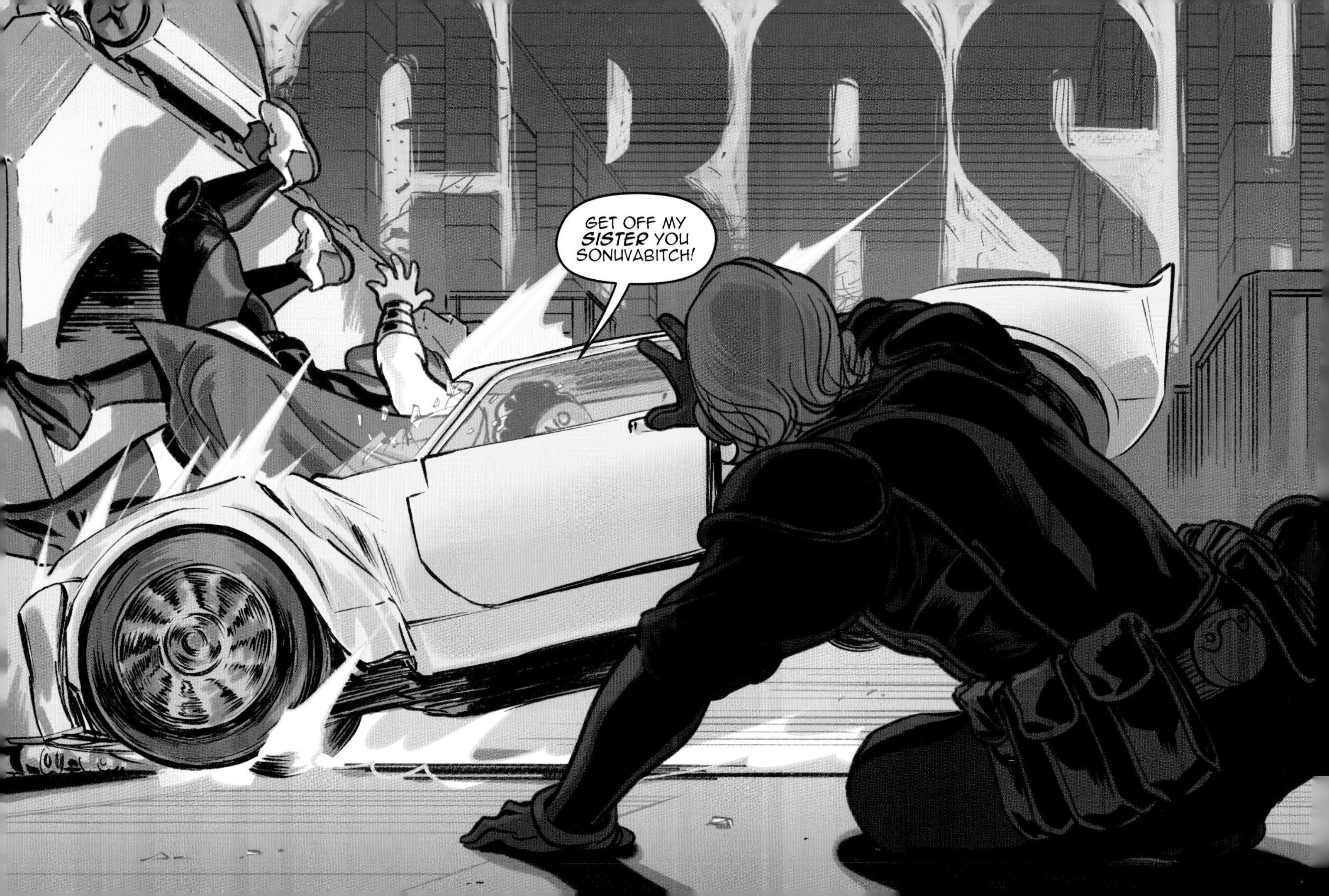
GET OFF MY *SISTER* YOU SONUVABITCH!

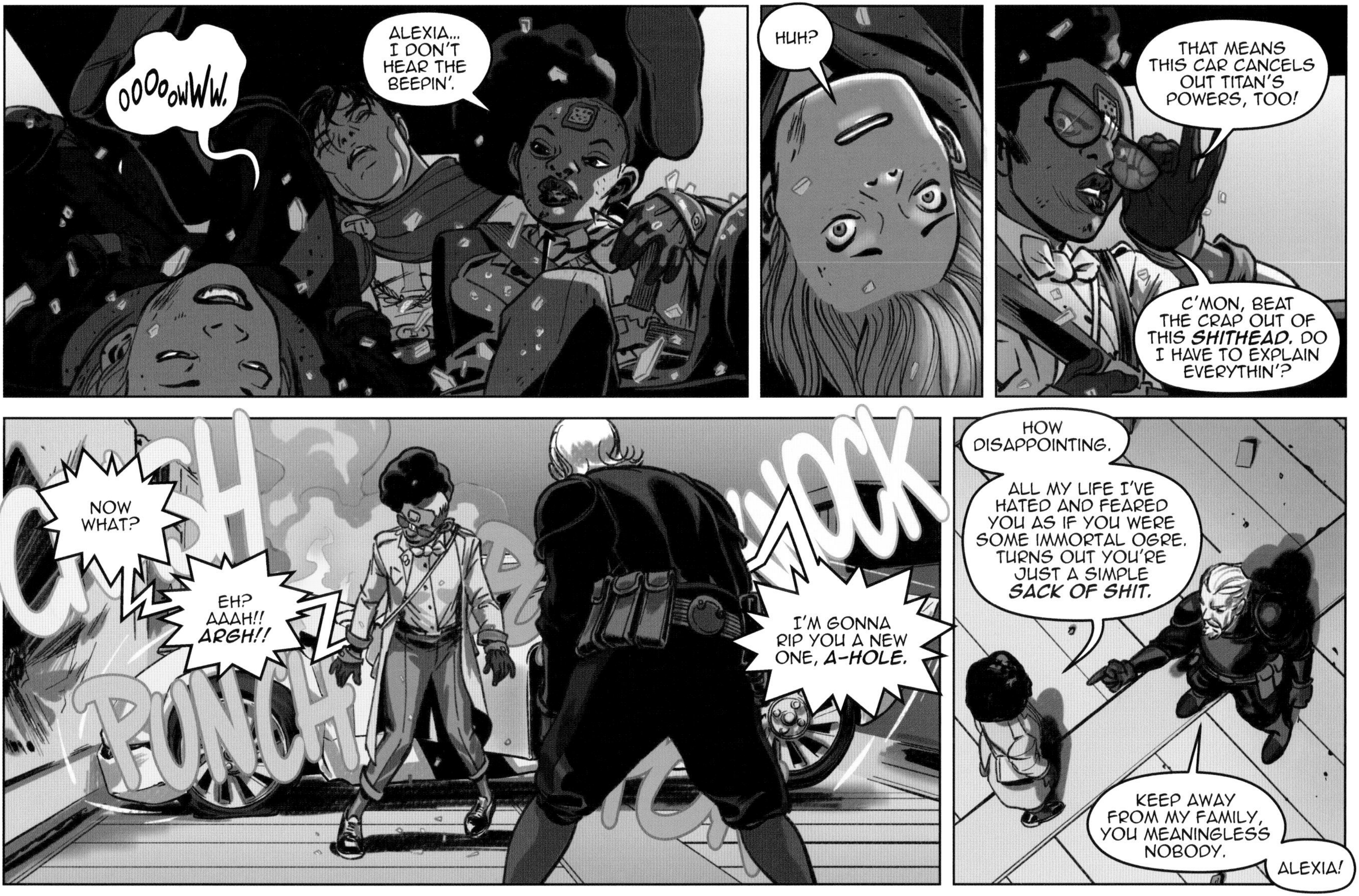
OOOOOWWW.
ALEXIA... I DON'T HEAR THE BEEPIN'.
HUH?
THAT MEANS THIS CAR CANCELS OUT TITAN'S POWERS, TOO!
C'MON, BEAT THE CRAP OUT OF THIS ***SHITHEAD.*** DO I HAVE TO EXPLAIN EVERYTHIN'?
NOW WHAT?
EH? AAAH!! ***ARGH!!***
PUNCH
I'M GONNA RIP YOU A NEW ONE, ***A-HOLE.***
HOW DISAPPOINTING.
ALL MY LIFE I'VE HATED AND FEARED YOU AS IF YOU WERE SOME IMMORTAL OGRE. TURNS OUT YOU'RE JUST A SIMPLE ***SACK OF SHIT.***
KEEP AWAY FROM MY FAMILY, YOU MEANINGLESS NOBODY.
ALEXIA!

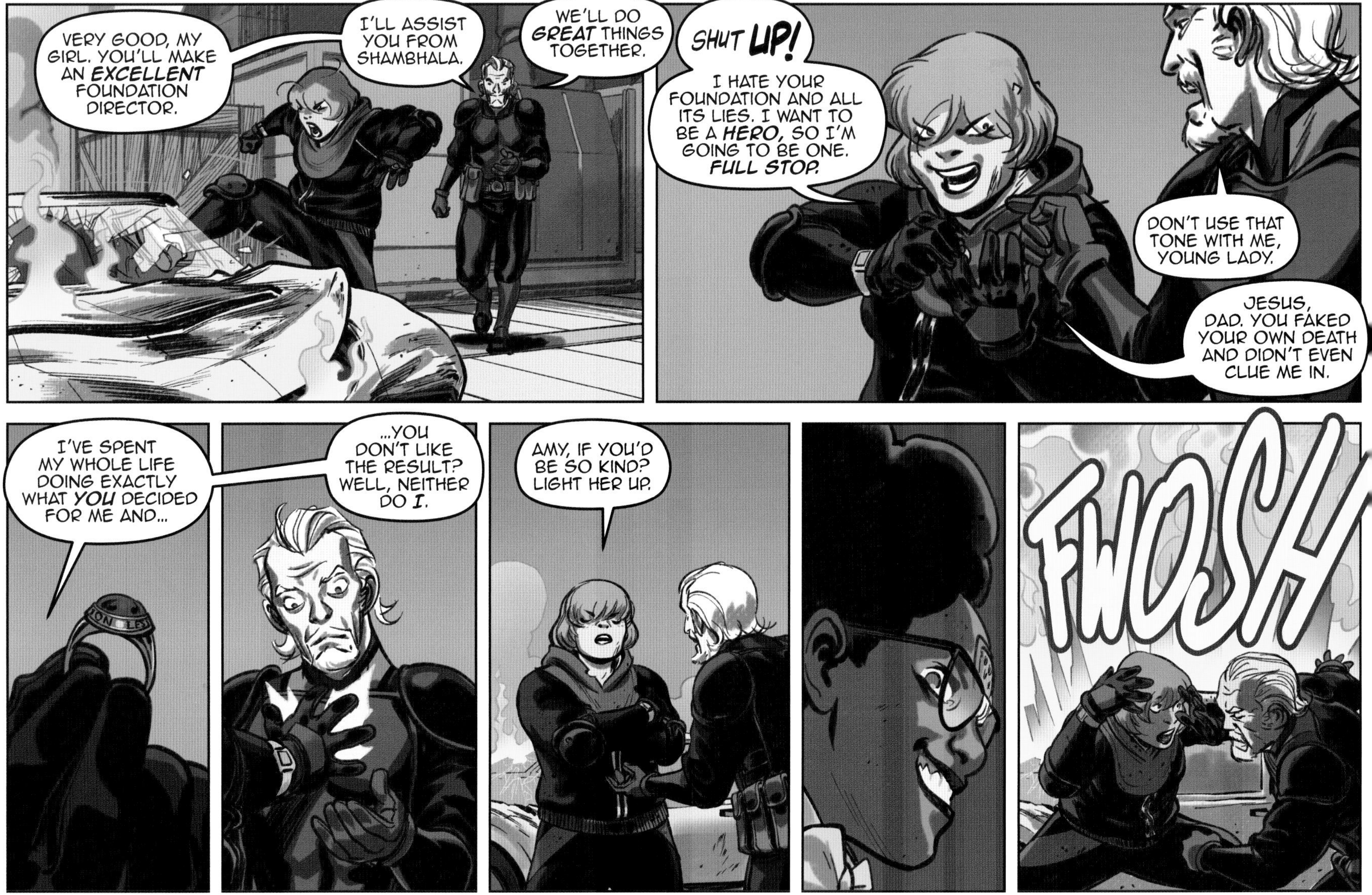
VERY GOOD, MY GIRL. YOU'LL MAKE AN EXCELLENT FOUNDATION DIRECTOR.
I'LL ASSIST YOU FROM SHAMBHALA.
WE'LL DO GREAT THINGS TOGETHER.
SHUT UP!
I HATE YOUR FOUNDATION AND ALL ITS LIES. I WANT TO BE A HERO, SO I'M GOING TO BE ONE. FULL STOP.
DON'T USE THAT TONE WITH ME, YOUNG LADY.
JESUS, DAD. YOU FAKED YOUR OWN DEATH AND DIDN'T EVEN CLUE ME IN.
I'VE SPENT MY WHOLE LIFE DOING EXACTLY WHAT YOU DECIDED FOR ME AND...
...YOU DON'T LIKE THE RESULT? WELL, NEITHER DO I.
AMY, IF YOU'D BE SO KIND? LIGHT HER UP.
FWOOSH

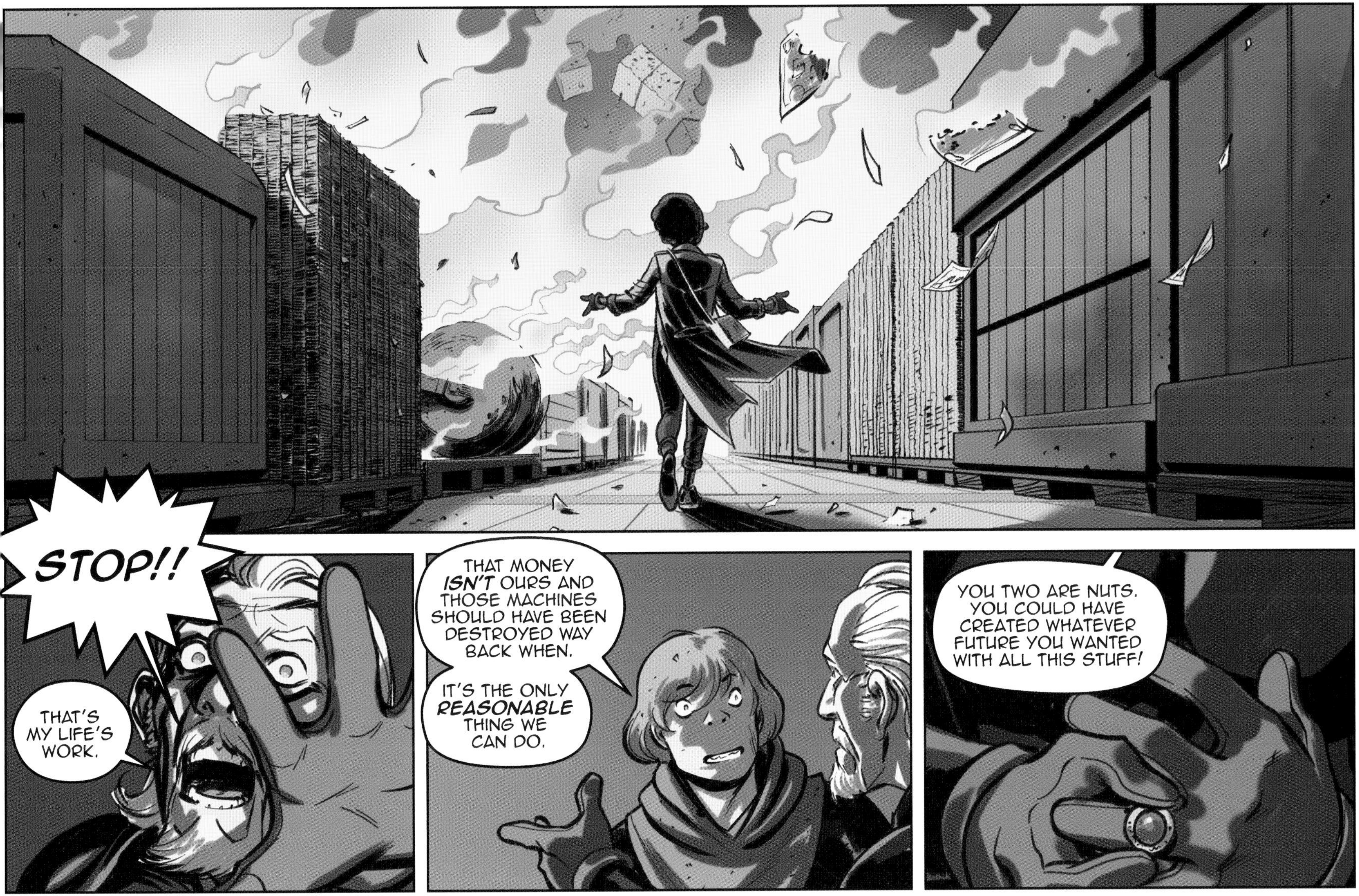
STOP!!
THAT'S MY LIFE'S WORK.
THAT MONEY *ISN'T* OURS AND THOSE MACHINES SHOULD HAVE BEEN DESTROYED WAY BACK WHEN.
IT'S THE ONLY *REASONABLE* THING WE CAN DO.
YOU TWO ARE NUTS. YOU COULD HAVE CREATED WHATEVER FUTURE YOU WANTED WITH ALL THIS STUFF!

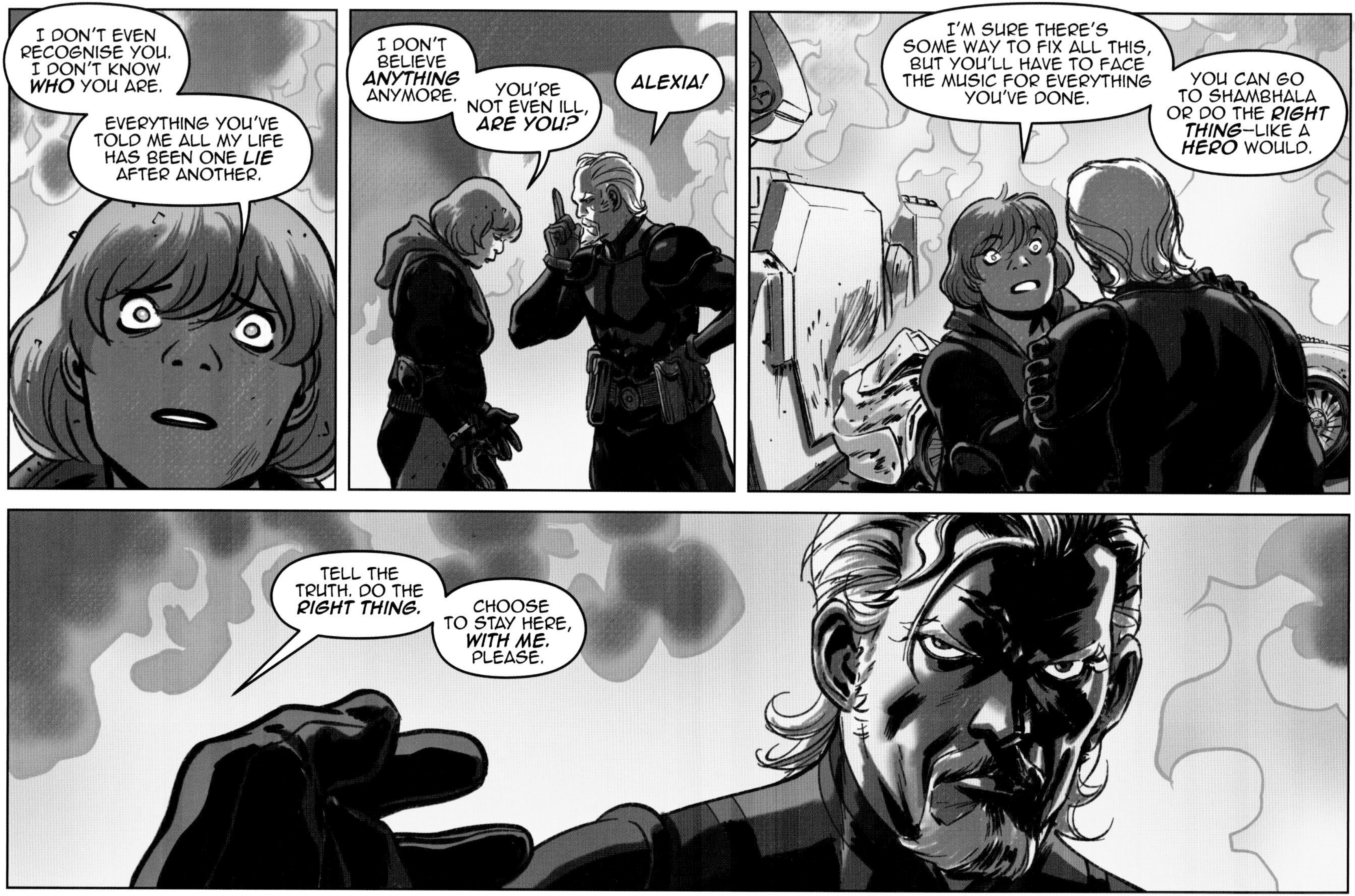
I DON'T EVEN RECOGNISE YOU. I DON'T KNOW **WHO** YOU ARE.
EVERYTHING YOU'VE TOLD ME ALL MY LIFE HAS BEEN ONE **LIE** AFTER ANOTHER.
I DON'T BELIEVE **ANYTHING** ANYMORE.
YOU'RE NOT EVEN ILL, **ARE YOU?**
ALEXIA!
I'M SURE THERE'S SOME WAY TO FIX ALL THIS, BUT YOU'LL HAVE TO FACE THE MUSIC FOR EVERYTHING YOU'VE DONE.
YOU CAN GO TO SHAMBHALA OR DO THE **RIGHT THING**—LIKE A **HERO** WOULD.
TELL THE TRUTH. DO THE **RIGHT THING.**
CHOOSE TO STAY HERE, **WITH ME.** PLEASE.

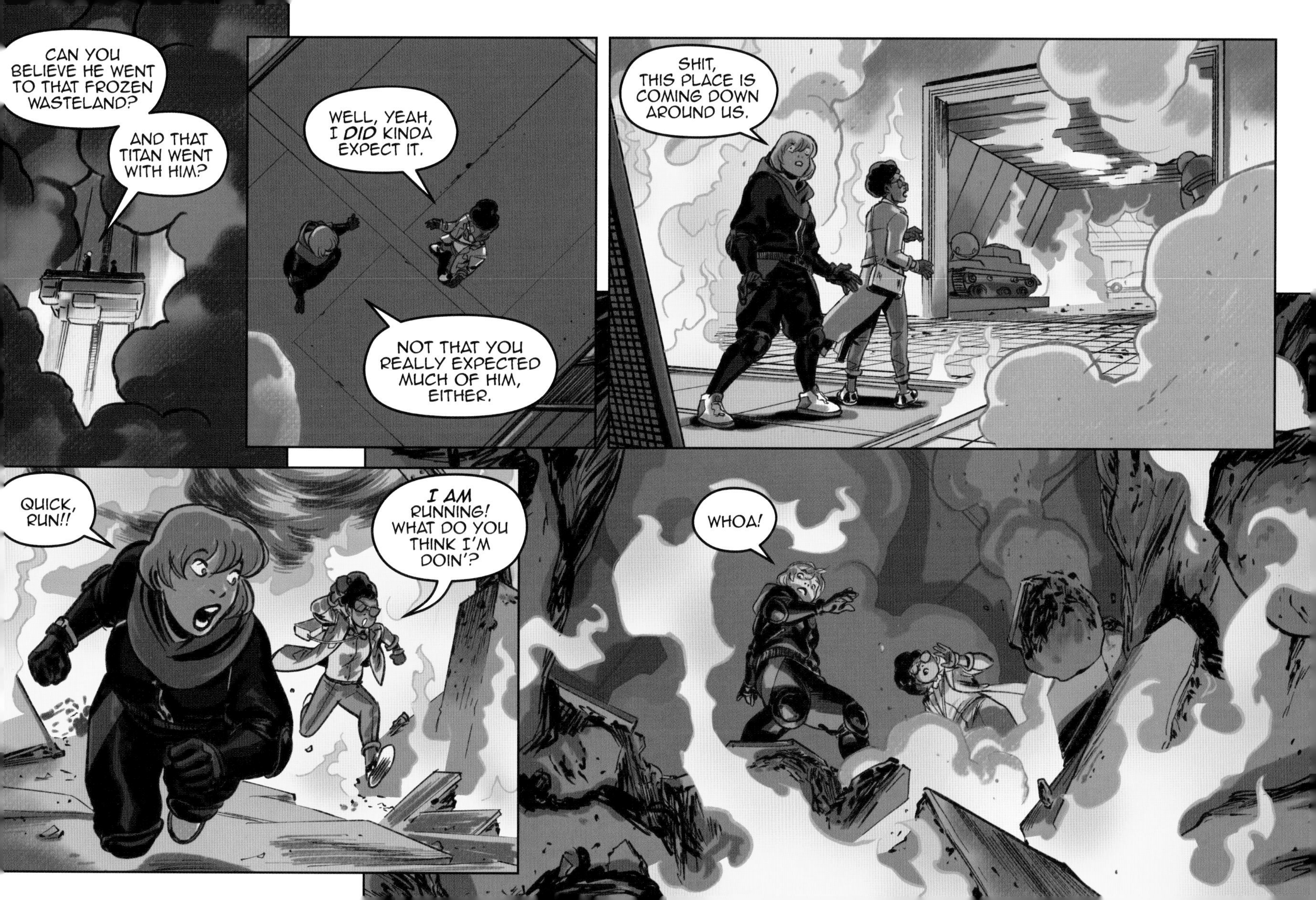
CAN YOU BELIEVE HE WENT TO THAT FROZEN WASTELAND?
AND THAT TITAN WENT WITH HIM?
WELL, YEAH, I *DID* KINDA EXPECT IT.
NOT THAT YOU REALLY EXPECTED MUCH OF HIM, EITHER.
SHIT, THIS PLACE IS COMING DOWN AROUND US.
QUICK, RUN!!
I AM RUNNING! WHAT DO YOU THINK I'M DOIN'?
WHOA!

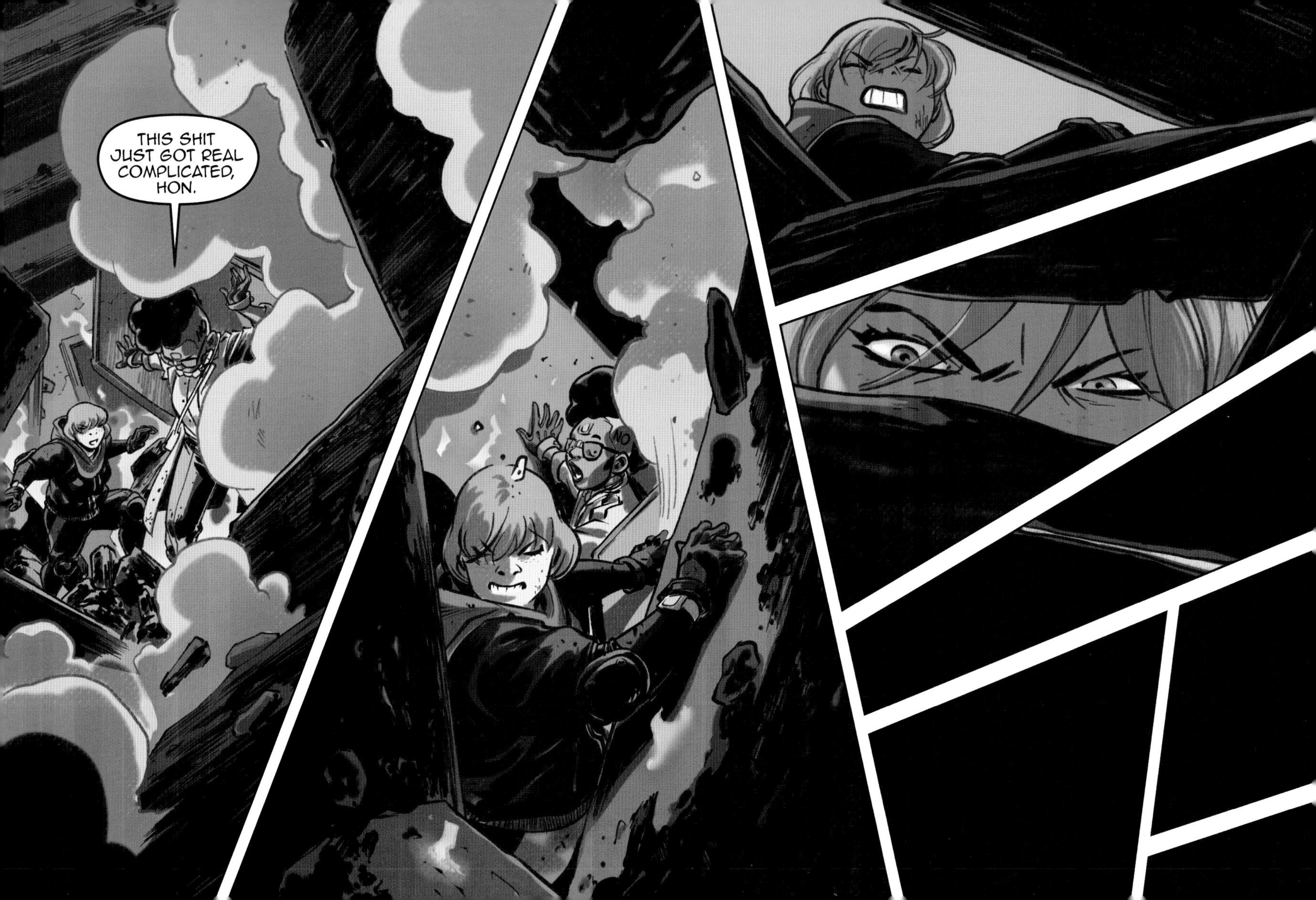
THIS SHIT JUST GOT REAL COMPLICATED, HON.

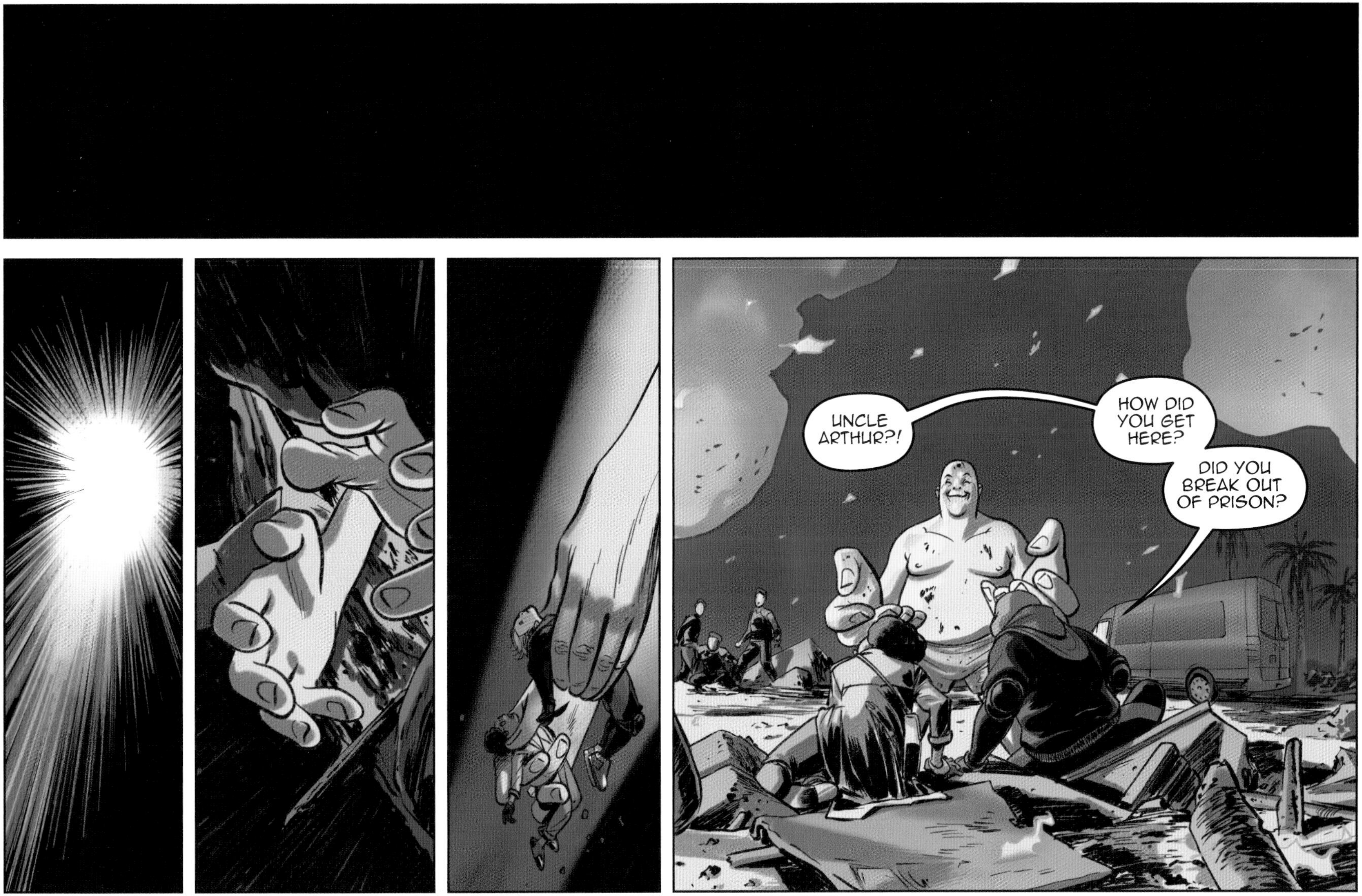
UNCLE ARTHUR?!
HOW DID YOU GET HERE?
DID YOU BREAK OUT OF PRISON?

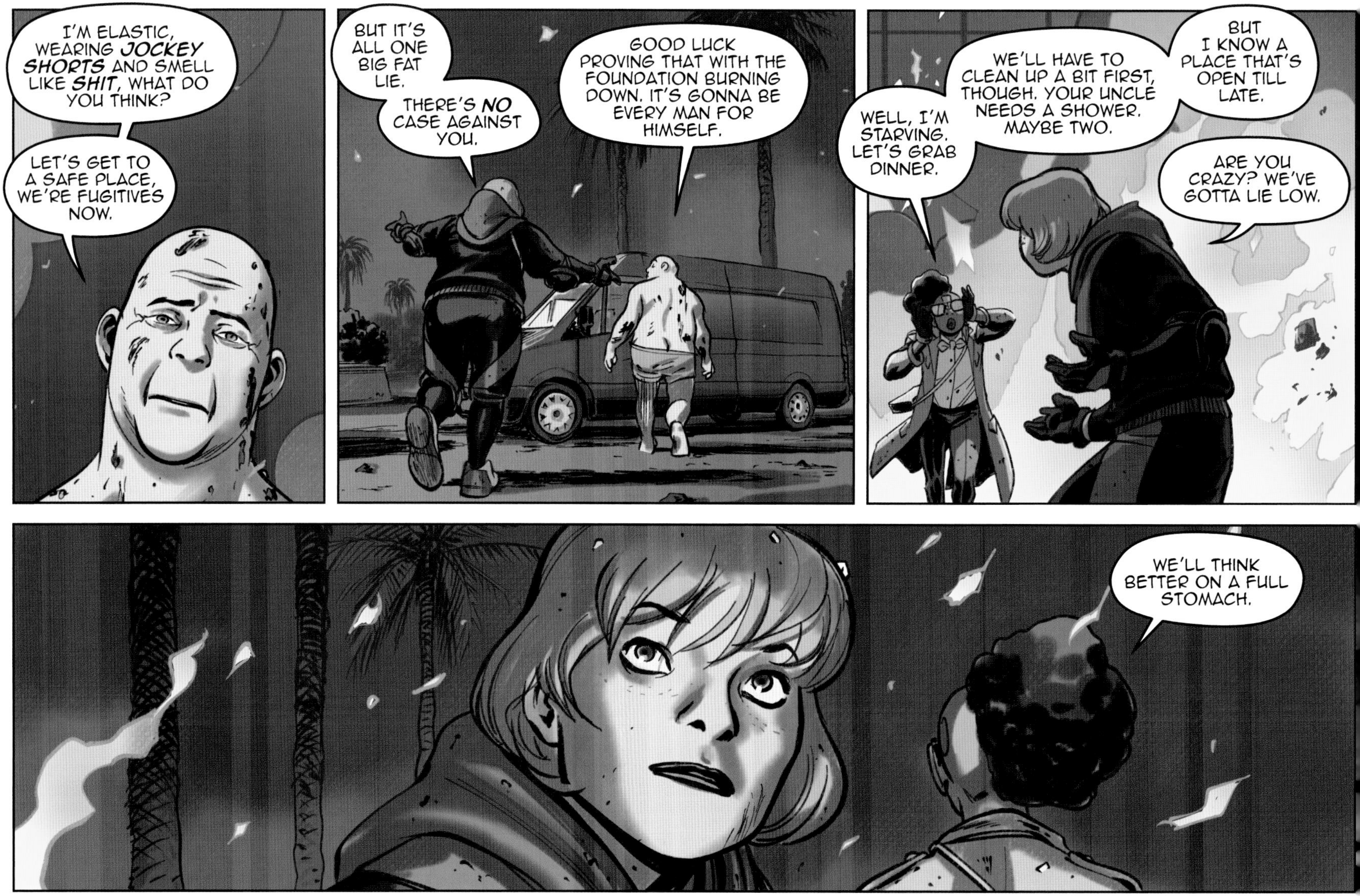
I'M ELASTIC, WEARING JOCKEY SHORTS AND SMELL LIKE SHIT, WHAT DO YOU THINK?
LET'S GET TO A SAFE PLACE, WE'RE FUGITIVES NOW.
BUT IT'S ALL ONE BIG FAT LIE.
THERE'S NO CASE AGAINST YOU.
GOOD LUCK PROVING THAT WITH THE FOUNDATION BURNING DOWN. IT'S GONNA BE EVERY MAN FOR HIMSELF.
WELL, I'M STARVING. LET'S GRAB DINNER.
ARE YOU CRAZY? WE'VE GOTTA LIE LOW.
WE'LL HAVE TO CLEAN UP A BIT FIRST, THOUGH. YOUR UNCLE NEEDS A SHOWER. MAYBE TWO.
BUT I KNOW A PLACE THAT'S OPEN TILL LATE.
WE'LL THINK BETTER ON A FULL STOMACH.

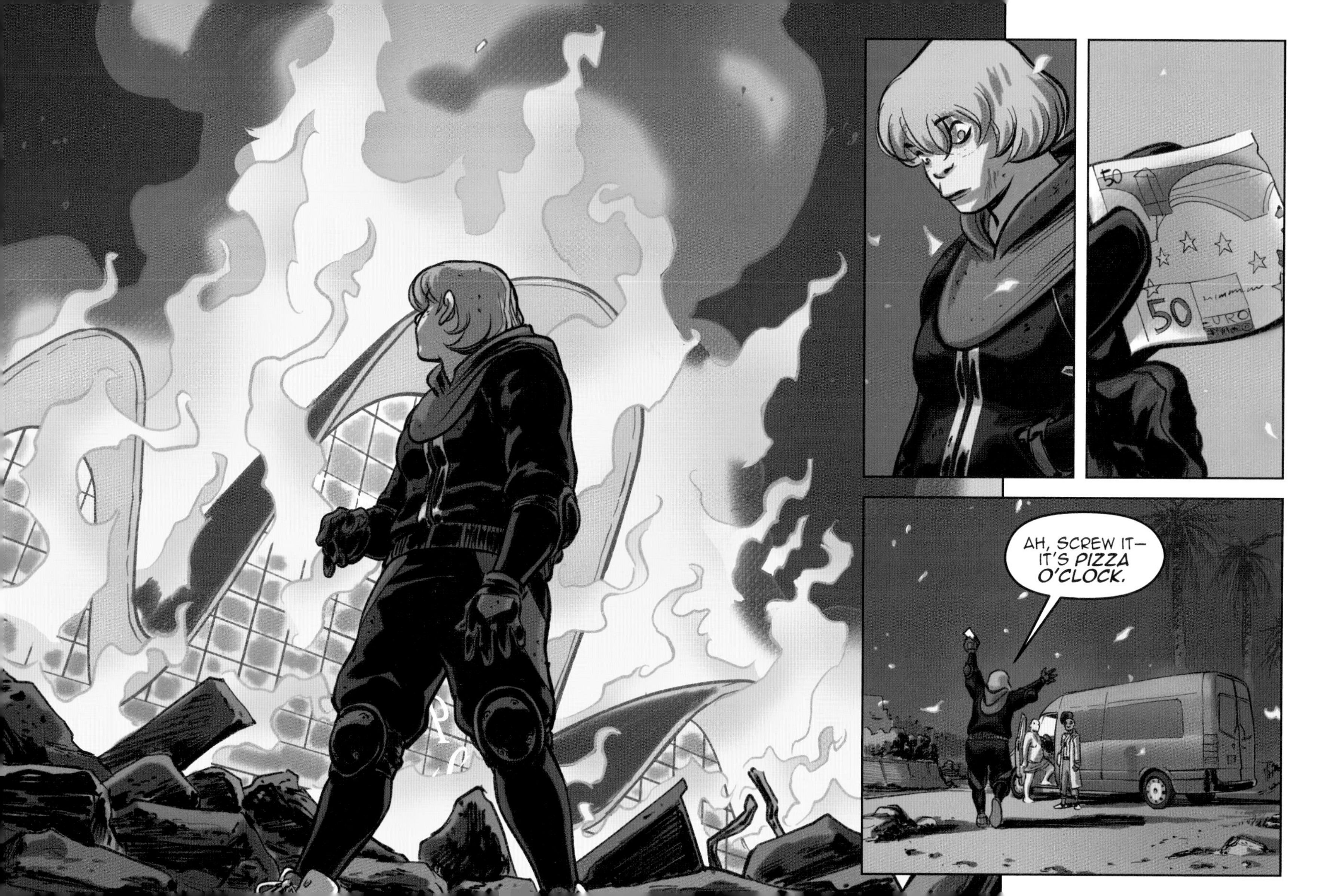
AH, SCREW IT—
IT'S *PIZZA O'CLOCK.*

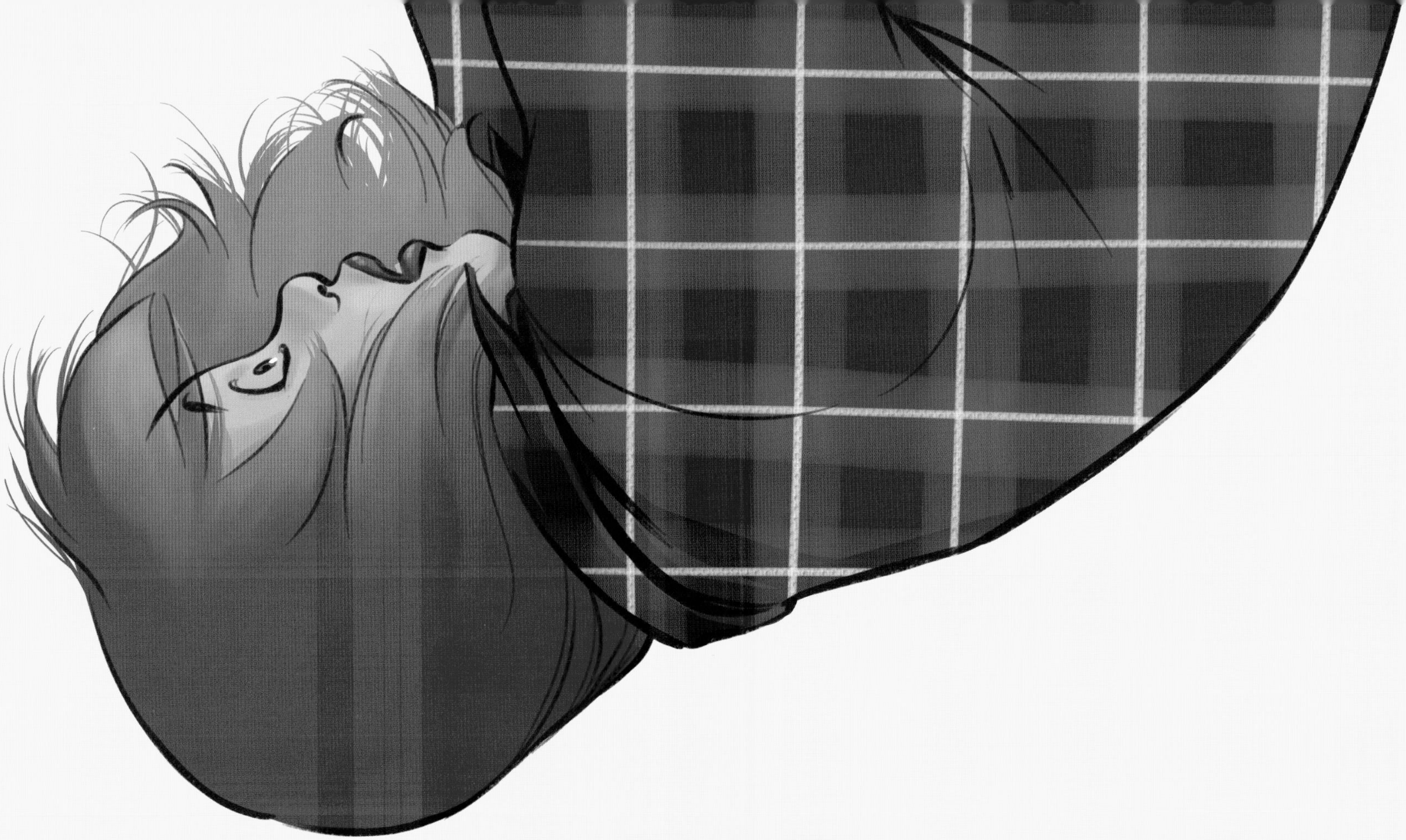

Concept Art & Sketches

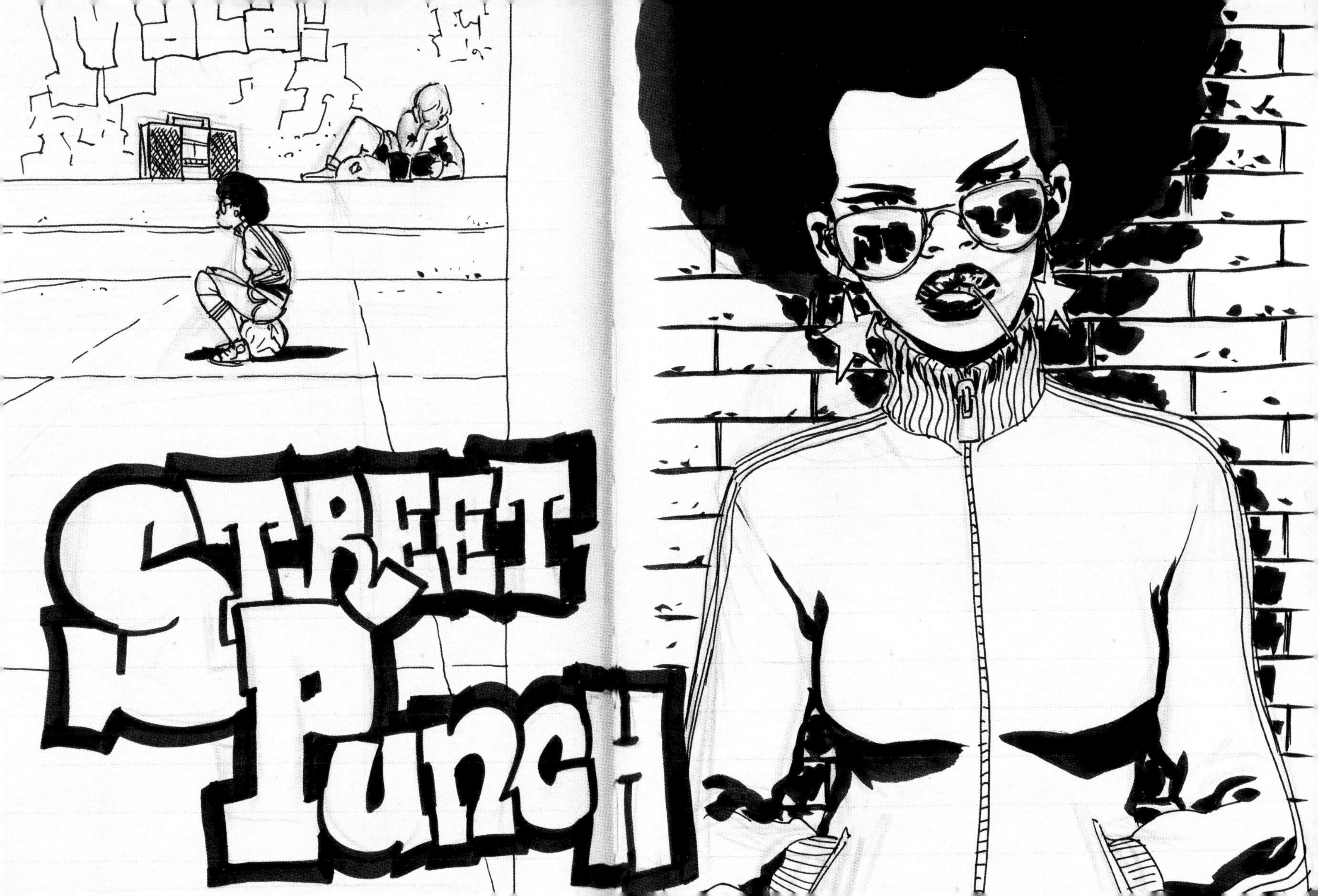
STREET
PUNCH

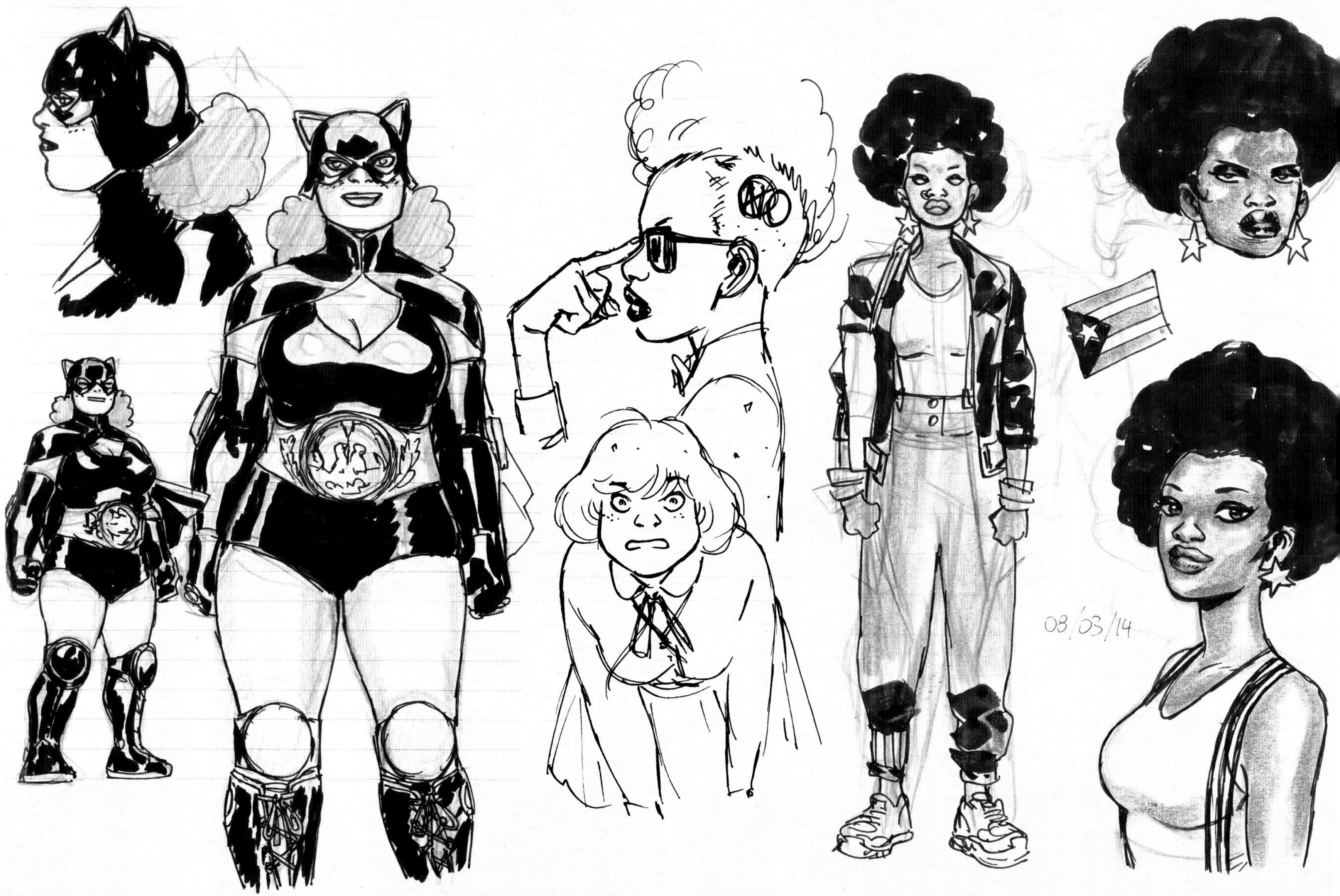
08/03/14

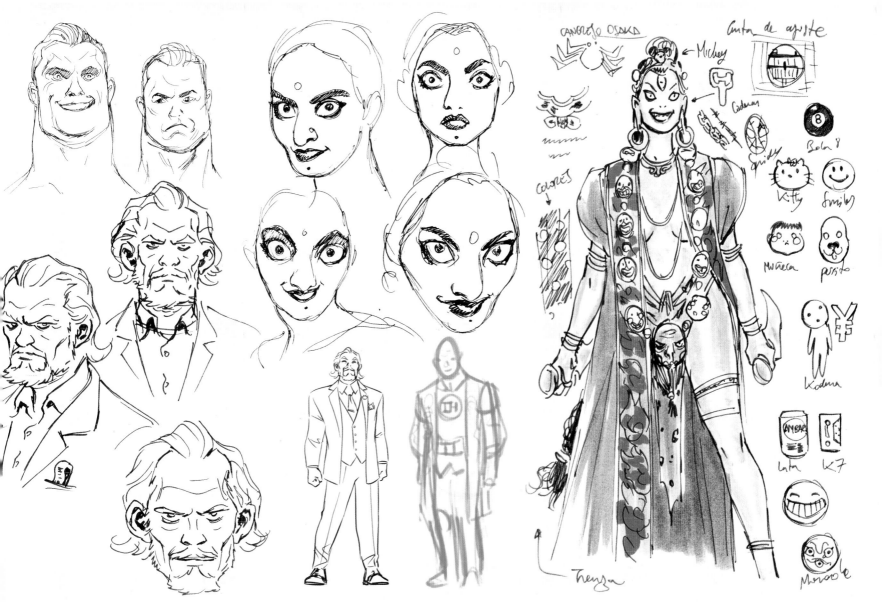

CANGREJO OSUKA

Cinta de ajuste

Michey

Caderas

COLORES

Bola 8

Kitty

Smiley

Muñeca

Perrito

¥

Kodama

AMBAR

Lata

K7

Treyza

Maroole

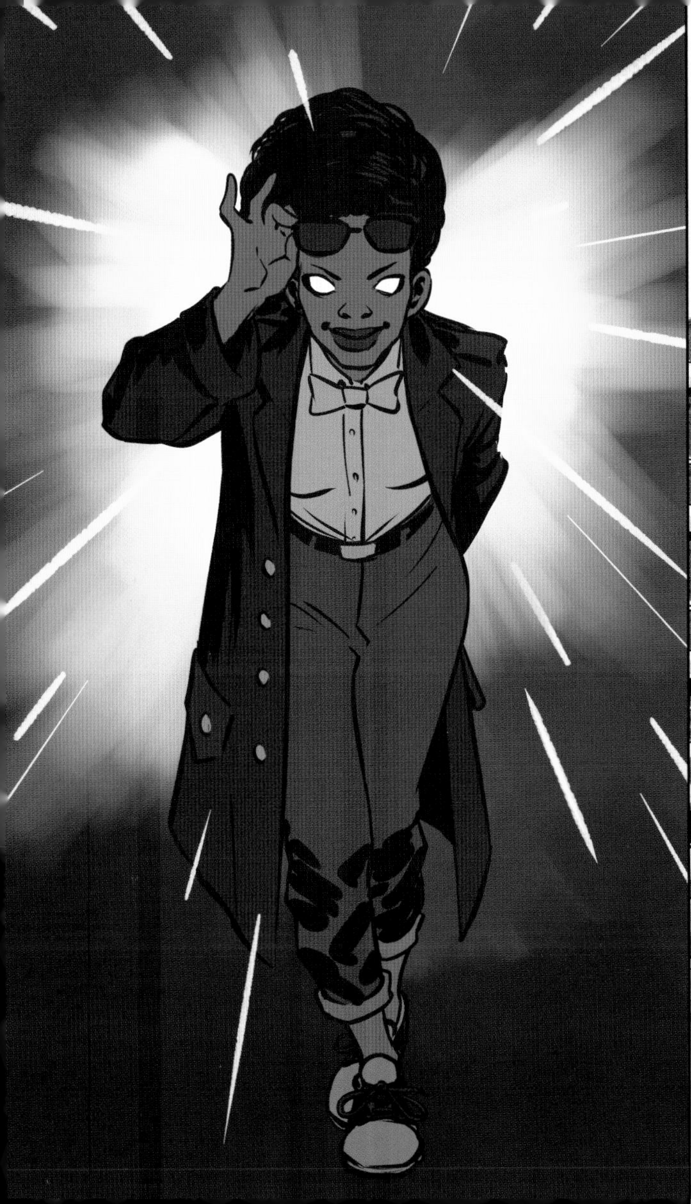

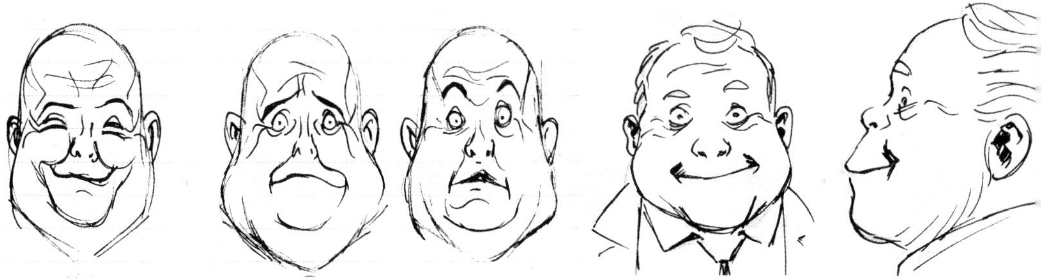

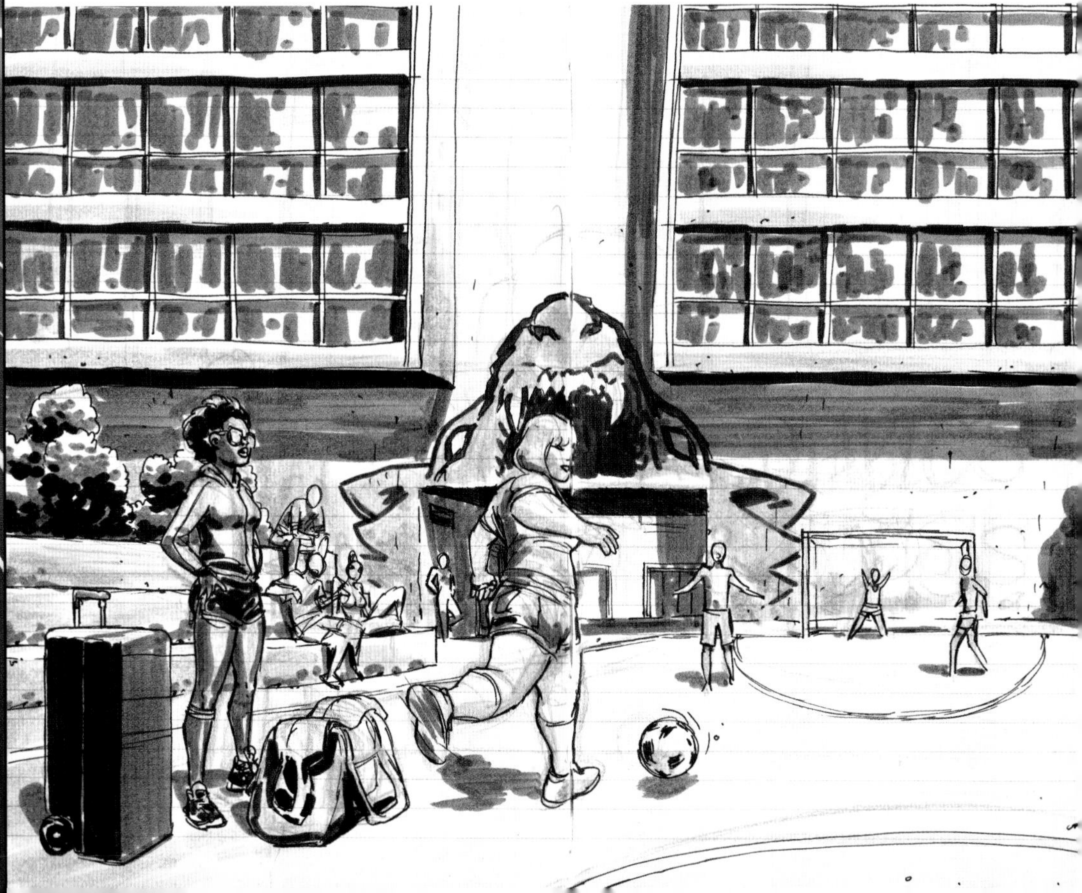

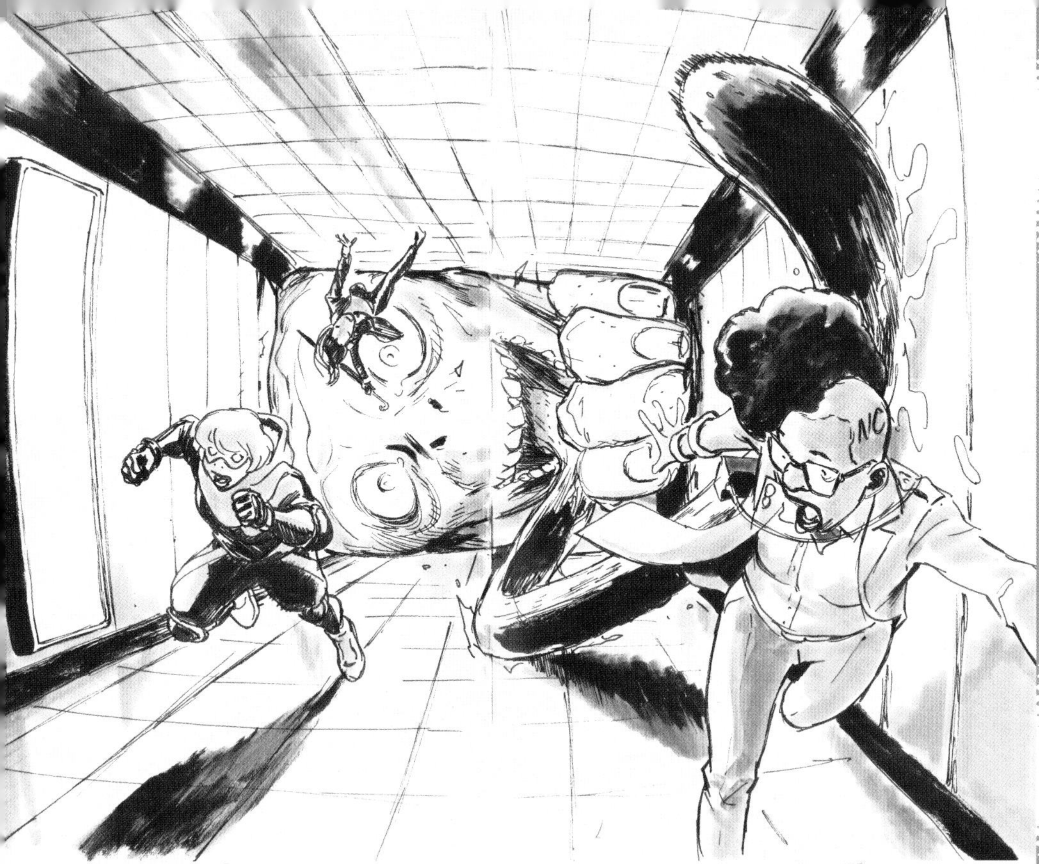
NC

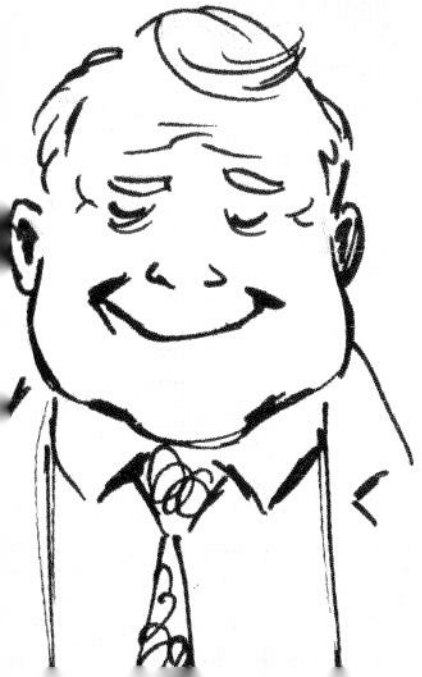

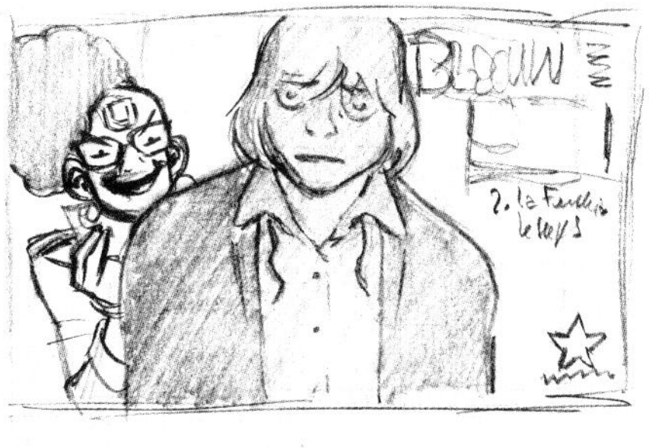

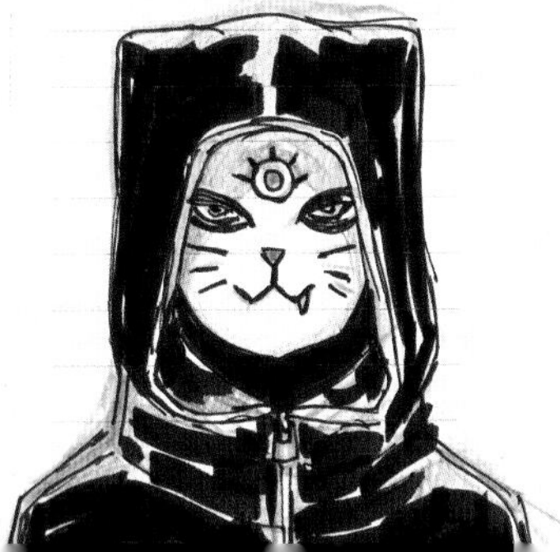

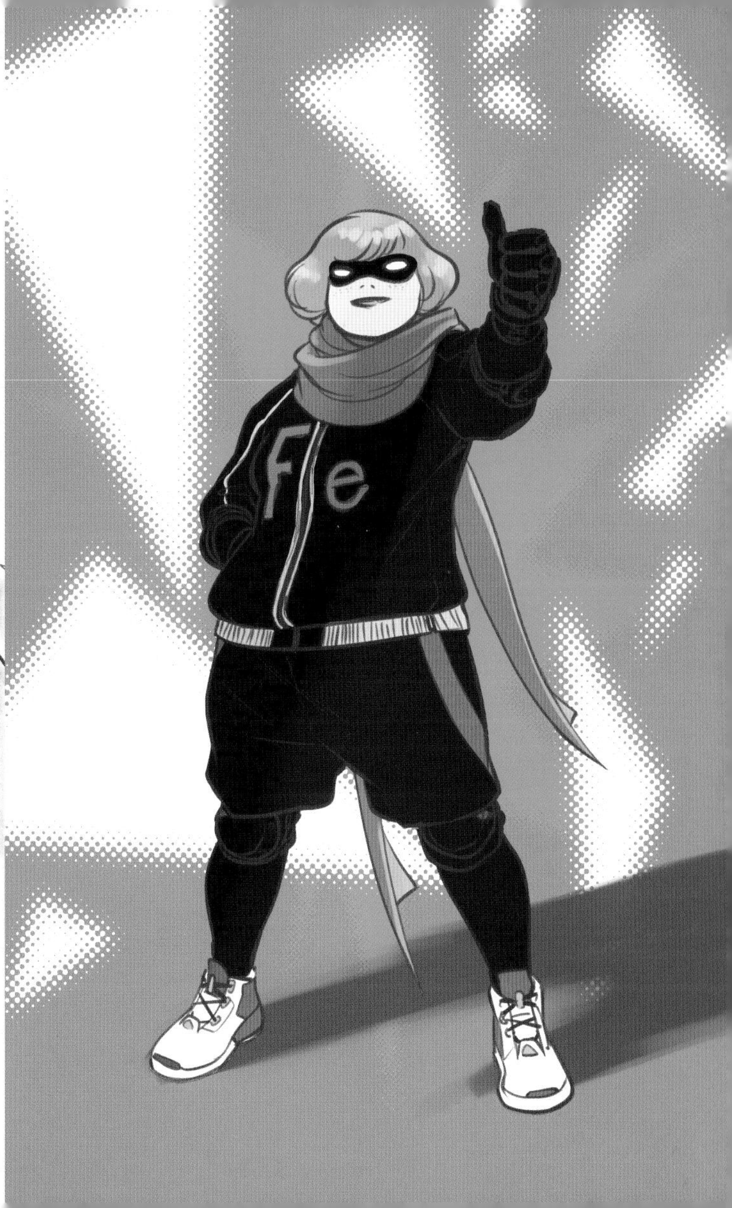
Fe

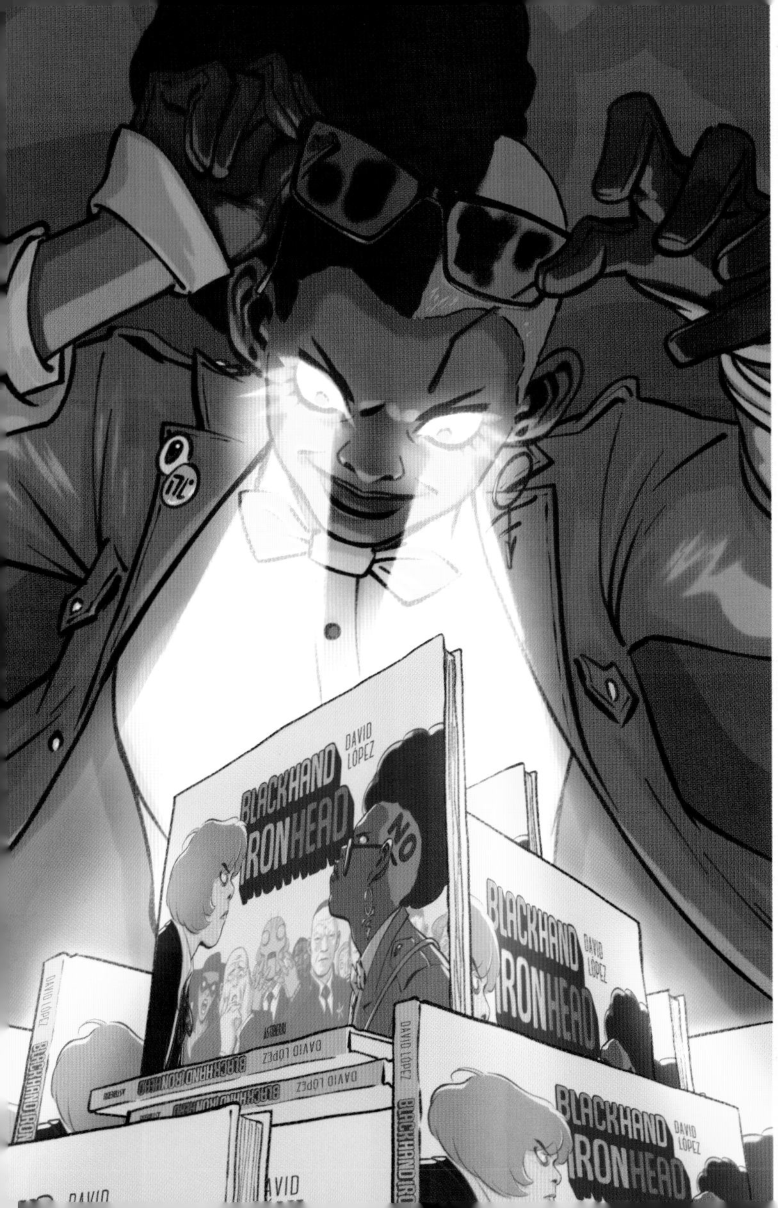
BLACKHAND IRONHEAD
DAVID LÓPEZ
NO
BLACKHAND IRONHEAD
DAVID LÓPEZ
BLACKHAND IRONHEAD
DAVID LÓPEZ

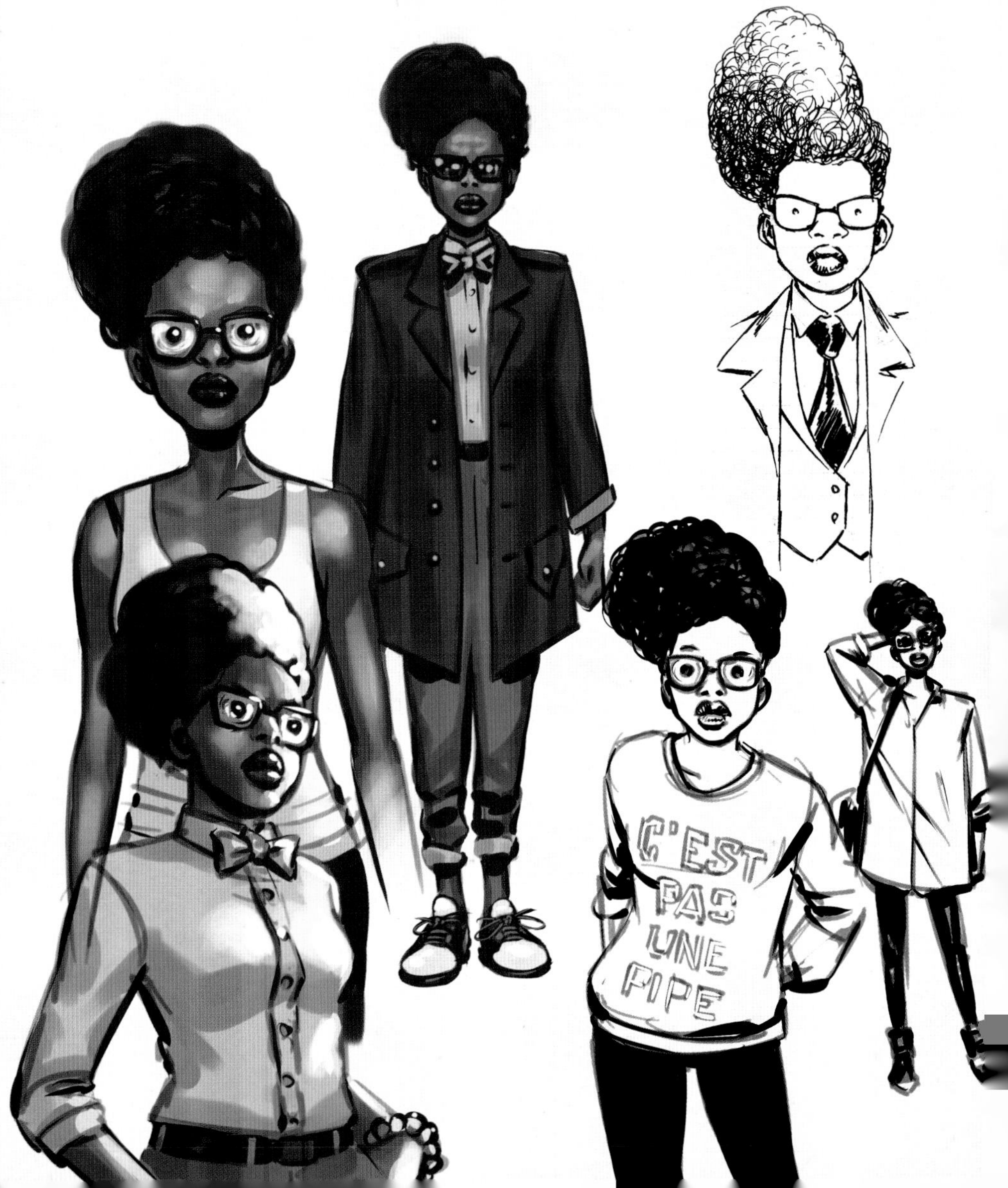
C'EST PAS UNE PIPE

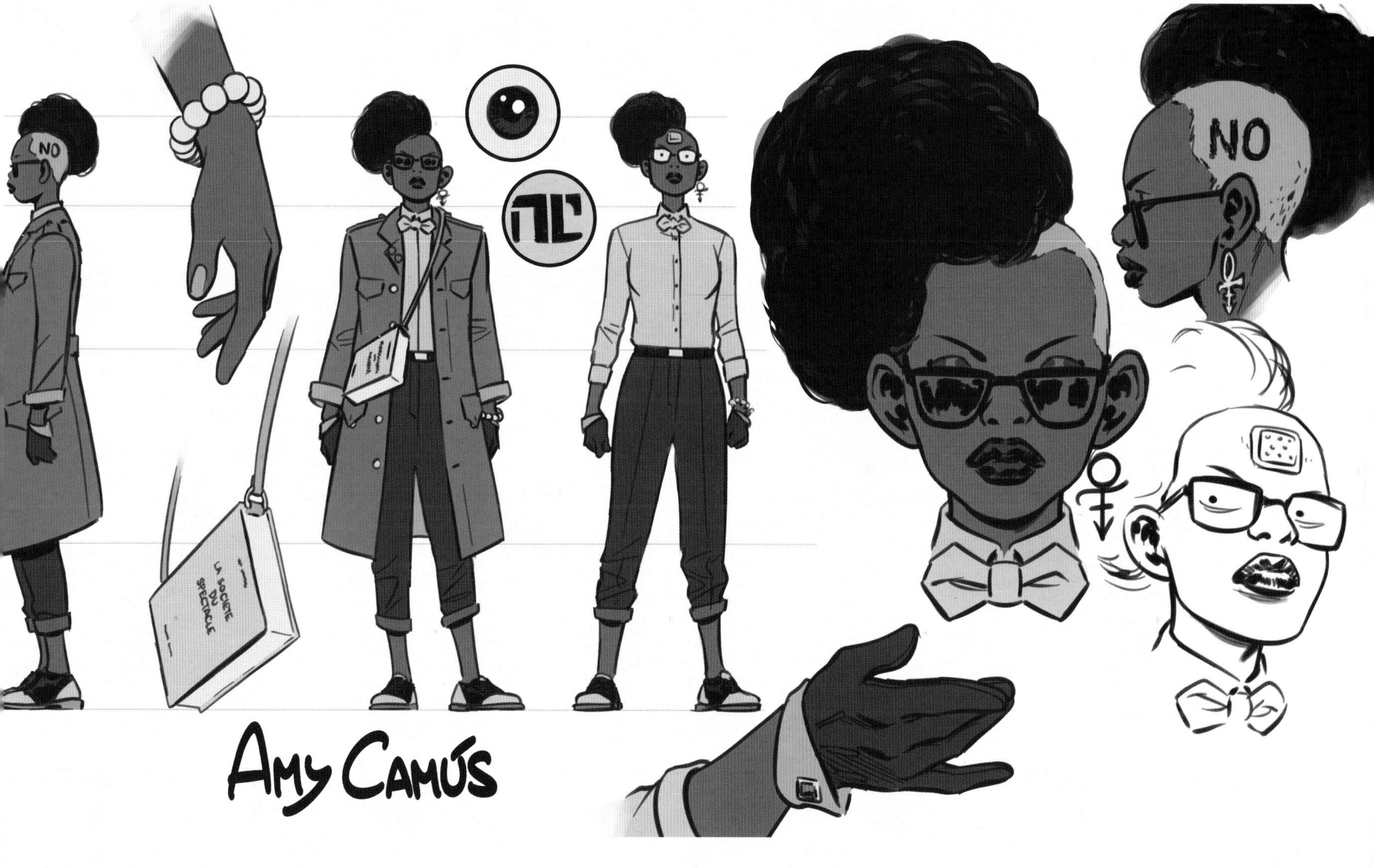
NO
LA SOCIETE DU SPECTACLE
NO
AMY CAMÚS

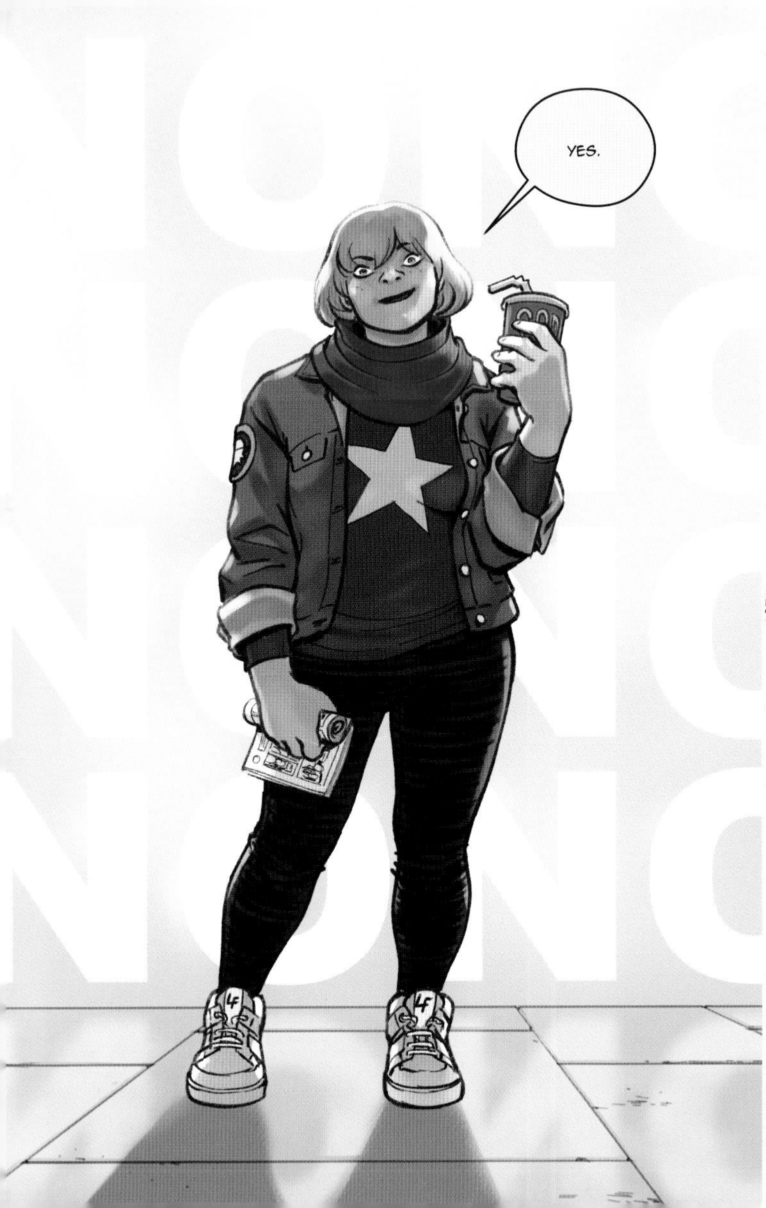
YES.

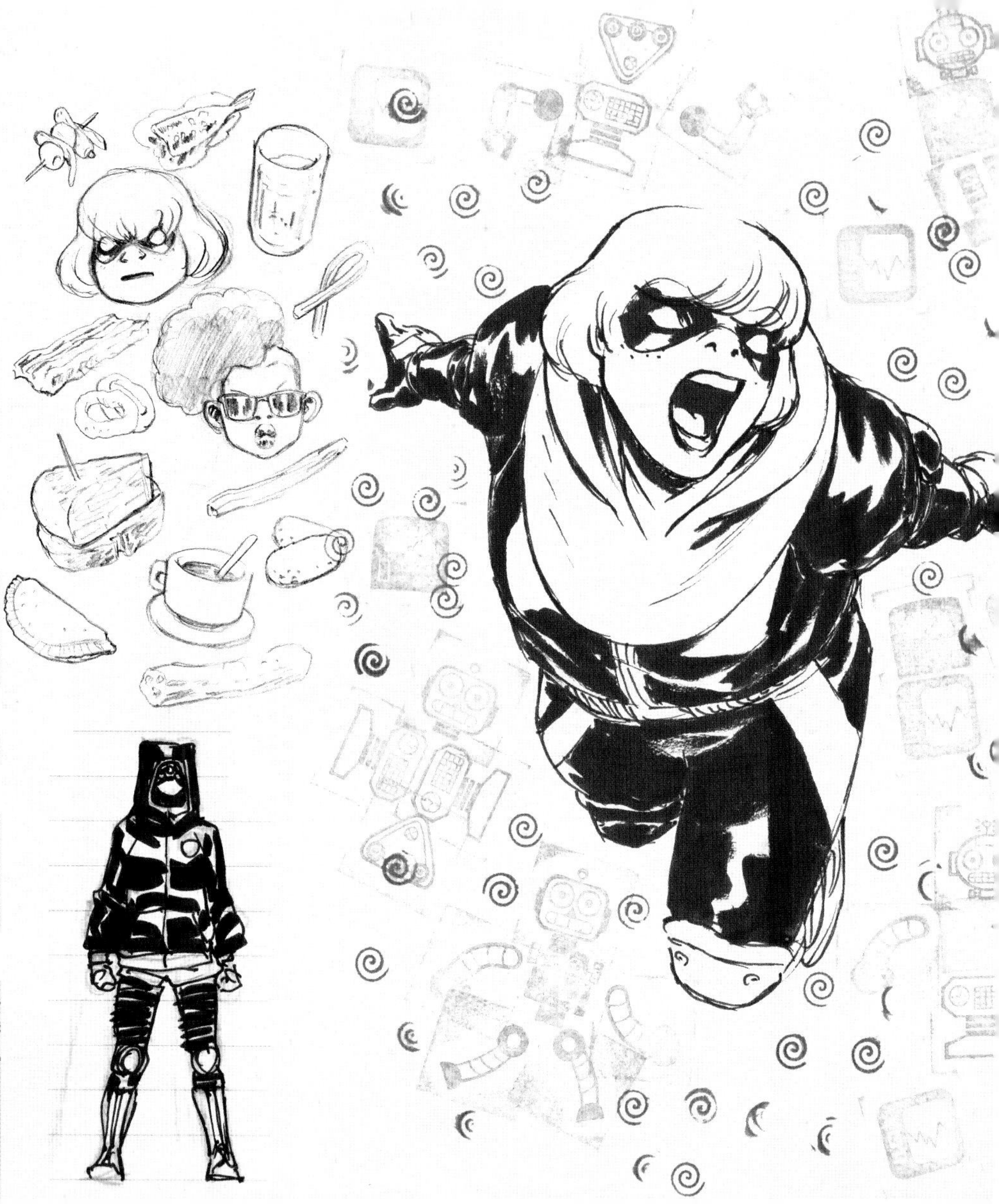

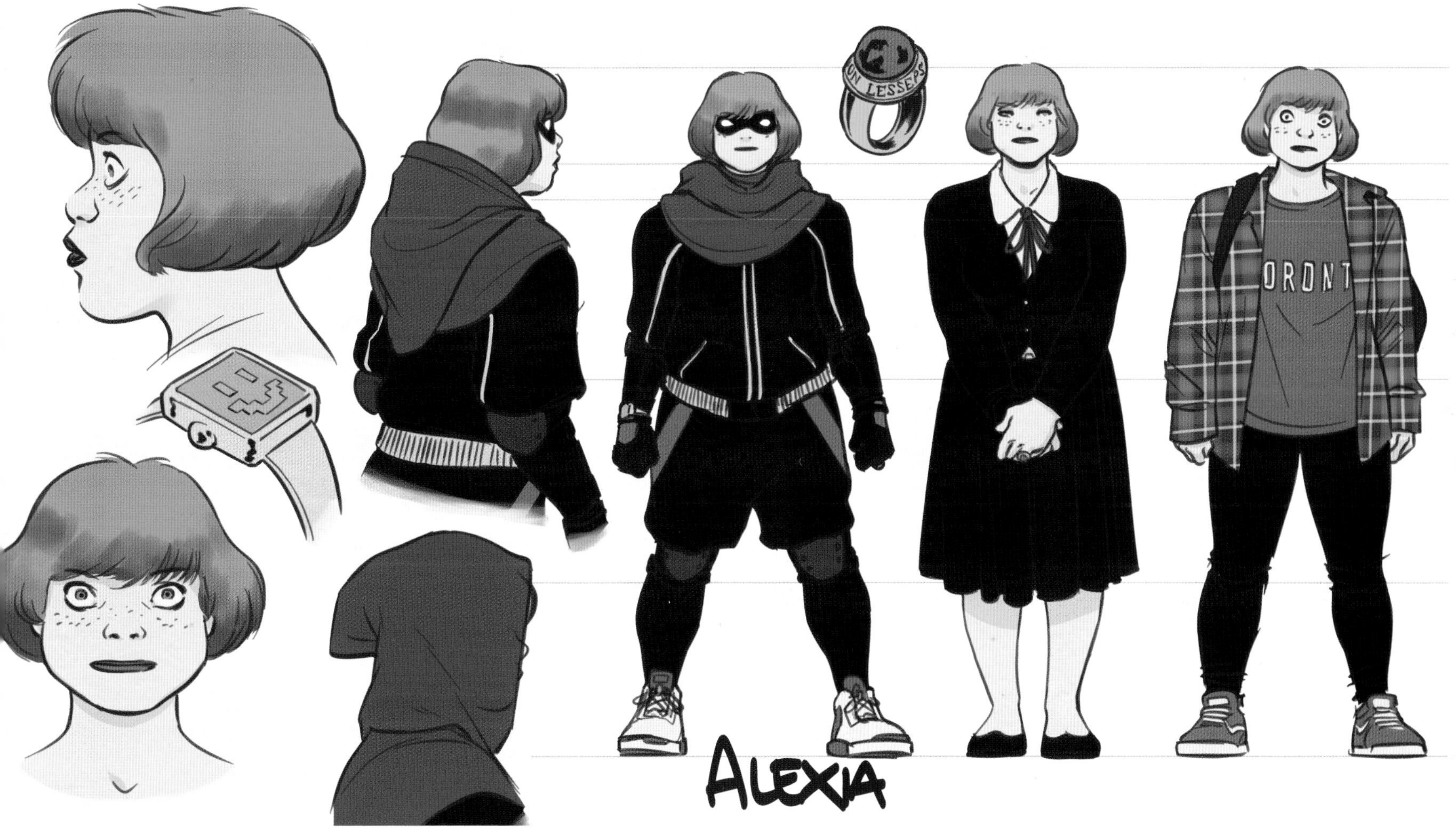
UN LESSEPS
ORONT
ALEXIA

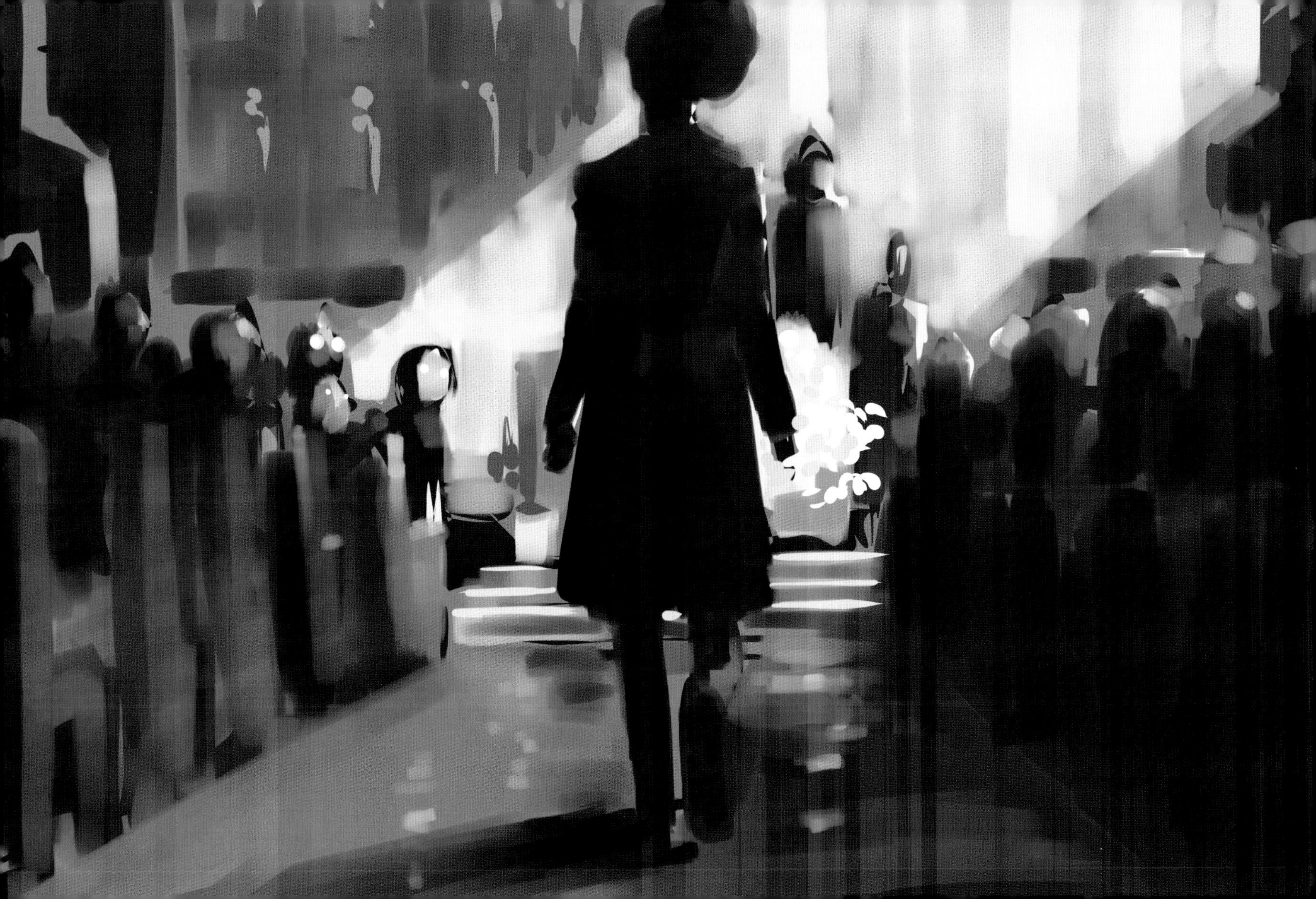

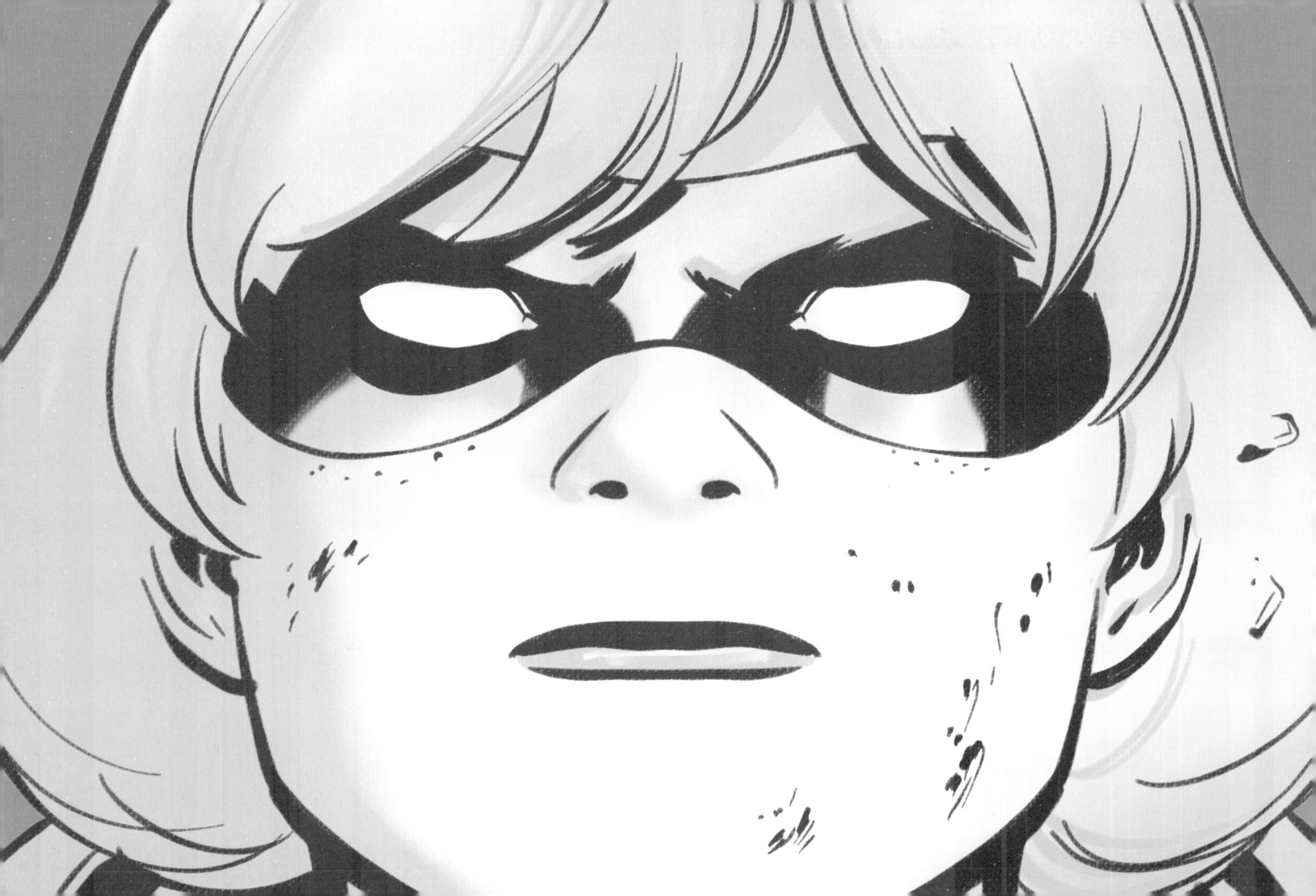